She wouldn't talk. She'd look at him with those little black eyes, primp up that cat's mouth (divided upper lip running to two black slits of nostril) and laugh all over her face.

Her *face*, he called it. To the Aleutians that meant more than eyes-nose-mouth. It meant the whole outward person, and their aura-cloud of life. *Persona* might be better, but it was too formal, too rarefied in English usage. Face would have to do. He had no idea what she saw as Sid's face, except that it wasn't the sun-scoured whitey-haired goblin he saw in a mirror.

He knew from the way she laughed that there *was* dirt: but she wouldn't tell. She particularly wouldn't gossip about Clavel. She revered the 'Pure One' – the Aleutian who admired humans so much he raped one. Sid gathered that Clavel was one of those celebrities whose legendary goodness withstands all attacks from the facts. Like Gandhi or Robin Hood. The rape of Johnny Guglioli the saboteur was regarded as the end of the Expedition's innocence. Yet it was not Clavel's crime that had passed into Aleutian mythology: it was his remorse. *The Grief of Clavel*. To them that was the title of the first contact story.

Typical! thought Sid. *What about* The Grief of Johnny Guglioli?

GWYNETH JONES

NORTH WIND

VISTA

First published in Great Britain 1994
by Victor Gollancz

This Vista edition published 1998
Vista is an imprint of the Cassell Group
Wellington House, 125 Strand, London WC2R 0BB

A catalogue record for this book is
available from the British Library.

ISBN 0 575 60248 1

Printed and bound in Great Britain by
Cox & Wyman Ltd, Reading, Berks

98 99   10 9 8 7 6 5 4 3 2 1

'I admit that I am one of those who would gladly break their neck for a wager, and that no schoolboy could be prouder of his pluck and agility than I am. That's because I'm undersized, and because all undersized men always want to do everything big men do . . .'

George Sand, *Lettres d'un Voyager*,
trs Sacha Rabinovitch
and Patricia Thomson

1: North West Frontier

'In those days,' grumbled Dr Bokr, 'they were the ones who wore quarantine. And we went anywhere we liked.'

The doctor had been telling a story about his first stay on earth. His last words were spoken aloud and in English, disturbing the golden, resin-scented silence. The Aleutian sightseers started and looked at him accusingly. Bokr quickly reverted to informal speech.

⟨Sorry, forgot myself.⟩

Perhaps there was no need to be nervous. Aleutians had come out from the post to visit these relics often. There had never been any trouble: though sometimes they'd been aware of curious watchers, keeping out of sight. But the trading post was on the northern frontier of Aleutian presence. An hour's journey away by jeep a war was raging.

There had been war on the giant planet – the same war, breaking out in one place as it subsided in another – for much of the period since the Aleutian shipworld arrived and settled in orbit around earth. Some people had longed to interfere, convinced that they could teach the benighted locals to abandon their superstitions and live in peace. Others had reminded the rest that they had no reason to feel superior. There was no armed conflict on the shipworld because they were a single nation. War was a normal feature of international affairs at home. At least the locals had no proliferating weapons. They couldn't do each other much lasting damage with their limited armoury.

The traders had retreated from trouble spots, consolidated where they were welcome, discreetly refused to take sides: all had been well. But suddenly, for reasons no one could understand, the Expedition was in trouble. The 'Government of the

World', the local body the traders had always dealt with, professed itself no longer able to protect them.

The staff at Expedition Headquarters at Uji, in Karen state north of Thailand, claimed that there was no cause for concern. Naturally, it was a matter of pride to remain equally calm on the frontier. But this was not the time for making provocative formal speeches about the burden of quarantine. It was known that the locals could be eavesdropping, even in a spot like this. The Aleutians waited, half afraid of a lightning strike out of the blue sky.

Nothing happened. They relaxed, laughing at themselves.

Goodlooking laid his hand on a slab of worked stone, and looked up. The scale of this relic astonished him. A massive grey-golden wall rose far above his head. It was webbed by a network of dark lines so regular and so harmonious that the effect was completely lifelike. But these dead stones had been cut and set mechanically by the hands of local people or by non-living machines. He stretched his fingers, so the quarantine film glittered in the sunlight. It looked soft but it was very tough. The film covered him entirely, over his clothes and every scrap of exposed skin. It shimmered in front of his eyes. He breathed through it: when he opened and closed his mouth it stretched and shrank.

On earth, he told himself. *Life is separate. Every being is separate. They do not grow their machines or their buildings from stuff impregnated with their own life. The animals and plants I see around me are separate, whether they are wild or tame. They are not designed by the secretions of farmers or gardeners. Nor are they escapes that have survived and gone their own way, from food-making changes that primitive people started long ago. Our wanderers, that they call 'mobile semi-sentient cell colonies', are passing information between us all the time. The locals, the humans, don't have that means of contact.*

The spaces between us are filled with a mist of common self. They are each alone, and it seems natural to them. They are afraid of our cloud of presence.

The Aleutians wandered in the circle of turf enclosed by the giant walls: Bokr, the post's physician and Panisad the trader, who were signifiers like Goodlooking; plus eight of the ordinary staff. These were artisans, technicians and domestics who, like the majority of Aleutians, never used spoken language.

Goodlooking found a fallen block and knelt down, using it as an armrest. He was tired. His disability made any physical effort exhausting. At home or in the shipworld no one would have dreamed that he could join in an outing like this: *out of doors, into the wilderness!* He was an unlikely recruit for the Expedition. He was here because Lord Maitri, the head of his household, was the chief trading officer at the frontier post: and Maitri was also, for this life, Goodlooking's beloved and indulgent parent.

The Self moves in mysterious ways. The last child Maitri had nurtured in his body had been a technician. The child before had been the great Clavel, one of the original captains of the Expedition to Earth. Clavel the Pure One: who was so little like a trader, but whose influence was so important to them. This time Maitri's offspring had turned out to be his own dim, disabled librarian. But Maitri loved all his children equally. He was the kindest of lords. Lives ago, he had practically invented the post of 'librarian' for his invalid dependent. He knew his ward longed hopelessly to visit the giant planet: therefore he had arranged it.

So here was Goodlooking, equipped with a double set of underwear against the rigours of the climate; and a formal name. In Aleutia your identity was never in doubt, it filled the air around you. Only important people had personal names, descriptive tags that might change from life to life or mood to mood. But on earth everyone had to have a fixed title, local style. It was an Expedition tradition. They had dug out Maitri's babyname for 'Goodlooking', since he had no other. Then, in the middle of his visit, the locals had turned hostile. And whatever the people at Uji said, the situation was obviously deteriorating. It wasn't his fault, but Goodlooking knew he'd become an embarrassment.

He smothered a rueful sigh. He would not have missed being Maitri's ward, or coming to earth, for fifty other lives. The risk of sudden death didn't bother him. One more shortened life was neither here nor there in his feeble career. It was the little things

that marred this wonderful privilege: that woefully inappropriate name, which he detested. The feeling that he was a
nuisance. The slight falseness of his position as Lord Maitri's
ward . . . Every hour was full of tiny stings.

In the silence, he was aware of his disability. All the staff of
the post belonged to Maitri's household, but Bokr was the only
one of these people that he knew well. Their use of the Common
Tongue, the silent language of their expression and gesture, was
unfamiliar. He could follow the gist. But he did not have the
key, the intimate knowledge of their past lives that would have
made every blurred phrase transparent.

At home, which for lives had meant on board the shipworld,
it didn't matter that he found communication difficult. He lived
alone in his little closet buried deep in the house, with Maitri's
private records, immersed in the moving images. Ironically, he
knew plenty of famous and important people: including some
famous inhabitants of this giant planet. He knew every gesture
and every incident of their recorded lives. But he was never
likely to be on a picnic with *them*.

Dr Bokr appeared at his side: materialising without warning,
as people seemed to do even in plain sight when they were
wrapped in the quarantine film.

⟨I hope the adventure isn't too much for you, librarian.⟩

His tone was casual. His kind, professional eyes told his real
feelings: *poor cripple*. Goodlooking tried not to recoil from the
blast of concern.

⟨Everything's so yellow!⟩ he declared brightly.

⟨Indeed!⟩ Sure that he had the invalid's attention, Bokr mod-
erated his gestures. He knew that Goodlooking could understand
the Common Tongue perfectly, regardless of quarantine – if
familiar people put themselves where he could watch their faces.

⟨Somehow we all thought that once we made landfall, it
would be the same as being home. But now it's the shipworld
that seems homelike, though it isn't like *home* in the least . . .⟩

He settled companionably by Goodlooking's block, and spoke
of the naked white radiance of the homeworld sun: the way it
rained down on you in the wilderness when you were right away
from any city, unfiltered by the presence of life. In the shipworld,
light dispersed from the bluesun reactor faded from blue day into

indigo night, never reaching full darkness or the diamond blaze of noon. Earth's sun was an improvement. But if you were an outdoor person . . . If you had travelled in the mountains – as Bokr had done once, with the great Clavel – this brassy glow was no substitute.

⟨Now that we know how tough you are, little invalid, you'll have to come out to the wilderness with me.⟩

When he talked about his previous trip to earth, which had happened in his last life and was part of his most recent recorded memory, Bokr seemed to be describing the distant past. When he talked of the homeworld, which he had left – in earth terms – thousands of years ago, he spoke as if he'd been there yesterday and planned to return tomorrow. It was natural. On earth, times had changed. The lost home remained frozen in their minds in the state in which they'd left it. But it was no wonder earth people found the Aleutian concept of time confusing.

One life, thought Goodlooking, awed by such deprivation. *To awake into consciousness, as a child wakes, with no one to tell you who you are. No one to show you your possessions, no one to bring records of your past that will teach you how to be yourself. One life and then nothing: out of darkness into darkness!*

⟨Shall we make it a date?⟩ suggested the doctor, with a roguish twinkle. ⟨You and I, out to the wilderness. We could lie down together under the stars, how about it?⟩

Goodlooking smiled vaguely.

There was an aura of mystery around the librarian's incarnation this time round. It was because he was Maitri's ward, and because Maitri made an unwarranted fuss of him (in some people's opinion). A rumour had got about that he was not really the librarian, but the truechild – the fated lover – of someone very important. He'd been given a false identity at birth to hide him from his lover's enemies. One day, when he was old enough or when the danger had passed, his real status would be revealed.

To find 'another self' was the Aleutian ideal of romance. Such a meeting was unlikely. There were millions of possible selves on record in the shipworld: and there was believed to be a 'natural prohibition' on the same person being born twice in the

same generation. But young Aleutians dreamt of finding their
'trueparent' in the previous generation, while romantic elders
searched young faces for their 'truechild'. If someone important
(and romantically inclined) thought he'd found such a treasure,
maybe he'd want to hide the baby. A person like that might well
have artisans, medical technicians, who could fake anything.
The rumour was absurd, yet plausible enough to have earned a
dim, disabled librarian some surprising attentions.

Goodlooking could have asked Maitri to deny the story. But
his lord seemed not to notice the gossip and Goodlooking
couldn't bear to broach the subject: *Maitri, am I a prince in
hiding?* He'd feel so stupid. He'd decided to ignore the whispers,
and pretend he didn't understand the hints. However, he was
not flattered. He did not see why he should be grateful for
proposals directed at the supposed secret celebrity.

'I was thinking about permanent death,' he said in clear
English. 'Such a sad idea.'

The doctor stared. 'Permanent death? Yes, horrible. Pure
superstition. Their physiology may be odd, but essentially they
must be the same as the rest of us. A person is a person.'

He answered the formal speech in the same mode, as politeness
required: but his face was a study. He could hardly believe that
he'd been snubbed, and by the meekest of his patients.

Shortly he got up and moved away with a dignified shrug and
headshake which cunningly managed to convey two messages:
telling Goodlooking that he was grieved that his kindness had
been misinterpreted; while letting the rest of the company know
he'd merely been making sure the invalid was not overtired.

It isn't sensible, thought Goodlooking wryly. *If they really
believe I'm a disguised prince, with a fated lover in my future,
why are they surprised when I turn them down?*

The Aleutians strolled about, admiring the stonework and the
plants and the scuttering, flitting scraps of wildlife. Goodlooking
settled against his block, gazing into the sunny air – the sunlight
that wasn't good enough for Dr Bokr – and catching fragments of
conversation; the occasional quiet word of English from the
signifiers. It was the official formal language of the Expedition.
It had been the most widespread local dialect when they arrived.
It wasn't so useful now, but the habit remained.

⟨It was a funerary room of some kind . . . Naturally the bodies have vanished, but why is the building still here? Why hasn't it changed into something else? In my experience if you leave *anything* lying about out of doors . . . What? How old? Hundreds of 'years'. Or is it millions? I'm not honestly sure.⟩

⟨Remind me, what exactly is a 'year'? It's a unit of measurement, yes? But is it of space or of time?⟩

He was glad to be ignored for a while. To Maitri's librarian the modest company at the trading post was a mad social whirl. It would have tired him if he'd felt quite at ease. As it was, he was only truly comfortable alone in his room: or chatting with the post's local interpreter, the 'halfcaste' Sidney Carton.

Sid had become important to Goodlooking. When he wasn't feeling well Sid would sit with him for hours, entertaining him with tales of old earth. The 'halfcaste' did not find it odd that Lord Maitri went on caring for his grown-up invalid child, and the 'secret identity story' couldn't mean anything to him. His friendship was sincere. The others called him impertinent. They said 'halfcastes' were a shifty lot. But Goodlooking knew that Maitri trusted Sid.

He'd been staring upwards absently, through the branches of the pine trees that surrounded this sunken chamber. Thinking of his friend, he gazed at the person who was looking down without at first feeling any alarm. The local's ruddy features were divided by that jutting growth they called the 'nose'. From the bottom of it sprang a flourish of black, bushy facial hair, seeming to defy gravity. At this angle, everything looked upside down. Those swollen purple lips could be a single grotesque eye. The deep-set, white-ringed eyes could be two small open mouths with white teeth.

The local was fully dressed, his clothes covered in marks of status and fashion. He must think the Aleutians looked funny. It had taken the traders some time to realise that people on earth *never* slobbed around in public in a state of undress. They must have created a ridiculous impression in the early days, when they went to grand receptions in their bare overalls. What did he see? A party of slick-haired, flat-faced people in long underwear making silly gestures at each other, in the effort – normal people overdid it – to converse through their quarantine.

The librarian realised that his mind was babbling in panic.
⟨Doctor!⟩

No one noticed his feeble alarm. But others had seen the face.
Bokr straightened his burly frame. His height was imposing. He
towered over most locals; as over most Aleutians. He spoke in
the dialect of the region. The person answered. Goodlooking
caught the word *archaea*, old things. The face retreated.

'He wanted to know what we were up to,' announced Bokr
calmly. The trading post staff exchanged glances. Their guest
looked at the ground, embarrassed. There were things he was
not supposed to understand. 'I think we should be getting back,'
Bokr went on casually. He gave the invalid a smile of mild social
apology. 'I'm afraid you won't see the ancient palace today.'

'Never mind,' replied Goodlooking automatically. He could
only help by joining the charade. 'Another time.'

Panisad, the minor trader, put an arm around his shoulders.
⟨CONGRATULATIONS,⟩ he told Goodlooking, *earnestly distinct*,
to make sure he was understood. ⟨YOU KEPT YOUR HEAD.
YOU WERE AS GOOD AS AN OLD HAND. YOU'RE ONE OF
US!⟩

They had all seen the frank murder in the local's eyes, and felt
the threat and hatred. Nobody mentioned these things. Someone
fetched the droms. Bokr took the invalid in his arms to carry him
up out of the tomb. Through the trees the shape of the old palace
could be discerned, it was so near. Goodlooking knew that he
would never see it now. He would not leave the trading post
again, until the evacuation shuttle – which was surely on its
way – came to take him. He would never see these stones again,
nor the yellow sun nor the blue sky. Suddenly he was horrified.
Had he really wasted such a precious hour brooding on his
neurotic wrongs? But it was too late for regrets. The adventure
was over.

The Aleutian pipeline ran north to south across the Argolid
plain: a regular trace of darker soil, diminishing until it disappeared into conifer plantation. It was part of a pump that was
drawing thick, foul brine from the gulf of Korinth and churning
out clean water at Nafplion to the south. Where it passed near

the site of ancient Mycenae, above the road from Argos to Korinth, Sid Carton was at work: supervised by Maitri.

Sid was chipping away at a splash of grey concrete that marred the neat dark band. Anti-Aleutian protestors had dug up the channel and poured in a plug of quick-hardening liquid stone, which they had laced with a wide-spectrum bactericide. They'd done no harm. The technicians at the trading post monitored their water plant constantly, and were unconcerned. Aleutian industrial bacteria could deal with anything the locals threw at them. But Maitri liked to keep his pipeline looking nice.

The protestors were amateurs. On either side of their plug, the 'pipe' of sterile soil that surrounded the bacterial flow was broken. There was every chance that alien micro-organisms had made a break for freedom: an ironic result for the anti-Aleutians. But Sid had seen too much of the realities of so-called Total Quarantine Enforcement to be upset about this. The living power tools used by the Aleutian artisans had to be kept inside the quarantined compound, and they had no local-style equivalents. Sid was using a hammer and chisel on the concrete. They were his own. He liked to see himself as a simple, old-earth handyman. And if something needed fixing in his quarters, he didn't want aliens nosing around. If you lived with the Aleutians you learned to keep your territory clearly defined. Otherwise they'd be all over you.

It was hard work. Sweat trickled on his forehead. The film, which he had to wear the same as the aliens, licked it up with a million tickling mouths. He squatted back to scratch the itch. His slickly encased hand dropped, defeated. Quarantine was a pain.

Maitri dropped into an animal crouch beside him.

'Let me have a turn.'

They were half-hearted bipeds, slipping easily and strangely into a four-footed gait. They'd been called *man-sized baboons in clothes*: it was close enough. The hairless, noseless muzzle of a super-sentient monster with formidable fangs leaned cosily by Sid's shoulder. He was careful not to flinch.

'No thanks, sahib. Your prestige is my safety. I don't want some partisan with an antique Kalashnikov to come over the hill and spot one of the immortal superbeings stooping to manual labour.'

But the sunburned landscape was empty. Nothing local had passed on the crumbling strip of road all afternoon.

'No messages at all,' mused the alien gloomily.

Ostensibly they were here to chip concrete. In fact they'd come out so that Sid could scoot down the road, to the place where the modern town of Mykini had been resettled when the Aleutians moved in up here and the former Mykini was razed. The prefabricated huddle had been abandoned before it was finished, but there was a functioning public cablepoint. Sid sneaked down there often, on his weekly half-day, to keep up with the human world's news. (The feudal Aleutians were bemused by the notion of private 'holidays' and 'working weeks'. But he'd squeezed this concession out of them.)

They didn't like human telecoms. All their technology involved living material, tailored secretions that oozed from the skins of their artisans. In some sense everything they used and touched was a physical extension of themselves, and every communication was mediated by living physical contact. They had their own science of audio-visual records, but it was almost exclusively for religious purposes. They were immortal – at least in their own estimation – and had no dread of death itself. But they called the place on the other side of a screen *the deadworld*. They feared the unliving images on their blurry video screens. The idea of interacting with the dead scared them. To talk to someone who appeared to you in there; or to a free-standing *dead* image, or to answer a voice propagated through emptiness as *dead* signals: this was, for an Aleutian, very like speaking to a ghost.

Maitri's staff would have been shocked to know that their tame local went in for eerie native rituals. But Maitri was a special kind of Aleutian. Sid had few secrets from him.

'Nothing,' he said. 'Cable cut somewhere up the line, complete services collapse. This is a very bad sign, Maitri. Our local amateurs wouldn't cut cable.'

The Peloponnese had been encabled for longer than the Aleutians had been on earth. Rural encablature had been a matter of regional pride back then. The population had shifted further into the cities and the system had fallen into disuse. The public points had remained as lingering beacons of global civilisation. Sid's beacon had gone out.

'What about the LOE GPS system?'

Lord Maitri was a 'Japanese', which meant he'd been a member of the original landing parties. The aliens' first patron on earth had been an ex-Japanese billionaire. That was where the Sanskrit names came from. Sanskrit being, Sid had been told, a sacred language for Japanese Buddhists. Sid grinned a little nervously. Maitri was very knowledgeable!

'Low-orbit ephemeral satellite communication's no use to us. It's controlled by the military. And the snowflakes get shot down right off if something's going on.'

Involuntarily they both stared around. They were unarmed, in accordance with the Landing Party Treaty.

'Is it "Men" I'm looking for, or "Women"?' demanded Maitri.

Sid groaned. 'Both: if we're very unlucky.'

'Of course. I understand that. There are *biological males* on the "Women's" side, and *biological females* on the "Men's" side.'

Aleutians were 'hermaphrodites', to borrow a human term. They could all give birth, and there was no strict equivalent to the male role in their reproduction. Maitri pronounced the technical terms with care. Sid looked at him suspiciously, wondering if the boss was being deliberately obtuse.

The alien's shoulders lifted. The planes of his face moved upward under the glinting quarantine film. This complex shrug was their smile. Bared teeth meant something else. But Maitri never snarled. He was the most gentle, the kindest of baboon-fanged telepathic superbeings.

'I must say, it does seem odd. Individual treachery is one thing. But this en-masse mingling, between two nations at war, still strikes me as bizarre.'

Sid was tired of trying to explain the Gender War to Aleutians. 'It's not "the Men versus the Women". That's *your* perception. It's about an attitude of mind. About ways of relating to the cosmos, to the WorldSelf, as you would say.' He attacked the concrete violently. 'I don't know why you're complaining to *me*, anyway. I'm not involved. I'm a halfcaste. Why can't you remember that?'

Maitri considered his human friend. He remembered the first meetings between humans and Aleutians. When the whole giant planet was in the grip of 'Aleutian fever', there had been some locals who went to extremes. They cut off their noses, they gave up talking aloud. They had their 'male' or 'female' bodies altered in imitation of the ungendered traders. They declared themselves immortal and searched human moving-image records for traces of their past selves. Their fellows had called them 'Aleutian-lovers', and regarded them as crazy. Now they clustered wherever Aleutians could be found, hungry for contact with their idols. They were called 'halfcastes' – a term that had nothing to do with the facts. The 'purebreds' (another term that made no sense), both Men and Women, despised them.

Sidney Carton came from the halfcaste community: this Maitri knew. But his human appearance was unmutilated. He'd kept his nose intact, and – as was obvious even in roomy overalls – the *male* lying-down equipment. He spoke English for preference, though he could understand the Common Tongue. He used deadworld communications without shame: and he did not seem to regard his employers with undue reverence. To Maitri, all this was proof of Sid's good sense. The others didn't agree. Unfairly and inevitably, Aleutians despised the 'halfcastes' as much as other humans did. Even more unfairly, people were suspicious of Sid because he *didn't* make a grovelling fool of himself. Maitri sighed. He remembered humans with whom one could be friends, he remembered mutual respect. Somewhere along the way that meeting had been lost.

'Maybe you should cut off your nose after all,' he teased. 'Your nose and . . . um, so on. That might help.'

The opaque goggles Sid wore over his quarantine didn't conceal his disdain. 'To me, being an Aleutian-lover is a spiritual thing.' He studied the end of his chisel. 'Mutilation is a mug's game, and "halfcaste" is an idiot word. There's no such thing. We can fuck each other, I have heard tell. But the congress is sterile. To get a real halfbreed Aleutian-human, you'd have to grow the bugger in a vat. And who'd want to do that?' He looked up, the blank goggles challenging.

The alien shrugged. 'Who indeed?'

Sid resumed his bashing. 'Truth is, I don't know what I am.

I'm not a Man, not a Woman, not an Aleutian. Whichever role I take, I feel like one of the others playing a part. That's why I call myself Sidney Carton. He's a character in a drama-movie, chiefly famous for pretending to be someone else. He's played by the lovely Dirk Bogarde in my favourite version. It's called *A Tale Of Two Cities*: a tragedy of human redemption.'

'Ah, a former life. We must view the tape together,' said Maitri politely. 'When we have a quiet moment.'

To the Aleutians, watching stuff on a screen was a sacred ritual. You were either 'learning to be yourself' by studying the records of your past lives, or you were saying your prayers by studying the adventures of other selves. That was their religion. They worshiped the Ur-Self, WorldSelf, in its myriad aspects: each aspect an Aleutian person. When the landing parties arrived and saw humans glued to their tv screens night and day, they couldn't grasp that humans didn't feel the same. They still couldn't grasp the difference: not even Maitri. Aleutians were like that: not good at changing their minds. Drama-movies, subscriber-soap, news, sport – they took it all to be records made for religious purposes.

The funny part was that the average Aleutian trader was no more 'religious' than your average human sinner. They went to church all right, because they were in the grip of a state religion. They weren't *keen*. Maitri in fact had a rare love of the records for their own sake . . . like someone having a passion for temple dancing or church music. But you could hear in his voice what he thought about Sid's humble prayers. Alien says: 'Oh, yes, Sid, I'd love to come to the temple and make *puja* with you.' Alien thinks: *how nice for them to have such childlike simple faith* . . .

'Some of my proudest moments,' agreed the unregenerate Sid solemnly. 'I would be honoured to share them with you. Can we go back indoors now, sahib? I am not achieving anything.'

Maitri didn't answer. 'I wish I knew what the problem was,' he said after a silence. 'Is it the disc plant?'

The Aleutians, having secured this toehold in the north on the strength of the Mediterranean Pump, had started manufacturing 'discs' – discrete energy packs: Aleutian organic batteries that looked like hand-sized cowpats but packed an amazing charge.

This was against the rules. The Government of the World had persuaded the Greeks to turn a blind eye: and in fact it had transpired that the aliens did hardly any trade.

When Maitri had arrived a year ago, he'd been full of plans for livening the place up. He'd envisaged open house at the compound. He'd seen himself settling down for long chats with Sid and the Mycenaeans about the work of his favourite human clerics: the Revd Wim Wenders, the Revd John Huston . . . the Very Revd Miss Jane Austen, perhaps – though Aleutians, who only 'read' the movies, found that spiritual leader's reputation mysterious.

It was not to be. Lord Maitri had not realised how much things had changed since he was last around. He'd been forced to resign himself to the new order, to Total Quarantine Enforcement and a complete absence of social contact with the locals. His interpreter, having nothing to interpret, had become the trading post mascot. Life had settled into a dull routine, enlivened only by the arrival of a sick librarian. And then the world-wide protests had started, spreading swiftly even to depopulated rural Greece.

Sid squatted back. 'No,' he said wearily. 'No one minds your contraband cowpats. Maitri, you *know* what the trouble is. It's the Himalaya Project. If you people agree to leave their bloody mountains alone, everything will be fine.'

'Bloody?' repeated Maitri absently. 'Why "bloody"?' He made a gesture of dismissal. 'It can't be that. Don't be silly. There must be something more.' He produced a bleak solution to the mystery. 'I think you've never forgiven us, truly, for the Rape.'

Sidney Carton laughed. 'Nobody remembers that old story.'

'I wish Clavel were here.'

There was another silence. The alien's dark eyes were blank, his attention turned inward.

'Thank you for being so kind to Goodlooking, by the way. Conditions here are hardly ideal for an isolate . . .' *Isolate* was not a term you would use when the librarian was about. Goodlooking could take it. He was a tough little person in his way. But who would want to know himself the cause of the flowering, deep inside, of yet another of the countless bruises life inflicted on that lonely and secret soul?

'Yudi has promised me a shuttle,' he announced.

Sid had resumed a desultory tapping, because he didn't know what the alien wanted from him at this moment. Maitri had gone into a very Aleutian mode: crouched there in unreachable thoughts, coming out with these gnomic pronouncements.

'That's good. When's it due to arrive?'

The alien shrugged. 'Yudisthara won't let me down.' He stood and held out his hands, palms open. Each lacked a little finger. The skin was loose and open-pored. His fingernails were the trimmed claws of a beast in clothes: a fairytale monster.

'We are different, but we are not so different. Your Self understands mine. If it were not for the quarantine your chemical essence, your pheromones, would be mingling in the air with mine and telling me your news. Aleutians go home? Most Aleutians would prefer to go home: if we knew the way. But I am not one of them, Sid. I love this planet. I do not see why I should not stay.'

Abruptly he dropped to the ground and loped off, to survey the empty road with keen anxiety.

ΑΛΛΟΔΑΠΟΣ ΠΗΓΑΙΝΕΙΣ ΟΙΚΙΑ

It seemed as if the whole of the Argolid had dropped into a pit of silence. The limestone crags above the conifers glowed golden and indigo against the summer sky. Sid pulled off his trusty goggles and glowered at the scrawled Greek lettering, half effaced by his chisel. Aliens go home! It was not a new idea. But in close on a century, it had never had so much support.

The first Aleutians had arrived on earth under the command of the three captains: Rajath the trickster, Clavel the poet – the one they called the Pure One – and Kumbva the engineer. They were a small party of private adventurers. The world from which they came was a ship lost in space, a wandering hulk that had blundered into the solar system by chance. The people of earth didn't know that. They welcomed the visitors with delirious excitement, hailed them as superbeings, angels, saviours. Rajath the trickster had been quick to take advantage. He discovered that the 'locals' believed his people had travelled instantaneously across the galaxy from a fabulously advanced world of superbeings. He eagerly agreed that this was so. The nature and location of the shipworld out in orbit became a guarded secret.

Then the aliens killed a human, and a terrifying standoff developed: terrifying to both parties, but again the humans didn't know that. Rajath had bluffed his way through that emergency, and the 'superbeings' seemed unassailable. Those few humans who saw the truth and dreaded the future were helpless. Meanwhile Clavel, the romantic young poet, had fallen in love with a 'local': a USSA journalist called Johnny Guglioli. Clavel believed that humans and Aleutians were one flesh, aspects of the same cosmic WorldSelf. He recognised Johnny as his 'trueparent', his genetic twin born in the previous generation and therefore, in Aleutian mythology, his perfect, fated lover. But Johnny loved a woman called Braemar Wilson, the secret leader of the anti-Aleutian resistance group called White Queen.

Johnny was a friend to the aliens, he refused to join in Braemar's plans. But then Clavel tracked Johnny down and, overcome by passion, raped him. This incident loomed large in the alien imagination, because of Clavel's otherwise spotless reputation. It was hardly mentioned in the human records. But it changed Johnny's mind. He and Braemar Wilson located the Aleutian shipworld and somehow got themselves out there, determined to blow up the aliens' bluesun reactor.

They could have succeeded. But the infant Government of the World, convened to deal with the aliens, had also located the ship. The saboteurs were detected. The humans, rightly or wrongly, decided to warn the Aleutians and Johnny and Braemar were caught. The aliens executed Johnny – a light enough sentence, in their terms, because they didn't know (most of them still didn't believe it) that humans were not immortal. Braemar, sent back to earth, escaped from custody and died from unrelated causes a few years later. That was the end of the tragical romance of first contact.

After that, the three captains had vanished from command. A different set of aliens negotiated with the Government of the World. They surrendered the territory Rajath had secured for Aleutian settlement in exchange for the right to set up a network of quarantine trading posts, radiating from their established headquarters north of Thailand. It seemed they had no further ambitions.

If you listened to the Aleutians, thought Sid, you'd believe that the whole of old earth – by which they meant anywhere outside their trading network – had been at war ever since. And they were mainly right.

He sat back on his haunches, fists balled against his ruddy cheekbones, brooding on the stupid mess of recent human history.

It had started with the 'Eve Riots' of the twenty-first century, when the downtrodden female masses of what was known as the Third World (a 'world' that seemed to have enclaves everywhere) took to the streets, demanding more pay and better conditions for their labour. A global conference had convened, in Bangkok, to discuss the problems. It was not meant to achieve anything. It was supposed, like the notorious 'Earth Summits' of the previous century, to be a brief indulgence for the bleeding hearts before a return to business as usual. Then the aliens arrived and decided, for reasons best known to themselves, to regard the World Conference on Women's Affairs as the seat of planet earth's government. Thereupon a whole package of worthy, virtuous reforms of human behaviour, *including* a better deal for 'biological females', became known as the Women's Agenda. After the sabotage crisis there was a backlash, and the Men's Agenda emerged. The Men were the traditionalists, and they included plenty of women who agreed that the traditional division of labour, responsibility and material wealth between the genders was natural and right.

It was more like a religious dispute than anything: dividing countries, continents, families – but only on the chattering and street-demo level. Then a European state called England took exception to the dire condition of an array of nuclear power stations positioned in easy radioactive-pluming distance from their south coast. The English weren't notably reformist. But this was a 'gender' issue, in the new terms. When the dispute became a shooting match, and then a conflagration that engulfed Europe, Northern Eurasia and parts of Africa, they called it the First Gender War.

Most humans of either party or biological gender hated the 'Men versus Women' and the 'Gender War' tags, but the names had stuck. By the time Sidney Carton was born, in England, the war in Europe had lasted for decades. After several false attempts at peace, there was no number attached any more: it was just *the war*. The rhetoric was long exhausted, there was little to choose between the two sides. Everyone was poor and everyone felt cheated of the riches and comforts that had vanished. Sid remembered being hungry and tired all the time. And he remembered being grimly grateful, though he rebelled against his own people constantly, that he did not have to join either faction of the vicious child gangs that roamed his estate. He remembered understanding, from a very early age, that it was crazy to be a halfcaste, but it was better than being one of *them*.

Sid's people had moved south to the enclaves. Many old-earth 'halfcastes' did that in the quieter years when travel was just about possible. In the enclaves, within their trading network, Aleutian influence kept the reformers and the traditionalists – the 'Women' and the 'Men' – living in reasonable harmony. The heretics who refused to have a gender were tolerated, if not welcomed, by the two communities.

While the human race was engrossed in this bitter squabble, the Aleutian traders had been quietly prospering, almost unnoticed: until one day they announced the Himalaya Project. They planned to set heavy-duty rock-munching microbes to level the peaks of the Himalaya ranges, thereby bringing refreshment to the climate of the subcontinent. It would take a few years, they thought. Maybe less. It wasn't the first Aleutian scheme of its kind, though it was the most ambitious. They seemed honestly amazed at the explosion of outrage that spread rapidly through the enclaves and old earth. It wasn't, they protested, as if the mountains were alive!

Everest, thought Sid. *Sagamartha. Mother of the Gods*. He lifted a handful of the storied dust of Greece, tissue of myth, seeds of soul, and crumbled it over his head. A world can be alive, without being saturated with the living cells of its sentient inhabitants. A world can be made sacred, by something other than biology.

But the Aleutians would never understand that. Sid grimaced horribly, his sun-scoured features creasing inside their wrapping into a thousand premature wrinkles. The dust slithered from the coat of film that covered a shock of hair the colour and texture of bleached straw. He had no sympathy with the purebreds' metaphysical angst. He didn't see what was special about a meat

– as it were – mountain. They were on record somewhere, surely. You could experience them anytime. Sid's dread was practical.

The Aleutian technicians admitted that there'd be a disturbance of local weather systems, and a rise in the deathrate: but nothing to notice, since there was a global war going on anyway. The effects would pass in a generation or two. The net gain in climate improvement was worth the cost.

In a generation or two . . . Sid thought of tons upon tons of rock and ice, shearing away. Of the sky filled with mountain dust, and the north wind rushing down out of the cold desert. He thought of the footage he'd seen of life after the Japan Sea cataclysm: a marginal upheaval compared to this one. Some scientists predicted that the inevitable cooling would tip the earth into a premature new ice age, a million years of winter. It hardly seemed to matter. Like a long drop, or deep water: after the first hundred, who's counting? But the Aleutians didn't understand that. They didn't believe in permanent death.

A flock of sparrows flew down and started to scratch in the disturbed pipeline for food. They'd be lucky . . . The purebreds were such fools. They woke after a hundred years and thought they could kick the aliens out, just like that. Sid watched the sparrows. *What I would like*, he thought, *is to have a house of my own, with a garden, and live in it and provide for my family. I could grow vegetables*. He wondered how long before an air transport from Uji could get here.

'There's only one way to shift them,' he told the little birds. '*Offer them an alternative*. Show them something better than what they've got. Otherwise *we are fucked*. Because nothing else makes it. Absolutely nothing we can do will touch them.'

Maitri came back on two feet, slowly, scratching the bristling gap where his nose should be. 'They're safe. I watched them to the turn.' His relief was touchingly obvious.

'No empty saddles?' The droms, engineered hybrids between horse and camel, were evil brutes, in Sid's opinion. But the Aleutians liked them. They were living machines: homelike.

'No empty saddles,' agreed Maitri, smiling.

'You should've cancelled that excursion.'

'Perhaps. But he'd been looking forward to it so much, we

didn't have the heart. An isolate, you know . . . There's so little one can do to make things right.'

Sid looked up. A gleam of vivid blue flickered through his stubby pale lashes. They were supposed to be telepaths. Sid knew the limits of that mythical ability. But like any human who had anything to do with them, he would not meet alien eyes directly if he could help it. For a moment he studied Lord Maitri covertly.

'Time to go home, Gunga Din.'

'Achcha, sahib.' The blue gleam vanished. The alien bounded away. Sid picked up his tools and followed.

The trading post stood alone under a hemisphere of antibiotic and carbon-strengthened glass. Once they were through the entrance lock, they were in Aleutia. The sightseers had just arrived. Domestics were leading away the droms. Goodlooking exclaimed, 'Sid, you've hurt your hands!'

He realised it was true. The quarantine started melting as soon as you were indoors. His palms were bare, and he could feel the blisters. Overcome by the unease that afflicted him when he met his alien friend in front of an audience, he dropped to one knee and flung his injured hands in the air.

'She cares! I believe she loves me!'

The Aleutians laughed, their faces brimming with soundless alien merriment. They thought Sid's routines with Goodlooking were killingly funny. A trolley was passing, carrying folded napery to the dining room. Sid grabbed a red tablecloth and flourished it. The cloth in a panic struggled to escape, but Sid would have none of that. He wrestled and brought it to sub-mission, cast it proudly to the ground and trailed it like a bullfighter's cape across the forecourt, singing:

> *L'amour est comme un enfant sauvage,*
> *qui n'a jamais connu la loi . . .*

In front of him stood a wide stone basin where an Aleutian gardener was trying to grow roses. Sid had forgotten what came next. 'Di-dada da! Di-dada da!' he chanted. He pulled a rose and flung himself at Goodlooking's feet, snatching another phrase out of oblivion. '*Si je t'aime prends garde de toi!*'

The aliens standing around applauded, human style: they

knew how to do that. Goodlooking recoiled from the broken stem of the flower. ⟨How horrible!⟩ She pulled herself up. ⟨Oh, I'm sorry. I didn't mean—⟩

'It doesn't matter,' Sidney told her, grinning. 'With a mug like mine, you get used to reactions like that from the girls.' He headed off for his quarters, swinging his toolbag jauntily.

Maitri took his ward's arm, and led him away. Sheets of quarantine film drifted from them as they walked and were nibbled up by the busy air. 'Don't let Sid's cabaret upset you,' he said. 'It's a form of shyness.' They had spoken English together since Goodlooking was a little child. Their shared passion for everything to do with the giant planet was a bond between them.

'I know that. But I wish he wouldn't call me "she".'

'It's natural to him. In the old days, they identified some people as feminine or masculine on sight . . . with uncanny accuracy, I may say, as far as it matters.' The Aleutians recognised among themselves a spectrum of personality traits, which seemed to match quite closely what humans regarded as 'masculine' and 'feminine' qualities . . . though to Aleutian perception many human males were feminine and many females were masculine; and of course either could be on the Men's side or on the Women's. All very confusing! But in Aleutia worrying if you were 'masculine' or 'feminine' was the sign of a trivial mind. 'Don't fret about it,' added Maitri, cuddling the thin arm close to his side. 'Nobody notices.'

They strolled, at a gentle pace. The Greek landscape shimmered through the glass dome, blurred by the silky cloud of Aleutian life. In front of the disc works, artisans were dolefully crumbling a pile of their products into dust. 'We're closing the plant,' said Maitri. 'I must go over there, to tell everyone how important their work here has been and so on.'

'Is it true?'

'No. But what's the first rule of good management, child?'

Goodlooking smiled. 'Praise.'

They reached a bench of local material, set where the artisans liked to sit and take the air. Maitri paused as if by chance. He folded himself down, drawing Goodlooking beside him. He knew his invalid's capacities to a step.

'You know,' said Maitri grimly, 'the Expedition has enemies out in orbit. They're going to use this against us. Where did we go wrong? That's the question. It *can't* be those mountains . . . ! I suppose we'll find out one day,' he decided wearily. 'The locals will tell us, lives from now, when they're not angry with us and it doesn't matter any more. That's the way people are.'

Goodlooking thought of his friend. Though Sid had no sympathy with the protestors, he dreaded the Himalaya Project. He had never put it into formal words. But Goodlooking knew that his fear was real, visceral: seeming beyond his rational control. He said nothing. It wasn't the moment for a mere librarian to tell Lord Maitri that he didn't understand the locals.

'I wanted to talk to you,' began Maitri. 'I'm going to be very busy. We may not have another chance . . .'

Goodlooking had known some crisis was imminent. But this struck him like a blow. 'Is the shuttle coming for me?' he cried. 'Oh, Daddy, I don't want to go. Let me stay with you, please.'

Maitri's nasal contracted. ⟨Ah, my dear!⟩

Goodlooking looked into his face: Maitri's arms went out. For a moment they clung together, Lord Maitri cradling the child in the curve of his body as he had done long ago. Then Goodlooking drew away, shoulders lifting in a tremulous smile.

⟨No farewell speeches,⟩ he pleaded. ⟨It's better not.⟩

Maitri smiled and nodded. 'Come then,' he said lightly. 'My brave child. We've time to console those artisans before we change for prayers.'

Goodlooking laughed, suddenly freed from a net of stinging slights. Nothing could cloud these last sweet moments of their intimacy. He would remember this day, when Lord Maitri came out of kindly duty to tell the librarian what a wonderful job he was doing. Dear Maitri! Praise!

Sid jogged through the blurred, furry walled passages, losing his quarantine to the nibblers underfoot and the tiny mouths in the air. Aleutian commensals of every size – tools, notepads, domestic appliances, furniture – bustled around him, from things like viruses to things as big as dogs and cats: every one of them derived from the body chemistry of some Aleutian or other.

Their main hall, where they ate and socialised, had been the

dining room when this was a human-type hotel. There was a
display case by the doors holding some reproductions of paper
pages, which he'd been told were from the hotel register. Labels
in English translated the illegible script, explaining nothing.
Virginia Woolf . . . Who she? Above them was a mugshot of a
scrawny geezer with jug-ears, done in low relief on a sheet of
gold. It looked modern, but Maitri said it came from the old
ruins. Sid didn't know if the gold was real.

Silent domestics were laying up tables. It looked grand and
archaic, like a civic banquet: and it *was* fairly grand, though
everything was disposable. In Aleutia there was no snob value
in having durable houseware. The snob value was in having
your famous housekeeper down with you from the shipworld
with a repertoire of exquisite designs stored in his glandular
secretions . . . The hotel was full of splendid Aleutian furnish-
ings: rich wraps, throws, hangings, couches, stools, video equipment: all of it alive, all of it liable to vanish and be replaced
overnight.

The food was probably equally fancy, but their food ranged,
in smell and appearance, from baby diarrhoea to snot soup.
Humans could eat it. But you wouldn't do so for fun.

The Silent were not slaves or possessions. Not they! They were
employees, colleagues, executives in the private company that
was an Aleutian household. There was no mechanical reason
why they didn't speak, nor were they elective mutes. It was
something switched off, he'd been told, in their mind/brain, so
that normal language was a blank. The Aleutians would put it
the other way round. To them everything in language – syntax,
metaphor, *he made his excuses and left* – was there in the
Common Tongue. The spoken word, you might say, was a rather
odd way of talking.

After evening prayers, the company would congregate in the
hall for supper. Then they'd clear the floor and dance. That was
something to see: when they had their formal robes on over the
eternal overalls, the coloured and patterned living stuff melding
and parting as they pranced around. After the dance, which had
no accompaniment but the rustle of their robes, they'd settle to
their music. Maitri's company included some talented people,
but the Silent were the best. Being Silent didn't mean you

couldn't sing. When they got together in ensemble, their mouth-music made the hairs on Sid's nape stand.

The Silent didn't appreciate local music. Whatever you tried on them they said the same: *too clogged, fibrous, tight, over-designed*. Too many notes, basically. But Maitri, who was so deft at knowing what everyone wanted, had dug out one of his souvenir tapes, something called 'Around the Parlour Piano', involving a bunch of Victorian-dressing history fans. They adored it.

The aliens did not sleep the way humans do. They napped and socialised in hall until dawn. Sid would wake in the middle of the night and hear the ensemble practising, mimicking the pure sounds of English words with eerie accuracy.

Be it ever so humble there's no place like home . . .

Bizarre!

The domestics smiled and nodded as he passed. They didn't look as if they were preparing to evacuate. Yudisthara would make them wait for the transport as long as he dared, Sid guessed. No one talked about it, but it was obvious that Lord Maitri wasn't in favour at headquarters. Lord Maitri the Japanese, intimate friend of the great Clavel, was a close associate of the three captains, who had been languishing in the political wilderness since the sabotage crisis. That was undoubtedly why he had been shoved off to this god-forsaken posting. It was natural that the regime which had ousted the captains should be wary of him. If Lord Maitri had returned to the scene, could the three captains be far behind?

The three captains were figures of legend in the human world. Rajath the trickster, Clavel the poet; and Kumbva, whose hunger for pure knowledge would never be satisfied. There were stories – which couldn't all be true, unless there was something badly wrong with Sid's understanding of Aleutian reincarnation – of the three, superpowered and capricious, secretly manipulating human history throughout the last century.

Sid often tried to get Goodlooking to give him the dirt on Aleutian politics. What about the shipworld clique called 'Dark Ocean', the people who wanted Aleutia to abandon earth? Dark Ocean people wanted to set off again, not to search for another landfall without awkward inhabitants, but to hunt for the lost homeworld. They'd had enough of the long adventure.

Did they really have secret agents in the Expedition, working to destroy it from within? Could it be true that the three captains were involved?

She wouldn't talk. She'd look at him with those little black eyes, primp up that cat's mouth (divided upper lip running to two black slits of nostril) and laugh all over her face.

Her *face*, he called it. To the Aleutians that meant more than eyes-nose-mouth. It meant the whole outward person, and their aura-cloud of life. *Persona* might be better, but it was too formal, too rarefied in English usage. Face would have to do. He had no idea what she saw as Sid's face, except that it wasn't the sun-scoured whitey-haired goblin he saw in a mirror.

He knew from the way she laughed that there *was* dirt: but she wouldn't tell. She particularly wouldn't gossip about Clavel. She revered the 'Pure One' – the Aleutian who admired humans so much he raped one. Sid gathered that Clavel was one of those celebrities whose legendary goodness withstands all attacks from the facts. Like Gandhi or Robin Hood. The rape of Johnny Guglioli the saboteur was regarded as the end of the Expedition's innocence. Yet it was not Clavel's crime that had passed into Aleutian mythology: it was his remorse. *The Grief of Clavel*. To them that was the title of the first contact story.

Typical! thought Sid. *What about* The Grief of Johnny Guglioli? *What about* The Grief of Braemar Wilson?

She's a funny little thing, he mused. The Aleutians varied as widely as humanity in physical appearance and bulk: some big as bears, some elfin. Some of them looked like humans with drooping shoulders and lumpy hips, some were much more weird. Goodlooking's *occluded nasal*, as they called it when someone had nostril slits instead of a gap, and her slight build put her on the human end of the scale. In certain moods he could see her as entirely human. It was an ambience. The mild-mannered librarian on the holiday of a lifetime – like Alec Guinness in the classic movie-drama *Last Holiday*. Goodlooking bore no physical resemblence to the glorious Alec. But the Guinness role in that movie was her. The secret boldness behind the diffidence, the dry observing wit: qualities you'd never

suspect if you didn't know her on her own ground, where she felt
safe.

Maitri had taken care to give her that ground on earth. He had
had shipped down with her copies of about half his private
library. Her room was stacked with the clumsy-looking alien
tape cassettes; a row of fat clunky alien screens went round the
walls. There was barely room left for Goodlooking's bed, a
meagre shelf for formal clothes; and her mixing desk.

She was a *video* librarian, of course. The Aleutians had never
gone through the phase of putting life's drama into printed
words. Print was reserved mainly for obscure technical manuals.
They'd passed straight from some kind of temple frieze picture
stories (the carving would've been done by tailored microbes) to
moving-image records. Goodlooking longed to get hold of local
classics in *incunabula* – by which she meant the books – for
Maitri's collection. But they'd be no more than treasured objects.

She'd told him that the most popular earth record out in orbit,
after *The Grief of Clavel*, was *Les Intermittences Du Coeur*, the
French tv serial of Proust. She'd tried to show him what made
Proust essentially Aleutian, flicking the images about, stopping
and starting and turning and interposing face on face. This
nuance in a smile near the end, to the *particular tone* of a scrap
of dialogue back at the start . . .

But Sid cracked up, imagining hordes of the alien working
classes descending on fortress Paris, storming the Boulevard
Haussmann, demanding to confess their sins and joys to the Revd
Marcel. She pulled down that cat-mouth at him, and the black
eyes got snappy. He couldn't get her to understand why he was
giggling.

If it hadn't been for her disability, he supposed she'd be in holy
orders herself. She'd be hearing confessions and processing them
into blurry generated-image video footage. Maybe that should
be *perceiving* or *absorbing* confessions. What the priests of the
Self did involved all their Aleutian senses. But it had to be a
flawed and artificial way of compiling the story of your life.
Some people – important people with a bohemian bent – went
really wild and made their own tape. The priests still did the
processing. What went on your record was your life as they saw

it: your experience filtered through the state religion. It sounded, he told Goodlooking, like a recipe for pure fiction.

'You mean, it's the same as your character records? Well, yes, of course. That's what we keep telling you.'

The traps of language.

He reached his room, which was at the back of the hotel, away from everybody except Goodlooking.

In the librarian's lair, whatever else was showing, she had a tape from *The Grief of Clavel* on one of the screens. In two-dimensional, fuzzy Aleutian gen-image, Sid could watch the saboteurs, Johnny and Braemar. Like most halfcastes, he knew these two well, though the rest of the human world seemed to have forgotten them. The babyfaced young man with those well-nigh Aleutian black eyes and coltish, gangling figure. Braemar Wilson with the mulberry red hair, sorrow and pain and fear etched into every line of her deliberate loveliness. Sid could watch Johnny going to his death, out there in the shipworld: walking with the executioner in a blue-lit cavernous hall through a crowd of alien faces.

He knew that for Goodlooking it was a beautiful, tragic, story about Clavel. He guessed she'd never thought how it might feel to be Sid, watching that story inside an alien stronghold.

He believed she still didn't know, which was an achievement for a human among the aliens. Sid was proud of the way he could handle himself in the Common Tongue. He didn't blab his intimate secrets in the twitching of his features. He could keep his private thoughts private as skilfully as most Aleutians.

The doors in their part of the hotel were converted to their specifications. This one was not. He shut it behind him and shot the bolt. He checked the ribbon of yeasted oily dough around the frame and slicked the seal back into place with his thumb. This was an old anti-Aleutian trick. It was supposed to keep wanderers out. The other tiny commensals were negligible. But the wanderers, those lice things that crept on Aleutian skin, that they ate off themselves and each other like baboons picking for fleas: they were the principal carriers of information. He'd never heard of them being used as spies. But he didn't want them in here.

It was believed that the wanderers were the key to the

physiology of Aleutian telepathy, and Aleutian immortality . . .
It was believed. Sid pulled a wry face. No human knew for sure
what went on inside an Aleutian body, much less in Aleutian
brain chemistry. Physical investigation was a big taboo. It was
dangerous to suggest the idea. But their genuine lack of interest
was an equally effective block. Their living science didn't
progress by leaps of theory. It simply *worked*, like life itself,
insensately trying this and that until something clicked.

Their knowledge of their own physiology had weird gaps.
When it came to interactions below the threshold of life, they
cut out entirely. What humans called pure science was to them
the preserve of a minority of eccentrics. *Electrons aren't things*,
a human savant had once pronounced. If electrons aren't things,
said the Aleutians, the hell with them.

He sat on his bed, a soft grey pallet unrolled on the floor. It
was an Aleutian product for the local market: what they called
half-killed and humans called sterilised. It was cosy, once you
got over the nightmares about being eaten by your bedding.

There was no need to make a mystery of it. The Aleutians
'communicated' over distance the same way they read each
other's body language so perfectly: by knowing each other very
well. They'd learned the responses by heart in those character
records. *Maitri* knew how *Yudi* would jump in situation A. *Yudi*
knew what *Rajath* would say if you asked him question Q. If
everybody acted in character, and it seemed they generally did,
the system worked. That was their telepathy: a feat of memory
and deduction.

Which is fine for them, he thought. *But if you badly need to
know what's going on in the human world, and you* don't
*happen to know the responses of the human brood-entity off by
heart, then it is time to call up the electrons and the photons.*
He pulled a small wadded bag from inside the folds of the pallet,
and whistled softly between his teeth as he put together the
components of his global-mobile. Let's find out if there are any
snowflakes in the sky. *Is there anybody there?* he chuckled to
himself. *Are my little spirit guides going to answer me?* He tried
to crank up a calm and merry mood whenever he used the phone,
in case his terror spilled out into the air around him. Is the

chemistry of fear a cosmic determinate? He preferred to take no chances.

The transmitter's tiny screen sizzled. *We have snowflakes!*

He tried to raise his boss. Not Maitri: the other boss. He failed. He was not perturbed. He was beginning to feel more relaxed about the situation. He was indoors, which made a grand difference to morale. The aliens were calm. What could happen? He decided to go to Trivandrum and talk to the children.

It was about time. They'd be forgetting what their parent looked like. It was a cruel shame he had to leave them for so long.

'I'm a tramp and a no-good and not fit to be a mother!'

He attached the contacts. Flip, flicker. The receiverless phone took his picture and fired the image to a low-orbit ephemeral, along with a tightly detailed set of 4 space coordinates. Sid sped a quarter of the way around the world, to the Malabar coast, into the heart of the Aleutian enclave band.

He was on the roof. It was in a horrible mess. *What can you expect?* he thought defensively. *I'm never here, because someone's got to pay the rent. How am I supposed to keep up with the chores?* He crouched among dirty cooking things, weirdly conscious of the heat and weight of the tropic air, which his image could not feel. The kids weren't in sight. Instead Jimi swung into view: shy and with liquid fawn's eyes, guitar slung around her neck (his neck! Sorry, Jim!), a pan of something in one hand.

'Sid? Is that you, Sid?'

'Of course it's me! Who does it look like?'

Correct me if I'm wrong, he thought, *but wasn't Hendrix quite a sharp young man? Sentimental, yeah, a soft touch, but definitely not an idiot. Not this time.* If we have to believe in reincarnation, he wondered bitterly, couldn't we make it a *touch* more plausible? But the halfcaste community in Triv didn't worry about that. It never struck them as odd how many world-famous global-village megastars had been reborn among them.

'Thank the Self you're here. We've having a hassle with Lydie. She won't go in the safe room.'

'The safe room,' he repeated, stunned. They could rely on

toleration, but they prepared for the worst. The safe room was
the refuge kept in a halfcaste home, ready in case of trouble.

'What's happened?'

Another figure in fancy dress hove into view: a scrawny
woman with lumpy peasant features and an air of iron determination. She came right up, invading his bi-location bodyspace,
peering from under the blue-bordered veil: spoke in her Common
Tongue that somehow conveyed a chi-chi accent, with grace-
notes of Albania.

⟨There have been outbreaks of anger against the blessed folk,
the messengers of God. We thought it best to take precautions.⟩

Sid felt sick. 'Bring her here!'

They brought Lydie, his six-year-old daughter. She was crying,
snailtracks of tears on her dark skin. She was furious with herself
because she wanted to be brave and couldn't hack it. She poured
out accusations against Mother Teresa and Jimi. Jimi chimed in,
defending himself. Mother Teresa began a saintly reproof. There
was nothing Sid could do. He couldn't hug Lydie. Or give Mother
T. a punch in the nose hole . . . (Sid had difficulty with mother
figures). He fought to find a controlling, sarcastic voice. He
established that Lydie's baby brother, little Roger, had settled in
the cramped, windowless refuge without a qualm. He sneered at
Lydia's rank cowardice. It was horrible to hurt her. But it
worked. Lydie went off with Mother Teresa. Sid was left with
Jimi, finally able to react to the news.

'You have anti-Aleutian trouble in Triv? Right, you weather
it, you know how. Don't do anything provocative. Stay indoors,
and don't worry about me. Don't let Lydie start worrying. Tell
her the trading post is going to be evacuated, we have air
transport on the way. It's true. Uji's sending a shuttle.'

The reincarnated guitarist blinked at him.

'They're sending you a shuttle? Oh. Sure. If you say so.'

'What d'you mean, "If I say so"?'

'Uh, the word among the purebreds is that the Aleutians
evacuated Uji days ago, and then the locals went in and
ransacked the place, burned it out. But it's human news record,
deadworld images. It's probably a pile of shit . . .'

Sid didn't say anything. His mouth was too dry.

'It's bad for us.' Jimi carefully worked out the obvious. 'The purebred news says they've gone, running scared. They don't seem like superbeings at the moment. Things aren't good for Aleutian-lovers.' He tailed off. 'I wish you were here, Sid.'

'I have to go,' croaked Sidney. 'I've been on this line too long. Do your best, Jim. I'll be home as soon as I can get there.'

He disassembled the phone and hid it. He sat scratching at a patch of grey scale on his wrist. If you lived with Aleutians, you learned to tolerate temporary infestations. It would go away.

He wiped his trembling hands over his eyes. *Maitri's wrong,* he thought. *There is no shuttle. How long have we got? A few days, certainly. Relax, Sid. Breathe deeply. Make a plan . . .*

2: Well Built Mycenae, Rich In Gold

In the main hall, the company would relax together through the night: napping, chatting, making music and playing games. Goodlooking left them soon after supper as usual, and went to his room. He took off his dancing robe and folded it carefully away. Robes were made to last longer than most Aleutian artefacts and this was a nice one, a gift from Maitri: a lovely clear blue, but plain enough for the librarian's modest needs. He sat at his desk, but couldn't think of any work he wanted to do. The moving images on the screens around his walls were a comforting background presence, speaking silently in their familiar language. But there was nothing he wanted to watch.

An hour away, war was raging. *What you have to remember*, Bokr had explained, *is that the 'females' are smaller, and they're the obligate childbearers for both broods. The 'males' are generally bigger and stronger, but they can't bear children. You can see it's a situation that's bound to lead to friction.*

Sidney Carton had told him it was not true that men couldn't have children. The miracles of modern medicine, he said, made any fool thing possible. But he didn't approve. Sid had two kids of his own. But they were proper children, borne by two lovers of Sid's who were women: or maybe 'halfcastes' who were still physically female, the way Sid was a 'halfcaste', yet still physically male.

The details of human reproduction were confusing. But in the image of Sid, carrying away his children like trophies from the enemy camp, Goodlooking glimpsed the unappeasable hunger of the childless side, the lives upon lives of psychic oppression they had suffered. Equally, he'd seen records of the appalling war atrocities against biological females. Brrr . . . He was quite glad, in ways, that he was going home and leaving the Gender War behind.

I'm going to miss Sid, he thought. They had spent hours together in this room – talking about old earth, switching from formal to informal speech like intimate friends; slipping by degrees from discussing other people's records to sharing their own hopes and fears. The librarian smiled to himself. He'd been told that the locals, including Aleutian-lovers, babbled with embarrassing candour in the Common Tongue: you didn't know where to look. Sid wasn't that kind of idiot. Goodlooking still knew things about the trading post mascot that would have shocked most of the company. But he would not betray Sid's trust.

He decided to get ready for bed. He took off his shoes, shucked off his overalls and laid out the battery, each type in its bulb of cultured skin identical to his own. One by one he squeezed the evening doses on to his palm: swallowed the intestinal ones, inhaled the respiratory ones, moistened with spittle the inner surface of his wrist and coaxed the muscle-and-skin ones on to the damp surface; where they oozed and vanished. Mugging cheerful reluctance (he hated this part), he delved into his underwear and inserted wriggling life into his *place*.

He changed his toilet pad. He didn't need to, but taking his medication made him feel as if he smelled bad. As he scrumpled the used one into his wastebin, the inevitable wash of commentary swept through his mind: consoling, irritating, hurtful; the things he knew people said and felt about his condition. He endured it.

The librarian was isolate. His body produced no wanderers, or very few; and could not assimilate other people's mobile cells. It was a rare condition, and incurable. The deficiency was so bound up in his chemical identity that there was no way of correcting it which would leave *Goodlooking* in existence. Synthetic wanderers gave him partial communication, and allowed him to lead a fairly normal life. But they didn't proliferate in his body, they had to be replenished daily; and he had to spend his nights alone. The doctors said other people's wanderers might invade him while he napped and make him ill.

He lay down on his pallet, feeling tired but restless. He would have liked to stay with the others tonight. In a sense it was silly not to. It hardly mattered if he got ill now. But he'd felt he'd be letting the company down if he didn't behave exactly as usual. They were traders. Traders are born to take risks. It's part of their obligation, essential to their identity. Maitri's company counted it a point of honour to accept the luck of the game without any fuss. Goodlooking breathed the populated air, wondering what messages it carried that he could not translate.

He had known that the anti-Aleutian crisis was serious, and that Yudisthara at Uji had no answer except to hope it would go away. If he was normal, Maitri would not have had to take him aside to explain the rest. The truth was all around him, shed by the bodies of the experienced traders. There was no shuttle from Uji. There would be no evacuation. Disaster was closing in on the trading post, and no one would escape.

⟨Don't be sad,⟩ he thought, willing the feeble chemical caress towards Maitri. ⟨I have no regrets, none at all. It was time for us to part.⟩ The others would be thinking that Lord Maitri's grief was overdone. It wasn't as if Goodlooking was an infant. This would be more fuel for the 'disguised prince' rumour! Goodlooking cringed: and then laughed at himself. It didn't matter any more. He should have taken Bokr's offer while it was going.

He rolled over and tucked his face into his folded arms. How long was it since the librarian had lain down with someone? Too many lives. But making love is nothing, if it isn't an act of physical communication. Few people wanted to lie with an isolate. Anyone who did had some humiliating motive . . . vulgar curiosity, at best. The way Sid spoke of his lovers, as fleeting partners in not very friendly encounters, had struck a chord of rueful sympathy with Goodlooking. Like Sid, he remembered none of his 'sexlife' experiences with unmixed pleasure.

But he still wished he'd taken Bokr up on that offer.

He curled himself down in the pallet in his underwear, thinking he'd dress again in a moment. He must have dozed. He woke with a tremendous, heart-thumping jolt, as if from a nightmare. He was lying sprawled across the floor. What had happened? The lamps that clung to his walls gave off their dim night-time glow. What were those noises? Were people shouting?

He picked himself up and crawled back to the envelope of

bedding. Blurred sounds of voices and footsteps reached him; and the sharp rattle of local deadweapon fire. Goodlooking didn't stir. He knelt in an agony of tension, for so long that he fell into a kind of trance.

At last the door of his room softly opened. Sidney Carton stepped inside. He was carrying a small tray with a beaker on it. Goodlooking jumped up. He clutched his desk and grabbed wildly for Maitri's favourite tapes. They were copies, but he felt he must save something. He realised he was in his underwear, dropped the tapes and groped for his clothes. Then his mind cleared. There was no shuttle waiting. This was the end.

Still clutching his overalls, he looked at Sidney Carton wondering, why the tray? It was a dead thing, it must belong to Sid. He found himself staring at a large black object that was tucked in a belt loop of Sid's Aleutian overalls. It was a local pistol. Goodlooking had seen it before. It belonged in Bokr's collection of souvenirs.

⟨Sid? What are you doing with the doctor's firearm?⟩

Sid's face was almost ugly, and full of deadly meaning.

⟨*I'm going to destroy you.*⟩

Goodlooking recoiled. Instantly he knew that Sid could not have said that. Goodlooking must have misread him, projecting terror on to terror. He calmed himself.

'I didn't want to be in the way,' he said aloud. 'I thought I'd better stay here. Have you been sent for me?'

'I've brought you a nightcap,' said the halfcaste, in a voice nothing like his own. 'Maitri says you're to drink it.'

Goodlooking took the beaker, but did not drink. He could not make sense of Sidney Carton's demeanour.

⟨I don't think Maitri sent you.⟩

He spoke hesitantly. He felt half paralysed, as if he was dreaming. But Sid must have read something in his face: because he swooped, grabbed the hand with the beaker in it and pinned Goodlooking's other arm against his side. Goodlooking fought silently, but the liquid spilled into his mouth. He could not stop himself from swallowing. The grip that held him didn't give up till it was gone. Sid let go, breathing hard.

⟨I'm sorry—⟩ he gasped.

Goodlooking dropped to his four feet and ran. He reached his

door, and was out in the corridor. Desperation gave him strength
he had never possessed before. He ran through the hotel, his
limbs giving way under him, reeling from one wall to the other
along the corridors. He was aware of lamps darkened and fallen,
of air that tasted of death. As he came to the main hall there
was smoke everywhere; and flickers of fire. But he was not afraid
of what was happening there. Fear was behind him, in Sidney
Carton's face.

The hall doors had been ripped down and hung in tatters,
leaking vital fluid. The hall was full of local soldiers. They were
pressed around the walls, their big dead lights trained on a space
in the centre. They had the remaining company lined up two by
two facing that space. Beyond it lay a tattered heap of bodies.
Those who waited for their turn were joking and chatting
informally, or maintaining a dignified silence. Some crouched
on four feet, in too much pain to worry about appearances. In
the middle of the floor four soldiers held down a naked figure,
bloodstained tatters of a brown overall trailing from its wrists
and ankles. Another soldier, buttocks bared, pumped and thrust
at the figure's belly. The soldiers were yelling with laughter that
was like screams of agony. No sound came from the Aleutian.

⟨No!⟩ cried Goodlooking. ⟨Maitri! No!⟩

A hand dragged him back. He fell, flung himself upright, and
struggled desperately to join his friends. An inexorable will
dragged him away. ⟨Maitri, Maitri!⟩ he wailed. The walls of the
corridor had turned black and red, they swayed wildly. Gaping
mouths and eyes looked out of them.

'Come on! There's nothing you can do!'

Goodlooking's will to resist suddenly gave way. He would have
collapsed, but Sid hauled him to his four feet. They crawled back
into darkness. Goodlooking was swimming in blood-hued
visions. He lost track of what was happening, until he felt by the
change in the air that they were outside the building.

⟨Be quiet!⟩ Sid's grip told him, in a reflex of panic.

Light assaulted them. There were more soldiers everywhere,
soldiers and jeeps grinding up the night in the ruins of the
shattered dome. Two of them were separate from the rest,
conferring, haloed by a blaze of white. One was stocky, with a
white scarf wrapped thickly around his head and a bush of facial

hair. The other was tall and slender. As he turned, a badge glittered on the shoulder of his uniform: a golden leaf.

'Shit!' breathed Sid. 'Ochiba!'

They had not been spotted, not yet. Sid studied the frieze of light and movement. ⟨Now,⟩ he muttered. ⟨Let's think about this . . .⟩ Goodlooking was gazing at something pale that lay in a glimmer of viscous movement. He realised detachedly that it was Bokr's hand. The rest of the doctor's body was a black hummock beyond, one wrist jutting out. Wanderers crawled in the gap between, feebly trying to make good the damage. They were dying.

He heard Sid grunt: 'This'll do.' The halfcaste had got hold of something palm-sized, rounded and heavy. Goodlooking saw him rise to his feet, bent double to avoid the light. Sid disappeared backwards and then reappeared, running out of the shadow. A soldier yelled. Sid's arm swung in a level arc. The big white light on their left exploded, with such violence that they were flung flat on the ground.

'Shit! It was a grenade!'

Goodlooking heard that choked gasp, and nothing more. He fell into unconsciousness.

He came awake, moving. He was being carried on Sid's back. They were climbing between thin, dark shapes that loomed out of the darkness: trees. His cheek was against Sid's shoulder. Through the stink of blood and burning from Sid's overalls he could taste the resin of the pines. *Oh no*, he thought. *I'm outdoors without quarantine.* Something other than the trees appeared: a bulk of stonework. He realised that Sid had carried him from the hotel to the *archaea* in the conifer plantation. *He must be exhausted.* As he thought that, Sid suddenly dropped to his knees. Goodlooking slid to the ground.

They stumbled on, hand in hand. Once, Goodlooking baulked and tried to turn back. But his will was broken. He let Sid drag him onward through a maze of black walls with cold, dark, empty air above them. Then Sid picked him up and carried him again, down an endless series of steps. And then, abruptly, Goodlooking found himself tumbling from Sid's back on to a bed of stones. How cold the stone felt. How dead!

'Where are we?' he whispered.

'It was a water cistern, I think. I found it when I was poking about in the ruins, months ago.' A shuddering sigh came out of the darkness. 'The entrance isn't obvious . . . I don't know if we're safe. I couldn't think of anywhere else.' There was a faint fumbling. Reddish light welled. Sid appeared in lamplight, his face an abject mask.

'They came out of nowhere,' he whispered. 'They must've used a rocket to blow the dome. It wasn't proof against military assault. Why should it be? It was supposed to be there to protect humans from *you*. There was nothing I could do. All I could do was get you out. I'm going to put out the light. I don't think it can be seen from above but—'

Side by side, they crouched in the renewed blackness: listening with taut-strung attention.

There was a long silence. Goodlooking stirred at last.

'Have you ever been raped, Sid?'

'Not since I was a kid.'

'What was that drink? Were you trying to poison me? Thanks. But you should have told me—'

Sid winced. 'I'm sorry about that.' He started, realising what she'd said. 'No! I wasn't trying to poison you. It was oneiricene: a local entertainment drug, mixed with brandy. It was the best I could do. I thought I'd get you drunk and it would make things easier. It was stupid, I'm sorry.'

'Have you any more?'

Sid laughed, a choked breath. 'You learn fast.'

He felt the librarian moving closer. She lifted the pistol from his belt loop. He let her take it. It was her weapon as much as his. Maybe she knew how to use an antique firearm. It would be good if one of them did.

'Is this loaded?'

'Yeah, I made sure. Much good it'll do us against an army.'

Sid was thinking of the safe room in Trivandrum. What did the horror of this night mean for his children? When humans have lost all rational fear of the aliens, what happens to Aleutian-lovers? He heard a faint click: and suddenly understood where the conversation had been heading. He yelled, flung himself on her, frantically wrestled the muzzle of the ancient revolver out of her mouth. The struggle was over instantly. Her bare arms were like flowerstems. He was afraid he'd snapped her wrists. Shaking, he stuffed the pistol inside his overalls.

'Why d'you do that?' she wailed. 'What's wrong with you?'

For an Aleutian, death is an excursion trip. Sid mustered his disintegrating forces. 'Because I'm going to get you out of this. Somehow. You're going to stay alive.'

There was no answer, but the silence felt defeated. He hoped she'd given up. The way he felt about all Aleutians just now, he couldn't cope with any more suicide attempts.

'The rose was dead,' said Goodlooking, very softly.

Sid wiped the tears from his face. That small, decent voice out of the darkness didn't deserve his hatred. 'I don't think they're coming after us,' he said. 'Try to sleep, or something. We'll make a plan in the morning.'

Goodlooking lay down on the stones.

It was strange to think he had been so close to this place, a few hours ago and in another aeon. He had come to the ancient palace after all. Maitri had told him about the people who used to live here: Clytemnestra and Agamemnon. It was one of those bad relationships, Maitri said, that closes on people like a trap. They'd lost their great household, lost everything, and the Gender War had swept them apart. But whenever they met in the same life, they'd probably fall together into the same cruel spiral as before. The poor devils.

Dear Maitri, thought Goodlooking. *So many stories. A giant planet full of stories, for us to collect.*

When he was seven and getting too old for birthdays, a religious health visitor came to do a development check. It happened in the character shrine at Maitri's house. Sacred moments were playing on the display screens. Someone was making a confession in the chaplain's room. Goodlooking, distracted by the hum of holy communion in there, knew that he had not done well. He didn't recognise the things they showed him. He didn't *feel* himself to be the person in the librarian's records. The health visitor took Maitri aside, and Goodlooking was left unhappy and frightened. He was afraid they'd say he needed another bone-marrow infestation.

Through the open doors of the shrine, something came flying: a little violet sail, rimmed in deep purple. It had eyes like tiny flames.

⟨Sir, what is that?⟩ he exclaimed, excited. ⟨Sir, I don't think we have a record of a thing like that!⟩

It was the moment of recognition. He had become himself.

⟨It's called a flying thing,⟩ said Maitri, beaming. ⟨People have started growing them, for fun, in imitation of the flying things on 'earth'. We have found a giant planet, you know, since you were last with us. We have made landfall.⟩ Then Lord Maitri dropped to his haunches without a thought of dignity, and hugged Goodlooking hard. His eyes were brimming with tears. He must have been worried, recognition had taken so long.

⟨Everything's going to be all right,⟩ he said. ⟨Don't you worry about what anybody says. You are my dear child, and everything's going to be all right.⟩

In the cave, Goodlooking closed his eyes. Little violet sail so pretty; memory, so sweet. Goodbye Maitri, for a while.

3: Travellers

The hotel had been burned to the ground. The soldiers had used some accelerant so violent that the fires were already out. Plates of fused glass rose like giant tattered petals around a smouldering ruin. Sid kicked through the mess where his room had been, and caught a faint rainbow glimmer in the charred litter. It might have been the remains of his global, it was hard to tell. The army had vanished. The plain and hills, scorched turf and ranked conifers, stretched quiet and silent under a calm blue sky.

From the traces that remained, it looked as if they'd piled the Aleutian dead in the main hall, which had been the heart of their firestorm. He skirted that area, trying to avoid the scraps of blackened tissue that floated in the air. The droms' stable was intact. The droms were dead inside it. What harm had they done? They were grown by *humans*. Standing over their tumbled bodies he suddenly wept: for his good master, for the whole gentle, fearless crew. It wasn't their fault they couldn't understand. The faces of the noseless monsters were human in his memory. He looked up, wiping his filthy hands across his filthy face. He saw a large shape lurking in the back of the stable, and caught his breath . . .

He went back to the underground cistern, where Goodlooking was crouched in the dimmest of lamplight. 'They've gone,' he said. He dumped the bundle he was carrying and dropped down beside her on the stones. 'No sign of any survivors.'

⟨No.⟩ No need to tell her that. Their eyes met, lingering: as if they were friends trying to recognise each other in a dark crowd. Last night they had been Maitri's librarian and the trading post mascot. Who were they now?

'Thank you for keeping me from killing myself,' she said aloud. 'The last thing I want out of this is a criminal record.'

Suicide was a crime the aliens took seriously. It had to be. Or who would stick around to pick up the pieces after a cock-up like this one? 'I couldn't find your medicine. Not a chance.'

Her shoulders lifted. ⟨It doesn't matter. I'll survive for a few days.⟩ From her expression, she'd be glad when they were over. 'You'd better take me to the Government of the World.'

Sid shook his head. 'I don't think so, kid. They were always *your* sponsors. If aliens can be massacred, the Government of the World is looking to save its own multiple neck. I don't think they'd protect you.'

'Then take me to the ICI.'

'*Who?*'

'The ICI. The corporation. Clavel joined them after Johnny died, so he could serve the human vision of WorldSelf as Trade. They're not involved in the Gender War. They won't have forgotten Clavel. They'll shelter me.'

Sid laughed. He didn't mean to laugh, but her idea of life on earth was too much for his shattered nerves. 'Sorry,' he told her. 'I'm sorry, but the days of corporate power and neutrality are long gone. It's no good. We're on our own.'

He pushed the bundle between them, but didn't open it yet.

'I'd better explain some things. The soldiers we saw last night came from both sides of the war. The stocky bloke with the turban was an officer of some Allied force, I'm not sure which. *The Allies* is a blanket term for the traditionalist side in Europe. You'd better get to know some of these names, because everyone knows them. The woman was from *Ochiba*, which is a reformers' army, Swiss-based. It means "fallen leaf" in the Japanese dialect. They were founded by reformist Japanese who settled in Switzerland after the Japan Sea cataclysm. You know about that, don't you? You know Japan disappeared in an earthquake not long before you people arrived?'

She nodded – a tiny duck of the chin that was their nearest gesture to a human *yes*, though it meant something more neutral: *I see*. You had to watch out, because it could easily be: *I see what you mean, but I disagree*.

'Ochiba is the "army of the rejected wife". I don't know why a fallen leaf means a rejected wife. But to Ochiba "the rejected wife" means mother earth. They're mother earth's most ferocious defenders, they're complete fanatics. If they're with the Allies, we're up against a Gender War truce. It won't last but they've banded together, these whole armies of *crazies*, to drive you people out. It's what I was most afraid of. I warned Maitri—'

And Maitri told me a shuttle was coming, he thought. *So much for their damned mental-model telepathy.* But he understood that Maitri had known the truth. When he declared '*Yudi will not let me down*', Lord Maitri was lying, and it was such a *human* lie. They were unarmed. Their own people could not or would not save them. What could they do but put a good face on things and pretend their disaster was all in a day's work? He wondered if they'd known exactly what would happen. Maybe. They'd tried everything . . . He wondered what it was like to be locked in this madhouse with no hope of escape: not heaven or hell or oblivion.

He hated himself. He had been betrayed, not by the aliens but by his own residual, idiot faith in the fairytale. He'd believed nothing terrible could happen to the superbeings. Now he was lost in space: no global, no cable, no hope of rescue. But somehow he had to smuggle an invalid alien through a country he didn't know, that was crawling with heavily armed maniacs who were slavering to tear her to pieces.

'This is my plan. We're going to disguise ourselves, especially you, and head for Athens. It's our nearest city.'

Cities had become relatively safe places, because urban populations were still mixed: so far. You got terrorism and assassination squads, but no old-style population destruction. Modern warfare was guerrilla warfare in the countryside, on a continental scale; no massive air-raids, no strategic nuclear strikes. Just the slow, almost accidental murder of a civilisation.

It should make sense to her. To an Aleutian, a 'city' was an enclave of life: life on every scale sharing the same myriad-aspected identity; life creating and tailoring a microclimate and whole biosphere to the will of the sentient inhabitants. Their shipworld was a city like that, a city in space, built around the trap that held the bluesun. Their homeworld was netted with 'cities', joined by tendril-corridors of life: while outside in the

wilderness balls of blue lightning prowled, the wild bluesun
reactors that could be trapped and harnessed like great dangerous
draft animals . . .

He pulled himself up, out of a vision of the *reality* of that alien
place. 'I'm sorry,' he said. 'My mind's wandering.' How could he
give her confidence? 'It'll be like a game. No, wait: you don't
have games. It'll be like Johnny and Braemar. The saboteurs.
We'll be like Johnny and Braemar on board the shipworld when
they were sneaking to the reactor chamber, trying to pass for
aliens.'

She hunched there in her battered underwear, a dun quilted
bodysuit with a pocket in the crotch for their sanitary arrangement. She looked so pathetic, his poor librarian. If he was lost in
space, where was she?

'You'll need another name. Goodlooking doesn't sound right.
How about Bella? It means the same, in a better dialect.' He
watched to see how she'd take it. She hesitated: her shoulders
rose a little. ⟨All right. I'll be Bella.⟩ Sid grinned, his spirits
enormously lightened by that alien smile.

'That's my girl.'

⟨But this is a bit embarrassing: I need a new toilet pad.⟩

He shook his head, with rueful pity. She was going to have to
take so much, and he knew how little things rankled with her.

'No. You'll be travelling as a human. If I had any pads we'd
have to leave them behind. You'll have to do like the natives
do.'

He bent over his bundle, giving her privacy while she handled
the bad news. 'This is called a *chador*.' He spread the dark folds.
'An honour cloak. It'll cover you from head to foot. It's female
costume, worn by both sides. By males too, sometimes. A
chador's a useful thing, when you don't feel like facing the world
. . . There are clothes to go under it. I had some of my wardrobe
stored in the stable, you see, that's how this stuff survived. Fact
is, I was expecting that shuttle, but I didn't know if there was a
place on it for me. Sadly, I hadn't got round to moving my ration
box.' He passed over these revelations quickly. 'We'd better
change.'

Aleutians didn't like to be naked, but she made no fuss. She stood and peeled down her underwear, toilet pad and all. She scrumpled the outfit up, mugging distaste. ⟨Pooh, nasty.⟩

Sid had not meant to look, but he couldn't stop himself. The pull of the grotesque drew his eyes. Aleutian skin had no red or blue tones. The whole human range from indigo-black to milk-and-roses was missing. Some of them were darkly olive, like the smoke from a fire of green wood; some a startling acid yellow; some very pale. Goodlooking was as white as a swan in twilight. She stood in the dull chemical light, frail limbs glimmering. He could see the line of the vertical cleft in her lower belly. On her breastless torso there were two small dark marks. Sid drew in his breath, responding in spite of himself to a girl's slight body, naked in shadow. He had stolen the swan princess's plumage. She was his captive. She turned, and caught his eye.

His fairy princess had the face of a child that had starved to death: black eye sockets, black nostril slits, lips shrunk so tight the outline of the teeth showed through.

⟨Which is my underwear?⟩ she asked calmly.

'It doesn't matter. They're both the same.'

Bella showed no interest whatsoever in Sid's manly physique. In human clothes again, and slightly shaken by the undressing incident, Sid took out a compact. He smeared his fingers with gel and rubbed them through his hair. He smudged in brows and lashes with his fingertips, peering into the tiny mirror. He didn't use cosmetic drugs. They were too chancy. With gels *you* decided when it was going to wear off. Dark hair, sun-damaged skin. He was reasonably nondescript, if no one noticed his eyes.

⟨Sid?⟩

She was looking at the compact. Aleutians didn't use mirrors. To them a reflection was a kind of natural deadworld phenomenon: it was creepy. He put the case away hurriedly.

'I don't think we should go anywhere,' she announced, with trembling firmness. 'We should stay here and wait.'

'Oh? For whom?' Caught off balance, he snapped at her. 'The rescue shuttle? I don't think so. I think Uji has evacuated anyone who was going, and everyone else is dead. And I know as well as you do that the shipworld won't send help. They won't back up the Expedition, unless something much worse than this happens.'

(his inner eye forced on him the scene in the main hall last night: what could be *worse than that?*)

He saw from her face that he was right, or at least she believed the same. They were all dead. He felt grief, panic and chaos surging beneath the thin skin of his determination. It made him cruel. 'But excuse me, what do I know? Maybe there are more Aleutians on earth, unbeknownst to the Expedition or the Government of the World. The brood's an organic computer. I suppose you can write yourself in or out of the system if you know how, change your chemical handle so your own parent wouldn't know you. I've heard about these Aleutian masters of disguise. Is it true? I'd dearly love to know.'

⟨I don't know what you're talking about.⟩

'Oh, please, have no secrets from your native guide. I suppose they're hunting for the instantaneous-travel device, the one Johnny and Braemar used to reach the shipworld? The occult secret of human science the Aleutians have been hunting for ever since?' He curled his lip. 'Don't tell me you believe in that.'

⟨Of course not. Don't be silly.⟩

Her puzzled smile jolted him. She didn't know what he was talking about, and he was going crazy. Get a grip, Sid!

'Ridiculous, yes. I'm sorry I raised the subject. And we are leaving at sunset.'

They went up the steps until they could see light, and waited for it to fade. Sid didn't feel hungry, but his mouth was horribly parched. In the pipeline there was plenty of water. But you couldn't get at it: it was locked in the slurry of the bacterial flow. He kept his anxiety to himself. Bella complained of neither hunger nor thirst.

'Let's go,' he said at last.

She climbed slowly, a few steps at a time. The pale mandorla overhead, shaped like a woman's sex or two hands folded in prayer, was filled with gold. Sid was carrying Bella's shoes and the chador. It was good woollen cloth, and he guessed – not yet realising the awful significance of this – that the invalid would find its weight a burden. He waited until she was beside him. Sid was not a tall man, but her head barely reached his collarbone. She looked up, questioning: why had he stopped? He touched the scarf he'd wrapped around her starved-child face. 'You're going into a different world,' he said. 'You have to trust me out there, Bella. I'm on your side. Truly. Remember that.'

They stepped out of the womb of stone.

He sat her down to put the shoes on. She'd tried, but she couldn't seem to manage it. Their 'baseball boots' gave you no idea of how weird an Aleutian foot was. Bella's foot was broad in the ball, ridiculously narrow in the heel, and had a kind of lockable arch. Her clawed toes were as long as fingers, and heavily padded underneath. He worked the one-size plastics in his hands till they were soft. When he tried to ease them on, he discovered that her pads were raw and bloody. He knew that they felt pain, the same as humans.

'Why didn't you *say*?'

⟨It was the running last night. I don't know how I did that, I can't run! It's nothing, it'll mend soon.⟩

'Don't worry. I can carry you.'

He dropped the honour cloak over her and picked up the whole bundle. She was no heavier than a six-year-old child, but he was very tired. They got down the hill with frequent halts. He kept to the trees for as long as possible, though he was fairly sure the skies were empty. The Aleutians were terrified of flying eyes, bugs, spy satellites. It was ironic. The humans thought the aliens read their thoughts. The aliens were convinced that humans watched and listened to every move they made . . . He wished he didn't have to take her to the hotel ruins. He put her down outside the stable, so she wouldn't have to see the droms. She'd been fond of them.

'Wait there and see what I found!'

The jeep had not been a hallucination. It was solid, untouched under its shroud of Aleutian tarp. The darling machine started first time. There was easily six hundred klicks level driving in the discrete-energy stack. Sid dropped his head on his hands, tearful with gratitude. Then, suddenly inspired, he groped in the deep shelf under the dash. He found a pack of stale chocolate biscuits, and a full two-litre canteen. 'Well, thank you little Sid,' he breathed. Little Sid had an ingrained habit of tucking supplies away. 'Thank you, my rotten childhood!'

The jeep crawled out of the stable, silent and lightless. Sid jumped out, elated. 'How about that! And look here: food. Water!'

Bella was staring at the place where the main hall had been. His stomach churned in sympathy. 'Don't think about it,' he told her. 'It's over. They're safe home, waiting for their next turn.' It was what she believed.

⟨What's *that*?⟩

He saw the large, pallid figure moving behind one of the rags of the burned dome. 'A suit!' He whispered, numb with shock. He pulled out the revolver. 'Stay here.'

The bulky doll moved lightly over the ruins, stooping and rising like a feeding bird. Sid followed, feeling dizzy; light-headed. He couldn't tell if it had anyone on board or not: the gait was smooth. Either way, its sophisticated senses must find Sid's trail, of this morning or last night. It would find the Aleutian clothes in the cistern cave. If he didn't stop it from searching, whoever had sent it would know that aliens had survived here. He saw it raise its big head, with a listening air. He'd been spotted. He was a warm moving manikin in its fields of perception.

He ran and hid in the disc works. The walls were blackened but standing. They held the shape of Aleutian utility architecture, knotted and lumpy as if woven from tree roots. Sid let the suit take a step inside, and dropped from his perch above the doorway. It toppled. Sid tore at the helmet's seal, a suit's weak point. He was hampered by the revolver, still clutched in his hand. The suit rolled and Sid was pinned, staring into a square of gleaming black. A gauntlet closed over his face. He swallowed a great gulp of something that was not air. *He could not breathe, his eyes teared, his lungs were bursting* . . . Something moved, over the monster's shoulder. To his horror he saw the blurred outline of Bella, without her cloak, with a rock in her strength-less hands. Something went *thunk*. The gauntlet came loose, and instantly Sid got a hand and arm between himself and the carapace. The suit recovered quickly from that fly swat. It was trying to get its glove back over his face . . . BLAM!!!

Sid crawled to his knees, while the echoes rolled. His head was ringing, his eyes bleared, his throat was on fire. The suit lay still, a blackened hole in its chest. Sid reeled away, found Bella and clutched at her: his face buried in her shoulder, his lungs heaving. Flowerstem arms hugged him, until he managed to stop shaking and stood upright.

'I told you to stay put,' he quavered, trying to be funny.

⟨Is it dead?⟩ she asked. ⟨What is a 'suit'?⟩

They crouched on either side of it. Sid tugged the helmet unit. He didn't know this model, but he knew the seals would release easily if someone inside needed resuscitation. It came away without resistance.

'It can be a robot. They can walk about on their own.' A woman's face looked up at him, shocked and sad. 'But often a suit is worn by a businessman. Businesswoman, in this case. What they used to call a *plumber*, when Braemar Wilson was around.'

Adrenalin made him garrulous, he hardly knew what he was saying. He pulled off a gauntlet, lifted the slack wrist and showed Goodlooking a broad silver bracelet incised with a pattern of crossed branches and flames. 'This is a Campfire Girl. United Socialist States Special Exterior Force. She's from the USSA.'

⟨But they don't leave their quarantine.⟩

'Ah, like most truth: not quite true. They used to be called the policemen of the world. Maybe they still feel responsible. The SEF keeps an eye on things over here. Sometimes they shoot trouble, if they think they can get away with it.'

The Socialist States had decided long ago to keep the aliens out. The Special Exterior Force kept watch over the infested old world, but at a price. They lived and died in their own quarantine, they could never go home. They were dedicated people. Her suit would have become armour at a touch. But in an armoured suit you felt trapped. You didn't stiff it until you were actually under fire, whatever your officers said. *I'm sorry*, he told the dead woman silently. *I've never killed anyone before, not in the real*. He replaced the helmet and the glove. He and Bella looked at each other across the ominous body.

⟨What was he doing here?⟩

'I don't know. Monitoring the protest and the truce: just routine, I hope. But we should not hang around. It is not a good idea to kill a Campfire Girl . . . We'd better get you covered again.'

For speed, he carried her back to the stable. They drank half
the canteen between them. Sid got the jeep out on to the road
and lowered its wheels. They set off towards Korinth in the dusk.

'It's about a hundred and fifty klicks. There may be roadblocks.
We'll bluff our way through. The jeep's panel has no map system.
We wouldn't want aliens to have maps, would we? . . . So I'd
rather stay on the road. If we're challenged, keep quiet. Give
them a silence, nine times out of ten the other person will fill it.
Let them make up their own story. You concentrate on giving
them a good impression "informally", in the Common Tongue:
you know, tell 'em you're normal and everything's fine.' Beside
him the cone of dark cloth didn't stir or make a sound.

Sid began to relax enough to worry about the suit. 'Probably
she was working alone. She'll have left a flier somewhere near.
When she doesn't check in, it'll go back to the mothership or to
base. They don't tangle with old-earth authorities: definitely not
with the gender warriors. With luck the suit's working record
will convince them she was killed by a random Greek
bandito . . .'

Suddenly there were lights ahead. They were the headlights of
a long armoured vehicle, half blocking the road. Sid's relief
evaporated. 'Get in the back!' They were being flagged down.
There were figures in silhouette, helmets and weapons. He
slowed. He prepared himself. A hand rapped at the window. Sid
stuck his head out. 'Who are you lot?' he demanded.

The woman was wearing green fatigues, a green supple bala-
clava with a nightsight and telecoms band. She wore the Fallen
Leaf with additions that identified her as a captain of the Franco-
Suisse NVDA (military wing). 'Who are *you*, soldier?' she coun-
tered, in accented English. Narrow dark eyes raked him.

'Irregular undercover forces, ma'am. Ordered to Athens.'

'*Bon*. Ther jeeep is requisisioned.'

'Hey, what about my orders?'

'We're heading thar way. We'll give you a lif'. Get in the back.
Captain Hassan,' she yelled. 'We have transport!'

The Swiss tapped the coms' unit by her ear, and addressed a
subvocal mutter to the troops in the crippled personnel carrier.
The other captain, despite the name, was a heavily built West
African type with a smooth, humorous face. He wore the red-

flashed blue uniform of the Western European Union, an Allied army. Sid leaned back, nerves thrumming, noting how the woman had tacitly assumed control. As they do. Oh, this truce couldn't last.

'Lights, Hassan: and drive it, don't trust the *panel*. These roads are vile. Goddess, what a day! Did you hear the news, English? We have burned out the nests. Not one is left on earth!'

'So it's not true that half of them got away, ma'am?'

'*Quoi?* Well, some they evacuated, it's true. Why not? We don't kill for killing's sake in my army, soldier.'

He hadn't looked at Bella, he was pretending vividly that she wasn't there. But he hoped she caught that news: slight comfort.

The Swiss was searching for controls she wouldn't find, in dawning wonder. No direction finder, no tvs, no radio: no telecoms.

'Where did you *get this*?'

'Liberated it from the Mykini looties, ma'am. They weren't going to be needing it.'

She exploded. Slammed her hands on the dash. 'You see what we're up against, Hassan!' She swivelled around. 'DON'T CALL THEM NAMES. NEVER CALL THEM NAMES. They're telepaths, fuck it. They could be listening even in orbit. And if they weren't, it's a question of self-respect. They are *the Aleutians*! You see what that "looties" makes us seem? Like children!' Appeased by Sid's earnest nodding she settled back. 'Did you have any part in the orgy, soldier?'

'Not me, ma'am. Nothing further from my thoughts.'

'Good. I detest that.' She swivelled around again. 'Who's your friend?' Sid suddenly knew that putting Bella in the chador had been a deeply flawed move. In the dark with a scarf round her face she might have passed. Ominously shrouded, her alien-ness was subliminally *dead obvious*. He was pinned in the Ochiba woman's stare. He tried desperately to intensify the message of his expression, his manner, his everything: *I'm a nice boy, I'm one of us. Whatever I do is normal.* It wasn't working.

Without warning, a zinging burst of blue-white shot through the cab. '*Abaissez-vous!*' yelled the Swiss. Hassan dropped over the stick, as if in swift obedience. The jeep careered to the side of the road, rammed and rolled. The Swiss scrambled out, rifle in

her hands, jabbering into her coms' reed. Sid pulled himself free,
dragging Bella. He swung her up in his arms: ran and fell and
ran again, until the noise had diminished and the dark was
complete.

'Looks like the truce is in trouble,' he remarked.

He had collapsed, face in the grass. He was clutching a fold of
the chador in one hand: in the other, the biscuits and the strap
of the water canteen. He rolled over. Stars looked down.

'Some Aleutian you are. Didn't your great Clavel live for
months among the locals at first contact, and no one suspected?'

He sat up, pressing the heels of his hands into his tortured
eyes. 'We lost the jeep. No probs. We'll be safer on foot.'

That night he carried her in bursts until he managed to blunder
into another plantation. Then they slept on a bed of slippery
pine needles, under the chador. It was for Sid a headlong fall
into oblivion, while whatever happened happened between the
squabbling armies on the road.

In the morning he looked at her feet and found the blisters
perfectly healed. They set out to walk to Athens. It was not such
a bad plan. It was summer, dry and warm. Sid had no maps but
there were roads to follow, and the distance between them and
the megapolis was not impossible. Sid knew it would be slow.
He reckoned it could take them ten days, even double that. It
didn't matter. It would be all the more time to think about what
he was going to do next.

But there was a problem. Bella could not walk.

She didn't refuse, she didn't complain. She would creep along
for fifty metres, and wilt to the ground. He thought she'd slept,
as far as aliens slept, and was as much recovered as you could
hope for. She simply couldn't do it. He had not known this. He'd
never seen her use any kind of cuddly organic wheelchair. He
realised now that was because Aleutians didn't think that way.
She was a cripple: being helpless was part of her obligation. If
need be, there'd always be someone to carry her. He guessed
she'd never walked more than a few metres at a time, unaided,
in her entire god-knows life.

It was like leading a toddler. He coaxed. He cajoled, he teased
her, he praised her, he carried her. They tried having her go four-

footed, though that was dangerous. It was no better. They set off at dawn. By the time Sid gave up, in the heat of the day, they'd hardly covered enough ground to daunt an energetic caterpillar.

There was another problem. They were crossing a desert. No food was grown here. There was only the aromatic scrub, and the swathes of marching softwoods that served the Greek Federation Accelerated Biomass Power Grid. Sid knew there were a few fortified villages. There'd been the place where he went to buy his human rations. But he wouldn't have dared to go back there, where he was known as the aliens' interpreter; and they came upon no others.

There was hardly any water. Twice, when the canteen was empty, he had to leave Bella and search alone, getting frantic about her safety, before he found a stream.

Sid began to feel as if he was going mad. She had not spoken to him aloud since they left the cistern cave. She was not going to speak aloud until this ordeal was over; you could see it in her eyes. He couldn't cope. He had lost his grip.

The uncertainty was terrible. He was speaking to her and he didn't know what he was saying. She was telling him things with her silence, but what? *He could not know for sure until she spoke.* For Aleutians it was normal to let things flow. Everybody worked from their own version of the multiple script. They never knew exactly how far all the scripts agreed, until somebody 'made a speech' and collapsed the wave. And then no one could prove what had really been going down before . . . If you were an Aleutian you could express what you liked in the Common Tongue. It wasn't evidence. No one could hold you to anything unless you were a signifier and they could get you to put it into formal words. What a way to live. It was unendurable.

Sid babbled to fill the silence.

'You'd better familiarise yourself with human customs. We'll start with cricket. You have eleven men on each side. The side that's in to bat takes turns to hit a ball, the side that's in to field stands around trying to catch the ball. Somebody throws the ball towards the batsman. Not at the batsman: a crucial distinction. Placing your fielders is an underrated science. You have long leg, short leg, mid-off, mid-on, deep cover . . . Right beside the batsman we have silly mid-on, so called because it is a *very* silly place to stand. Come on, sweetheart, one more step. Let's see if we can reach that rock. No, not this rock. The big one over there. I bet you can.'

He told her not to worry, the Aleutians would be back. The purebreds were fools, they'd forgotten all they'd ever known. When Braemar Wilson tried to blow up the bluesun she wasn't *joking*. She had seen the future. You wouldn't get Braemar imagining you could throw the Aleutians out, and have them stay out . . . kill them and have them stay dead. Sometimes he sang to himself, holding her up against his shoulder as they stumbled.

> The north wind will blow,
> And we shall have snow
> And what will poor robin do then? Poor thing . . .

'You don't understand, do you?' he demanded. 'You've never met a weather system like ours. Your techs can't imagine it: they don't *imagine* things. The north wind will blow, down out of the freezing desert, and, sure, it will cool India. *But what else will it do?* You have tame weather. Ours is wild. Wild as a bluesun.'

He told her she mustn't think he was a protestor. He was absolutely not involved in this vile, stupid business. He was a faithful and true servant. 'But we have to get on, Bel. One more step. And another. Good girl, clever girl. One more.'

On the fourth night from the hotel they came to a ruined Christian chapel, on a ridge that they were following above the road. Sid hoped that it was still the right road. They had walked, if you could call it that, from dawn until noon and again from late afternoon until twilight.

'Look at this,' crowed Sid. 'Five-star accommodation for madam!' The chapel was a roofless barn, thickly carpeted in ancient animal droppings. 'Plus, I can get you a discount for the shit. It's not very fresh, what an oversight.'

They'd had to give up the idea of her wearing the cloak. He unslung it from his shoulders and tucked it over her, and poured some water into the canteen cup.

'You're to drink that. You hear? No nonsense.'

Aleutians didn't drink like humans, they took most of their

liquid in their soupy food. She had merely stared at him reproachfully when he tried to make her eat biscuits. He'd had to mush them up in water in the cap of the canteen. Now there were no biscuits left, she'd decided to refuse to drink. It was true the stuff tasted weird. He was afraid the canteen wasn't working any more, and they were drinking raw stream water contaminated with God knows what. But that wasn't the problem. He suspected she was trying to save their water for Sid: which he wouldn't allow.

He scowled awfully. 'Drink it. I can find more.' She inserted a drop or so between two rows of narrow, close-set white teeth; and returned the undiminished cup to his hand, with finality.

⟨Thank you. That was delicious.⟩

It was cold that night. He sat with the alien cradled in his arms, staring at the broken cross above the stained white gable wall. He didn't know what day it was. Or night. He'd got used to living with the aliens, who didn't seem consciously to *measure* anything. He heard howling close by, and a rapid scuffling of animal feet: a pack of wild dogs.

Sid was a city creature, along with most of the population of the human world. He'd never been out of sight of people and packed dwellings until he came to Mykini. He'd seen footage about fruits and berries: edible tubers? What had happened to all of that? Somebody had emptied Mother Nature's larder, or maybe it was the wrong time of the year. He wouldn't know. Where there are predators there must be prey. He could've hunted whatever the wild dogs hunted . . . if he knew how to start.

His left arm was around her. His right hand gripped the clumsy souvenir firearm. He had to have some illusion that he could protect the kid. But they had seen nothing of the armies since their jeep had been requisitioned. Bella was going to die of hunger and exhaustion, not by violence.

It was so cold they couldn't stay still. They walked on by moonlight. At dawn, the fifth dawn, they reached a highway. The sky was dyed violet and rose between hill masses ahead. A road bridge lay sprawled across the bed of a shallow river. In midstream, where it had been swept away completely, a causeway of shored-up stones crossed the gap. Sid left Bella under a pillar of the bridge at the western bank, and went to fill the canteen. He dipped his head in the stream. It was icy cold.

He remembered, back at the trading post she had said she wanted to collect *incunabula*.

So he had gone down to the cablepoint and found out the meaning of the English word. They were free with their English translations. He'd had to decide what *a manuscript text from before printing* must mean in context. He had scoured the abandoned houses. The failed resettlement had been looted thoroughly and often – odd how there are *always* looters, no matter how depopulated a place gets – but he found a printed book: printed in English script, and brought it back in triumph. She was very touched. She put it reverently aside. Sid was disappointed.

'Aren't you going to read it?'

⟨Unfortunately, I can't read.⟩

'Wait a minute. You're a librarian!'

⟨I can memorise the shapes of the letters. I know what they're supposed to do. But nothing happens in my mind.⟩

She couldn't see why this was funny. It was her obligation.

Not being able to read was part of the genetic make-up of the person known as Maitri's libarian – along with his disability, his skill with the alien mixing desk, his courage in adversity and thin-skinned cringing over trifles. Along with the subtle traits, whatever they were, that made Sid call his companion feminine. But to herself, she was not a human girl. She was a . . . a polyp, torn from the multiple life of Aleutia. How could she survive?

She was asleep or unconscious when he came up from the water. He knelt beside the meagre body. Her ears, half hidden by the black slick locks of 'hair', were convoluted cups of gristle set horizontally instead of vertically. Some aliens could move them like animal ears, but Bella wasn't good at that. She could only manage a little twitching, like a human's party trick . . .

He felt fiercely protective, possessive. He had done everything for her. He'd shown her how to take down her pants to pee. But he could not keep her alive. The swan princess does not translate into the human world. His memory was stacked with images from a childhood spent in front of a screen. *Find yourself*, they'd ordered him. But now he found Bella. She was the immortal girl, seduced into leaving Shangri-La, in *Lost Horizon*. She slept: a tiny old woman so ancient that every scrap of human appearance had been wrung out of her. She had left her immortality behind, and the brutal weight of time had fallen on her. 'Most old,' he murmured. 'Most old, of anyone I have ever seen.'

She would die. And the north wind would blow.

Her eyes were open. He started: but she wasn't looking at him. She was watching the flowing river. Her eyes were brimming with the alien tears that filled their eyes but never fell. She turned her head slowly. ⟨Sid, I can't go any further. Please don't make me. Let me fall asleep, and wake up at home.⟩

Sid. Informally, she didn't use the meaningless noise. It was '——' a kind of *hey you*, but personalised. It hurt. He had barely eaten for days. He was in a weak, emotional state; he couldn't stand any more of this.

'You're coming with me to Athens.'

⟨To the city,⟩ she repeated, with a faint smile. ⟨And then?⟩

Sid didn't want to discusss that. 'We need food. I'm going foraging. You stay here.'

⟨Yes, go, please. Don't watch me die. I don't like it.⟩

'Stop that nonsense! I'll be back soon.'

He stood. At once he dropped again. There was a crowd of people coming up the old highway. They came like a broad murky tide. Their scouts were moving in the trees on either side.

⟨What is it?⟩ she demanded feebly. ⟨The armies?⟩

'No. It's travellers.'

Humanity on the way from nowhere to who knows where, refugees without a destination. They were human locusts. Travellers recognised two categories: *one of us*; and *consumable*. Sid stared around wildly, but it was far too late to get out of their way.

'Lie still!'

⟨Will they kill us?⟩

He flung the chador over her head. 'I don't know! Lie still!'

They were spotted, of course. They were taken to the line of motley vehicles, around which foot passengers and animals herded and ambled, to a chicken-shit motorised camper van that clearly belonged to someone important. A thin, respectable looking old man was brought out.

He looked the fugitives over carefully. A small crowd gathered, while in the background the river crossing went on. Vans and carts rumbled on to the causeway, amid shouted instructions. Around the chicken-shit van dogs sniffed and barefoot children milled. A bony pair of grey horses searched for blades of grass in the old highway paving.

'Speak English?' suggested the old man.

Sid took a gamble. 'I am English. Sir.'

Laying claim to native ownership of the world's best surviving contact language was risky. But it often impressed old folks. The patriarch clasped his hands. 'Ah! English!'

Sid bowed modestly. His glance flickered over the crowd. The women were heavily veiled. He saw glimpses of bright skirts flashing above bare, scabbed ankles. The young men were hefting exotic weaponry. Some of them wore fresh fragments of Allied or Reformers' uniform. But they didn't look seriously military. The atmosphere felt peaceful.

'And your friend?'

'She's my wife. Naturally, English too.'

The patriarch and his people considered Bella. They sensed something, some threat. Before he saw it coming, two young men gripped Sid by the arms. Another two grabbed Bella.

Sid yelled, 'Leave my woman alone! Don't disgrace me!'

His appeal to their customs was in vain. A third man pulled off the chador, while two kept close hold of the dangerous unknown beneath. *Please*, begged Sid, not knowing what he was pleading for. For her to be Clavel and convince the travellers she was as human as they. For her to grow wings and fly.

The crowd recoiled. Wah. Bleggh. Euck.

Someone yelled, with disgust and pity. Sid didn't have to recognise the Eurasian dialect to understand. 'She's a halfcaste!'

The old man was silent for ever. 'What are you doing here?' he demanded at last. 'Don't you know the aliens are gone and the armies are hunting down anyone who's had dealings with them?'

'We were heading south, for the enclaves, to get away from the war. We were on the road when it started happening.'

The oldster shook his head. His compassion was weary and genuine. 'I don't know where you can go now.' He looked at

Bella. 'Poor child. What horrible things you do to yourselves. You can travel with us, if you wish. But keep her covered.'

Sid could have fallen to his knees, sobbing in gratitude. He wanted to kiss the man's feet. The patriarch, with a kindly wave of his hand, ended the audience. The traveller women closed in: hands darting, eyes flashing, tongues jabbering.

At close of trading the fugitives had a cooking pan, two beakers, one with a cover; a metal spoon, a firelighter, a packet of Breakfast Special Indian Tea powder, three large potatoes and a bundle of fuel and water chitties. The travellers had the canteen, Sid's compact, Sid's shoes and the revolver. Plus Sid's handprints to be copied for credit-matching. They thought they'd done well, Sid was equally satisfied. He'd have liked to hold on to the revolver, since its value was obviously depressed at the moment. However it was better to trade while they were in the mood for trading. They would certainly return in a different frame of mind for anything valuable they hadn't been able to secure.

Someone came along with a present from the old man: two cartons of naturlait; and with permission – as they seemed tired – to ride in a freight van. They were taken to it and clambered aboard. Sid downed half a litre of milkoid liquid, watched her do the same and fell into deathlike sleep, one arm flung over his precious burden.

The convoy was heading north to a famous winter fair on the Black Sea. They reported that the truce had indeed barely survived what was now called the Protest. The anti-Aleutian raiders were supposed to have returned to their normal business. But stray fragments of Ochiba and Allied units remained in the area, scrapping with each other and dealing savagely with anything remotely like Aleutian sympathy.

The travellers were traditionalists by custom, but they weren't partisan. On Sid and Bella's second day they fell in with an Ochiba field hospital. They regarded this as a windfall. Everyone who was ill in the camp trooped over there. They insisted that Sid must get something for his inflamed eyes. It became impossible to refuse, and he was afraid to leave Bella alone. They found themselves in the field hospital compound, standing in line with the rest.

By the time their turn came with the doctor, Sid was so frightened he was perfectly calm. She was working alone with her instrumentation. 'Speak English?' she said automatically, as she put him in the diagnostic couch. 'Don't be afraid. We treat anyone. We treat Allied soldiers if they come to us.' She gave Bella in the chador a nod of respect, and flushed his eyes out with a cool, soothing spray.

'What d'you do when you're not treating casualties?' asked Sid, making nervous conversation.

⟨I kill men.⟩

'Excuse me?'

The doctor's eyes moved over the couch's readings: her face and body told her story in the Common Tongue.

⟨Yes, it's true. I am an assassin. I'm a doctor in Athens. In my spare time, I kill men that my group has identified as targets. Men who rape their children quietly at home, keep their women in fear, and go out to abuse and destroy the world. But it's over. I am not going back. I have a husband and two sons. I love them. They are safe in America. I am with Ochiba now. I will join my family when the war's over.⟩

She looked into Sid's face: not aware of having spoken.

'Do? I was a civilian doctor. I have joined Ochiba now. You're shocked. Don't you agree that the Men must be stopped? There are biological males in my group, Alecto. They agree.'

'I don't think killing is the answer,' croaked Sid.

'It is the only answer left. There's no serious damage. Rest as much as possible. You'll be fine.'

They'd been the last in line. They walked slowly, agonisingly slowly, back to the camp. They'd established squatters' rights to a pitch beside their freight van's back wheels. They had no near neighbours, the 'halfcaste' stigma gave them space. It was deep dusk. Bella took off the chador. They looked at each other in wide-eyed surmise, and shuddered in unison. They had no doubt that the woman had told Sid the simple truth. She was a doctor: and in her spare time she killed men.

'Why do you care?' asked Sid bitterly . . . meaning not only

Alecto's work but the whole madness of the war. 'You don't think killing people does them much harm.'

⟨Why do *you*? You think people can only be killed once.⟩

He was silent, admitting her point. He didn't know which was more terrible, the war zone itself or its evil penumbra of urban terrorism: psychopaths in the home. The traveller women were tending their fires, cooking food, mending clothes, minding children: and hiding themselves assiduously under the black veils from the enemies who shared their lives. Who raped them and beat them regularly. Not all of the women or too often, but enough to keep them scared. Enough to keep their dreaded female power from breaking free. He thought of the Women's Agenda, and the Men's, and how muddled it had all become since the shooting started. But the Aleutians were right. The real war, the war behind the war, was the one between men and women . . .

'You know what,' he said. 'Johnny and Braemar couldn't have been lovers if they'd met now. It would've been impossible.'

⟨They were on opposite sides then.⟩

'Yeah, but it wasn't the same.' He shook his head. 'No, I'm wrong. There are millions of people in old earth cities right now for whom nothing's changed. The men are like spoiled kids and the women like mommas frightened of their own children, but they're not aware that it has anything to do with this cosmic battle which is being fought for the soul of the world. They're still thinking: it's not *my* business, it won't happen *here*.'

He'd fetched water and put the fire together before they went to the doctor's. He lit the chunks of compact, put the pan of water to boil and stared at it miserably.

⟨You're thinking of your children.⟩

'I'm afraid they're dead.'

Maid-monster Lydia. She'd been a mean, wilful, beloved little *monster* since the moment she could breathe unaided. And sweet Rog: the gentlest, most forgiving baby in the world. Sid had always wanted children. In his wary forays into the sexual arena he'd deliberately chosen partners who'd get a kick out of being pregnant, but would be bored by the babies. And he'd been wise enough not to act too keen. Neither of the mothers suspected she

was doing what Sid wanted when she dumped his offspring on
him.

⟨You don't really think that.⟩

He sniffed. She was right, but . . . 'I don't think they're dead?
Yeah, well. I have my supposed "halfcaste" Aleutian sense of
how the plot went, which tells me *nothing terrible happened.*
But my human reason tells me it's just when you think you
know something that probably you're definitely wrong. And
there's the others.' He mentally reviewed his scatty housemates.
'They're like kids themselves, they're hopeless.'

Bella started to move into the dog-jointed Aleutian crouch:
thought better of it and drew up her knees, wrapping her arms
around them. ⟨So why did you take service with Maitri, and
leave your people behind?⟩

'Because someone has to pay the rent.' How could he explain
the situation in his adopted country to an Aleutian? 'You see the
country where I live, Kerala, is a Community State. There's only
one household,' he translated. 'It's run by the Women. You can
be a member of the company, a citizen as we call it, if you're a
Man or a biological male. Not if you're a halfcaste. So who's
going to feed me and mine? I have to take work wherever I can.'

⟨Why don't you stop being a halfcaste? Is that possible?⟩

'It certainly is. The purebreds love a repentant looty-lover.'
He gritted his teeth. '*But I'm not one of them.*'

He saw the sneaky movement of her shoulders: *Sid is being
unreasonable.* He knew that particular little smile of old. It was
different now they were no longer playing Gunga Din and the
colonel's daughter. The pan began to bubble. Stirring it, he
dropped in pinches of Breakfast Special powder, then added
naturlait until he had the ideal, creamy, caramel brew. Sid was
proud of his tea. If they could get nothing but tea, naturlait and
potato gruel, it wouldn't be a bad diet. He poured, watching her
covertly. She had recovered quickly from her exhaustion. She
hadn't noticed, he guessed she was still in some kind of shock.
But after days without her medicine, starving in the wilderness,
she was stronger and healthier than he had ever seen her . . . He
wouldn't comment on this. He wasn't supposed to say *anything*
that would start her wondering. They waited for the tea to cool
in the midst of the vast, muted stir of the camp ground.

'Look,' he said. 'There's the moon.' It was a young moon, sailing in the turquoise afterwash of sunset.

⟨It's beautiful.⟩

'You have two, don't you? A genuine satellite, quite big, and a kind of lump like an old boot.'

Bella gave him a curious look. ⟨I live indoors. I've hardly seen the night sky, except on a screen.⟩

He handed her a beaker. She looked up into his face, and touched his cheek. ⟨What's this glittery stuff?⟩

'Oh.' He rubbed his jaw. 'It's beard. I don't like gene therapy. I use a depilatory. If I can't get it, then after a few weeks' – he shrugged apologetically – 'I grow bristles.'

⟨How peculiar.⟩

He chuckled. 'We aim to please.'

Aleutians touched each other all the time, but the butterfly caress of her fingertips had a different meaning and Sid knew it. He was kneeling, smiling at her, and they were closer than they had been in any necessary intimacy on the trek. A certain attraction had existed in the trading post, between Gunga Din and the colonel's daughter. They had both, Sid thought, dismissed the pull as something that would never happen. But that was in another lifetime.

He said ⟨Bella, would you by any chance like to . . . ?⟩

⟨Sid, would you . . . ?⟩

Sid beat a retreat. He sat back. He clasped his hands between his knees to stop them shaking.

⟨Yes,⟩ he said. ⟨Yes. I'd like to lie with you.⟩

He had been brought up a halfcaste, and she had no preconceptions about aliens. A human was a person to her.

⟨To take our minds off things,⟩ explained the librarian sensibly.

Sid turned and casually – it took enormous determination – put his hand on her arm. He discovered that the last few seconds had changed this into an astonishingly arousing act. She looked at him doubtfully: and they kissed.

He found that there were symmetrical runnels from the base of her throat, skirting the flat muscle where her breasts would have been. Fingers run in there made her shiver. Her hands slid under his shirt, searched his body: pulled at his nipples. He thought of the thing that they kept in the fold in the belly, called the claw. But he'd gone too far to turn back. He pushed the loose shirt down over her shoulders, and hunted his mouth and tongue along the grooves in her eager flesh.

⟨Shall we go inside?⟩ he asked.

They climbed into the freight van in that shamefaced way of lovers retiring, though no one was watching and nobody cared. The travellers did it in the open. Sid had seen and heard the furtive rhythmic movement in the primitive privacy of darkness: the couplers sure as animals that no one would have the indecency to disturb them. But Sid and Bella were indoor people. Inside the van they took off their clothes in darkness, and hurried together for fear of losing their nerve. Sid forgot entirely that she was not a human woman. His prick slid inside a moist cleft that did nothing to dispel the illusion . . . and was *met* there, by something that clasped it with a wild grip, so terrifying and so delightful he almost died. Desperate tremors ran through him: and then burst into convulsive spasms, while her body flowed liquid against him, melting and radiating in a hunger, an oblivion of connection, until they both lay still. He rolled away. Lay on his back on the dusty wagon floor, sweaty and ecstatic.

'Johnny Guglioli didn't *like* that! What a weirdo! Bella, can you cook? If you can cook, I think we should get married immediately!'

She stirred; he felt her sit up and peer at him in the dark.

⟨I can't cook. Why should I cook?⟩

'It was a joke, Bel. Hey, was it okay for you?'

This was a joke too. He knew it had been glorious for her. He didn't take the credit. How could *it* fail, after abstinence and such days of terror; and since they were friends? She bent over him very quietly. Her soft breath touched him.

⟨Shall we do it again? And maybe take a little longer?⟩

In the morning they were still lovers, though Bella had not said a word aloud.

She couldn't act the woman. Getting an Aleutian signifier to cook and clean would've been like trying to teach a fish to ride a bicycle. So Sid did odd jobs for barter and became adept at the domestic tasks of the camp; a regular in the social mill around the water tanker. The traveller women looked on him with scandalised pity, regarding his 'wife' with the resentment they'd reserve for a major courtesan. How right they were!

They crossed the great canal, and the megapolis drew near.

The travellers had a van full of sophisticated listening gear. They could avoid any firefight on the ground. They feared most the Allied robot fighters, the mad dog-planes that roamed the sky above their masters' path, launching into random attacks on anything that moved. One afternoon there was a squealing siren from the listening van that sent everybody running. People swiftly hauled out inflatable shelters of the most advanced battlefield model. The camp became a field of giant missile-resistant mushrooms. The outer ranks, the young men, scattered into the landscape. Sid and Bella dived into their freight van. The raiders passed, without doing any harm this time. Sid lit their firelighter, which doubled as a tiny lamp. Bella sat up in a pile of sacking bales.

'Are you all right?'

They had never investigated the contents of those bales. Sid thought it was probably toxic waste being moved illegally across moribund 'national borders'.

⟨Sid, look at this.⟩

A sack had split. It was full of cowpats: Aleutian discrete energy. It dawned on them without rancour that this explained somewhat the patriarch's kindness. If soldiers found the alien goods, the two 'halfcastes' could take the blame. Bella picked up a disc and held it beside her ear, like a local recording eye.

⟨Tell me, local person. How satisfied are you with Aleutian products? Very satisfied? Quite satisfied? Could we do better?⟩

Sid considered. 'Well, it's the names. That's my one complaint. In my culture a product's name is critical. It's supposed to be witty, relevant, possibly surreal—'

Her face in the light of the flame was bright with laughter. ⟨You don't like the *names* of things? That's absurd!⟩

He looked up at the cat-elf perched on her bale of contraband, giggling, and secretly smiled.

⟨What's the matter?⟩

'A wish granted. I had wanted to see you laugh again.'

They made love with undiminished delight, agreeing that this staggering gift of pleasure, which he called sex and she called *lying down*, made you wonder why you'd ever doubted the existence of a good God. There were moments when it crossed Sid's mind that they could stay with the travellers for ever. They were dead to the world. No one would know. But Bella didn't say a word. She never collapsed the wave, she would not give a name to what was happening. And Sid never asked her why she didn't.

The plantations ended. They came out of the wilderness into an industrial zone. The landscape burgeoned into fat welts and blisters of factory shapes connected by a maze of enclosed walkways and freight and passenger transport tubes. Huge exhausts pumped stale warm air, a permitted effluent, into heat-ex walls that stood glittering like giants' mirrors.

One morning Sid told Bella it was time to part company with the travellers. They bundled up their things and left without goodbyes. Sid had traded their stock of fuel and water chits for a part-spent megapolitan cashcard. He took her down to the metro station by a little-used outdoor entrance. The place was deserted. He had no fresh news, but he guessed the Protest and the threat of the armies was keeping people at home. The gate to the platform was closed by a twinkling barrier of light.

He put Bella in front of it. 'This here is a *gate*,' he told her. 'When you come to one of these you have to feed it. A handprint, or a contact film of your handprint will do. Or you can feed it cash, which is,' he translated, 'a card like this, which carries an allocation of your household's resources. Don't try to get through without feeding them: it will hurt.'

He checked the card, the barrier dispersed and he gently pushed her ahead of him. It reformed behind them.

'Now we're in livespace, which means camera eyes are watching us. Don't be afraid. If you don't wave a weapon, or try to jump on the line, the monitoring doesn't exactly *see* you. But you mustn't take off the chador in a place like this.'

He knew that she must be terrified. All this stuff was *the deadworld*, evil, nasty, native rites. But he couldn't comfort her. When they left the travellers they had passed through a barrier as insubstantial and effective as the photochemical gate.

'*Elefsis!*' she said suddenly.

The name of the station was displayed over the platform, in Greek and English lettering.

'I thought you said you couldn't read!'

⟨Read? I was looking at the pictures.⟩

The curved walls held a succession of rich, three-dimensional images, the universal decoration of old earth: cheaper than paint.

⟨I know this story. Maitri told it to me. This is where 'Persephone' – a young Woman, the truechild of someone important – was kidnapped by the Men. The Women had to make big concessions to win her back. It was a turning point in the war for the Men around here.⟩

She 'talked' in the chador in gestures that were massive, compared to the tiny flickering of Common Tongue. The name 'Persephone', spoken aloud, struck Sid uneasily. He didn't know it, but he felt he ought to.

'Don't mug like that,' he told her. 'It looks bad. I don't know, maybe you're right. I don't know much about the war in Greece: but the Men are winning down here, that's true.'

On the platform lay three ears of wheat bound in a red cord: *There is no death.* It was a signal that European halfcastes used. Elefsis was an important place to them, Sid wasn't sure why. He was glad to know that at least one Athenian gender-heretic had survived the violence.

He stared at the token, feeling cruelly divided. What was he going to do with Bel in Athens? He had pounded to ecstasy in her arms, crying inside: *I would not change one measly, virtual particle in the sum of things that made you!* It was Johnny Guglioli's last declaration of love to Braemar, spoken on the execution floor: the height of romance in Sid's halfcaste soul. But that couldn't be right. He and Bel couldn't be lovers. The attraction between two outsiders at the trading post should have been *useful*, making his job easier. It shouldn't have gone any further, and he was sorry it had got out of hand.

But if she would only say the word . . .

He knew that she would not. The reserve that had risen between them had two sides.

They travelled a long way on the metro train. As it approached the city centre a few Athenians joined them. No one showed interest in the glum young man and his veiled companion.

He left her in an outdoor park, a few stations beyond the Plaki on the way to the airport. It was a neglected spot, in a city where to brave the outdoors for any reason was eccentric. A booth meant to dispense snacks and information stood in a grove of withered pine trees. It was non-functional, but the doors had seized open. He told her to stay out of sight and he'd be back.

It was getting dark when he returned. She was outside the booth beside their bundle of camping kit. She'd taken off the chador. In the gloom she looked very human: a ragged, grubby, homeless waif.

'It's much as we'd expected,' he told her. 'Your people have retreated out to orbit. The Government of the World has joined in the general rejoicing. The truce is over, the armies are no longer a serious threat to us. But anti-Aleutian feeling's very strong.' He paused. 'I've bought us some air tickets. I'm going to take you to Trivandrum with me. It seems like the best option. I know Triv, I can hide you there. And when things are calmer—'

⟨I thought air travel was terribly expensive.⟩

'Ah.' He wasn't sure what to make of this. 'I bought the tickets on credit. I'm sure your folks will pay me back.'

He produced food: naturlait, a carton of squashy rice pudding, another of naturfromage. 'I finished the cashcard in a good little mart near the travel office.' He fished out their spoon from the bundle, opened the pudding and stuck it in.

'Try this. You'll like it. This is Bella-friendly food.'

She took the carton, without a smile. Sid was overwhelmed by a wash of silent rejection. She'd been like this since he had told her it was time to leave the camp. He couldn't stand it any more.

'What's the *matter* with you?'

She said something he didn't quite catch.

'Are you trying to tell me the holiday romance is over? Well, fine. I knew that. I wasn't expecting you to *marry* me.' Her face glimmered, sour-sweet. 'What's funny? Aleutians do it. We know you do. Rajath was married to Aditya the beauty. Maitri used to be married to a security officer, I forget the name.'

⟨Oh, contracted partners . . .⟩ The librarian drew herself up, with dignity. ⟨You should have told me you expected to be paid.⟩

Sid gathered that, to Aleutians, 'marriage' was a form of licensed prostitution. This addition to human knowledge made his cheeks burn. He was shocked at Maitri. She ate three spoonfuls of the pudding and laid the carton aside.

⟨I'm not coming with you.⟩

'What?'

⟨I'm extremely grateful for all you've done.⟩

'You can't stay here!'

She shrugged, quietly confident. ⟨Yes, I can.⟩

Sid's jaw dropped. She had seemed so rational. But then, how could she be rational, ripped from her living world? He realised that he must be seeming as cold and strange to her as she did to him. The time they'd spent with the travellers had been an illusion. They'd stepped out of it the way you leave a game: both of them disoriented and miserable in the real. But he was too much on edge to be gentle.

'Oh, I see. It's the rescue shuttle again. It's due here any moment, I suppose.'

She looked at him, oblivious to sarcasm, as if it was none of his business. ⟨Something like that,⟩ she agreed distantly.

Sid gritted his teeth. 'The Aleutians have gone. You're alone. You have to come with me. I found out about the situation in the enclaves. It was rough, but it's quiet again. We know you can pass as a halfcaste. In my home town I can keep you safe. It won't be for ever. It might not be for very long.'

⟨I know that. Your people will invite us back soon.⟩

And the north wind will blow, thought Sid, with a surge of anger. He had no illusions. The aliens would return, and in at least as strong a position as before. He didn't need to be told this, so *casually*, by the alien whose life he'd saved.

'Talk sense. You're isolate. If there's anyone, in the shipworld or lurking on earth, who doesn't believe you died at Mykini, they couldn't possibly find you. So tell me more. Who exactly is it you're expecting?'

She gave him a reproachful look: but no answer.

'I'll make you a deal,' he said. 'Our cruiser leaves late tomorrow. If you're here in the morning, you come with me.'

Suddenly the fight had gone out of both of them. They retired inside the booth. It had been used by other vagrants. There were scraps of litter and heaps of human turds in the corners. Bella settled where she could see out: presumably watching for her rescuers.

⟨I lost my records.⟩

'Maitri's library? They were all copies, surely?'

⟨I don't go to confession very often. There's no reason, nothing happens to me. But I had confessed at the trading post, before things went wrong: the first time in this life. It's lost. Being isolate is relative. Sometimes I have a partial remission. This time I've had no wanderers at all. Without records, when I come back it'll be as if I was never Maitri's child.⟩

'You can make another tape.'

⟨It won't be the same.⟩

To his human senses she was silent and motionless. He understood – if he did – the way Aleutians understand each other: because he knew so much.

'I'm sorry,' he said.

She sighed. ⟨So am I.⟩

Deep in the heart of the night two aircraft landed, one shortly after the other, in the park. The first was like a large bird. It tried to fold its wings, and made an awkward scramble of the movement. The second resembled an insect. Two pairs of long transparent vanes lifted, rotated, and slotted neatly over its abdomen. An Aleutian emerged from each machine. One, gangling and loose-limbed, wore the eternal dun overalls. The other was dressed in a red cossack tunic with white ribbed silk breeches tucked into high red boots. They stood, measuring each other.

'Nice bit of *schmutter*,' said the older of the pair.

When these two had last been on earth together, Rajath the trickster had been much older than Clavel. Worldly and bold, he had dominated the romantic young poet. In this life the balance was reversed. It was the first time they'd met, in person. Clavel, equipped with the bleak assurance of a middle-aged idealist, slowly smiled: enjoying Rajath's disadvantage.

Rajath straightened his tunic.

'I'm sorry about Maitri,' he announced.

⟨It's over.⟩ Clavel dismissed the conventional sympathy.

⟨I suppose the engineer will be along soon?⟩ grumbled Rajath, accepting the brusque drop into informal speech.

⟨Kumbva? I have no idea where he is, or if he's on earth. I'm not in his confidence. He's dropped out of sight entirely.⟩

⟨Maybe the Protest got him,⟩ suggested Rajath, brightening. ⟨What about you? What was it like in . . . in your area?⟩

The presence of the other two captains (if Kumbva was alive) was clandestine. The Aleutians knew that Clavel was on earth, but he'd kept the location of his retreat private. ⟨I'm a discreet divinity. I had no trouble.⟩

⟨Didn't Yudi try to evacuate you?⟩

⟨Yudisthara knows I can look after myself. But I'm afraid you've suffered. It's unlike you to be travelling alone. Did you lose some people?⟩

Rajath's splendid local clothes were, at a second glance, rather soiled and battered. ⟨Lose? I'm travelling light this trip, that's all. I did have a little trouble. It doesn't matter. There's a game called 'stock exchange' one can play in Moskva. You can win a fortune in an hour's play, come out and find your tea hasn't started to cool—⟩

⟨I find that one dull,⟩ remarked Clavel. ⟨Too linear.⟩

Rajath laughed. For a moment they were in sympathy, over a taste for local pleasures that would have appalled Yudi.

⟨I love the games,⟩ said Rajath. ⟨But what a mess the planet is in: war and ruin everywhere. What *happened* to the place?⟩

Clavel showed teeth. ⟨Us.⟩

The trickster considered this novel idea. ⟨Nonsense,⟩ he decided; and moved restively. ⟨Shall we get down to business?⟩

Clavel looked at the small building under the trees. ⟨I suppose,⟩ he said at last, ⟨you imagine that you are here to collect my property for your employers in orbit.⟩

Rajath was hurt. ⟨Colleagues. You mean colleagues . . . Look here poet, you had your chance. If you wanted 'your property' – and I dispute that a person can be anybody's 'property' – why didn't you take him before?⟩

⟨I had my reasons.⟩

⟨Well, never mind. Here we are together: can we do business?⟩

Clavel showed teeth again. ⟨I don't trade with traitors.⟩

Above them, a few stars competed with the half moon in a hazy sky. ⟨I resent that,⟩ said Rajath. ⟨You started this, and essentially it was for your own profit. We're not so different.⟩

The other stretched his rangy limbs. ⟨In that case, since we're alone and evenly matched: shall we fight it out?⟩

⟨Let's not be vulgar,⟩ temporised the trickster uneasily.

⟨By all means, let's not be vulgar. Let us agree instead that it may serve both our purposes to let this game run a little longer.⟩

Shortly, the bird and the insect crafts took wing and escorted each other away.

Sid woke with a start. He rolled over, his heart racing, and struck a light. Bella was beside him. He checked outside. Nothing was stirring. He knelt by her, shading the flame in his palm. He had remembered that Persephone was the daughter of a goddess, who was kidnapped and carried away to the land of the dead: another lost immortal girl, like the one who left Shangri-La. He looked down at Bella. Did she really whisper *I'm married*? No, but in the Common Tongue she had told him; though she could hardly bear to explain it, that she felt committed to someone else.

'You poor sod,' he muttered. 'You poor little sod.'

He put out the light and lay down, filled with guilt and pity; and determined not to give way to either.

4: ON THE FACE OF THE WATERS

Maitri's librarian, who had been called Goodlooking and was now called Bella, lay waking in the safe room in Sid's house in Trivandrum. As he rose into consciousness other rooms fell from him. His study-bedroom in Maitri's library; a neat row of pallets in a ward for sick children. A soft toy snuggled against him: dear friend loved and lost ages ago.

He saw the soldiers pouring through the shattered dome. Maitri trying to reason with them. Trying bombast: 'I must protest! This is an outrage!', that sounded ridiculous from Maitri. Light suckers were falling, writhing in the flames. Bokr stared at his own severed hand, a moving clot of wanderers seethed over the gap, dying. *Who took my revolver? You should have lain with me, kid. It would have been a bond between us* . . . Bella's Aleutian memory made no distinction between what he had seen and what he knew intensely of how events must have been. He lay with closed eyes, enduring the images. They would fade. In another life, good things would blot out the bad. In another life, those soldiers would make amends. *Everything must happen*, thought Bella, knowing that horror and grief would pass, and he would recover his trust in the even-handedness of Time.

He remembered his journey with Sidney Carton from Athens to this place. There had been a metro train to the airport, and then a succession of air-cruisers. They blurred into one. The cruisers were like metro trains, and the metro trains were not so different from city transport at home. He had no perception of flight, or of the vast distances. He and Sid had been carried through blank hours in a series of dead buses, full of people who were equally, eerily void of life in the Aleutian sense . . .

When they'd reached the last airport it had been night. Sid
had spoken to the driver of a tiny dead vehicle. The driver
laughed, and said (Bella caught the meaning, though the words
of a strange regional dialect were indistinct), *'The halfcaste
street? Don't be afraid to say so. The killing is over, thank God.
You people can relax.'* Neti-neti, he said: not this, not that.
Bella gathered this was another local term for Aleutian-lovers.

He remembered being hurried past an open doorway where
local faces stared out of a half-lit gloom. Up narrow, dark stairs
to a door that was firmly shut. Sid had lit their firelighter, his
hands shaking. He tapped, then knocked, then banged and
yelled. Finally it opened. A thin, dark-skinned halfcaste without
a nose saw Sid, burst into tears and fell into his arms. That was
Jimi. In the room above they met Mother Teresa, Bob Marley,
Superman and Father Roger Casement. Noor Jaan was not at
home: and Cactus had been poorly and was asleep.

The children were there, Lydia and baby Roger. When he saw
them a long, desperate tension, that had been within Sid since
the massacre, suddenly melted. He dropped to his knees, holding
out his arms. *I will be grateful for ever*, vowed the librarian,
rising from sleep, *to the WorldSelf, for letting Sid's children be
all right*.

When the children had been greeted, Sid had told his housemates that Bella was an Aleutian and would be staying with
them. They were thrown into panic: exclaiming, fussing, grovelling. Sid had taken Bella away, to this place that was the safe
room, and left him alone.

It had been a relief to escape from the 'she' expression. But
he'd decided to keep the name 'Bella'. It would be souvenir of
this adventure, if he ever got home again. He felt the chafing of
a coarse, oversized toilet pad. He needed to change himself. He
opened his eyes, thinking of what Sid had called the 'native way'
of dealing with the problem. If this was the alternative, he could
come to regret that peculiar freedom. He got up and changed,
stuffing the dirty pad in the bin. The toilet stand held a roll of
'cleeno', a trade-goods cloth made of living material 'half killed'
for the local market. Sid had told him he could use it to clean
himself. He tore a piece off and wiped doubtfully at his lifeless
skin. It felt disgusting. He didn't want to be rude, but – he stuffed

it in the bin. The clothes that Sid had put out for him were
Aleutian in style but made of local fabric. He didn't mind
material that was decently dead. He dressed and returned to the
pallet: and settled there informally, knees and hips reversed.

The room had no windows and no visible door. It was stacked
with emergency supplies: liquid, food, first aid. Dim light came
from trade-goods light suckers on the walls. In one alcove stood
the toilet stand, a wastebin and a huge carton of the clumsy
pads. In another there was a minimal character shrine: a screen
and a shelf of records. This was the place where the halfcastes
would barricade themselves in, if their enemies attacked the
house.

He had to escape from here. But how? And to where?

Bella wasn't sure exactly when he'd realised he was being
kidnapped. On the night of the massacre Sidney Carton had
come to his room and blurted out *I'm going to destroy you*. But
the weird terror Bella had felt then would have meant nothing.
People can't be held responsible for what they do or say, in the
Common Tongue, in desperate situations. No, it wasn't then.
But his suspicions could have begun the next morning, when Sid
went out to see what was happening and left the librarian alone;
and he had started thinking. Certainly he'd been wary enough
to conceal his surprise at the halfcaste's slips, his familiarity
with things a simple interpreter shouldn't know: at Sid's increasingly thin story, all round. But it was the 'suit' incident that
finally convinced the librarian he wasn't imagining things.

Sidney Carton was a secret agent. His pose as a superior kind
of halfcaste – too self-respecting to mutilate himself or to
slavishly accept Aleutian culture – was a bold, cool bluff. He
was an anti-Aleutian fanatic who had installed himself in
Maitri's service as part of a carefully prepared plan. He had been
taken unawares by the Protest and by the massacre . . . as Sid's
friend, Bella was glad to feel sure of that. But he had managed
to escape with the prize anyway: Maitri's librarian!

It sounded bizarre, but nothing else fitted the facts. For some
reason the anti-Aleutian fanatics, and also the mysterious
'Campfire Girls' from the forbidden territory of the USSA, were
desperate to get hold of Bella. It was as if they'd heard of the

'disguised prince' rumour, and were convinced that Maitri's librarian would make a valuable hostage.

Bella glowed with embarrassment. In the wilderness, and notably on that night in Athens, he had let his imagination run away with him and half believed the rumour himself. He cringed inwardly at the memory, crouching close on the strange pallet, feeling that his most secret fantasies had been laid bare. But everyone has silly fantasies. He was glad to say that the idiocy had passed: leaving only a residual feeling that it would actually be rather unpleasant to find out *that you were someone else*.

Possibly the anti-Aleutians believed that the librarian possessed some information, some secret hidden in Maitri's records, that could be used against the Expedition. Perhaps Sid had been supposed to kidnap Maitri himself, until the invalid librarian appeared and presented a softer target. Bella couldn't think of any such secret, but maybe it was something he knew without understanding its significance . . . He abandoned the puzzle. Whatever he knew or didn't know, whether or not he'd been kidnapped by mistake, he couldn't let the Expedition's enemies – Maitri's enemies – keep hold of an Aleutian hostage.

Sid had left him in Athens, to get instructions from the boss – via the deadworld, Bella surmised, disliking the idea. Sid seemed so normal, it was nasty to think of him talking to ghosts. He'd returned with air tickets to Trivandrum. The inference was obvious. Sid's evil boss, the ominous figure who dominated Sid's unconscious silent confessions, was in the city.

I'm going to destroy you. He remembered the horror that had filled him when Sid came into his room. It was so strange: in the midst of a massacre it was gentle Sid who had terrified him, because Sid looked on the killing as an Aleutian might have done. He was frantic, he was flooded with the usual emotions. But *he knew it didn't matter*. The destruction that he promised was something different, something *effective*. In Sid's boss, the Expedition was up against a genuine enemy: a well-informed, ruthless fanatic, in the same mould as Braemar Wilson.

He bore Sid no ill will. No one chooses their loyalties. He wanted to remember for ever Sid's patience and tenderness in the wilderness, in those dreadful days when there'd been neither kidnapper nor victim, only two lost souls together. He wanted to treasure the memory of the lying down they'd shared: that had been lovely. If he got home alive he was determined to brave the embarrassment and make a full confession, so it all went on his record. Meantime, how was he to get out of here?

He was amazed at himself. He didn't know where this courage and energy was coming from. He was sure it would evaporate the moment he tried to do something. But he felt, strangely enough, unusually well and strong after his ordeal: as well, at least, as on his very best of days in normal life. It must be the air of earth, he thought. The emptiness that others found so harsh and enervating was a blessed relief to the isolate. Suddenly he stretched out on the pallet, hiding his face. The air was empty, he was *alone*. The loss of Aleutia was as real to him as to a healthy person physically bound into the meshes of life. He was dead to them, he was utterly deserted. It was awful.

In the room she liked to call their main hall, Mother Teresa kept a row of pallets for the dying poor of Trivandrum. She had never had many customers. The halfcaste way of death was too quick and casual for her; and the destitute of the Community State didn't like *neti-neti*. She'd carry them in here, half dead, and somehow they'd manage to crawl out again. When Sid went in there, the morning after he brought Bella home, he found the ward abandoned for the duration of the Protest, the pallets almost buried under a tide of shambolic untidiness. After long days in which the household had hardly dared to open the window shutters, the atmosphere in the long room was dank and foul.

He'd caught Mother Teresa emptying the freeze-dry toilet. She turned her back on him. She hated to admit that her family used a thunderbox. But Clark, her eldest, had an appetite for lip-smacking purebred food: *masala dosa*, *idli*, hamburgers, *gulab jamum*. The waste products of his gorging couldn't be contained in an Aleutian-style sanitary pad.

Sid lifted heaps of dirty clothes, and poked at jumbled utensils. Clark was lying on a string bed, poring over the flickering pictures of a comic. Mother Teresa, a feminine halfcaste, had never had the chance to make dramatic changes to the woman's body that had borne her three 'wards'. But she'd tried hard to

make her children into genuine freaks. Clark was an object
lesson in the perils of cheap prenatal gene therapy. He raised a
face divided by a severe cleft palate, shifted his sexless bulk
above the flipper legs that could barely carry him.

⟨What're you looking for, boss?⟩

It was heartbreaking to know that his mother had paid a small
fortune, *real money*, to have some quack turn her child into a
sort of human walrus. 'My sunglasses. Have you seen them?'

⟨Sorry.⟩ Clark settled again, groping a greasy package of
sweets. ⟨Can't help. I'm doing my character study.⟩

'Superman is a *fictional* character, for God's sake.'

⟨So's 'Sidney Carton',⟩ responded the hero, unmoved.

'You don't know that.' Sid grinned. The beast was harmless.
'You weren't there.' The second of the brood was twisted up on
a battered cane armchair in a yoga pose, staring at the ceiling.

'Bob? *Bob!*'

As a foetus Bobby had been declared, by a less than usually
rapacious quack, unsuitable for prenatal meddling. He'd started
having his features rearranged surgically now he was grown: a
cheap option as far as the nose went, but he had grisly ambitions
for his hip joints. He was a devout telepath.

'BOBBY! HAVE YOU HAD MY SUNGLASSES?'

⟨Leave him alone,⟩ snapped Mother T. ⟨Can't you see he's in
conference with his lawyers?⟩

The halfcastes were stuck with the twentieth century as a
source of past selves. Further back, there weren't any moving
images. Further forward, you ran into a modern 'deadworld'
tech, which the Aleutians spurned. The time trap meant that
the gender-heretics were stuck with the sex-roles of the past.
They didn't care. They weren't reformists. For most of them,
there was no agenda: be like the Aleutians, that was the whole
thing.

Some of the most favoured icons were unconcerned: they got
together socially. Spiritual ownership of other identities (physical resemblance was not a big issue) was fiercely contested
around the enclave band; usually by freight mail. If you were
really devout, you could squabble via telepathy. There were
halfcaste lawyers who would brazenly *bill* the fools for legal
consultation in this mode.

'Oh, excuse me, Mr Marley, sir. I didn't realise you were in astral multiphon-conference. Let me step over these heaps of meltoptics here. Where's Noor?' There was a conscious silence between the brothers. Bobby grinned in his networking trance, without opening his eyes. Clark sniggered. Sid judged from this that the bold girl had gone down the mall to play virtuality games: a pastime totally forbidden to halfcaste youngsters.

He turned, with a shrug of complicity (they weren't bad kids): and found that Mother Teresa had brought out her Aleutian cooking stove. She was feeding it with pieces of shrivelled turd.

Mother T. had scrounged her proudest possession from the Aleutian Hotel. The halfcastes who lingered around the compound sometimes used to come away with alien cast-offs, sterilised to conform with quarantine rules. The 'stove' was a room-cooler. It had not been grown to run on turd, nor to heat to cooking temperatures: but you could make the cruder commensals do anything, really. It helplessly gulped the waste and began to glow. Sid turned away, hating to see a living machine mistreated – and suddenly, horrified, remembered Bella.

'Are you crazy? Get that thing out of sight!'

He sprang across the cluttered floor. Mother T. squawked and threw herself in the way. They ended on the floor together, in a scatter of dried human dung. The room-cooler wriggled off under the furniture. Clark and Bobby raised an ironic cheer.

Sid squatted on his heels, head in his hands, furious with the whole stupid muddle of the halfcaste world. 'Are you crazy?' he demanded again. 'Suppose the landlady walked in and saw it? You know the way she walks in here. Remember who we've got upstairs!'

⟨She knows what we are. And she hasn't been near us since the violence.⟩ Mother Teresa snorted, scar tissue round her clumsily bared nostrils flaring. ⟨Don't talk to me about danger. Where were you, when they were burning halfcastes in our streets?⟩

She was shaking. She'd give her life for Bella, without question. The poor, brave, pitiful old bat. He saw, lost in those evasive button-hard little eyes, the longing to be good that had made her choose her saintly name; that bound her to this tattered, idiotic cult of the superbeings. He picked up his sunglasses, which had been under the bag of dung.

'She won't be here long,' he said. 'If I forgot to say it last night: thank you, for keeping my children safe.'

Father Roger was reading his Office, sitting tranquilly on the narrow cot in his cell of a room. As Sid came in his eyes continued to flicker over the moving glyphs on the flat reader in his hand. His godson was sweetly asleep beside him.

Sid fidgeted, peering at mementoes. Here was a papal blessing, all the way from Lima. Roger had been a priest before he became a gender-heretic. A reformist by conviction, he'd *recognised himself* in the person of a minor hero of that persuasion from the early twentieth century. It was his bad luck that the RC Church had subsequently decided to canonise Roger Casement, crusading anti-racist and homosexual martyr, with a batch of similar types in a move to gain reformist credit. The Reunited Catholic Church was unhappy about reincarnation. It felt a lot worse about a priest who was a reincarnated saint. Rog had been terribly demoralised when Sid first met him, struggling to find his way. Poor Rog! The Protest wasn't going to have helped his case. But he was patient. Wasn't it the Aleutians who said, 'time's cheap'?

'Roger? I don't want to interrupt, but—'

'Mmm?'

'Suppose—?' Sid broke off: tried again. 'Suppose you knew something important about someone, something crucial? But you couldn't tell them without betraying a vital secret . . .'

Father Casement looked curiously at the restless young man. 'A moral dilemma, Sid? That's new for you.' He shook his head. 'You'd have to tell me more.'

Sid straightened a framed flat reproduction: a pencil sketch of a gaunt, kindly looking masculine Caucasian. He glanced from it to the plump Tamil priest with a discreet nose-chop. Asking a saint for advice on a business decision. What did he expect?

He sighed. 'Thanks anyway, Roger.'

On the floor above, the kids and Sid had the smaller back room, Jimi and Cactus shared the other. Sid found Cactus at home alone, in the character shrine alcove, lying gazing at the screen. Cactus was often ill. He'd had gene therapy meant to give him an Aleutian gut, which had left him with a digestive system that could not digest much.

He was an unusual alien-lover. He didn't know who he was, but he was sure he was someone quite ordinary. He spent his time tracking carefully through news coverage, forgotten game-shows, prehistoric mall monitoring – anything that Jimi could find in the secondhand bazaar – waiting for the moment of *recognition*.

'Hiya, Cactus.'

He was called Cactus because he had hardly any hair. What there was of it grew in spikes, each a single horny growth, with bare puckered scalp between. They watched the screen in companionable silence. It was a fossiled infotainment feature about sewage treatment, with a large cast. At a break for some surreal animation, Cactus stopped concentrating and made a shy speech. 'I'm glad you're back, Sid. We missed you.'

'I missed you too. I'd have been here if I could.'

'It wasn't so bad. We stayed indoors. But what're we going to do now, without the aliens?'

That was what they all wanted to know, though it was only Cactus who had asked out loud. How are we going to live, *Sid*? It had to be Sid. No one else was going to think of an answer.

The feudal Aleutians didn't strictly speaking pay their servants. Lord Maitri had given Sid practical and generous presents when he took the halfcaste interpreter into his service: a bale of organic batteries, bolts of cleeno; water tablets. The household had been living on the sale of these goods for the past year. But the small remaining stock was useless now.

'They'll be back.'

'I don't want to sound disloyal. But what if you're wrong?' Cactus's anxious face crumpled. 'We can't give up being looty-lovers because the purebreds threw them out. It'd be a betrayal of our whole lives. But how are we going to survive?'

Sid perched the sunglasses on his nose, and smiled wisely and mysteriously. 'Don't you fret. I'll think of a number.'

Cactus nodded. 'I'm sure you will, Sid.'

'In fact, my prickly one, I'm on my way up town, to wheel a deal that should keep us cosy for a while.'

⟨Car chases,⟩ murmured Cactus, gazing at his friend. ⟨High-priced secrets, privileged information, disguises, fights in alleys, showdowns with Mr Big. Oh, Sid, I'm glad I know you.⟩

'Couldn't have put it better myself. Wish me luck.'

Before he'd become Maitri's child, the librarian had usually spent his infancy in a children's ward. Most people who bore an isolate quickly decided that the baby would be better off under specialised care. The shipworld or at home, it had been the same. For more lives than he cared to remember he had passed straight from some hospital or other – if he survived – to his study-bedroom beside Maitri's library, and scarcely left his lord's house again. He had almost no experience of his own: only his knowledge of the records, and the thin replenishment of his prosthetic wanderers. *There's one consolation*, he thought. *I will be no more helpless in the streets of this city than if I was at home*.

Sid had never explained how he had acquired his adult dependents. He was like Maitri, the librarian decided: who drew people to him by gentleness alone, and anyone who once joined his household stayed for ever. They were certainly loyal, which was awkward, because Bella needed help. But loyalty can be deceived . . . He was sorry he wouldn't see Sid again. It was a shame to have parted so awkwardly, both of them feeling guilty and preoccupied. He resolutely put the sadness aside. It couldn't be helped.

Someone had brought a bowl of soup. He'd found it by his bed when he'd woken from a brief doze. He had judged that it would not be poisoned, so he'd eaten it and found it very good. He picked up the bowl, let himself out of the safe room and made his way to the roof, where he knew he would find the weak link in Sid's company.

The halfcastes lived in a run-down area near the temple, on the border of the reformists' part of town. As Sid marched confidently up the MG road – called after Mahatma Gandhi, like the main road in every second town on the subcontinent – the character of the street display changed. The frequency of block-high shimmering pages of sacred calligraphy increased. They became more literal, less stylised. In the gaudy Hindu projections there were fewer forests of chaos, more conventional gods and demons. Underfoot, the vivid, hardwearing and highly engineered sidewalk turf gave way to plain white instant stone. There were few women on the street, and many of them were veiled. There were more teksis and fewer buses. He was in Man Town. But the change was not violent. Kerala was a reformist state where reformists and traditionalists lived together peaceably: as on a larger scale the reformist states of the subcontinent lived in peace with their traditionalist neighbours.

Battery buses threaded the teeming pedestrian traffic, teksis swooped and dived. A heavy monsoon rain began. Sid put up his umbrella, but kept his dark glasses on. They hid his blue eyes, and that wasn't all. Up here the MG was a strutting ground. Keeping your eyes covered was a way of avoiding the glowing stares of challenge and staying out of fights. Sidney Carton swaggered, cocksure: occasionally pausing to brush some imaginary injury from his spruce white cotton suit. He felt safer in Woman Town. *Everybody* felt safer in Woman Town. But he enjoyed coming up here: it was a thrill. It stirred his blood with ancient pride. Safety isn't everything.

He stood, deliberately, and took a good long look at one of the burned-out buildings. He'd never noticed that so many Community Retailers carried Aleutian goods. But the subcontinent had been the Aleutians' favoured trading area for a long time. There was an affinity between alien and Indian culture. Hindus believed in reincarnation and were as indifferent to change as the aliens; while Muslims had their Aleutian submission to fate, and their rigid recklessness. Where else on earth would you find such an insidiously, immovably feudal society, or such a blurring of the distinction between repetition and diversity? A hundred thousand MG roads, why not? But favour and affinity hadn't saved them from the Himalaya Project. That was the aliens for you, decided Sid gloomily. You thought you understood them. You started thinking this understanding proved that *the whole cosmos made sense*. Then *pow!* Complete breakdown.

He wished he hadn't told the others that Bella was a real alien. They wouldn't give her away on purpose, but they were such fools, and she was so helpless. But he wasn't used to deceiving them. Maybe he'd have to move her, think of some-

where else. A group of youths were pouring solvent on a clump
of strange greenery: Aleutian weeds, escaped from the hotel
compound. Sid thought of the wild breaches of quarantine that
the Protest had caused: *so damned stupid* . . . A young face with
blacked-out eyes turned and glared. Sid hurried by, into the foyer
of an old-fashioned high-rise hotel. It was a place that foreign
alien-watchers had favoured before the Protest. The lobby was
deathly quiet. Two Arab-states men in flowing white robes were
taking coffee. They watched him over their newsreaders.

'Mr Thursday,' he told the receptionist. 'To see Mr Sunday.'

He was expected.

He knocked on a sheeny grey door that was redolent of another
age: of minibars and faxed news updates and closed circuit tv.

'Come in, Sid.'

He entered and was confronted by a towering Samurai warrior:
scaled armour, venomous eyes, sword raised high. He dodged, he
feinted. The sword swept through his body, cleaving him from
shoulder to groin. Sid groaned in exasperation.

'Sit down.'

The Fat Man was ensconced with his back to the light, behind
a secretary-desk. His white-gloved hand proffered an antique
chair made of padded hessian and metal tubing. Sid approached
warily. There was a spider on the seat. Sid disliked spiders. He
laughed and poked at the thing fearlessly. His whole hand went
through the *chair*. He lost his balance: reached out to his left.
The chair vanished and reappeared on his right.

'*Why* do you always get me?' he demanded.

'It's my timing,' explained the Fat Man. 'Which is superb. And
the fact that your raw perception is fooled. *You* know the
difference between trickery and reality by context, if nothing
more: the spider on your chair has to be a joke. But your senses
have to be told. It makes a little delay.'

'Is the chair real now?' asked Sid patiently. He knew it was.
His senses could tell when the game was over. He sat down.

'Well.' The Fat Man steepled his gloved hands and peered
largely over them. 'Is there a way through the doors of death?'

Sid grinned. 'Some kind of looty fantasy, isn't it, that
expression? Something about being able to walk into a tv screen
and come out on the other side of the galaxy? It sounds like a

dumb tourist's misunderstanding to me. Seems to me if you tried that, all you'd get would be a bumped nose. Suppose you had one.'

They laughed.

The Fat Man was a veteran, legendary Aleutian-watcher. His grasp of the alien question, in all its aspects, was renowned through the enclaves and old earth. His long and close association with the halfcaste Sidney Carton had started one day when Sidney, not yet a teenage single father, just a rebellious halfcaste brat, met a large and fat tourist who was wandering insouciantly in the *neti-neti* area of Ernakulum, the coastal town where Sid's people were living. Sid had heard the fat tourist asking: '*Is there a way through the doors of death?*' The other kids hooted, gaped dumbly or ran. Sidney was intrigued. He had followed the stranger. The Fat Man had pretended not to know he was being followed, until he walked into Bimbis the confectioners, ordered a sumptuous heap of cakes and invited Sid to join him. Then he had begun to talk: about the aliens and the saboteurs, about the sciences of earth and Aleutia, and about the wildest dream of all.

He said he was looking for the instantaneous travel device. It was not a myth. It existed. The saboteurs had used it to reach the alien shipworld undetected: and then the secret had been lost. The traces that remained were certain enigmatic phrases, buried in old earth's mass of recorded data, a few microns of gold in a mountain the size of the planet: like that one, *there is a way through the doors of death*.

Sid had known he was hungry for more than food, born hungry. He had never known what he was hungry for, but he recognised it at once: *something impossible*. They'd been partners ever since. The Fat Man had filled Sid's empty mind, taught him alien lore and human science. He'd taught Sid to read and write, explained to him the workings of history. Sometimes he would disappear for months, pursuing other business. Sometimes he would arrange for Sid to take service with the aliens, in deepest cover. Afterwards Sid would answer strange questions, and the Fat Man would never explain what he had learned.

For all Sid knew, this sorcerer had a whole college of apprentices scattered over the globe, and 'Mr Sunday' was one of many aliases. But Sid, 'Mr Thursday', thought not. He believed that no one else shared the great alien-watcher's lonely, crazy quest. The Fat Man slipped a small package across the desk. Sid pocketed it without a glance. He knew what would be inside – milk tokens, school-meals vouchers, cablesoft-stamps: the paper money of the Community State's grey economy. The landlady would know what to do with them.

'Well, Mr Thursday?'

Usually they managed to stay in touch no matter where Sid was. Sid's boss had a weakness for gadgets, especially fancy telecoms. Sid was conscious of the gap in the record: the days of his trek with Bella, and in the travellers' camp. He put that time firmly out of his mind.

'She's in my house, unharmed, secure.' He had taken off his glasses when he entered the hotel lobby. His darkened lashes flickered. He could feel that packet in his pocket. 'I think we should tell her what's going on. She's not *merchandise*.'

'Oh.' The Fat Man pondered.

'I think she should know who she is.'

'Ah. The question of Aleutian identity.' He leaned back, gazing thoughtfully at Sid. 'The wanderers are very important. Those louse-like red bugs are cell-colonies which are *sentient*, in that they replicate not only the individual's whole genetic identity, but also his current emotional status, his current skills: his whole life-status, condensed into chemical signals. We believe that a neural model of the entire brood entity, similar in principle to the "homunculus" perception map in the human, exists in each Aleutian mind/brain. When they consume each other's wanderers, this model is updated. Every update is repli-cated in the reproductive tract, where each Aleutian – as we know – carries the full complement of the brood's genetic material. Thus, the Aleutians are not true "telepaths". They have no psychic powers. Their knowledge of each other, reinforced of course by the character tapes, is based on physical contact and chemical reaction, however rarefied. But in a sense they are true immortals. When a new "Clavel" is born, that bundle of chemicals really does "know" what happened to Clavel in his last life . . .'

Sid was looking increasingly depressed. 'Chemicals don't *know* things. Conscious memory can't be passed on like that. And even if it could—'

A white hand lifted mildly. 'A debatable point.' The big man's face grew bleak. 'I'm reminded that the physiology of their reproduction explains why to an Aleutian rape has the same meaning – if you can call it that – as the human act. When they *lie down* together, as they say, the exchange of wanderers, a polite constant in social interaction, becomes a flood. Wanderers are directly absorbed through mucus membranes, sometimes in enormous numbers. Thus, their love-making, as in the human gestalt, is essentially an act of chemical communication. Rape, as among humans, is the means of imposing a stronger party's version of events on futurity.'

There was a short silence. Both of them had liked and admired Sid's alien employer.

'Such futility.' The big man fisted his hands. 'Oh, my Sid! Everyone on earth is rejoicing at the *success* of the Protest. You and I know better. Why have human beings become so stupid? The Gender War has rotted their minds. I wish I knew how it happened. How did the battle of the sexes become such a disaster?'

'It was the Aleutians,' said the halfcaste, forgetting to protest that the war wasn't really about gender. 'The problem was always there. But everyone believed, deep down, that it couldn't be solved. Men and women were complementary halves: two sides of the same coin. Then the Aleutians came, and each of them was a *person*, nobody's better or worse half. The women saw the aliens: with no one forcing sex on them; having children and not getting their pay docked for the privilege; and so on. The men saw the same aliens doing what comes naturally with no thought for the consequences, and nobody having unrealistic expectations or nagging them to behave. They both said to themselves: if the Aleutians don't have to put up with that shit, why do we? The superbeings made it valid for everybody to be a person. But – cut it any way you like – that means there's twice as many fullsized humans in any given area than there used to be: and still only one planet. Naturally, there's a war.'

'The fat man was impressed. 'Quite a speech, Sid.'

He shrugged. 'Don't quote me. That's a too-close contemporary and worthless opinion. When it's over, they'll say this war was fought for purely economic reasons. They always do.'

The Fat Man nodded. 'Naturally. As the aliens say, trade is the human world's state religion: one must pay one's respects.' He relaxed his big fists, and seemed to shake off gloom. 'Back to present business. Is everything still going smoothly?'

'She won't talk to me,' confessed Sid. 'I don't know if I mentioned that, when we last spoke. Not a formal word. It gets on my nerves, I admit. My mother never talked to me. When she died I was six, and I'd never heard her voice. My Dad – I thought of him as my Dad – brought me south, and he *never said a word* to me either, all the time until we split up. It seemed reasonable to them, and I'm grateful they let me alone over the therapy. But, you see, it puts me in a bad temper when people won't talk. I'm sick of the Common Tongue. I'm afraid I'm making her dislike me.'

'Oh?' The Fat Man was concerned.

'No, don't worry. She doesn't suspect a thing. She thanked me for stopping her from committing suicide.'

'A good point. Though I don't think an invalid would have had any trouble getting off. The aliens discourage suicide, but they can be broad-minded in defining "death from medical causes".'

'She wouldn't see it like that. She's too conscientious. And innocent. She's a complete baby.'

The Fat Man regarded his protégé with grandfatherly affection. 'A baby! You know, Sid, it's hard to catch an Aleutian measuring anything. But the Office of Aleutian Affairs at the Government of the World has established that the shipworld observes a "year" about one and one-sixteenth as long as ours. It's deduced, and the deduction seems reasonable, that this is the length of the original planetary year.'

'Yes, so?'

'According to my sources, "Maitri's librarian" has been alive, "this time" – as the aliens say – twenty-three and a half shipworld years. The comparison is inadequate, since we haven't established the average Aleutian lifespan. But it would appear that in human terms your "baby" is a year or so older than you, Sid. Aeons older, of course, in theirs.'

Sid grimaced impatiently. 'Fine, she's a grown-up—'

'Why did you use the name "Bella", by the way?'

'She needed a local name. It came to mind.' Sid's eyes were veiled, his tone slightly defiant. 'I want to tell her.'

The Fat Man steepled his white fingers again. 'Johnny Guglioli and Braemar Wilson, the saboteurs. They reached the shipworld, they attempted to blow up the bluesun reactor, they were caught and Johnny was killed. The aliens on the shipworld were not aware that there was any mystery about Johnny and Braemar's means of entry until after the crisis. Braemar Wilson escaped on her return to earth, and was never questioned. Nobody asked: *how did they get there*? Or if the question was asked, investigation was quickly abandoned.

'But I know and you know, Sid, that there was no forced entry to the shipworld, nor any spaceplane launched from earth.' He raised his hand to forestall an interruption. 'Agreed, my cautious Sid, evidence could have been concealed, evidence could still emerge. So much data has been lost and mislaid, the answer to the mystery may be perfectly simple and may yet never be found. But so far, at the least, we can say that the mystery remains. And we know, for certain sure, that powerful interests on earth and in orbit believe that Maitri's librarian holds the key. The key, oh most precisely, to the kingdoms of heaven.'

He held up his hands again: both of them. 'You will not tell *him*.' Sid's boss gave a slight ironic emphasis to the correct Aleutian pronoun. 'For his own safety, he must not know. Don't believe in the fairytale, Sid. The aliens are not angels. And never underestimate them. When you next have to rescue Bella, you may be up against much more serious opposition. You are likely to have to deal with ruthless, corrupt, villains: who can read your body language, my Sid – yes, yours – and *the situation* so minutely that they might as well be reading your mind with a bright green psychic ray.'

His tone was so grim, as he spoke of the green psychic ray, that Sid laughed. 'It sounds hopeless, Fat Man. What am I supposed to do when I'm faced with these hardened criminal superbeings?'

Mr Sunday's unwonted gravity dissipated. 'Try thinking about cosmology. Or high-energy physics. I guarantee you, every Aleutian in the room will fall into a catatonic trance.'

He sat back, reached into a pocket and brought out a slim, pearly screen case the length of his large palm. 'Look at this, Sid. A new toy. There's a cam that goes with it, a little flying thing. We've been talking for long enough. I think we should have a peep into the safe room.' Something winked from between the gloved hands, a flickering mayfly. It zipped through the air, nipped between the blinds and vanished. There was a pause, in which the rain grew loud and Sid began to frown. A gossamer screen unfolded: glimmered, fizzed and cleared. They watched a slow pan around a dimly lit, low space.

'The cam can't burrow through solid walls,' explained the Fat Man in a whisper, as if the insect wing monitor might hear him and flit away. 'When it can't get nearer to the target location, it embeds itself in the last barrier and builds a picture from heat, echo, residual light . . .'

'That's our safe room, all right,' Sid confirmed, slightly piqued. Didn't the Fat Man trust him? But then, jaw dropping, he gave a wail of disbelief. The room was empty.

He ran into the street. There was a teksi stand outside the hotel. He leapt on to a greasy saddle. The meter bleeped: *tell on me to the town hall, would you . . . ?* He scrabbled in his pockets for a con-film, slammed the fake palmprint on to the contact, gunned the stick. The machine shot away in a fountain of puddle water. The Fat Man murmured, 'Such impetuosity!' He put his screen into his pocket: rose with ponderous grace, took Sid's umbrella and went to find some tiffin. He adored South Indian food.

Under an awning made of Aleutian trade-goods waterproof, Lydia had cleared a space in the roof's clutter. She wiped the grisly-looking cement with a rag of cleeno, and used the same spongy grey rag to wipe her hands. Taking a water tablet from the box, she broke off a fragment and put the rest back. She dipped wheat flour out of a bin, crumbled the Aleutian powder into it and stirred it around till it was moist.

She kneaded flour and water dough on grimy cement with her grubby hands, in perfect safety, occasionally poking at her charcoal brazier. Aleutian trade goods made domestic hygiene easy for the poorest and least competent of their customers. Anything the cleeno had touched was free of harmful life for hours. The water scavenged from the air by the cryptobiont powder was distilled to exacting purity. As she worked she hummed a wordless song. Small people, winged and dressed in flower petals, played around her. A miniature turquoise pony jumped over the flour bin. Lydia giggled. Suddenly, she looked up.

⟨Hello,⟩ said Bella, standing in the rain holding the soup bowl. ⟨It's your hated rival.⟩

Lydia stared. 'I spat in that soup,' she announced.

To an Aleutian it was an odd insult. Bella accepted it in the spirit intended. He returned the stare calmly. Sid's children were not mutilated. Lydia's nose was narrow and straight, her eyes level, her mouth cleanly sculpted. Contrary to Aleutian lore about local reproduction, she did not look in the least like Sid. But Sid had said that didn't matter. *Race is bullshit*, he said. *Culture is everything. I don't care who they look like: they're my kids now.*

His fierce love was returned. Bella knew that last night, as she stood in her daddy's arms looking over his shoulder at the alien guest, Lydia had divined in an instant everything that had happened between Bella and her father: and in the same instant had silently declared war. Her jealousy was Bella's opportunity.

⟨Come in out of the rain,⟩ said Lydia at last, accepting that they were to parley. Bella was drenched. He ran his hands over his soaking clothes, dumbfounded.

⟨Don't you have rain?⟩

⟨Not like this.⟩

Bella knelt under the waterproof sheet, gazing at the rods of silver that lanced from the sky. Lydia, pretending indifference, picked up her lump of dough. The flower fairies came out from hiding. The tiny turquoise pony approached, and sniffed at the alien's knee. Lydia was smiling slyly. Bella gasped.

⟨What's that?⟩ He saw the fairies, and gave a convulsive start. ⟨What are they?⟩

'They're toys, don't be scared. They're deadworld things,' she added spitefully. 'They're a kind of *matte*. Don't you know what

a matte is? It's a deadworld image. You can have them any size.
They can be the size of city blocks, for decor. Or you can wear
them, or you can play with them. See?' She showed a round
medallion strapped to her wrist: made an adjustment. The pony
reared and tossed its tiny, sparkling mane. 'I control them. Don't
worry, I won't let them hurt you.'

⟨*Could* they hurt me?⟩ asked Bella.

Lydia gave the alien a sour glance, disappointed at the tone of
calm interest. But she noticed that Bella didn't reach out to
touch. She didn't answer the question. 'Mother T. hates them
because they're anti-Aleutian. But my daddy bought them for
me, so I don't care about her.' Abruptly, the pony and the flower
fairies vanished. Lydia put her griddle to heat on the brazier.
⟨Anyway, you shouldn't be here. Daddy told you to stay in the
safe room.⟩

Bella watched the halfcaste girl's averted face. ⟨You know Sid
is a secret agent, don't you?⟩

Lydia's mouth tightened. ⟨I don't know what you mean.⟩

⟨Well done. Admit nothing, just listen. Sid's cover is blown. I
have to find somewhere else to hide before he comes back, or
he'll be in dreadful trouble. Can you help me?⟩

Lydia looked around: her large white-circled eyes wary. ⟨How
do you know—?⟩

⟨I'm a '*telepath*',⟩ explained Bella. ⟨You know that. I found
out by '*telepathy*'. I have a plan, but I need help. You must help
me to reach the Women. *Or Sid will die horribly*.⟩

Lydia's soft dark cheeks had grown pinched and grey, her eyes
enormous. Bella almost felt guilty, it was so easy.

⟨The Women?⟩ she quavered. ⟨Why?⟩ Suddenly her face cleared,
her eyes brightened. 'Ah,' she said aloud. 'I know what you
mean to do. Yes, I can help. I'll take you to the temple.'

The temple had once been a particularly holy place, forbidden
ground to any but devout Hindus in sacred dress. Nowadays a
diminishing band of priests sat in the cloisters chatting, or
performed gentle rituals with ash and flowers, rarely troubled by
worshippers. The carved courtyards belonged to the parakeets,
the palm squirrels and the bats; and the occasional sightseer.
The temple stood between Woman Town and the nest of alleys

where the halfcastes, the *neti-neti*, lived alongside the poorest of the poor. Children of all three communities used the approach as a playground: it was neutral territory.

Lydia had been kept indoors since the violence began. Most of the time she'd been shut up in the safe room. She'd lain awake listening to the mobs of purebreds prowling, yelling threats and smashing fragile walls; breaking windows and setting fires. She was still forbidden to go out. But the aliens were gone and for days the city had been quiet. When she and Bella arrived the neutral playground was busy.

A group of purebreds, Women and Men's children, were playing cricket in the rain. A gaggle of little noseless brats ran around the cricket pitch, rags tied over their heads for imitation gaming visors, deep in an imaginary virtuality game. By the sacred tank, some halfcaste huckster stalls had reappeared. Before the Protest, the halfcastes had been the storytellers, fortune-tellers and tinkers of Trivandrum. They had a magical knack with faulty decoders or old video equipment. Lydia glanced at the stalls, feeling reassured. She scanned the approach for faces she recognised: and turned to find that Bella – shrouded in the chador – had crumpled to the ground.

'What's wrong? Are you sick?'

Bella got to his feet and looked back in amazement at the descent he and Lydia had made from the *neti-neti* roofs.

⟨No,⟩ he said weakly. ⟨I was . . . surprised.⟩

'Remember to speak aloud. Purebreds *hate it* if you talk in Common Tongue in front of them. Always say words.'

She took Bella to the pavilion. It was a den built out of irregular sheets of shado – the Aleutian heat-absorbing material – up against the outer wall of the temple, well hidden under a mass of purple-flowering creepers.

'It's still here,' crowed Lydia. 'I hoped it would be. I helped to build this! But the purebred kids think it's theirs.'

It was empty. They settled in its shelter. 'Keep well back. See that Woman girl, going in to bat? That's Hafzan. D'you know what "going into bat" means?'

The chador nodded.

'She's the one. Her family are deprogrammers. Do you know what that is?'

'No.'

'It's when purebreds kidnap halfcaste kids to turn them back into purebreds: give them noses and fix their brains so they can't speak Common Tongue any more. In Kerala it's against the law. But if they can get you to say you want the treatment, then it's legal. I'm going to tell her you come from Goa. All your people were killed and you've lost your memory. That way you won't have to make up lies and remember them. Daddy says always keep the lies to a minimum.' She folded her arms complacently on her skinny knees. 'Daddy says being a halfcaste is a spiritual thing, we've no need to cut our noses off. I'm not sure. I'm going to decide when I'm older.'

The tall girl in white stood gripping her bat, in a slightly hunched pose that was full of springy tension. From far away the bowler ran. His white-clad arm seemed to float in a beautiful, aspiring gesture. There was a loud crack. Hafzan half stumbled, half crouched into a short run. Her partner crossed her coming the opposite way. Bella saw the configuration of fielders come to life, as if in response to a chemical touch. He remembered Sid's dogged voice in the wilderness.

'I wish you could see Daddy play. He's a terrific bowler. He can bat, too. I'm going to be the same. You can see it, our style is identical. I am his truechild, you know. I haven't told him yet. I want him to recognise me for myself.'

How young Lydia seemed! But Bella didn't laugh. He had rarely known affection for a parent. But he remembered feeling the same way about Maitri, when he was too young to understand that it would be grotesque for a parent and child to be lovers: ⟨*I'm your truechild, Daddy, I'm sure I am.*⟩ Maitri had never laughed at him.

The sacred tank was surrounded by decrepit iron railings set in a kerb of stone. The devout had bathed in this green, glaucous pool, used it for washing clothes and drunk the water for hundreds of years – without serious ill effect, as long as their general health was good. More recently the tank had shown signs of commensal infestation. It was a widespread problem. Some people said all the ground water in India was affected, through Aleutian irrigation projects. The *neti-neti* and the poor claimed that bathing in infested water would cure any disease. There'd been no investigation of this claim in Trivandrum. The infestation had been ignored before the Protest, and escaped attention at the height of the violence. This was about to change.

As Lydia and Bella watched the cricket match, two rival processions were converging on the temple. A column of Men, all of them biological males, marched into the temple approach first. They were dressed in white, and led by a gaunt old man in a green turban and flowing snowy robe. Youths in the front ranks unslung the metal drums they were carrying, and stacked them. Close behind, coming up from the south of the temple, was a party of Women with a few biological males among them. The Women's procession was gaudy. Music played, and bursts of light sprang into the air. Everyone in the front ranks was wearing a matte-mask. A glittering phalanx of demons, beasts, goddesses, trees, walking mountains, advanced on the tank: and started to make another pile of containers.

'I wonder what's going on!' exclaimed Lydia.

The halfcastes at the huckster stalls were not curious. They had hurriedly started to pack up. The children playing the imaginary virtuality game stopped and stared. The cricketers attempted to continue play. Hafzan shouted: 'Get on with it! Bowl!' A lone scrawny old man emerged from the water and stood in his underwear, gaping through the railing.

An eight-armed goddess, with a weapon in every hand and a necklace of skulls over her blood-daubed breasts, consulted with the green-turbaned imam. Everything seemed friendly.

⟨Maybe we should go home.⟩ Lydia was torn between commonsense and determination. ⟨Maybe we can grab Hafzan as she goes by—⟩

A crystal-clear amplified voice cut through the rain.

'The tank is ours and we will cleanse it! This is Women's Town!' A chorus rose from the masked ranks.

'Hammerhead! Hammerhead!'

The cricket match collapsed. The *neti-neti* children vanished up into the safety of the roofs. The cricket teams and the hucksters' customers drew together, uncertain whether or not this was going to turn dangerous. Before the imam's side could reply, a new figure burst on to the scene. A halfcaste in garishly coloured Aleutian overalls, with a mass of fizzy black hair, came running from the site of the market stalls. Without a word he swarmed over the railing, his guitar swinging from his neck.

'It's Jimi!' cried Lydia. 'He must have been at the market!'

Jimi ran down to the water, till gold-flecked scum was slapping around his ankles. 'You can't clean them out!' he shouted. 'The Aleutians are everywhere! In your bodies, in your blood, in the air you breathe. They are the future. You'll never get rid of them! It's too late!'

Lydia gave an inarticulate wail. The bystanders scattered. Men and Women from the rival processions poured over the railing and through the gate. Jimi ran. He turned, stooped, and flung handfuls of scum at his pursuers, spattering them with the alien miracle – and then he disappeared under a tide of bodies. There was one wild splash.

'*We've got to save Jimi!*' sobbed Lydia.

Bella thought Lydia had better save herself.

⟨Run for it, hated rival! Now, while they're distracted!⟩

⟨What about you?⟩

⟨Go on!⟩

Lydia scuttled. Bella knew he couldn't have managed to get up on to the roofs again. But in any case he didn't intend to run away. He tried to feel calm. He told himself the deadworld images were illusions. They were not *dead things walking*, drawn out of void forces. It was done with fearo-things. Maitri had told him about those human chemical signals, like wanderers but not so efficient. They could be used to produce hallucinations. Maitri said that was the basis of most local 'magic'. Pheromones, that was it.

He pulled off the chador, and stumbled across the cricket pitch to where the processions were mingling in battle. An eight-armed monster stood in front of him. Out of the hallucinatory forest of arms a real hand grabbed him.

'Hey, little halfcaste. Get out of here! Are you trying to get yourself killed?'

He raised his face. 'Please help me. I want to be human.'

Monster confronted monster.

'My,' said the goddess, impressed. 'You certainly need help.'

*

By the time Sid arrived it was over. Fragments of the hawkers' booths were strewn in the mud. Patches of the water's surface were still burning: empty fuel drums rolled about. The combatants had taken their casualties away with them. They'd taken Jimi, too. Lydia had turned back as soon as she realised Bella wasn't behind her. She was sitting by the gate in the railing. Her father propped his teksi and came towards her.

'Bella's gone.'

She nodded, and burst into tears. 'I'm sorry, Daddy! I'm sorry!' Sid collected pebbles and started chucking them, idly, into a puddle. Loss and hurt bewilderment hit him, like a tank running over his chest. *How could she do this? She belongs to me!*

5: DEUS PROVIDEBIT

'Men have no natural authority!'

The voice was the voice that had spoken to Bella from the mask of an eight-armed monster. The speaker was Katalamma Pillai: a young Woman of vigorous, athletic presence, dressed in a smartly tailored emerald green tunic and trousers. She was sitting cross-legged on top of a low storage cabinet in her mother's office.

Katalamma had brought the fugitive halfcaste home to her mother's house: a pleasantly old-fashioned establishment in the green heart of Woman Town. B.K. Pillai was a distinguished reformist lawyer. This was her office. The large room was lined around three walls with cabinets stacked with record media: tapes, discs, cards, charged paper, flat-readers; printed books. A few clerks were at their desks, visored, deep in research: but public office hours were over. At her own desk, B.K. was helping Bella to complete her application for reverse gene therapy.

'Look at the traditionalist marriage ceremony. In every culture in the world, "traditional" marriage is a ritual of submission, a formal abdication of authority. The aliens are right: we are two nations, we have been at war for aeons. Marriage is the surrender ceremony, repeated and repeated, of the Women's last defeat. Every social function Men have was stolen from us as war booty. When we have won back all that was ours, Men will spend their time making themselves beautiful and strong, so that we can choose the best of them to fertilise our seed!'

The lawyer was sitting by Bella, watching the text of the application as it scrolled — with a small patient smile for her daughter's ebullience. 'Can biological males have natural authority?' she inquired mildly.

Katalamma shot her a reproachful glance. ⟨I don't want to discuss that.⟩ The status of 'biological males' was a vexed question for young reformist activists. 'The aliens,' she continued, on smoother ground, 'unmasked themselves when they announced the Himalaya Project. We thought they were our partners, but they demanded submission. They are "Men" in gestalt, as the anti-Aleutian fanatic Braemar Wilson warned us long ago.'

'The aliens are not our enemies,' murmured B.K. 'It's true that they have changed people's lives, in the enclaves. But who knows? The Age of Information – all those deadworld networks – was coming to a natural end. Human priorities are always changing. Why be self-doubtful? In Kerala we have a Community State that owes nothing to alien influence: a system which will provide without a qualm the expensive treatment this young woman needs. The Aleutians are simply foreigners—'

Katalamma sprang from the cabinet and strode across the room (in her arrogant step glimmered the shade of a blood-dripping vengeful goddess). The far wall was covered by a depth-projection of the earth, selected to physical geography: a beautiful and engrossing decoration.

'Was it simply foreigners who did that?'

She stabbed a finger at the Panama Trench, which Expedition artisans had dug through the isthmus between the two Americas. It gave the vast reaches of the USSA a natural quarantine barrier in the south to match the sea passages in the north.

Bella, to whom earth was a series of destinations with blanks in between, didn't know the scale of the wall projection. The trench looked tiny and harmless. She knew the Expedition had acted in good faith, believing that the work had been approved and accepted by their customers. But she trembled. If the two Women started to revile the Himalaya Project, surely anger would sharpen their perceptions. They would know that their 'repentant halfcaste' was actually Aleutian.

So far everything had gone well. The story devised by Lydia had been accepted without question. The halfcaste community in Goa, a state further up the coast, had been massacred in the Protest. Nobody expected Bella to give a coherent account of her flight from that horror. And she had found it easy to convince them that she 'wanted to be human'.

It was a matter of translation. If you are a permanent invalid, you must resign yourself to your fate, otherwise life would be intolerable. But the bitter revolt of the normal person trapped inside never goes away. *I am not normal, but I long to be.* Oh yes, it was easy to keep on saying that, in the Common Tongue. Dangerously easy!

'Please don't start on the Himalaya business, Katalamma. You know my views. The Aleutians are, as I said, ignorant well-meaning foreigners. They were trying to help us and they made mistakes. The situation has had human parallels. Who should know that better than the people of India? We must not forget that Aleutian trade goods have made an immense difference to the poor: far more difference, more quickly than we could have made with political solutions.'

She stopped the scrolling document. 'Here we need your signature, Bella.'

Bella looked up, remembering to make the 'she' expression. Since she'd taken refuge with the Women, it made sense to present herself as female: and she was used to it, from travelling with Sid. 'Signature?' She wasn't sure what it meant, in this context.

'A thumbprint is perfectly adequate . . . Oh.'

The lawyer had started to lift Bella's hand: a hand lacking the little finger, dead white, and with a crepey texture as if it had been held too long in water. She realised an oversight. Bella hadn't yet been examined by a doctor. Though this girl was desperate to be human again, she was a halfcaste. It would be cruel to subject her to those deadworld devices so soon after the horrors of Goa. The poor child was going to suffer enough medical indignities, once her therapy programme began.

B.K. held the strange little hand uncertainly –

Katalamma bounced across the room (Katalamma walked as if she could barely stop herself from leaping into flight): and peered. The person known to her fans as 'Hammerhead' was not troubled by undue sensitivity.

'Looks human enough. You should get a print.'

'Place your thumb on the screen, Bella.'

Katalamma stayed to watch, with a proprietory air.

'I want you to apologise to the imam,' said B.K., in a firm undertone. 'For that disgraceful affair at the tank. He's an old man, he deserves respect. The way you behaved, you are no better than the mobsters of the Protest, who will be prosecuted for their crimes if I have my way. And I *will* have my way.'

'My people didn't have anything to do with the violence. We intended the Protest to be reasonable, limited, justified.'

'Intended! Ha. You knew what would happen.'

'It was the Men,' muttered Katalamma sulkily.

'Always the Men! What would you do without that alibi?'

Sid had told Bella that the humans hated the terms 'Men' and 'Women' to be used for their political division. They preferred 'traditionalists' and 'reformers'. But here in the enclaves, alien and human usage of the gender-words blurred together.

Katalamma glowered, pushed back her cuff and tapped the pillbox strapped to her wrist. The Kali mask leapt into existence.

'Switch that off. You know I won't have it in my office.'

'Why not?' demanded Kali, in Katalamma's voice. 'It's a lesson for Bella. Attend and learn, new human! For a hundred years the aliens have been destroying our deadworld networks—'

'Ha. The Gender War can take most of the credit for that!'

'Don't listen to her, new human. It was the aliens, just as much. Well, we can't argue with them, they are superbeings. I am Kali. I enjoy chopping things up. The deadworld is no longer a network, it has scattered into a million, million forms. I have all the power of the *void forces* here on my wrist. I am Hammerhead the hidden virus, the avenger who will one day arise!'

B.K. applied Bella's thumb one last time. 'I will teach you to read, Bella. And maybe to write. It is the best gift I can give you: the gateway to a great world of knowledge that is in danger of being lost for ever. Empowerment does not lie in *gadgets* that can be stolen from you or smashed. There, that's finished.'

She lifted printed sheets as they emerged. 'You're making yourself ridiculous, Katalamma. Your father and I gave you a good Keralan name. Why not use it? You're too old for a gamer's handle.'

'You called me after a sea goddess. Hammerhead *is* a sea goddesss.'

Katalamma's real hand grasped Bella's, and held it to the controls of the deadworld toy. Smoke engulfed the desk and Bella: blue smoke, *water*. Deep in an illusory depth of field there moved a huge, sleek, limbless body. It rushed forward silently: a commensal with a flattened, flanged head, an eye at each end of the extension. It was a tool, obviously, but for what purpose? It turned on its back. Bella gasped. A mouth opened on rows of jagged teeth. 'That's a hammerheaded shark,' said Katalamma's voice, high and thinned as if by a great distance. 'A goddess of the sea. Sharks are female-ordered, fearless, powerful. That's why I chose the name. But don't look at the teeth, look at the gills. That's how she breathes, by pushing the water through there as she swims. If a shark doesn't swim, they say, she dies. Mummyji says the Aleutians were trying to help us. *We cannot be helped*. We must live in our own way, develop in our own way. Or else we die.'

'Hmph,' said the lawyer. 'Very poetic.' But she seemed mollified. Sincerity could always move her, even in her own child.

'Now, Bella: bureaucrats must have hard copy! We could despatch a print of your application to the fax room at the Health Department straight away, but we will avoid a delay of some weeks if we take it to the post box.'

The post box was out at the gates of the garden, an immense distance for Maitri's librarian. But Bella was still enjoying a period of well-being, which was doubtless built of terror and would end in complete collapse. She reached for the battered chador. It was never out of her sight. Mother and daughter silently exclaimed in pity.

'No, my dear,' said B.K. kindly. 'Not the cloak. There is nothing wrong with the chador. Everyone should have the right to wear the chador: but not every day! You have "recanted". You are safe from the hooligans.' She paused. 'You know, deprogramming therapy can take a long time. It may never be complete. Do you understand? Being human is something that starts on the inside.'

⟨I understand.⟩ Bella recollected herself. 'I understand.'

'Good. Wait, there's one thing we must do before we send off this application. We must ask my husband's permission.' B.K. smiled tenderly. 'He is the head of this household.'

The Pillai house was set back from the street in a wide and rather wild garden. At the front of the building steps led up to a gabled porch, the entrance to the law offices and the family's rooms. The ground floor was an open, pillared hall: a caravan-serai for passing Pillai dependents, for pilgrims; for any poor traveller who asked for a place to stay. It was lunchtime. A rice tiffin was being served at long tables. B.K. led Bella through the bustle to the back of the hall, where there was a fish pool in a square stone basin. Mrs Pillai's husband was there with one of the guests: a holy woman in the white robe of a Hindu widow, whose pilgrimage had been interrupted by the Protest.

'Ravi—'

'My dear?'

Mr Pillai was in Brahminical dress. The sacred thread traversed a meagre fluff of grey on his lean, naked breast. The hair on his head, gleaming black, was twisted in a bun. Between him and the holy woman lay a flat reader, displaying some abstruse, distant work of God. Ravi Pillai was a devout reformed Hindu.

'Ravi, my dear, we are going to post Bella's application for reverse therapy. Is that all right with you?'

Ravi looked up from the star-filled abyss. 'Of course.' He made an effort to return to the mundane. 'I hope it goes well. I will pray for you, Bella . . . if you don't mind.'

'I don't mind,' said Bella shyly. The lawyer's deference to her marriage partner made her uneasy, since it was so obvious that B.K. was in charge. But Ravi didn't seem to mind.

B.K. glanced at the screen, indulgently taking an interest. 'Seeking for God in the stars? You know best, my dear: but I remember my Einstein. If there has to be a "centre" to the universe, though why there should be such a thing I don't know . . . Then it is here in our garden, my dear, as much as anywhere.'

'If there is heaven of bliss,' murmured the holy woman, 'it is here, it is here, it is here – '

B.K. spoke English as a matter of reformist principle, as the language of post-nationalism; and Malayalam, the language of

Kerala, with her traditionalist friends. But she beamed in delight at the holy woman's pure Urdu.

'Ah! Once, *guruji*, I read those words, on the walls of the palace in Delhi. I have been a traveller myself, you see. But we must leave you if we're to catch the post. Bella?'

Bella was staring intently at the holy woman, who remained bowed over her reader. Nothing of her could be seen except the dome of a shaven skull rising from an ample heap of drapery.

'Bella? Have you fallen asleep?'

A fold of white cloth moved in an impatient, amused gesture.

'I'm sorry,' said Bella. 'I'm coming.'

'This is the husband-worship of a Hindu housewife,' complained B.K. as they walked. 'If Ravi wants to support a whole college of shady indigent ascetics for life, his will is law and I must feed the lot of them . . . But the *evidyane*, the seeker-after-truth, is a genuine scholar. I feel that, don't you? A truly inquiring mind.'

Bella faintly agreed.

Bella had settled quickly into this ordered household. She washed with water; and coped with human sanitary arrangements (profoundly grateful for Sid's training). No one asked her to eat hard foods, but she ate dahls and curds, and found them tasty. All strangeness ceased to register. She was an Aleutian, she expected familiarity and found it. If there had been a separate video library in the house, she would have been happy to move in there indefinitely. Why not? Since Maitri was gone, there was no reason why she should not find another patron for this life: and B.K. Pillai was kind. She was safe among the Women. Neither Sidney Carton nor his evil boss could reach her.

She had been given a bedroom of her own on the clerks' floor. This, too, was soothing. She was an isolate, she'd always spent her nights alone. She went to it, after walking to the post box, to rest. The chador was folded over her arm. A ceiling fan stirred the warm, moist air. There was someone sitting on her narrow bed-with-legs.

It was Sidney Carton.

He looked up, and smiled with his mouth. His hair and brows and lashes were pale again. 'Hiya, Bel.'

She dropped the cloak.

'I've a friend,' he said conversationally, 'who thinks this kind of thing has deep existential implications. I'm here, you see, where I am. I'm also wherever it is you are: somewhere in the future, from my point of view, and somewhere else in space. I jumped the gap, like an electric current: actually as a map of photochemical impulses, or something like that. Let me experiment. Is bi-location really happening?' He screwed his eyes shut: the thick pale lashes squeezed between ruddy corrugations. He opened them again. 'Nope. Nada. You're there, I'm here. Or the other way round. This isn't happening. Try to touch my hand, you'll see.'

She didn't move. After a moment, the hand dropped. 'This is a letterbomb. I have to tell you that. It's the law, anywhere in the human world. I have to *announce* "This is a letterbomb" in case you get the idea that I'm a psychotic episode.' He laughed, then became serious. 'This is a recorded message, Bel. It's no different in principle from someone talking to you out of a screen. But for you, I know, that idea's scary enough.'

⟨I'm not afraid!⟩

'What can I tell you? We gave Jimi a grand send-off, once we'd got his body back. I think we invited the whole halfcaste population. It's lucky he couldn't attend the festivities, really. You know what he's like at parties: gets all shy, drinks too much, does stupid things. In fact, if I seem a little strained, it's because I'm still hungover myself.'

And so he went on, gossiping about his housemates and his children, as if this was Goodlooking's room at the trading post. Until suddenly, mid-sentence, he disappeared.

Bella came down at twilight for evening prayers. A Tourviddy bus from the countryside had taken up temporary residence in the Pillais' garden. The guests in the caravanserai, ignoring the modern entertainment available from an array of cable-consoles, settled every evening for the old-fashioned movies. Bella had 'attended evening prayers' dutifully each night . . . humbled by the casual, relaxed attitude of the locals. For them, obviously, prayer was a natural part of life. No one put on a special face to come to church. She slipped in at the back, knelt and briefly covered her face. She tried to attend to the service.

It was a confession of murder: the ugliness of the story conveyed by high camera angles and sidelong, voyeuristic traverses. It was clear that the murderer was someone famous. The priests had been both too cruel and too kind in their editing, leaving a sense that murder was *very* vile; but that to do something vile was glamorous if you were important enough. In Aleutia this sort of thing would have been considered unfit for public worship. Bella didn't know if that was right or wrong. It's almost *too* lifelike, she thought. One would think those were not generated images, but real people . . .

She couldn't concentrate.

Sidney Carton!

People chatted out loud and passed snackfood. A baby was crying in one of the front rows. She'd seen it, a big-headed, sickly thing. It was always crying. If it was so ill, why didn't they gently let it die? In any hospital Bella had ever known, it would have been down for *nursing care only*.

⟨You aren't attending to your prayers.⟩

Bella jumped as if she'd been stung. The *evidyane*, the holy woman, was kneeling beside her and had softly touched her arm.

⟨*Aliens always watch a movie as if they're going to be asked questions afterwards. But not you! You have a talent for masquerade.*⟩ The large bundle of white rose up and moved off into the shadows, to the water tank; and waited there.

⟨Watch!⟩

A hand slipped out of the drapery and showed her what seemed to be a paper cut-out of a fish, like the friendly local commensals that lived in this pool. The hand moved. Almost immediately, a silent fountain of little, glittering creatures burst from the dark surface of the water. They multiplied, crisping the air into fractured rainbow patterns.

⟨Give me back my fish.⟩

Bella suspected a practical joke, but picked the one real cut-out from the air. Nothing happened. She handed it over.

⟨Ah. How did you do that, I wonder?⟩

⟨Is it a joke, sir? I'm afraid I don't get it.⟩

⟨There's a joke. But it doesn't concern you. Come.⟩

The pilgrim led Bella up a narrow outside stairway and into the back wing of the house; into a small, bare and dimly lit room. B.K. would have put her husband's pet scholar in a good guest suite. But the pious widow was indifferent to comfort, and had preferred this austere little closet. As soon as they were in the room with the door shut, the pilgrim folded back the robe which had been pulled over that shaven head. The Hindu widow vanished. Someone kind and wise – at once cheery, formidable and somehow very innocent – studied Bella. Both of them had dropped the 'she'.

'Yes,' he said, in English as perfect as Lord Maitri's. 'I'm an Aleutian. You know me, and I know you, librarian.'

'Sir—!'

He forestalled Bella's respectful greeting. 'Please, I'm travelling incognito. Call me "Seeker-after-truth". I like the name.' He settled on his pallet, a local-made bedding roll which was spread on the floor beside a stack of curious baggage: local baskets, boxes of strange design, messy paper-wrapped bundles. His wide and bristling nasal flared in amusement at Bella's dumbfounded silence. 'How do you like *my* masquerade? Much can be done by simply lying about one's appearance. It's a trick of confidence. But look at this.' He bared his throat and arms. 'Did you notice? No wanderers!'

⟨I noticed, yes.⟩

The pilgrim smoothed a hand over his glossy crown. ⟨I have no wanderers, and yet I am not an isolate. I detect reproach. I wouldn't try on another person's disadvantages for fun, Maitri's librarian. Its the only way I can travel as I like to, among the people. They fear our wanderers. Without them I am inconspicuous and – for Yudi's sake – one could argue that I am not breaking quarantine. It's a reversible inhibition; easy once you know how. The hair loss is a side-effect, but all to the good. They find our hair odd.⟩ He smiled warmly. ⟨I gather you're not dead, librarian?⟩

⟨No.⟩ Bella folded to the ground, joints reversed. ⟨I know everybody thinks I am.⟩ At the Seeker's nod of invitation, he spoke formally. 'When Lord Maitri's company died, I escaped with our halfcaste interpreter. He brought me to Trivandrum. But then I decided I'd be safer on my own.'

He couldn't bring himself to say more. It suddenly seemed impossible that *Maitri's librarian* should have been kidnapped!

⟨Very wise,⟩ agreed the other placidly. ⟨The halfcastes are shifty types.⟩

⟨But, sir: I don't quite understand. You were travelling on earth for pleasure?⟩

⟨For pleasure? Exactly. I am a student of the local culture. I was on my way to Kaligat, from Bhutan: and here I am on the coast of Malabar, don't ask me how. Never mind. My treasure may be hidden anywhere on earth.⟩

⟨Treasure?⟩

⟨Incunabula, librarian. Lost text records.⟩

⟨Ah!⟩ Bella's attention kindled. ⟨Text! Maybe the originals of 'Miss Jane Austen'?⟩ It had been a blow to Maitri's librarian, who could not read, when he discovered that the pre-moving-image works of earth's greatest clerics were for ever out of his reach.

⟨Not quite. I'm after some important scientific data.⟩

Like most Aleutians, Bella regarded obligate scientists with a mixture of dubious respect and mild scorn. They were called 'engineers', but it was a courtesy title. Their technicians and artisans did the engineering. Scientists were dreamers. As they themselves admitted they dealt with exceptions, vagaries, anomalies, imaginary rules for imaginary cases. None of their *pure mathematics*, *pure physics*, *pure mechanics*, was any use in the real, living world. At the worst, an engineer was a kind of magician, dabbling in the occult. At the best he was a mystic: driven to seek knowledge of the Self beyond the realm of life, in the unknowable void. Bella had no doubt in which category Seeker-after-truth belonged. He was no less uncomfortable. Mysticism wasn't his kind of thing at all.

⟨How interesting,⟩ he remarked feebly.

⟨Huh.⟩ Seeker-after-truth positively snorted. ⟨*Interesting*, indeed. You are very kind! Yes, absurd as it may seem to you, instead of collecting the works of 'Jane Austen', I have spent years on earth trying to trace a lost technical work by a local engineer called 'Peenemunde Buonarotti'. Ah, you know the name?⟩

⟨Of course, sir. 'Peenemunde Buonarotti' is the engineer who doesn't believe in aliens, in the story of *The Grief of Clavel*. He's the one – or is it 'she', I'm not sure – the saboteurs visit before they leave earth for the shipworld.⟩

Seeker-after-truth snorted again. ⟨In the story of *The Grief of Clavel*,⟩ he repeated bitterly. ⟨A minor character! A walk-on part. The greatest thinker, the greatest mind we have ever encountered! 'Buonarotti' is my patron in spirit, librarian: the lord I would serve through all the lives to come, if it were possible. 'Peenemunde Buonarotti', is the inventor of the instantaneous travel device. Oh. You find something funny?⟩

⟨I'm sorry. Not exactly funny, sir. I was surprised. Isn't the, er, the instantaneous travel device a myth?⟩

The scientist gave him a calm, penetrating look. ⟨No. I believe not.⟩

⟨But how can it be real? Their best technology is like ours only inferior, isn't it? Except for the 'deadworld devices': and they're trickery. It's done with 'pheromones', that give people hallucinations . . .⟩

⟨No, it is not. Their science of the deadworld is real.⟩ Seeker-after-truth laughed at Bella's doubtful face. ⟨You're a librarian. You must know a little about the meaning of the term *instantaneous travel*. Which is sometimes known as 'faster than light' travel, or, as we say, 'faster than life'.⟩

⟨Yes. Faster than life. That's why it is impossible.⟩

⟨That's why, librarian, it is impossible unless one could travel *immaterially*, through the deadworld.⟩ Seeker-after-truth stretched out a broad hand, the colour of greenish woodsmoke. ⟨You will have heard the 'missionary' persuasion in the ranks of the Expedition speak of the humans and ourselves as 'no different flesh'. By which those worthies mean that humans can and should behave just like Aleutians. 'Buonarotti' teaches that we are *no different mind*.⟩

He slipped casually into formal speech. 'It was this teaching that led to her being known at first contact as "the scientist who doesn't believe in aliens". Apparently Braemar Wilson tried to recruit Peenemunde into her anti-Aleutian resistance movement. The attempt failed, though she may have become a grudging sympathiser. Peenemunde's teaching is not partisan. She believes that we are one mind, not for sentimental reasons, but as one of the conditions of existence. We are self. And the self: Aleutian, human, yours, mine, WorldSelf Itself, is made not of flesh but of a stuff Buonarotti calls information.' He turned his hand from side to side in the empty, dimly lit air. 'The information is the reality, and it is not bound by time or space or material.

'Nothing possessing mass can move faster than light. Or "faster than life" as we say, having perceived the same limit from a different viewpoint. As the speed of the body approaches that boundary its mass becomes infinite. To move it faster would require an infinite force, which is nonsense. What Buonarotti suggests is that an informational self, under certain conditions, might be freed from the constraints of physics. The implications are tremendous. The humans think in terms of fabulous speed of transit. To you and I, non-location is the vital point. If our selves could escape from space and time, we could be everywhere at once. That would have to include being home again. Do you see?'

⟨A little, sir.⟩

Seeker-after-truth chuckled. ⟨Well, at least you are polite.⟩ He lifted his blunt face, listening. ⟨I think the service is over. You should go.⟩ He reached out his smoky hand and pulled the librarian close in a warm hug. ⟨They must not see us together much, or any amount of plausible lying in the Common Tongue won't hide what we are. But though we are both 'isolate' I am near. You're not alone. Oh, and librarian . . .⟩

Bella had risen to leave, respectfully: showing throat.

⟨Sir?⟩

⟨A piece of advice. *Don't* try any mistaken 'missionary' kindness. You know what I mean. Do not interfere with that baby.⟩

Bella had not mentioned the ghost. But he found that Seeker-after-truth had somehow disarmed it, making a deadworld apparition seem a matter-of-fact and harmless thing. It seemed Sid had tracked Bella down. But he was helpless: he could only pester his escaped prisoner with local trickery. Bella was safe from him.

There were other dangers. Hafzan Zamani the deprogrammer, the cricketer from the temple approach, had discovered that the

Pillais had a repentant halfcaste. She came to the house daily to investigate the 'new human'. At first Bella had managed to be too ill for visitors. But as her incongruous health and strength increased B.K. encouraged the friendship.

Hafzan took Bella home and showed her round the Zamanis' sumptuous biosphere house, which was glassed over like an Aleutian trading post. They watched war atrocity records of rape, liposuction, clitoridectomy, footbinding, and Hafzan showed Bella round the meadow and the desert suites: the main hall with its miniature forest, the river that ran down through the house in falls and pools. She said that biosphere houses were a preparation for life on Mars: and this was Bella's downfall.

'Why Mars? It would take so much work. What's wrong with fixing up this place?'

Bella spoke without thought, caught in the trap of casual formal speech. She was instantly transfixed in horror.

Hafzan gave her a long stare. 'That's halfcaste talk.'

'I didn't mean anything. I love the Himalayas.'

'You're lucky to be here, you know that, don't you? You know what we did to the aliens? We dragged them out and *raped them*, the way they raped . . . ah . . .'

'Johnny Guglioli,' supplied the librarian, helpless to his obligation.

The deprogrammer scowled. 'Yeah, him. We raped them and we burned them, we had our revenge. In some states of India, they're still dragging halfcastes out of hiding. They pretend they want to be human, to save their skins. *But then they start talking like halfcastes*: and they get burned alive!'

Next afternoon, Hafzan invited Bella to come with her to town. She didn't dare to refuse. They travelled by bus: past the temple, and the software house where Katalamma 'worked' (where she could occasionally be found, that is, gossiping with her friends about the two great topics, politics and how to stay unmarried). They got down in Man Town, among the tall, shimmering street displays. It was a rare rainless day in the monsoon, and hot. The unveiled Woman girl strode along, affecting not to notice the hungry stares of the Man Town young men. Bella followed, in shalwar kamise under the chador, clutching a copy of her deprogramming application in her pocket and repeating frantically, ⟨*I've stopped being a halfcaste. I want to be human!*⟩

Hafzan led her into a side street. A single deadworld display stood in front of a narrow entrance in a long, blank wall. It was a free-standing image of two huge blue-skinned humans, with rolling red eyes and red tongues lolling in fanged mouths. They were armed with broad, glittering blades, like giant versions of the ceremonial dead knife used by an Aleutian executioner.

A machine like a metro station gate stood between the figures. Hafzan fed it with a sheet of film out of her waistbag. Bella remembered Sid's explanation. A handprint was an identifying signal, carrying information about a person's status and right to services. In Kerala, she'd gathered, every adult had a print on record, and nobody used the secondary 'cash' system they had in Greece. Some of the film copies were quite legal. But Hafzan's expression inspired Bella to ask:

'Does your mother know you're using that?'

Hafzan grinned, seeing through this gambit at once. 'You have to be accompanied by an adult,' she said aloud. 'Come on, inside.' The entrance hall was full of moving coloured light. 'Are you a Christian?'

The terms Christian, Muslim, Hindu referred to local societies or factions: their significance was obscure to the Aleutians. Bella had no idea what was going on. She didn't know what to answer.

'I'm feeling ill,' she pleaded. 'I should go home.'

Hafzan ignored this. 'Mama says most halfcastes come from Christian backgrounds. It's because your religion doesn't give you a social framework. Chota Lal Benedict, who married B.K. Pillai's elder daughter, Hammerhead's sister, is a Christian. None of it means much, except for the holidays. I don't believe in God. But you'd better be a Muslim. I'll convert you.'

She grinned slowly. 'You don't know what this place is, do you? That's why I asked if you were a Christian. They go to hell if they play the games. This is a virtuality mall.'

Somewhere in Bella's memory forgotten tourist information muttered of *unspeakable orgies*.

'Don't be scared. It used to be worse than this. In the old days, you had to get into a body bag and lie down with sensors sticking all over you. The bag would paralyse your body and your mind would go off into the gameworld, and if anything happened to that bag you were dead. If you got too scared in there: yeccch, disgusting! It's different now, it's done with visors. Take off your cloak, you can't play in a chador.'

They passed through a double door, that opened at a touch and closed behind them; and entered a blue-lit narrow gallery that seemed to circle a large space of darkness. It was lined with high-backed chairs. Bella could hear a tiny rustling: the sound of cries, of running footsteps. It was coming from headwraps that hung from the backs of the chairs.

'This is the spectators' gallery.' They seemed to be alone, but suddenly Hafzan was whispering. 'It's not much of a mall. In old earth they have games that suck your mind out. Wait there.'

Bella stood, horrified. She felt as if the whole human population of earth was aware of her. She was suspected, she was being tested. She would have to go through with this, to prove her humanity. But what *was* this? She had no idea. The terms *game* and *mall* and *virtuality* wouldn't resolve in her frightened mind.

Hafzan reappeared, full of furtive daring and excitement.

'We're sorted, come on.'

Bella tried to seem eager: and walked slap into an invisible barrier that was hard enough to sting and bruise.

'Not like that! Get your kit on. You can't play naked!'

Minutely, from the gallery seats, came an inarticulate babble: mad wails, whimpers of horrid pleasure, pounding hearts, orgiastic panting. 'You have to be eighteen,' whispered Hafzan. 'You can get in the gallery on an adult contact, but you can't buy a game without showing proof of id. So we get in here, and we wait by the arena exits. When someone comes out with spare time, we take their kit before they rack it. The gamers let us. They know the system's not fair. I'm thirteen, and this is a kids' game really. I could play it legally almost anywhere, except in Kerala.'

'Why do they come out with spare time?'

Hafzan laughed. 'Try it and see.'

Bella took the odd-looking wrap and put it around her head. No screen appeared in front of her eyes. The world *vanished*.

Hafzan's voice spoke, inside her head.

'If you try to take off the visor while you're inside, *the sensei*

will stop the game and we'll be in big fat trouble, so DON'T DO
IT. If you want to get out, head for an exit. You can always do
that, you'll see. You'll find yourself out of the game and *then*
you can take off the visor. If you score well enough, you get
more time indefinitely, but you don't have to worry about that.
You have three minutes and nearly ten secs, it's long enough.
When your time's up, your wounds will stop regenerating and
you'll find yourself exiting. Hold out your hands.'

Something hard and long slapped across her outstretched
palms. Bella was turned, and pushed backwards into the darkness. The voice in her head shouted, 'GO!'

She was falling, through infinite space.

She was standing, a strange weapon in her hands, in a paved
courtyard. It was night, firelit. Around her rose the walls,
towers, battlements of a vast fortress. The sounds that she had
heard in the gallery had grown to fill a flame-shadowed immensity with the cries and clamour of battle. Hafzan was with her,
but the girl had put on a mask like the Kali mask. She had
acquired a fanged muzzle, and the stance of a creature that runs
on four feet though it can walk on two. She looked almost
Aleutian, apart from the coat of hair. Red flames flickered behind
her and danced in her gaping pupils. As the voice spoke in Bella's
head, Hafzan's fanged mouth moved.

'If you stand there doing nothing, the sensei'll start feeding
you the book. Don't bother, you don't need it. It's a shoot 'em
up, there are no rules. All you have to remember is: we're
monkeys. Monkeys are the ones with tails, demons are the
enemy and they look fancy. Let's go.'

They ran and loped, knuckling the knobbly stones. The night
was hot, and there was a smell of singed hide. From somewhere
close came the dull thumping of a battering ram. They joined a
huddle around a monkey officer. Accepted at once, they were
sent to attack the fire-arrow demons on the west stair.

Bella was appalled, fascinated, horrified. *She was in the
deadworld!* A player ran at her. His mask was gaudier than
Hafzan's, he had no tail. He must be a demon. Bella stepped out
of the way of his weapon, aimed her own at where his head was
going to be in a moment. The demon fell.

⟨Is that right? Is that what I'm supposed to do?⟩

No one answered. They were monkeys. They were gone.

She was in the deadworld. Dead things, *void force things*, surrounded her mind, separating it from the real. But the world was still out there, it had to be. As her stunned impressions settled, Bella began to grasp the conditions. The deadworld entity that had taken over her perception managed the space of a real arena as a three dimensional maze. There were some material fittings – ladders, chutes, suspended walkways. The demons and monkeys were marshalled round and around the circuit, kept apart or allowed to rush together, experiencing a huge bewildering castle.

Something arbitrary as a shift in a dream happened to the attack on the west stair. Bella found herself high on the battle-ments alone, and saw a demon far away firing at her. She put up a hand automatically to fend off the missile, and was clutching an arrow shaft. It was on fire. Her hand was burning! Sticky fire clung to her palm. Bella screamed. She saw her monkey flesh burst into raw red and black blisters, glimpsed the white glisten of bone, felt the intolerable pain . . . Then she was on her knees, crouched against a wall, whimpering, watching the skin reform.

This is fun?

After that, she took care to avoid injury. She killed demons with her club, which became with practice more than a blunt instrument. It began to spout accurate fire when she pointed it. She discovered that in certain spots the castle was *permeable*. There were places where walls could be walked through. There were appalling-looking drops that didn't exist. There was an invisible staircase. You could use these trick trapdoors to sneak up on the opposition, or vanish out of trouble. She began to kill more demons. It was, in a strange way, relaxing. There was no room in your mind for grief, fear or anxiety about the real.

She started to wonder, vaguely, what had become of Hafzan.

AIEEEEEENEEEEEENEEEEE!

It sounded like a fire alarm. But the violent red glow was coming from her own weapon. *Head for an exit*. In a panic, Bella ran for the gateway she saw ahead of her. She passed through the wreckage of a pair of massive metal-bound doors.

The castle vanished. She was in nothingness. She pulled off the visor. Floor materialised under her feet. She was in the spectators' gallery. She was standing in a bay between racks of visors and weapons. Figures converged out of the gloom. A crowd pressed around her, there was a confusion of voices and Common Tongue. People laughed. Someone said, '*Congratulations, kid.*' A hand patted her shoulder, eyes smiled. The crowd dispersed. Some tossed their kit negligently into the racks and walked away. Others revisored and dropped back into that other world. Bella was left facing a small group of players, all of them young. Hafzan was among them. Bella gathered these were her friends. One had the sliced, concave face of a genuine halfcaste.

'What happened? What did I do?'

Hafzan's friends knew about the 'new human'. They stared hard, passing informal comments freely. '*Holeface,*' muttered one. 'Lay off,' warned a Man boy. 'In here, we're all gamers.'

'You said you'd never been in a mall before,' Hafzan accused. 'Then you go and score a limit! Are you a spider?'

'I don't know what that is.'

'A pro. A trapdoor user. Why didn't you *tell* me?'

'You won a free game,' said someone. 'Wanna play? I've still got some time. Shall we play?'

The young humans didn't move. They glowered at her, still panting: their hearts thumping, eyes wild, faces glistening. Bella, the cripple, was not out of breath. She felt a rush of petty triumph. She wanted to do it over again. She looked at the weapon and the wrap in her hands. She had seen a demon, a big man, drop his weapon and run: fleeing in orgiastic terror from the unreal battlefield. *How can I have beaten them?* she thought. *I'm a cripple.* It was not horror of the deadworld, but another emotion she didn't understand, that made her put her kit down.

'Anyone can have my time. I don't want to play again.'

That evening Bella knelt on the edge of the congregation in the pillared hall, watching moving images of the Self in cheerful aspects of song and dance and courtship. She could not follow the story. Seeker-after-truth's voice came out of the shadows, softly speaking English. 'In old earth these days, they laugh at the idea of passive-audience entertainment like this. The cult of watching puppets on a screen is dead, out there among the humans. They have other ways of enlarging their experience.

Alien influence has affected the enclaves people more than they know.'

He touched Bella lightly. ⟨Come.⟩ They slipped away.

'I've been shopping,' announced Seeker-after-truth. 'In the Connemara market.' The incunabula that he collected came in odd forms. He had shown Bella obsolete record-media converted into jewellery, armour, knife blades: inlaid in carved wood, fused on to wall tiles, made into clothes and bedding. He tossed out a wide shawl that was woven from thread-fine, indigo-bloomed tape.

'Pure coralin, from before the first war! It's a splendid find.' The material slipped through his fingers. 'But what's recorded here? Who knows? My artisans will have to work on it. And you, librarian, what have you been doing with yourself?'

⟨I did something terrible.⟩

'Ah. And you want to tell.' His eyes were very kind. The locals called him a 'holy woman'. The Seeker was no cleric. But in his strange way, Bella felt that he was closer to the Self than any confessor Bella had ever met.

'It was the deprogrammers,' he explained formally. 'I'd made them suspicious. I played a deadworld game, to show them I wasn't an Aleutian. But *I* won. It was an imaginary battle. I'm an invalid, an isolate. I've never used a weapon! I don't know why, but it was winning that felt terrible. I felt like a thief.'

⟨The games sensei are experts at tapping potential. Perhaps there is a hunting beast hidden in every thinking being's mind. Perhaps it's true that we are better hunters than they. Others have found it so.⟩

The Seeker was smiling: a complex, rueful smile.

⟨But your response to the moment of truth is unique, librarian. He Who Puts Down His Weapons. I wonder how that would go in Sanskrit?⟩

Bella was not exactly surprised to learn that other Aleutians had tried the games. He was isolate, but he understood some-thing of what went on off the record, on earth. But in the Seeker's complicated smile he glimpsed a whole secret history: and dropped his eyes, alarmed. He didn't want to know any more!

⟨Please don't laugh at me. How could I have a landing party name? I'm an invalid, a silly, trapped holidaymaker . . .⟩

Sanskrit names, from the sacred language of the Aleutians' first patron, were generally reserved for the three captains and their original crews.

⟨I am not laughing,⟩ Seeker-after-truth told him gravely. ⟨You deserve the honour.⟩ Suddenly he became less solemn. 'The Zamanis are not bad people. They are bigots, but scrupulous in their methods. But Hafzan is a bossy young brat. Your handling of her challenge does you credit.' Formal English seemed to come to the Seeker as easily as the Common Tongue. He brought a paper packet out from the folds of his white wrapper.

'Have a sweet? A gulabjam. They're very good.'

They looked like solid shit and smelled of dead flowers.

⟨No, thank you.⟩

'Hard food won't harm you. It's no more than a question of accustoming your insides, by degrees. You should make the effort, it is worthwhile.' He popped a sweet into his mouth. 'Let me show you one of my best finds. It's from an archive of a scientific journal: almost perfectly preserved, and so clearly coded! My staff were able to do a complete restoration. Take a look. There's a whole article by Peenemunde Buonarotti – in English, of course – that comes up wonderfully. I carry a copy with me everywhere.'

He opened a page on a flat reader-screen, and pushed it over.

⟨As you know, sir,⟩ Bella pointed out diffidently, ⟨Maitri's librarian can't read.⟩

⟨Did I know that? Perhaps I did. But you can look.⟩

The seeker's enthusiasm was so convincing Bella almost expected the screen to blossom into a magic doorway. Nothing happened. The black marks squirmed. With difficulty he could make them keep still. ⟨Look here, especially.⟩ The Seeker touched the screen with a short, square-cut claw. ⟨That phrase: *Deus Providebit Sibi Victimam Sacrifici.* Do you see it? Study it well. It has no place in the article. It is a sign. It is one of the signs 'Buonarotti' left for me, on the trail I follow.⟩

⟨What does it mean?⟩

Seeker answered formally. 'The words are from an obsolete dialect. In English it would be, "The Lord himself will provide a

victim for the sacrifice". It's a line from a Bible story. You will
know of the Bible, of course, though probably not at first hand.
There are few satisfactory moving-image transcriptions from
that collection, though I believe in parts it is very fine. The
victim and the sacrificer, and God. It is a triune you often find
in their mystical records. These three aspects seem to define the
condition of selfhood, in local philosophy. In the Bible fable,
someone called Abraham is ordered by God make a sacrifice. The
sacrifice is to be the murder of his truechild, Isaac. He prepares
to obey, but at the last moment God intervenes – satisfied by the
gesture, apparently. It's an odd story. Perhaps if it were translated into images you could explain it to me, librarian. But as to
what Peenemunde means by that promise: I don't know.'

He shut the reader with a sigh, and grimaced at his heap of
scavenged relics. ⟨Perhaps I'll never know!⟩

⟨I suppose it is too dangerous for you to go to 'Germany'?⟩

The mystic frowned at him. ⟨Why do you say that?⟩

⟨To 'Peenemunde Buonarotti's' workplace. I suppose you can't
search for your incunabula there, because of the war.⟩

⟨The war has never restricted my movements.⟩ Seeker-after-
truth seemed piqued at the imputation. 'Unfortunately,' he
added in English, 'Peenemunde Buonarotti's university campus
was contaminated in a radiation accident around the outbreak
of the First Gender War. Whereupon, as you no doubt remember
from *The Grief of Clavel*, she retired to the enclaves and did no
further scientific work.'

⟨But 'radiation' isn't really dangerous, is it? I think you should
look where the work was done. In my experience, whenever an
image or a record has been misfiled or mislaid, it *always* turns
out to be near where I first thought it should be. I search and
search: then suddenly there it is, where it was all along!⟩

He'd become animated, relieved to find an aspect of the
Seeker's quest that he actually understood. He retreated.

⟨Not that I would know anything, sir.⟩

But Seeker-after-truth was following his own thoughts. ⟨No, it
won't be in 'Germany'. Physical location would have meant
nothing to him. He could order his treatise on instantaneous
travel copied out in a library thousands of miles away, have the
record hidden by remote machinery, and then order every other

trace of it to be destroyed: all without involving another living soul. I am convinced that's exactly what he did, leaving nothing but the signs to tantalise me.⟩

In the Seeker's absorbed musing, he dropped his careful use of the 'she' pronoun. Peenemunde became a person, a fellow scientist. ⟨He knew that I would come. He wanted me to come, to rescue his glorious child from oblivion. But he couldn't bear to make it easy. And how can I blame him? How must it feel to be a 'mortal', and know that you must hand over your life's work to an 'immortal superbeing'. . . or see it lost for ever . . .⟩

⟨Why couldn't he give it to the locals?⟩

Seeker-after-truth started, as if he'd half forgotten the librarian was there. ⟨Why, indeed? I have my suspicions. But for whatever reason, he hid his secret completely. You won't find a single human scientist who believes in the device.⟩

Bella couldn't resist the thought that this was probably because the device didn't exist. He kept it to himself.

⟨If all else fails, sir,⟩ he suggested kindly, ⟨one day you'll meet 'Peenemunde' in person. Everything must happen.⟩

The Seeker gave Bella another of those long, penetrating looks that made the librarian feel small and stupid.

⟨We will not meet. 'Peenemunde' is dead.⟩

⟨Oh . . . You believe in permanent death, sir?⟩

⟨They don't come back,⟩ said the mystic. ⟨I have studied their culture and I've come to believe that. They do not come back. Not the way we do.⟩ His tone was suddenly brusque, so that Bella wondered what he'd done wrong. He began to fold the coralin-tape shawl.

'I don't think you'll have any more trouble with Hafzan Zamani. I will be leaving Trivandrum soon. You stay where you are, I'll make sure that Yudi knows where to find you. But as we may not get another chance, we'd better talk about Sidney Carton.'

Bella started. ⟨Sid?⟩

'Sidney Carton,' repeated Seeker-after-truth, with a trace of a smile. 'The halfcaste interpreter who helped you to escape. Forgive me if I'm wrong, but informally you've led me to understand he turned out to be a suspicious character.'

Bella had felt that Seeker-after-truth could not be interested in his silly story. He was sure that the mystic had encouraged this impression. The other Aleutian must have changed his mind. He was watching Bella now with a keen and most unmystical expression.

⟨I don't know what to say. It will sound so farfetched. I don't know anything for sure.⟩

⟨Try me,⟩ suggested the other. ⟨Informally, will do.⟩

Bella drew a breath, and tried to order his thoughts.

⟨Well, he is not like a halfcaste. He hasn't changed his appearance trying to look like one of us. But Maitri trusted him, so I did too. But when he rescued me, I couldn't understand why. He had one of those dead firearms. If he wanted to save me from unpleasantness, why didn't he kill me? He's not ignorant, he knows Aleutians don't have permanent death. That was the first thing that made me wonder: and then it was obvious he'd been prepared to take off and *take one of us with him*. Then gradually I was sure. There was nothing you could use as evidence. But we were alone together in the wilderness for days. Informally, as you know, they can't keep their secrets. I tried not to let him know I suspected him. He brought me to the nearest city and then he went away and talked to someone. He came back with airline tickets. He said he bought them on credit, but before that he'd told me he was poor, a 'masterless man': where would he get credit? He brought me here. But I'd thought it out. I knew I had to get away, before he delivered me to his evil boss. I knew I could pass as a halfcaste, we'd found out that. I thought I'd be safer with Women than with Men, because they're more tolerant of halfcastes: and because Sid's a man, I mean a male. So here I am.⟩

⟨Resourceful librarian! But what had you thought out?⟩

Bella drew a breath. ⟨I believe Sid's an anti-Aleutian fanatic. Like 'Braemar Wilson'. I don't blame him. I'd want it on record, if this became official, that he did nothing unfair. He's brave and kind and clever. But he kidnapped me.⟩ Bella refused, even informally, to mention the 'disguised prince' rumour. ⟨I don't know why. Somehow some people had got the idea I was important, for a plot to destroy the Expedition.⟩

⟨Can these anti-Aleutians be really dangerous?⟩

The Seeker's tone was neutral, but Bella found that he'd grown confident. ⟨Yes! You see, they're like 'Braemar', they *understand*. To Sid and his boss, the Protest was a hideous waste of time. Sid knows too much about us, more than any local should. He described the homeworld to me, once. It was eerie. It was as if he had been there.⟩

⟨You thought that? Interesting!⟩

⟨The Government of the World has never studied us, because they're afraid to offend us. The halfcastes have their own ideas, and don't want to know the truth. Only 'Braemar Wilson's' people tried to find out things, as you would of a real enemy. Sid is the same. I think his gang is *very* dangerous . . .⟩ Bella remembered another telling detail. ⟨Oh, and it's a little thing, but he called me 'Bella'. He said it was a translation of Maitri's petname for me, which was Goodlooking, you know: silly, but I had to use it, for earth. It isn't.⟩ The librarian shrugged dismissively. ⟨The root is different. But 'Bella' was the name of 'Johnny Guglioli's' child. That's not something even a halfcaste would know casually. As you know, the story of *The Grief of Clavel* isn't famous on earth. For me it was too much of a coincidence: a name *sneakily* connected with the saboteurs, on top of all the other little slips . . .⟩

Seeker-after-truth frowned. ⟨Librarian!⟩ he muttered.

Bella quailed. He didn't blame Seeker-after-truth for being annoyed. He had explained things poorly. He'd made his story sound feeble, overheated and childish. He crouched low.

⟨I'm sorry I bothered you, sir. You're right. I see it now. There's no mystery. I was imagining things.⟩

⟨No.⟩ Seeker-after-truth gently tugged the librarian's nape, lifted him and drew him close. ⟨No,⟩ he repeated. ⟨I don't think you were imagining things.⟩

He seemed to consider how much to reveal. ⟨I will tell you this much. There *is* a plot, and the Expedition *is* in danger. You have become involved in a treasure hunt.⟩ He chuckled softly. ⟨Yes, a romantic treasure hunt. You don't believe in the instantaneous travel device, my sensible friend. But there are folk who do: and not all of them are harmless wandering scholars. Some are anti-Aleutian fanatics. Some are humans who have no interest in aliens one way or the other. Some are Aleutians who have never visited the giant planet and have no sympathy with the

Expedition. Some〉 – he smiled grimly – 〈are traitors in our own ranks. Yes, traitors with Sanskrit names. If you think about it, you will see that news of the device could be very damaging to the Expedition, if our enemies reached it first. From what you say, it seems that these people have . . . mistakenly decided that you have information they need.〉

He stroked the slick dark head that was resting against his shoulder. 〈You will return to our world soon. You should be safe from further kidnap attempts. But I'm going to ask you, very informally, to keep your suspicions to yourself for a little while. Be discreet about 'Sidney Carton'. Will you trust me?〉

〈Of course, sir!〉

〈Good. I hope I can be trusted . . . in the end. You've kept the name though, I gather? In spite of its associations?〉

The librarian's shoulders lifted. 〈It's a souvenir. I've never had an adventure before. And surely won't again.〉

〈But you seem to take to them. 'Like a duck to water', as the locals say.〉 The scholar pondered. 〈You are looking very well. The atmosphere of earth seems to be good for you. I could use a librarian: especially one with a natural disguise. It would only be while Maitri is away. I know one can't hope to poach from Lord Maitri's company! This is just a feeler, but what do you say?〉

Bella realised, astonished, that he was being offered a job.

He was silent for too long. Seeker-after-truth would think him impossibly ungrateful. But he felt overwhelmed. He thought of the outing to the ruins at Mykini: the yellow sunlight and the scent of the pine grove. That picnic had been an event like no other in his quiet existence. He remembered the librarian of that day with a desperate nostalgia.

I want to be myself again!

〈I'm sorry,〉 he said at last. 〈I don't think I'd do for your work. I'm not that sort of person.〉

Bella returned to his small room on the clerks' floor. The Pillai household was plunged in the death-like silence of night among the locals. He crouched on the narrow bed-with-legs, his limbs drawn into a knot and his face buried in his hands. He thought of the strange events that had gathered around him. He remembered

how Maitri had drawn him aside after the visit to the ruins,
before the massacre. What had Lord Maitri begun to tell him?
What was the news he had refused to hear, misunderstanding in
his usual isolate way? No. It couldn't be. He was Maitri's
librarian, no one else.

He trembled, and trembled, and finally – when he had grown
calm – Sidney Carton came to him: Sid, in Aleutian overalls,
with such a sad and lonely face. She – becoming *she* again to
enact Sid's desire – could not bear to send him away. She put her
arms around him. Sid slipped his hands along her shoulders,
inside her local shirt. His fingers found the grooves that should
have been melting and running with wanderers. He bent his
head and used his mouth to hunt the moist lips, too passionate
to notice there were no messengers there. His hands traced the
lesser grooves beside her spine. She could not help herself. She
pulled herself up and hard against him, so that he could feel
through her clothes the plumped, engorged rim of her *place*,
pressing against his belly.

Bella stopped it there.

The ghost of Sidney Carton had reappeared in this room at
random intervals, after the first time. Bella had searched and
failed to find any kind of occult device. He had told no one,
certainly not Seeker-after-truth. This haunting was a problem
that he would have to deal with alone. But the letterbombs were
not erotic. That was Bella's own idea. He crouched on the bed
and wiped his brimming eyes. 'Oh, Sid,' he whispered. 'What a
shame. What a waste.'

Bella didn't see Seeker-after-truth again. One morning soon after
their long interview, she went to the back wing of the house and
found a Pillai domestic sweeping out the pilgrim's empty room.

'Where did the *evidyane* go?' she asked.

But the domestic only gave a shrug, that cold smile which
never touched their eyes.

She didn't use the cablepoints. When the Tourviddy van,
which had remained parked in the Pillais' garden, showed taped
news bulletins at 'evening prayers', Bella perceived them as
timeless records of selves in interaction, rather than information
about current affairs. But she knew what was happening. The

humans talked about nothing else, formally and informally. Negotiations had begun between the shipworld and the Government of the World in Thailand. After half an earth's year away, the aliens were coming back. The human world had found it needed Aleutian goods, and decided not to let false pride get in the way of business. And some people had realised that alien presence was a bulwark against the spread of the Gender War. It was understood that the fate of the Himalayas could be discussed later.

The day Bella learned that Aleutians had returned to Uji, he knew he ought to reveal his true identity to his hosts before the rescue party the Seeker had promised came to fetch him. But the right moment never seemed to come. On a morning some days after the momentous news, he went to B.K. Pillai's office. It was nearly noon. The lawyer was alone, the rows of clerks' desks empty. Tattered ends of garlands, left over from the harvest festival at the end of the rains, trailed from the frame of the wall-sized world picture. Burning sunlit air poured through the open shutters. But this room, close to the heat-ex well that was the house's cool core, was never too warm.

B.K. was working steadily through the dregs of her in-tray. She was almost down to the level of pathetic requests from shady foreign charities. As she worked, she talked to herself in the Common Tongue. The language of her minute facial gestures was intelligible to the Aleutian who saw her as patron, benefactor, wise friend.

‹Katalamma will never marry. She should have been a boy, then it wouldn't have mattered that she isn't clever. It was not to be. Two is enough: and Daddy believes reproduction technology is sinful, except for childless people who are very unhappy. She will get pregnant; girls like my young goddess can never resist getting pregnant. Anything's possible these days: fused ova, manufactured sperm, out-of-body pregnancy (though she wouldn't want that, what prowess is there in that?). It will upset Daddy, but she won't care. They none of them want husbands, that generation. What's the use of keeping a vicious animal caged in your house? they say, feeling that their time has come and at last they are free. The young women like Katalamma don't know anything about how the war is going. I am afraid of the aliens. But without them there is only the war, growing nearer. The war which we reformers must lose, and every woman too: though so many of them refuse to see it. How can the people who hate war win, when we are driven into battle? It was not the aliens' fault, they only named what was happening, it was brewing for a long time. But it is too late. What is it the aliens say? *Once the weapons are out, everybody loses.*

⟨I must find myself some more useless work, to occupy my mind. I must make Katalamma believe I am glad the aliens have returned, to damp her anger. She trusts me still. I don't want her in trouble. There is no alternative, it's them or worse—⟩

She looked up. She was crying. The flowing human tears, that seemed so wild and excessive, ran down her face.

'Bella,' she said. 'Good. It's time we had a talk.'

Bella was trying to say, *There's something you should know.* She didn't manage to speak. She hoped afterwards that B.K. understood, and forgave her. But at that moment Ravi Pillai came into the room, treading the polished wooden floor softly on his bare feet.

'Mummyji?'

They went out together. Ravi stepped back, and said shyly to Bella: 'Please, wait here.' Bella sat down at one of the clerks' desks and waited, trembling.

At last B.K. Pillai came back, dressed in a gold-banded green and purple sari over gold gauze petticoats. It was the kind of thing she wore when traditionalist Hindu ladies came to tea: to curl on the Pillai sofas like large, gaudy kittens, eat sweeties and make pointed comments about Katalamma's marital status. She stood, smoothing the silk and smiling distantly.

'Please come with me.'

The aliens had arrived. In their dun overalls and quarantine film, they were in the caravanserai hall. They presented gifts of 'half-killed' Aleutian goods, carefully wrapped in quarantine. They made polite speeches in English. Informally they were extremely rude, under the mistaken impression that humans cannot understand the Common Tongue at all. But the language barrier was no obstacle to their flagrant amusement and disgust. Under the transparent film, tiny squirming blood-blisters wriggled over the skin of their faces, hands and throats. Bella had been expecting to be found, some time soon. But his head began to spin. Weakness overwhelmed him, he fell down in a faint at his rescuers' feet.

The Aleutian hotel had been burned out. Its gardens, which had been prized by locals and aliens alike, had been reduced to an ashpit. The rescue party had taken over another hotel near by.

As soon as Bella-who-had-been-Goodlooking, Maitri's librarian, was well enough, they held a small reception party for him in the room they'd made into their main hall. Bella arrived with a nurse at his elbow, still very shaky. The room was a gloomy place, decorated in a grim industrial shade of red. Ancient electric chandeliers hung from the ceiling; but the light came from sucker lamps.

He'd been bewildered by the size of the group. But he'd learned that the expedition to claim Maitri's librarian had been the first sortie from Uji since the return to earth. It had become a social event, and there'd been hosts of volunteers. Sarvanga, the leader of the party, presided over the gathering from a flat-topped partition that he had adopted as a hard, narrow dais.

⟨So here you are, back from the dead!⟩

'I'm very grateful—' Bella began.

Sarvanga brushed the formal thanks aside. ⟨Think nothing of it, little isolate. For the prestige of Aleutia it was important to recover you.⟩

⟨Don't keep him long, sir,⟩ murmured the nurse. ⟨He really shouldn't be out of bed.⟩

⟨Of course not, poor fellow. But there's this business of the local halfcaste.⟩ Sarvanga turned to one of his aides. ⟨'Sidney Carton', isn't it? What amazing names they have.⟩

'Lord Maitri's halfcaste interpreter,' the spruce young signifier supplied, very formal and correct. 'The chap's here now, sir. He's hardly been away since he found out we'd recovered Goodlooking. He seems to expect a reward.'

⟨Actually, I'm calling myself 'Bella'—⟩ No one noticed.

⟨Cheeky blighter,⟩ complained someone in the group. ⟨We rescued the librarian.⟩ Another of the company lifted his head, which was resting elegantly in the lap of a close friend, and

transferred a wanderer from his own naked throat to the friend's
mouth. ⟨I thought 'Bella' was hiding with some purebreds?⟩

⟨Sounds like an opportunist sort of beggar,⟩ judged Sarvanga.
⟨What really happened, librarian?⟩

Be discreet, he remembered.

⟨It's true that he rescued me,⟩ he submitted. ⟨He thought he
was 'saving my life'.⟩ (Anyone who could understand English
chuckled. The rest quickly followed suit.) ⟨But I'm afraid it was
more from greed than loyalty. I decided to dispense with his
protection as soon as I could.⟩

There was a murmur of approval.

⟨Isolate, too. Brave kid!⟩

Sarvanga deliberated. ⟨I know. Let's give him some money.
That'll get him off our backs without committing us to
anything.⟩

Bella felt that his audience was over. He didn't know what he
was supposed to do. At the moment his medication was only
confusing him. Someone emerged out of the brilliantly robed
crowd.

⟨'Bella', my dear . . .⟩

It was Aditya, in a robe of dark blue local silk trimmed with
gold: Aditya, whom the locals long ago had nicknamed *Beautiful
Girl*. Aditya the beauty was a leader of fashion, before whom Uji
society paid homage. It was easy to forget that he was also a
veteran of the Expedition. Bella turned with abject relief to a
face that he knew. Maitri and Aditya had never been close, but
they had served together.

⟨Poor thing, you're exhausted. Come away with me. I'm
longing to hear about your adventures! I'm so jealous. I *adore*
adventures.⟩

In the passage outside the 'main hall', ex-cocktail bar, Sid was
hunkered down with his back to the wall. No one had stopped
him coming in. They hadn't got their quarantine sorted yet. Sid
suspected that under the new regime, Total Quarantine Enforcement was on the slide. It would only matter when the Aleutians
wanted it to. He was holding Roger: who squirmed, silently
intent on escape. Lydia stepped on stray wanderers and imag-

ined, vindictively, tiny pinpricks of pain going through the owners of those little bugs: *ooch, ouch, eeech*.

'Daddy, how could she trick me like that? I'm a baby.'

'To Bel you're not. You're a person, same person you always were: a little shorter at present.'

'I hate her. I hope I never see her again.'

'You probably won't, after today.'

She danced off down the passage. The flooring was red, squishy and warm to the touch. Walking on it was like walking on warm raw flesh. Sid was glad that the returning aliens had set themselves up, without knowing it, in the one honest-to-God brothel in the whole Community State of Kerala. But he was afraid the insult was lost. They wouldn't understand and they probably found the gruesome decor cosy.

It was the Fat Man's idea that Sid should act the beggar. This charade was supposed to reassure the aliens about the strange behaviour of a halfcaste interpreter. If he turned up like an idiot, demanding a reward for saving the immortal's life, they'd know he wasn't a spy. Or so the Fat Man claimed. Hop-skip, hop-skip. Lydia was driving him crazy.

She came back and asked, 'Why do people have white skin? I mean the white that turns red, like yours.'

'Dominance display selection. I'm a fashion victim.'

'You could go and live in Sweden, you'd look ordinary there.'

'*I don't want to live in Sweden.*'

'Why don't you get it fixed?'

'I don't do gene therapy.'

'You had me vaccinated against periods.'

'That's different.'

She stood in front of him, arms folded harridan-wise. ⟨Don't you want to be like me? If you loved me, you'd do it.⟩ She was the mother demon in miniature. The aliens were right. At six she was almost adult, lacking nothing except height and a trifle of experience.

'Talk out loud. Don't speak informal in here, it'll lower your guard. You'll tell them things without knowing it.'

Figures appeared in the distance. The heel-drumming was over.

'Shut up, Lydie. Shut up and look pathetic!'

⟨Isn't it horrible about the gardens,⟩ chattered Aditya, arm in
arm with the isolate. ⟨How could they do that? Their own flesh
and blood. I know it *isn't*, but one can't help feeling—⟩

⟨Horrid,⟩ agreed Bella conventionally. He saw Sid, and stopped
dead. It was terrible to see him like that: his courage and his
power buckled down under his misery.

⟨Oh, Sid. Why are you *doing* this to yourself?⟩

He stared defiantly. ⟨Mysterious and important reasons, that I
can't possibly explain to you.⟩

⟨Leave him. It's not your problem any more.⟩ Aditya looked
back as he swept Bella away. ⟨Gosh,⟩ he marvelled. ⟨Can you
really follow them, when they mumble like that?⟩

⟨No,⟩ said Bella. ⟨I don't understand them at all,⟩

6: Beautiful Girl

The damage of the Protest, at the manor house at Uji, had been quickly repaired. This secluded valley in Karen State, north of Thailand, had been the Aleutian headquarters on earth since the earliest days of the Expedition. Little had survived of its local character. In the main hall of the house the single original feature that had remained before the Protest was a large bowl of glazed earthenware known as *Clavel's Fountain*. A natural spring, that rose from under the foundations of the house, kept it full of water. It had been respectfully restored, but the 'earthenware' itself was an artisans' imitation now.

Bella had spent hours here, in undisputed possession of the stepped plinth and the melancholy indoor pool. It was a good spot to lurk in peace. The post-Protest company found Clavel's Fountain gloomy, and avoided it.

Today the full company had assembled because Yudi was receiving visitors from the shipworld, but Bella's haven remained quiet. The grieving murmur of the spring water, trickling away in a hidden pipe to join the Uji river, reminded him of B.K. Pillai's fish pool, and of Sid. *Why are rivers 'melancholy' in Aleutia?* Sid had asked once. *Why do you people hate running water? Is it because it moves and isn't alive?* This had been somewhere on the journey through the wilderness, beside a most welcome stream. We don't *hate it*, Bella had told him. *Water's eerie, because it holds reflections that are living-things-not-alive. When it's flowing it's always in the wilderness: which is sad. And it flows away like life, never turning back. You call us immortal, but we feel time the way you do.*

Everything about his adventure had 'flowed away': except that he couldn't seem to leave earth. He had made a tactical

error in Trivandrum. Because he'd collapsed, he'd become the
invalid again. If he'd realised how he would be trapped, he
would have struggled to stay on his feet. Now it was too late.
We, the Aleutian 'we' which means society as an executive, had
decreed that he was not strong enough to travel, and he was
Maitri's librarian again: he couldn't fight the verdict, he *felt* ill.
It would be a sad return, without Maitri. The household would
be much depleted: by the loss of the frontier post company, and
by the inevitable drift of people finding positions elsewhere
while their lord was away. But he longed to be home.

He knew none of the new staff who had been recruited to
make up numbers after the Protest. To his weary ignorance they
seemed a dull crew: and silly, too. It had become the fashion for
everyone to go about surrounded by personal commensals. It was
for the prestige of the Expedition, they said. The most minor
trader had an entourage, and at popular times the hall seethed
with walking wastebins, writing desks, snackboxes. It was a
long way from the gallant romance of the landing parties.

Bella didn't know who they were trying to impress. Nego-
tiation with the Government of the World had been reduced to
an exchange of recorded messages. In the present mood of the
Expedition, it seemed likely that no locals would ever be allowed
in the valley again. It was necessary but sad. When Mr Kaoru,
the Aleutians' first patron, had willed Uji manor to the Aleutians, it had been a gift of friendship: a gift to his friend Clavel,
who had loved the valley in its native, melancholy beauty.
What would Kaoru think of the way things had changed?

There was a stir, up near the dais. Yudisthara was Silent. His
speechmaker had risen to propose a vote of welcome to the
honoured visitor. Traders with their comic retinues pressed
closer to the action. Bella stayed where he was.

As Lord Maitri's librarian, and lately his child, he had his own
view on shipworld politics. Yudisthara's visitor was minor roy-
alty. He was also a notorious supporter of the Dark Ocean
movement. Dark Ocean, the clique who wanted Aleutia to set
off again into the 'dark ocean' of space: to give up the earth and
return to the hopeless search for home. What was a friend of
that crew doing beside Yudisthara? The speech ended. The
company, signifiers and Silent both, broke into a vocal and

chemical chorus of approval. They were thrilled that the Expedition was getting attention from someone important. If you pointed out the Dark Ocean connection, they'd brush it aside. They'd say they 'weren't interested in politics', while Yudisthara was cravenly making up to the Expedition's enemies . . .

It was perhaps fortunate that Bella's medication could not diffuse the tincture of his bitterness very far. In the Common Tongue, he kept his expression neutral.

⟨I'm nobody important. What I think doesn't matter.⟩

⟨Yes,⟩ the company answered: in their patent indifference and in the chemical touches that drifted by. ⟨You're nobody. Strange things happened to you in the Protest. But that's over and we don't want to think about it. And we don't want to be unkind to an invalid, but you don't have much to offer socially—⟩

Bella smiled. It was the verdict he wanted. Indifference was balm to his shattered nerves. A carrier commensal had come into the hall, with something in its mouth.

⟨Packet for Maitri's librarian!⟩

Bella started. 'Oh, no!'

He didn't know he'd gasped aloud until heads turned. Denial was useless. He was taking his medicine. A genius of disguise like Seeker-after-truth could suppress or alter his chemical presence. Bella was helpless. The commensal arrived at his feet, glowing with triumph. Poor thing, it didn't know any better. From somewhere in the crowd came a sharp warning in English. 'Don't touch it, Bella!' It was good advice. But he was impelled to ignore it, driven by an idiotic need to pretend that nothing strange was happening.

There had been other messages like this, but he'd been lucky before. They'd been delivered to his room in Uji's sick bay.

⟨For me? Who could be sending packets to me?⟩

The wrapping was the same as before: thick, dead and slightly abrasive to his fingertips. He looked for the tab, meaning to avoid it at all costs: but he'd already touched it. An ethereal something leapt into existence. Briefly, a huge glistening bubble shone in the air. Then no margin could be seen or felt. A local stood among the Aleutians: angular at the shoulder, scanty at the hip; taller than some, smaller than most. His short light-coloured hair was roughly upstanding over his head. His lifeless skin was scoured red. His eyes, deep-set under craggy brow ridges, were invisible behind a fur of pale lashes. He made a speech.

'Gentle aliens, this is a letterbomb. It's a harmless form of photochemical communication, developed in the early twenty-first century. The letterbomb has always been used by innocent people denied the normal means of making their contribution to public life. Are you watching this, Bella? Also known as Maitri's librarian, also known as Goodlooking?'

⟨He's here!⟩ cried a trader excitedly. Bella wished the floor would swallow him. The ghost stared ahead blindly.

'I want you to know that I'm thinking of you. I think of you every hour of every day. I want to remind you that you have unfinished business on earth. Don't go back to Aleutia, Bella. Please! Don't leave! I need you desperately—'

Someone sobbed, ⟨*I'm going to faint! Make it stop!*⟩

The image vanished. Bella swooped and stuffed the packet into the maw of somebody's mobile wastebin. The commensal made frantic choking noises and its owner exclaimed indignantly, ⟨Hey! Stop that!⟩

⟨I'm sorry,⟩ gasped Bella, ⟨I'm sorry, everyone so sorry—⟩

A babble of comment rose up. ⟨Was that a 'letterbomb'? Isn't that a trick the fanatics used to use? Are there fanatics about? So much for our security!⟩ . . . ⟨Magic? Void forces? Nonsense. It's been proved that they do have wanderers: nasty things called 'fearo-moans'. The packet will have been infested with them. When it was touched they burst out and triggered a mass hallucination.⟩

⟨It's a pity the librarian destroyed the evidence.⟩

⟨Was the local a 'Man'? Is this to do with their war?⟩

⟨Don't be silly, it was the librarian's 'halfcaste' guide!⟩

⟨Oh, I see. Haven't I heard they were . . . close?⟩

⟨Well, an isolate, you know. Beggars can't be choosers—⟩

Someone ran up, arms wrapped dramatically around his belly. ⟨It's people like you, local-lover! You were responsible for the Protest! Kill them! Reprisals! Revenge the babes unborn!⟩

Bella was in despair. But rescue was on its way. Aditya the

beauty elbowed his way through the press, caught the shaking invalid in his arms and turned on the last speaker.

⟨Coward!⟩ he snapped. ⟨It's people like *you* who make the locals think we're spineless. Babes unborn! What nonsense.⟩ His generous nasal narrowed in spite. ⟨If you're afraid of the locals, you'd better not talk like that in here. Don't you know Uji is 'bugged'? You think anything hidden in the manor must have been destroyed in the Protest? You're wrong. You can never get rid of all those deadworld eyes. They're everywhere.⟩

The traders were wearing formal robes. Aditya, forever a leader of fashion, had come to the reception in his plain overalls with a few scraps of bizarre decoration. He made the rest of them look overdressed. But his passage through the small crowd, Bella in tow, was conducted with an imperious sweep and swirl. ⟨Poor Bella, what a horrid thing! Has it happened before? Oh, tell me later. What nonsense about the babes unborn. As if anybody knows why a pregnancy fails: or starts, either.⟩

It was commonly believed by Aleutians that the mysterious process of conception was triggered by stress. It was therefore argued by some that everyone who had died in the Protest had died pregnant: thus doubling the death toll.

⟨If fright makes people pregnant, I wonder how you explain Maitri, dear soul. He's the calmest person I know, and *ludicrously* fecund. How lucky you are, Bella. We say isolates are infertile, don't we? You never have to worry about the business.⟩

Bella was being swept towards the steps of the dais. He made a feeble attempt to escape, but Aditya wouldn't let go. ⟨You're to stay with me. I don't see half enough of you. Don't you remember, you and I were going to be friends? In a little while we'll go off somewhere and you can tell me what all *that* was about.⟩ Taking a wanderer from the bounteous supply on his own throat, he popped it into Bella's mouth. ⟨There. Now something for me, to seal our pact.⟩ He bent, and delicately nibbled one of Bella's synthetic messengers. He would gain little from the exchange, since the isolate's prosthetic wanderers didn't convey much information. But the gesture was kind.

⟨Ah, Maitri's librarian. Thank you for fetching him, dear.⟩

To Bella's horror, the informal remark came from Yudisthara. He shot the beauty a glance of shocked reproach. Aditya screwed up his shapely nasal in cheerful mockery. ⟨Don't be scared! He's harmless!⟩; and pushed the librarian forward. Bella had to creep up, obediently, to the chief executive's couch.

The Silent merchant either had not noticed the furore by the pool, or he was pretending he hadn't. As Maitri used to say: Yudisthara wasn't a bad sort, but he was a dreadful coward. He'd ignore anything for a quiet life. But the visitor from orbit leaned across from his place beyond Yudi, his robe clinging to him in splendid glossy folds.

⟨This is your lone survivor? He must have a tale to tell.⟩

Bella had been thinking of the important visitor as an enemy of the Expedition . . . and none of his concern. He suddenly realised that this person had command over an outward-bound spaceplane.

⟨Unfortunately, yes, gracious sir. I stupidly happened to escape. Sir, you are so wonderful and powerful and good, you make me brave enough to ask, very humbly—⟩

⟨Yudi!⟩ Aditya's glorious presence completely swamped the librarian's grovelling. ⟨You had something for Bella?⟩

⟨Ah yes, ahem.⟩ Yudisthara produced a sheet of flimsy mauve tissue. The librarian, who, in his modest dependent's life, had rarely *seen* a bank note, stared at it in bewilderment.

⟨It's yours. That is, it's the reward we decided on for the local chap who rescued you and came looking for payment. Money seemed best, it doesn't commit us to anything. When we tried to hand it over he'd disappeared. We can't have them saying we don't pay our debts. You'd better keep it. The chap was Maitri's servant, and as you're the only one of his folk around . . .⟩

Maitri was dead because Yudisthara had abandoned the frontier posts to save himself from unpleasantness. Bella kept his eyes lowered. Reproaches were useless. Everything has to be forgiven, or how can life go on? But he couldn't smile. Poor Yudisthara, flustered, gave a hopelessly inappropriate chuckle, and tucked the folded tissue into Bella's unresisting palm.

⟨There now. I hope you'll be well enough to travel soon.⟩

⟨I'm well now! Sir, can't you let me go?⟩

The august visitor had forgotten his fleeting desire to hear the survivor's tale. He thought enough attention had been given to this distraction. He raised his voice.

'Will somebody tell me something about the local scheme called "taxation"?' He was a linguist, and spoke excellent English, but he pronounced the unfamiliar term with caution.

Aditya laughed merrily. 'It's a marvellous idea,' he crowed. 'Every household has to hive off part of the company resources into a common store, to be spent on public works. Yudi absolutely *hates* it. He thinks it *promotes economic growth*.'

Hate was hardly a strong enough word. Economic growth was Yudisthara's nightmare. He lived in terror of seeing this cancer of the giant planet transferred to Aleutia. The economic world is a plenum. How can any part of it have net *growth*, except by devouring its neighbours: shrinking markets, destroying diversity, killing trade? The prospect was horrific.

⟨Aditya, my dear,⟩ he pleaded. ⟨I'm sure our visitor has other interests. Can't we talk about something more pleasant?⟩

Aditya laughed. The minor royal was waiting impatiently, ignorant non-trader greed glinting in his eye. Yudisthara bowed to necessity. ⟨I have a statement on the subject, if you insist, sir.⟩ He nudged his speechmaker.

Bella's chance was gone. The tissue money felt evil against his palm. He was trapped for ever, alone in a hateful crowd. He could not bear it. With a muttered excuse, he got up and fled.

His room was in the hospital wing, beside the character shrine. He reached the open gallery that linked the main hall to the shrine and stopped to recover, leaning on a low carved rail. The doors of the Chapels of Rest were behind him, a dull garden in front. The 'carving' was an artisan's imitation of local woodwork.

Before the Protest, Aleutian commensals had replaced most of the wildlife of the Uji valley. They were already coming back, covering the scars. The river – the river Clavel had loved – was channelled and hidden. The valley was roofed over with the membrane the locals had agreed to accept as quarantine. Beyond it lay the heliport, once more functional, where freight from the Government of the World arrived; and where Maitri's librarian had touched down. His throat was filled with life. He encountered, like a long lost friend, the disappointment he had felt that

day: when the magical *Uji* turned out to be a place that looked,
smelled and tasted just like home.

How impossible his whole adventure seemed, since he'd been
breathing Aleutian air again. Immersed in this medium he
couldn't be anybody but Maitri's librarian, the hapless invalid.
He couldn't understand how he'd survived at all, and seriously
wished he had not. He found it very difficult to believe that he'd
ever had those long interviews with Seeker-after-truth, about
plots against the state, secret history and mythical treasure.

⟨Hello, librarian.⟩

It was Aditya, alone.

⟨I'm sorry—⟩ began Bella. The beauty stopped him. ⟨Don't.
You don't have to apologise, no one noticed.⟩

Bella was touched. It was kind of the beauty to come after
him, kinder still for him to come alone. Aditya had no absurd
train of walking appliances, but he had his retinue of friends. He
had divined, as few people did, that for an isolate a group
conversation is stressful and confusing. He drew Bella from the
rail, a hand tucked comfortingly into his arm.

⟨You're staying in the hospital, aren't you? I love the way it's
next to the Chapels of Rest: so thoughtful and convenient.⟩

He touched a door, and led Bella into the dry chill of the
funerary rooms. The cold tables lay empty. The dead of the
Protest had been burned to black ash. There had been ceremon-
ies. But no bodies from the massacres would lie here, desiccating
and crumbling: returning, particle by particle through the slow
commerce of the air, into the life of Aleutia.

⟨And now we wait,⟩ said Aditya grimly, ⟨to find out if our
enemies stole anything from that mass of Aleutian tissue.⟩

⟨What do you mean?⟩

⟨I mean proliferating weapons. Don't be naive, librarian. Real
weapons, grown from inert enemy tissue. You know how commensals are grown, don't you? though you can't have your own.⟩

People who wanted or needed personalised possessions grew
them from cultures of their own mobile cells, doped with artisan
secretions. It was an absorbing hobby, if you had the knack,
though the results were often clumsy and disappointing.

⟨Yes, of course.⟩

⟨The weapons people do that with dead flesh: muscle, fat,

bone, blood. If you raised a weapon from an enemy's wanderers, the first thing it would do is commit suicide. From dead flesh, you can grow things that will seek their own kind and *destroy*. That will proliferate and destroy, on every scale, for ever.⟩

Aditya grinned ferociously, as if building weapons of mass destruction was a wild, exciting game. He loved excess.

⟨I don't think they stole tissue,⟩ said Bella. ⟨It wasn't like that. It wasn't very well thought out.⟩

⟨You're right,⟩ agreed Aditya almost regretfully. ⟨It won't happen, not this time. But one day they'll realise there's no other way to get rid of Aleutians. If they really don't know how to build our style of weapons, they'll learn. Then we'd better watch out!⟩

The walls of the funerary rooms were lined with memorials to members of the Expedition who had died on earth. Clavel was there: and Bhairava, the security officer who had once been Maitri's marriage partner. Spaces were being prepared for a host of others. Aditya's name did not feature on this roll of honour.

⟨I wish I was here. I can't think why I'm not . . . What a ramshackle crew we were,⟩ he sighed. ⟨And how horribly things have changed. I don't mean to be unkind to poor Yudi but⟩ – he shrugged – ⟨I've seen it often. Someone has a great idea, and you start out: everything's brilliant. Oh, it was splendid when we were the landing parties. Then something goes wrong – the sabotage crisis, you know. To humour the faint hearts, you bring in some 'reliable' people. Suddenly, the whole enterprise is in the hands of the sensible folk.⟩ (Aditya's disdain for the *sensible* was sting in the air.) ⟨Who somehow have the ear of the Big People at home, the ones who never paid attention to you. You realise the situation is hopeless . . . I'm not surprised that the three captains have walked away from Uji. It's dreary. I don't know why I came back!⟩

While Maitri was shunted off to the frontier and abandoned to a horrible death, Aditya – long-time confederate of Rajath the trickster; and Rajath's marriage partner in his last life – had been welcomed with open arms. It was unfair: but inevitable. Nobody had worried about Aditya's loyalties. It was well known that Aditya the beauty, too lazy and too wild to covet power for himself, liked to be near it. He had been Rajath's lover when

Rajath was in command. Now he was with dull Yudi: and no one at Uji thought it strange. The beauty's whims were famous.

Aditya stopped halfway down the honour roll.

⟨You don't approve of me, do you, Bella?⟩

Bella had been thinking that the traders had made a vulgar error. Aditya was loyal, in his fashion. Lying with important people was his hobby. But if Rajath turned up here in rags tomorrow, with one of his crazy schemes, Aditya would be involved, instantly. These two were not true selves, not at all. Yet the bond between them was enduring – and dangerous! He didn't want to spoil Aditya's fun. What's the use of being a daring rebel, if nobody disapproves?

⟨Well, maybe not.⟩

⟨You aren't going to show throat to someone who makes an obligation out of lying down with the powerful? Oh yes, I know. But you're wrong about me.⟩ He swivelled around, back to the librarian. His hands shaped the nipped waist and swelling buttocks of a female local: he cast a sultry look over one shoulder in a perfect Jessica Rabbit.

'I'm not bad,' he drawled. 'I'm just drawn that way.'

Bella laughed. The beauty became himself again, grinning in triumph. ⟨You see! We're 'soulmates'. I love the 'movies' too. We're even the same 'sex'.⟩ He crossed the chapel, and recaptured Bella's arm. ⟨They called you a 'she', and I used to be 'Beautiful Girl'. It goes to show, doesn't it, the 'Women' have a long way to go to get on the winning side in that 'gender war'. With all the Expedition to choose from, who do the locals pick as honorary females? A 'cripple and a whore'!⟩

At Uji, Aditya's wit was as revered as his beauty. Bella refrained from pointing out a couple of errors in this joke. He was not immune to the famous charm. He felt suspicious, and distinctly foolish, to be singled out like this: but he didn't want the conversation to end. He'd been heading for his room. This was forgotten. Arm in arm, they strolled gently. Aditya's darting informal chatter, peppered with spoken English, reminded Bella of Maitri. It was very soothing.

⟨How I envy you your travels. Ah, but you've never seen 'Paris'. I was there before the wars. Such a wonderful place! Do you remember a banquet they gave for us in the 'restaurant Jules

Verne'? You must remember: the lights, the city spread beneath us like a magic carpet!⟩

⟨'Paris'!⟩ sighed Bella hungrily.

⟨Of course you want to know if I met 'Marcel'.⟩ Aditya took on an air of mystery. ⟨He never goes out. But very occasionally, if he hears of someone who interests him, he'll issue a very private invitation . . .⟩

⟨Er, I thought he hadn't been alive for a while—⟩

Aditya paused. ⟨What was that?⟩

⟨I said, I wish I thought I had a chance to meet him.⟩

⟨Ah!⟩ Aditya squeezed Bella's arm. ⟨How wonderful it is to talk to someone with a soul, a mind.⟩ He stroked the isolate's wan cheek. ⟨'*Wee sleekit, cowering, timorous beastie . . .*' You peep out of your lair so shyly. But there's someone special in there. I'm pleased with myself for spotting you, at last. You're like a secret no one else has guessed.⟩

They were standing on the covered bridge that had once spanned the river. They looked down to where the water ran, buried and silent. ⟨I forgot about Clavel,⟩ said Aditya softly. ⟨They called him 'she' too, in the beginning. A cripple and a whore and a goodie-goodie. Poor 'Women', what a profile! But how we miss him. I mean Clavel. We need our Clavel.⟩

⟨I thought you didn't like him.⟩

⟨I don't exactly *like* the Pure One. But I feel that he's necessary.⟩ He grinned. ⟨It's no fun being wicked, if nobody's pulling the other way. He's alive and on earth now, we say. We say he'll return to the giant planet for all the lives to come: to mourn alone, until his lover comes back. I wonder when that will be.⟩

Bella said nothing. Aditya glanced at him sidelong. ⟨But I hate gossip like that, don't you?⟩

He changed the subject. ⟨About these 'letterbombs'—⟩ Bella stiffened. Aditya caught his nape and gently shook him. ⟨Don't go isolate on me. You have a problem: perhaps I can help. How long has your halfcaste swain been persecuting you like this?⟩

He had vowed to tell no one, but after what had happened in hall it was useless to lie. ⟨Since I was hiding in Trivandrum,⟩ he admitted. ⟨I was sure it would stop. I don't know how he gets the things into Uji. I haven't tried to find out. I was—⟩

⟨You hoped that if you ignored it, the problem would go away,⟩ supplied Aditya. ⟨You're 'only human'. I won't ask if you did anything to encourage him.⟩

⟨I don't want to talk about it!⟩

⟨Hush, I said I won't ask.⟩ He frowned: a lovely disturbance of his alluring face. ⟨Just a moment: I think I saw one of the outside-freight handlers with a packet much like that. You could try. . . Oh, but those people *won't* be questioned. *Run away and play*, is their response to a mere signifier. But one of my own Silent has a friend in the delivery office. Bella, will you let me take this in hand? You needn't be involved.⟩

Bella was ready to agree to anything that meant the subject was closed. ⟨Thank you,⟩ he muttered.

He felt Aditya studying his averted face with curiosity.

⟨Suppose it had come to the point, and the locals had sent you for their 'gene therapy'! Weren't you terrified?⟩

He shrugged. ⟨I've spent a fair amount of time waiting for non-urgent hospital appointments. I didn't think it was a big risk.⟩

Aditya's laughter was a glorious explosion. ⟨Oh, unexpected librarian! You are a 'cool customer'!⟩

He took hold of Bella's meagre shoulders, turned him around and smoothed the folds of his modest, borrowed robe. ⟨You mustn't pester my 'honey bunny' about your passage home. He's bothered over the 'Himalaya Project'. It must go through. They had to beg us to come back, after chucking us out with menaces. We're in the ascendant, and we must let them know it. But when Yudi feels pressurised, he digs in his little heels. You leave him to me.

⟨Life isn't so bad here.⟩ He smiled. ⟨You must stop fighting it, that's all. You must come to my little cottage, and meet my 'guru': a rather intriguing engineer I brought back from home.⟩ He slid Bella an oblique glance. ⟨His name's Viloma. You know him?⟩

⟨I don't think—⟩

⟨I expect not. He's a materialist: a believer in the consciousness that resides in dead matter. He's had, well, difficulties. I'm rather a 'port in a storm'. I'm a sceptic, of course. But I admit I'm fascinated by the occult: *our* occult beliefs, that is, not theirs, which are simply 'mumbo-jumbo'. You can judge for yourself. I'm sure he'll interest you.⟩

The tropic heat of Karen was tempered in this valley, and the sunlight muted. It was late afternoon. Light had left the tinted membrane and indigo shadows filled the soft air. Bella stared at the buried river and felt the blood drum in his temples.

It was happening again. Either he was going mad, or *something* was happening. Why should Aditya flatter and pursue Maitri's librarian? Even the beauty's fondest admirers would admit that disinterested kindness was no part of his obligation.

Don't do this to me. Please, people, stop it. Don't you know you could drive someone crazy? If you keep on telling someone he isn't who he thinks he is, it isn't funny, it's frightening . . .

The cry remained stifled, locked inside.

⟨I know how it is,⟩ crooned Aditya, smoothing Bella's hair. ⟨When you get the whole picture it blends together, the good and the bad. You see there's no difference really: it's just life, the way life is. But when you only get dribs and drabs, you feel anxious and slighted at every turn. Poor librarian. You must stick close to me. I'll look after you.⟩

Darkness. Darkness striated with light. A slow adjustment and the skeins of fire and dust take on the form of an amoebic entity, connected over vast distances: like stringy, runny, swirls of beaten egg pervading a glass of murky liquid. It's all moving around the inside of a limitless sphere. 'Space,' says the voice of the letterbomber. '*The final frontier . . .*'

Then light shines on a large, softbodied woman with a mass of heavy golden hair knotted up on her head. Though you can see her clearly in colour, she's staring upward at a cloudless dark sky. You may realise, if you are at all familiar with the night skies of earth, that there are remarkably few stars visible: but a handful of the scattered points are very large, brilliant and new to you. Are they planets? Air-cruisers, satellites? No, they burn with the deep stillness of the constellations. As the sequence moves on, the light that bathes the big woman picks out colour in the foreground. The undergrowth she's treading has subliminal strangeness.

'These are the *stardate diaries*. These sequences have been loose on the samizdat of old earth for a long time. They appeared in the cablenet after the death of a scientist called Peenemunde Buonarotti. Buonarotti's career ended when the First Gender War began in Western Europe. She's forgotten now.' The heavy woman begins to fade (into the past). There is another night sky: and then another; and another. The heavy woman continues to fade . . .

'Results,' says the letterbomber. 'Nothing but results, no working-out. Someone left a trail of strange skies, we think it was Buonarotti. At a later date something else appeared in the net. It's a list of real stars, some extremely far away from us here on earth. Several of them are stars that have been identified by scientists, in the past, as planet-bearing candidates. Those of us who know about the *diaries* believe the inference is obvious. Those stars have planets, and Buonarotti visited them. The stardate skies *were drawn from life*.'

I need a bit of contemporary newsreel, thought Sid as he worked, sitting on the floor with his desk inside the 'limitless sphere'. *I need Peenemunde Buonarotti: place her and fix on her physical appearance. Need that before pasting her on the night skies sequence. And the foregrounds need work. Buonarotti painted night skies because to her the stars said it all. But it's also hard to make a generated image of a weird planet look –*

Suddenly he stopped working.

'Cut the playback, Lyd.'

The night sky collapsed. Sid pulled off his wrap. In a bare, functional little room, Lydia Carton presided over a heap of dun-coloured boxes. Roger was lying on his front in the dust beside them: alternately chewing something and trying to poke it into a crack in the concrete floor.

'This isn't working,' Sid announced.

Bella had fled, and they hadn't a hope of kidnapping her again. The Fat Man had decided they would attempt to win her over to their cause by persuasion. It was his idea that Sid should make the content of the letterbombs seem personal. If they fell into the wrong hands, the aliens would see an infatuated looty-lover performing a native ritual. But Bella, who had spotted Sid for an anti-Aleutian, would know there was more to it.

Sid had become convinced that the Fat Man knew everything

that had happened between him and Bella. Pride kept him from protesting, because he was sure his boss already knew that the 'lovelorn' campaign was causing Sid *untold pain and humiliation*. But he had decided unilaterally to use the *diaries* this time. They were supposed to be pursuing Bella for the sake of information she possessed without knowing it. It should make sense to try to jog her memory.

The *stardate diaries* had been precious to Sid when he was a child. He knew they were faked. Anyone could see that. Buonarotti had been unable to take a cam with her on her trips. She'd constructed the images afterwards, from memory. That didn't make her journeys less real! He had been miffed when he introduced the Fat Man to them, and found him unimpressed. Now that he was older, he could understand the Fat Man's reaction. The diaries were part of the legend. He still loved them: and they were junk. But that wasn't what was wrong with this letterbomb.

No, he said to himself. *This isn't working. She has no memories for us. She's an innocent bystander. The poor kid!*

The situation was intolerable. Sid was the one who was going to be innocent of the Gender War crimes, full parent to his children: and all without giving up a nanometre of his beloved masculinity. He'd dreamed of someday finding someone – girl for choice, boy would do if he was happy in the role – who would play the glamorous girl to Sid's boy wonder, view fun and nostalgia. Someone like him, who rejected the Gender War yet loved the game of gender difference.

But what happened? Life and the Fat Man had turned Sid the parent into an absentee father, Sid the aspiring movie hero into an unmanly creep who had sold his girl for a handful of *milk tokens*: and finally had him pestering this poor alien – who probably wasn't interested in Sid at all by now – like some mindless crypto-rapist waving his dick in the dark park.

I can't stand it! I won't do it! I can't go on with this!

She only wanted to be left alone. But there was no chance of that. She didn't know it yet, but there was nowhere she could run to get out of the way of the crossfire. He couldn't save her. He could only do what the Fat Man said was right: and hope. He pulled the desk towards him again, miserably.

Lydia was on to him at once. 'Daddy, what are you doing?'

'Starting again, it was no good.'

What should he tell his photochemical penpal? *Cactus is still
in a dreadful state. I need to get hold of a skinny female-to-male
transsexual with big hair, who plays electric guitar like an
angel, view lasting relationship. Do you know anyone . . . ?
Fingered me straight off, did you? What a bloody cheek. I WANT
YOU BACK, you sneaky two-faced little alien—*

'Daddee! That's not fair! We've been here *hours*!'

Oh, and remember how I wanted to spend time with my kids?

'I'll be as quick as I can.'

'Daddy, there's someone coming.'

Footsteps sounded in the corridor. Sid ran to the door: jumped
up, grabbed the rim of the glassed light above it, hung there
peering. The studio was supposed to be empty today. He'd
borrowed the printkey from a friend of a friend.

'It's the management! Everybody out.'

He ripped his meltoptics from the boxes, grabbed his desk and
Roger, and discovered to his horror that the thing the toddler
had been masticating was Lydia's pillbox, the fx generator on a
wrist-strap. It was soggy with baby slime.

'Are you part slug, Rogie? I've often wondered.'

'I wanted that.' Roger spoke seldom but with decision.

'Ssh.'

He hooked Lydia by one wrist and hauled everyone through
the back window: an escape he'd checked beforehand. They were
in an alley. Their exit was blocked by a vast, knobbly-hipped
brown cow. She had a collar round her neck which would say,
in Malayalam squiggle, that she was milked for an anti-cancer
vaccine or some such thing. There were loud, inquisitive voices
from the studio. 'Get out of my way!' yelled Sid. 'You're not a
sacred animal, you're a pharmaceutical production line!' The
cow – they knew their rights – sneered. Sid barrelled through,
hauling Lydia behind him. She was squealing, '*Daddee. I left my
pillbox!*' God help Roger when she saw it. He burst out into Man
Town, without an atom of energy to spare for *creating the right
impression*. So much for the near-Aleutian skill that permitted
Sid to blend in anywhere. Such is the life of a saviour of
humanity, in ungrateful times.

When he next heard from the Fat Man, the campaign was suspended. The letterbombs were being intercepted.

The persecution stopped. Bella did not know how it was done, and he didn't ask. He became a daily guest at the beauty's 'little cottage'. In the old days everybody had lived in the manor house. Over lives, cottages had sprung up throughout the grounds: after the Protest they'd quickly been restored. The smartest of the company escaped to these private retreats whenever duty allowed, not even returning to hall for the night unless specially summoned.

There was a proliferation of unearned Sanskrit titles at Uji. Aditya's friends, disdaining this vulgar ostentation, had decided to call themselves after characters from the local classic *Les Intermittences Du Coeur*, the moving-image transcription of the popular works of the Revd Marcel Proust. It had been Aditya's idea, they told the new recruit – though Aditya, transparently vain of his genuine Sanskrit, was always forgetting to be *Oriane, Duchesse de Guermantes*. They'd have renamed Bella, but the isolate protested he'd get too confused.

The materialist Viloma had also declined the honour. He said that he'd been given his earth name by his spirit guide: who was Samhukti, a cleric who had been Rajath's chaplain at first contact and who was not presently alive. Viloma had been recruited to the Expedition by Aditya when everyone from Uji was back on the shipworld during the Protest. His previous history was obscure: and his idea of *consciousness residing in dead matter* couldn't have been more different from the mysticism of Seeker-after-truth. He held seances, at which – Bella gathered – the believers sat around a piece of cloth with a dead person's decayed spit in it (or some such relic), asked questions and were given vague replies – transmitted by Viloma, of course.

Bella wondered what Samhukti would have to say about all this, if he came back while Viloma was around. He found it hard to be polite about this sort of thing. He'd managed to avoid attending the seances, which took place at night when the isolate was safely away from the cottage on medical grounds. He was grateful that Aditya tactfully dropped the idea that he would be 'fascinated' by the medium.

He came to suspect – strongly! – that it was the bored beauty, who didn't want to lose a new toy, who was blocking his passage home. He found he didn't mind. It wasn't as if he had anything to go home for. He would get there eventually. Meantime it was actively pleasant to be summoned from his room in the sick bay by a fashionable and friendly young trader, and 'carried off' in obedience to Aditya's commands. It was flattering to be in demand, because of his knowledge of the tv serial of *Proust*. (They had adopted the names, but they were as irreligious as most socially successful people, and knew nothing of the record itself.) He was highly privileged. People said that Yudisthara had to make his appointments at the cottage days in advance.

One morning he was summoned by Albertine, the more sensual of Aditya's two closest favourites. Aditya was often casually brutal about Bella's disability, but he never forgot what it meant. He always sent someone in person to fetch the isolate. He noticed that Albertine was full of suppressed excitement, but thought nothing of it. The 'little clan' could get excited over very little.

Aditya was taking breakfast with his household in a nest of local silk cushions. Alison de Vere's *Black Dog* played around the walls of the cottage's tiny 'main hall'. Francoise, a domestic who was a talented musician, was singing to them unaccompanied, in a mid-twentieth-century arrangement:

> 'Who knocks?' 'I, who was beautiful,
> Beyond all dreams to restore,
> I, from the roots of the dark thorn am hither.
> And knock on the door . . .'

⟨Superb,⟩ sighed Aditya: and then, jumping up: ⟨Good! The librarian's here. Let's get ready for the outing!⟩

⟨What outing?⟩

⟨Oh Bella, you know! We've been planning it for days. I've fixed up a quarantined 'jeep'. We're going into town!⟩

⟨To town? You mean to 'Karen city'? But—⟩

⟨Please stop repeating what I say. Hurry and get ready.⟩

Bella saw that Viloma was watching him silently, playing with a small mirror that he wore on a metal chain. The medium's stare unnerved him, making him feel it would be

awkward to persist. His medication often muddled things,
plunged him into embarrassing lapses. Celeste was at his elbow,
holding a basin and a roll of cleeno. He backed off: he'd met the
nasty stuff in Trivandrum.

⟨What's *that* for?⟩

⟨It's called 'cleeno',⟩ explained Aditya. ⟨Don't look disgusted.
We should try our own goods, don't you think? We're going to do
like the locals do, and give ourselves a good 'scrub' before we put
on our quarantine.⟩

Celeste took hold of Bella with the calm, bullying air of any
domestic to a signifier he doesn't know well. Aditya was rubbing
his hands vigorously over his own basin. Bella was forced to
surrender. ⟨Are you sure this is a good idea?⟩ he pleaded, wincing
under the domestic's ministrations. ⟨Does Yudisthara know
we're going?⟩

The little clan laughed.

⟨Oh, Bella! You know Yudi always takes my advice on local
affairs.⟩ Aditya tossed his fragment of cleeno to Albertine, and
slipped a small local-made box out of an overall pocket.

'Cigarette, anybody?'

'I'd love one,' cried Gilberte and Albertine together.

'Why don't you try one, Bella? It's a local drug called oneiricene, you suck this lollipop. The drug doesn't work for us, but
the lollipops are charming, don't you think?'

'The drug doesn't work?'

'None of them do, except alcohol, which must be a cosmic
constant or something.' Aditya tucked small white sticks into
his hair, and twirled for the company. 'Tell me somebody? Yes?
No?'

By the time they had decided whether cigarettes in the hair
were fun or not, a driver from the jeep pool was at the cottage
door. ⟨Don't be a spoilsport, librarian,⟩ coaxed Aditya. ⟨You're
isolate and you miss things, and then you make a fuss: it's silly.⟩
He grew dignified. ⟨This isn't entirely frivolous. It is time we
showed our faces to our neighbours, in an informal way. Nobody
will make a move unless I do it first.⟩

Francoise was handing out boluses of barrier jelly. Aditya,
Viloma, Albertine and Gilberte were soon blooming from head
to foot in the sheen of quarantine film: and Bella too.

Their jeep passed slickly though the membrane where it came to ground level, and clambered into the trackless thickets that closed the southern end of the valley. There had been a road here once, until Mr Kaoru had advised the Aleutians to have it blocked. That was long ago. Uji had been becoming more separate from the human world ever since. The three captains had humoured the locals, participating in their needless rituals of deadworld communication. The last trace of those arrangements had vanished with the Protest, and would not be allowed back.

At length the jeep's driver hit on a local road. Buildings began to appear, and thickened. The jeep deployed its wheels. This was Karen City, a name resonant in Expedition history. The Aleutian party sat up and began to pay attention.

⟨I hope nobody makes a scene,⟩ muttered the librarian cravenly. ⟨I hate scenes.⟩

⟨I love 'em,⟩ grinned Aditya.

He was to be disappointed. There was no hostile reaction to the superbeings. Perhaps the 'bugs' of Aditya's bogey tales were a reality, and the locals had been forewarned and had time to compose themselves. Some traffic halted, some people stopped to stare. But the jeep went on its way unmolested.

⟨Poor things,⟩ sighed Gilberte, the aloof and sensitive one of Aditya's rival best friends. ⟨I always sympathise with losers.⟩

Albertine was a natural optimist. ⟨I expect they're glad to see us! They're probably longing for Aleutian tourists.⟩

No one was sure what to do next. Aditya, apparently satisfied simply to have broken out of Uji, had curled into a corner of the back seat, and relinquished command. Viloma had withdrawn into a forbidding gloom. Albertine and Gilberte made halfhearted suggestions.

⟨Is there something famous we could see?⟩

⟨Can we buy something? Who has anything we could trade?⟩

⟨Let's eat something weird!⟩

And, rather forlornly, ⟨Maybe we should go back now—⟩

But Aditya suddenly woke up and lunged at the jeep's window, impelled almost through the membrane in his eagerness. 'Look! There's a karyotype booth. I want to have my fortune told!'

⟨Stop, driver! Stop right here.⟩

Bella didn't know what a 'karyotype booth' was. He would not have considered having his fortune told at home. He wasn't that sort of person. But he got out obediently. In the jeep they'd been in the microclimate of Uji. The heat and weight of the air outside engulfed him. The smell and taste of it, through his quarantine, filled him with a shock of nostalgia for the trek, for Sid; for Trivandrum. It frightened him. He wanted to get back in the car. At the kerbside a local, a young man with his eyes covered by a green sun-visor, slid from the back of a spindly sort of teksi.

⟨Something wrong, librarian?⟩ It was Viloma.

He took Bella's arm. ⟨Oh, thank you.⟩ He didn't think the materialist had ever touched him or spoken to him directly before. The contact was not pleasant, but he was grateful for it.

⟨I felt dizzy, it's nothing.⟩

They followed the others up several flights of damp, dead cement stairs. The fortune-teller's booth had a medical air. It was very clean. A woman sat behind a counter. Non-living machinery clustered beyond a screen so frigidly clear it must be pure glass. Bella could not see a recording desk.

⟨Where do we make the record for 'her' to read?⟩

Albertine and Gilberte stared at the fortune-teller. ⟨You called him a 'she' word! Can you tell them apart straight off?⟩

Aditya laughed. ⟨Not *that* kind of fortune-telling. This is 'karyotype' reading. One provides a sample of tissue, it goes into those non-living machines. They make a print of your basic identity, what they call your 'genotype'. Then the fortune-teller gives you a personality reading, from 'her' charts.⟩

Bella felt that he was missing something important. He recalled Aditya's cheery lecture on proliferating weapons.

⟨*We give away tissue?*⟩ He must have misunderstood.

The others laughed.

⟨Don't panic, librarian,⟩ soothed Aditya. ⟨Not *inert* tissue. I'm not asking you to hand over a free gift of weapon-starter! A wanderer will do: there's no harm in that.⟩

⟨But we're in quarantine. And I'm isolate, remember.⟩ Bella attempted a laugh. ⟨I haven't many to spare.⟩

⟨Ah, but *fortunately*, we've brought along some freshly used towels. We'll take wanderers from them. It doesn't matter that yours aren't real. They were made to match you.⟩

Giggling, Albertine produced the soiled cleeno.

The Karen woman behind her screen watched the silent byplay between the aliens, and never stirred. But Bella saw that she was not impassive. In her reserved dialect of the Common Tongue she was saying that it made no difference. She wouldn't have to touch anything. The machinery was sterilised between clients. Since the Protest had failed and the aliens were here to stay, it was better to make a profit out of them somehow.

'I don't think we should do this,' said Bella, trembling but goaded into formal protest. He didn't know what was going on, but *something* was. 'This ritual is for locals. It's meaningless for us. We know who we are, what can she tell us?' He looked from face to face: 'Engineer, surely you agree?'

Viloma folded his arms. ⟨Aditya is my patron here.⟩

The boy in the green sun-visor came into the booth. His cropped head and the strangely knitted muscles of his bare legs gleamed with moisture. It must have started to rain. He spoke, in the local formal dialect. 'Is there someone here called Bella?' Without waiting for a reply, he came up to Bella and bowed.

'Message for you, miss. I'm a polite boy.'

The boy scooted out of the door. Forgetting that he was isolate and could not run, Bella leapt after him. He ran two-footed, hands encumbered by the package. There were people on the stairs, gabbling: they'd come to see the aliens. Bella broke through them into a warren of streets, and finally into a square walled with display windows. It was pumped full of air as dry and cold as a mortuary. The boy had vanished. Bella dropped into a helpless crouch, his head pounding, heart beating like thunder. There was no one about. He saw that there was a tab to pull this time. He pulled it. Sid leapt into existence. Inside the bubble it was a sunny afternoon on the North West Frontier, and Maitri was still alive. Sid was in his Aleutian overalls, holding a rose.

Si je t'aime prends garde de toi.

'I won't go away, Bel. I'm never going to leave you alone.'

⟨Another of them. Poor librarian.⟩

Aditya had caught up.

It was a short message this time. Sid vanished without speaking again. The rose remained on the floor of the street. Aditya dropped beside Bella. Boldly, he passed his hand through the illusion.

⟨It feels of *nothing*. How eerie.⟩

In the middle of the square there was a stone bench beside a plot of local greenery. Bella went over to it and crouched, knees reversed, head bowed. Aditya walked around the rose, studying it from every angle.

'I thought I'd put a stop to this.'

⟨It doesn't matter.⟩

Aditya came and sat beside him, and touched him gently. ⟨You don't really want it to stop, do you?⟩

Everyone seemed to know that Maitri's librarian had done lying-down things with his halfcaste guide. Bella didn't mind them knowing, or at least he didn't care. It was easier to talk about it, since he and Aditya were in quarantine: both isolate.

⟨I'm isolate,⟩ he said bitterly. ⟨Beggars can't be choosers. Yes, I lay with him. And I liked it. Lying down with him I wasn't disabled, he missed nothing. It was wonderful. But no, I don't want him hanging around. What's the point?⟩

Aditya sighed. ⟨I've felt the same. It's very sad. One can't take them home, poor things.⟩

In the beginning there'd been some local visitors to the shipworld. It hadn't worked. They were out of place and couldn't make themselves understood. The experiment had been abandoned. The Aleutians sat in silence, mourning Bella's loss.

⟨I've had an idea, librarian. Why don't we take a trip to the north? Into old earth? That should shake him off. I know there's a war going on, but it won't affect us. The Protest's over and I'm tired of Uji. I want to revisit the old haunts. We could go to 'Paris', and eat at the 'restaurant Jules Verne' . . .⟩

'I think the "Eiffel Tower" isn't there any more.'

⟨Isn't it? Never mind, there are other places.⟩

Bella watched the rose slowly fading into nothingness.

⟨I'm sorry about the 'karyotype' prank,⟩ said Aditya. ⟨It was just a tease. Do you forgive me? Say you do.⟩

It was Aditya's obligation to give pleasure. The right strokes flowed from him naturally, like the abundance of wanderers that told you how wonderful it would be to lie with him. There didn't have to be any plot behind his surprising enthusiasm for Proust, his sudden respect for Clavel the Pure. His whims were famous. He'd taken a fancy to the obscure isolate, and his natural skill did the rest. There need be nothing behind it . . .

Who is it who wants to be sure of who I am?

Bella thought of that question, which he was not going to ask. Somewhere in the days since Aditya had adopted him, he had stopped being frightened. He had been given a clue to follow in Trivandrum. The strangeness that had gathered around him since he arrived on earth was no longer so bewildering.

⟨What do you say? Will you come?⟩ Aditya poked him in the flank with a shrewd, silvered finger. ⟨What's the matter? Don't you trust me, librarian? You know, I do truly like you.⟩

Truth is prolix and inexhaustible as the Self. There is no need to lie, there is always some truth you can tell. The beauty's admiration could be genuine, why not? Bella's sadness over giving up Sid was real pain: it was also good camouflage. *Good heavens*, he thought. *I'm becoming a secret agent!*

⟨*Nobody* trusts you, beauty. But I've heard you're fairly harmless if Rajath's not around.⟩

⟨Oh, him. He's a child at present, you know. I can't wait . . . I mean, I can't hang around waiting for him to catch up.⟩

Bella laughed. ⟨All right. I'll come.⟩

They left the square arm in arm.

In the cottage, about an hour before dawn, Aditya knelt in front of a mirror. He was alone. Everyone else was asleep in the main room. Outdoors a blue glimmer dimly suffused the valley. Inside a single silver lamp burned: the flame alive and dead, visible and bodiless. A screen of imitation bamboo shifted, a figure slipped inside. Aditya continued to gaze into the mirror with the severe, absorbed attention that beauty gives to beauty: but with a different and strange glamour added to beauty's charm.

⟨You are completely mad,⟩ she said, without turning. ⟨Worse than mad, *stupid*.⟩

The intruder came and knelt behind Beautiful Girl, lifted a bunch of black ribbon-hairs and buried his face in her cool nape.

⟨You think Yudi will burst in and tear my throat out?⟩

⟨If he bursts in, it will be to offer you a nice cup of soup, I should think. *You know what I mean.*⟩

⟨It might have worked. It was worth trying. When are you going to seduce him?⟩

Aditya's shoulders lifted. ⟨The eternal masculine . . .⟩ she marvelled. ⟨That's an *incredibly* stupid idea.⟩

⟨But he'd be thrilled. He'd become your abject slave.⟩

⟨You speak for yourself. Feminine people are different. Besides: try to *think* for a moment. Why should I want to do it with a cripple? For fun? Out of vulgar curiosity? I'm supposed to be his friend. D'you think he'd believe I'd fallen in love? Don't be ridiculous. Maitri's librarian is not an idiot.⟩

The beauty's visitor conceded this.

⟨Do you think he suspects?⟩

⟨You tell me. He is a 'cool customer'. I'm sure he suspects *something*.⟩ Aditya's tone became modestly complacent. ⟨When was I ever not up to mischief? I believe he doesn't care. Maitri is dead, and somehow he can't get home (white teeth glinted). What has he to lose? I think he doesn't care what happens to him. That's what I believe, and I admire him for it,⟩ she added thoughtfully. ⟨I truly do.⟩

⟨Now you're trying to make me jealous. The eternal feminine!⟩

They laughed together silently, enjoying their alien game: perfectly innocent. ⟨You'll go on helping me,⟩ he coaxed, sure of her. ⟨Though you think what we're doing is idiotic and dangerous and wrong?⟩

The beauty smiled on him, mother and whore: unsparingly honest, endlessly indulgent. ⟨Will I serve you, though you are a childish, dangerous fool? Because, my dear. Because.⟩

On the morning after they arrived in London, Bella stood looking out of the window of her hotel room. It was a strange room, filled with ramshackle and gaunt non-living furniture that didn't seem to belong. Between the buildings he saw a figure worked in high relief on a slab of grey stone, the remains of a larger monument. A four-wheeled cab hummed by, interrupting his view. In Trivandrum young locals: Hafzan, Katalamma, had spoken of old earth with pride and envy. It was the *real* world, where humanity's life was lived. But it seemed to Bella that he'd travelled into the past. This remote city, untouched by Aleutia, was the earth of Maitri's first-contact records: full of dead vehicles, foul smells and grotesque sights.

Last night the Allies, their hosts, had taken Aditya's party on an excursion through the fitfully lit streets. In a night market they saw a stall selling live figurines: adult female humans, half life size. They sat or lounged on dusty draped shelves in scraps of bright-coloured clothes, gazing around them idly. Aditya instantly wanted one. But the stallholder had objected and the Allied soldiers burst into scandalised laughter. Their guide, a government official, said the figures were 'sextoys' – 'not sentient, but grown from living tissue. Like your commensals.'

Everything was in decay. But there was a scale of construction under the dirt that gave the Aleutians vertigo. London had been built by giants. The giants had vanished, or else something had shrunk them until they crept about the broken bones of their city, the size of wanderers.

Aditya came into the room and stood looking over Bella's shoulder. 'Who is that?' asked Bella. 'The statue?'

They had travelled straight to London, in long stages by

chartered air-cruiser. Aditya had decreed on their arrival that the signifiers had to speak formal English on all occasions. He wanted to relive the landing parties' triumphant world tours.

'Someone called Edith Cavell.'

'What does the lettering say?'

'You can't read, of course. If I remember, it says "Patriotism is not enough. I must have no hatred or bitterness towards anyone." Strange but true. They have their Clavel, we have ours, with the same obligation to goodie-goodie. Funny if they should meet!' He gave Bella a sly glance. ⟨The poet's retreat is around here, we think. Suppose you and I paid him a visit?⟩

'I think I'll wait until I'm invited.'

Aditya grinned at the reproof, but he was unwontedly serious as he looked at the statue: ⟨I told you the truth, at Uji. I don't like the way the Expedition is without Clavel. But you shouldn't put your faith in heroes. It's the way to get hurt. Only love people you know to be even more self-serving and wicked than yourself: that's my advice.⟩

Though England was supposedly secure, traditionalist territory London was unsafe, a haunt of terrorists and bandits. This didn't bother Aditya, but the constant interference of their military escort annoyed him. The tourists left almost immediately for Manchester, another city further north.

A few days later Bella was in a green garden on the outskirts of that place, looking at a small stone cross that stood half buried in wildlife growth. A select core of signifiers from the 'little clan' of Uji clustered around: Gilberte and Albertine, Viloma the materialist; and a dour almost silent middle-aged person who was Aditya's long-suffering housekeeper. Bella didn't know him and had not noticed him much at Uji. He'd been called *Morel* – another *Les Intermittences* character. There was a running joke about this, because they were trying to get Viloma to call himself *Baron Charlus*: and in the tv serial Morel was the Baron's faithless lower-rank lover. Neither Viloma nor the housekeeper seemed to find the idea amusing.

Albertine had Aditya's *Braemar and Johnny Guidebook* open and was scanning the frames. It was a local artefact from before the war, made for the Aleutian tourist market. Aditya had

produced it when they left Uji, and he unveiled his travel plans.
Albertine found the place and the little clan compared glyphs on
the stone with the recorded image.

CONSTANCE MARY WILSON
(BRAEMAR)
1988–2044

Fail again. Fail better.

A gardener who had followed them from the gates stood staring.
He was not hostile. He remarked informally that they were the
first *holefaces* he'd met. He was wondering why they were here.

Aditya, forgetting that it wasn't old-earth etiquette to notice
an informal question from a stranger, went over casually and
cast a friendly arm around his shoulders.

⟨You're surprised that we honour a hero of your resistance? But
I admire the saboteurs passionately! We all do. They were
prepared to give not only their lives, but more: to commit
genocide, to make themselves *evil*, for a noble cause. That's
superb. You may be surprised to hear it, but in the shipworld
'Braemar and Johnny' are almost as popular as 'Marcel Proust'!⟩

The gardener gaped. 'Marcel Proust?' he gasped, in accents of
panic and bewilderment. ⟨Don't touch me! Don't infect my
mind!⟩ He dragged himself free and fled across the graves.

'How odd—'

'I think he was afraid of you,' explained Bella.

Aditya recovered from the shock of having failed to charm.
'Nonsense. That's *your* fault, librarian. You and your obsolete
soap operas. He obviously despises Proust.'

The signifiers, having seen the required sight, drifted away to
peer at other graves: Albertine exclaiming what a charming idea
it was to plant the dead in gardens. Bella stayed by the grave.

For a short period, in the years before the war, Aleutians had
visited earth freely. Braemar Wilson's burial spot had been part
of a recognised tourist trail. There had been a trodden path to
this spot and stalls of Braemar memorabilia at the gates. Bella
preferred the melancholy quiet. He shared the poet-captain's
famous view of foreign travel. *People are the same everywhere,*

strangers are strangers wherever you meet them. Traffic hummed on the ancient road. From the ground the dead returned, particle by particle into the life of their world. The wildlife grasses stirred and murmured, and tiny flying things darted about. There was more lettering under the dates, inscribed within a smaller, elaborately worked cross. Bella peered at it. He always looked carefully at local lettering in odd places, in case he spotted Seeker-after-truth's password.

⟨I wish I could read.⟩

'It says, "For Valour". That's the Victoria Cross. The highest military honour we have. It was awarded posthumously, at the time of the Panama Trench crisis.' Bella didn't look around. He stayed very still, poised between exasperation and joy. He knew the voice, of course.

'They awarded her a posthumous rank as well. She's Captain Wilson. She'd've liked that. She was a confirmed-and-out traditionalist, our Braemar. She knew it was poisonous nonsense: the sex games, the nationalism, death and glory. She loved it anyway. I'm sure you remember the Trench incident. It could have been our first Protest, but it never got that far. A few governments made provocative gestures – like awarding the VC to the woman who tried to destroy you. It fizzled out and Braemar was forgotten again. You're the ones who remember the saboteurs.'

Bella turned. There was Sidney Carton. He was wearing dull green and standing barely an arm's length away, just within the encroaching shrubbery.

'What month is it?'

The corners of the apparition's mouth twitched, his stubby lashes flickered. 'It's June,' he said. 'It's a year since you left me. Why d'you want to know?'

He had wanted to know because Sid, speaking aloud about Braemar, was speaking informally about a dreadful lapse of time. Bella was not aware of one. He'd asked the question without thinking: he realised that the ghost had answered. This must be an interactive letterbomb. Then, like a breaking and reforming of reality, he knew that it was *Sid* standing there.

How long is a year? He saw Sid walking out of the safe room in Trivandrum: preoccupied, guilty and haggard from their long

journey. How long since that night? That interlude with Sid had
been a fantasy, an illusion . . . so he'd told himself. But Bella
had forgotten how real the illusion could seem. He couldn't
speak or move. There was a murmur of chatter, like a tinge of
Aleutian identity slipping through his quarantine. The others
were coming back. Sid vanished into leafy darkness.

Their host in Manchester was someone called Kershaw, an old
friend of Aditya's who had once worked for the Aleutian Affairs
Office of the Government of the World. Some of his men were
waiting at the cemetery gates for the Aleutians, in armoured
jeeps. His security was less officious than the Allied government
version, but it was impossible to get rid of an escort entirely.

Bella said nothing about Sid. The Aleutians returned to the
big house on Kershaw's fortified estate, where they had a sealed
suite, cleared of occult devices and the eerie amenity of indoor
running water, in which they could dispense with quarantine.
Bella went to rest as usual. On his way to rejoin the others he
met a human child with arrogant eyes, who was lurking on the
stairs.

'Are you as ancient as Aditya?' demanded the infant, peering
at him through the antibiotic screen.

'Aditya's not ancient!'

'She is! Old as old! My grandfather says so!'

The child scurried away. On the wall of the stairway hung a
large and bad still portrait, lifelike but completely lifeless. Bella
recognised the subject: *Ellen Kershaw*. This was the 'Kershaw'
who had been an Aleutian-watcher at first contact, the person
Aditya had known. She'd been dead for many years.

It wasn't that Aditya didn't understand this. He knew about
human mortality. But it meant nothing to him, so he ignored it:
Kershaw was Kershaw. In one of the halls below there was wall-
sized matte display of a big half-wild garden, mysterious in
twilight, with a river running through it. Bella had admired the
lovely scene for a while, before he understood that this was Uji:
Uji as it had been when Aditya was last on earth; as no human
alive had ever known it. Across so much that was the same, he
glimpsed the impossible disjoint, the abyss between Aleutia and
humanity that could not be crossed. It was time.

In the room they'd made their main hall, Aditya was curled

on a huge bed-with-legs, eating perfumed crackly sweets from a glass bowl and comparing maps of Europe in the *Braemar and Johnny Guidebook* with the modern versions.

The tourists' itinerary had changed. Aditya had decided that Paris was too dangerous, and was looking at Eastern Europe. He wanted to track down a particularly obscure site, a tourist coup on the *Braemar and Johnny* trail. It was a sarcophagus – a nuclear accident monument – which had an obscure connection with the saboteurs. Bella had wondered if Aditya's enthusiasm for Braemar and Johnny was assumed for his benefit: more librarian-stroking. He thought not. The other signs were that Aditya's fancy for an obscure invalid had reached its peak with the invitation to come on this trip. It was now rapidly waning.

⟨What's the matter, librarian? Are you ill?⟩ Aditya's curiosity was perfunctory. He tossed the maps aside. ⟨Oh, who cares? We'll have one of those cars that knows where to go.⟩ He choked, and spat out a mouthful of the snack. ⟨Augh! I adore hard food, but this is vile!⟩

⟨I think you're supposed to smell that, not eat it.⟩

Celeste swooped to deal with the mess. ⟨Beauty, don't be disgusting! What will the locals think!⟩

Their rooms were meant to be clear of deadworld eyes, but the Silent took it for granted that this was a good-mannered lie.

Aditya shot Bella an irritated glance. ⟨I thought I said we were to speak aloud. Don't just stand there, librarian. Eat.⟩

It was possible to eat while wearing quarantine, but it wasn't convenient or pleasant. Pureed and cooled food was sent up to them in their suite. It was uniformly vile, nothing like the Trivandrum dishes Bella remembered.

'I'm not very hungry,' he said in English, meekly accepting the beauty's inconsistency.

⟨Then get into your quarantine and robe. Quickly! You're isolate and you don't pay attention and then you make us all late. It's time to go downstairs.⟩

This household had no evening prayers. The only screens that were considered important were the banks of security monitors in the guardroom, and watching them was usually left to the machines. Instead of gathering in front of the movies or the 'tv news' the Kershaw clan gathered in a secure underground hall for a prolonged evening meal. The Aleutians joined the assembly after the tables-with-legs had been cleared of food.

Kris Kershaw, their host, had discovered that Bella spoke fluent English. He talked to her about the outing planned for tomorrow night, to a sensei club at Castlefield down in the city. Old earth's sensei nightclubs were famous, and Aditya had insisted on visiting one in spite of the risks. Kershaw was in good control of his informal speech: unusually so. But he was nervous. He confessed he found the beauty's attitude to danger alarming.

On his cheekbone, beside the opening of his left ear, clung a small black object like a cosmetic patch. It was his connection with the guardrooms. Sometimes in conversation he would stop talking and listen: and murmur briefly for the pickup on his throat. The big hall was illuminated by fiery balls of light that hung in the air: dead things alive and moving. Death in life was all around them. Bella thought how far he'd travelled since he had last seen his home.

He left the company early as usual, just as the guests had embarked on an exhibition of Aleutian evening dances. Gilberte and Albertine were performing 'Everything Says I' as a duet to the mouth-music of Aditya's Silent ensemble. One of the domestics had given him a light for the dark passages. It had been instructed to follow him at shoulder height. As they reached the stairway to the aliens' suite it darted away. Bella found it under the stairs, perched on a fat stack of glistening, brown-skinned mudpats. They were Aleutian discrete-energies: discs.

Kris Kershaw must have good connections. It was supposed to be impossible to get hold of Aleutian products this far north. The fireball sipped like a feeding insect. Bella watched it: thinking of the awkwardness of official tourism after the freedom of his life in Trivandrum, remembering Mykini and the travellers' convoy.

Tonight he did not feel like a secret agent. He didn't want to think about what these discs might mean. The apparition in the garden had upset him. It must have been a hallucination, or a new kind of letterbomb. Sid mustn't be here!

The light rose again to his shoulder. They climbed slowly – Bella was very tired – past false windows (there were no real windows in the outer walls, this was a house built for wartime) that showed monitoring of the Kershaw estate. Lights upon

lights glittered in the dusk, outlining squat towers and sparse
gardens, and the concrete ramps and walkways that linked long
bunker-like living halls. At the antibiotic screen, the fireball
drifted away. Bella pushed through a curtain of clinging gel and
went to his own room, away from the others at the end of the
corridor. A light by the bed came up softly as he entered, the
door closed behind him. The bed was local style, with legs and a
separate quilt. Sidney Carton was sitting on it.

Bella walked past the breathing ghost, sat at the head of the
bed and reached for his medical pouch. A hand closed over his
wrist. Sid spoke, in the Common Tongue.

⟨You look dreadful. You were better off without that stuff.⟩

Bella stared at the hand. Sid felt the shudder that went through
her: but she was not surprised, nor frightened. ⟨Please don't call
me 'she'. I know I'm small and weak and physically vulnerable.
I don't need to be reminded of it all the time.⟩

⟨Is that what you think it means?⟩ He released his grip. ⟨I'm
sorry.⟩ He nodded to the view of dark and glittering towers
through the room's false window. ⟨I was born on an estate like
this one. I never planned to come back.⟩

She was very still, her gaze unwavering. ⟨Are we being
watched?⟩

⟨Probably, but only by machines. Don't speak aloud.⟩

⟨Ah, I see.⟩

⟨Aren't you going to ask me how I got in?⟩

She shrugged a little. ⟨You're a secret agent. I suppose you can
do secret-agent things.⟩

Sid laughed, a silent glimmering. ⟨Remember, I said I'd never
leave you alone? You should have known I'd be around, as soon
as you left Uji. This is the first chance I've had. Your host let me
in. You see, he's what you'd call an anti-Aleutian fanatic.⟩

Bella barely reacted. ⟨Oh, is that it? I knew there was something funny.⟩

He smiled, a little grimly. ⟨Yes. An anti-Aleutian, but a good
friend of your friend the beauty. Kris is being paid – in discs and
other goods – to make trouble for the Expedition. He thinks his
alien friends have promised in return to kill the Himalaya
Project. I told him I needed to see you over a similar kind of
double-dealing: he believed me. Actually, I'm *very* interested in

Aditya myself . . . for the same reason you are, I guess. This business is getting complicated, Bella.⟩

Her quarantine had begun to disintegrate in the Aleutian air of the closed suite. She rubbed shards of it from her face: watching him carefully all the while.

⟨You mean, the treasure hunt?⟩

The letterbombs had never mentioned the *instantaneous travel device* by name. But there had been an acceptance, almost from the beginning, that Bella knew the truth: knew that she had been kidnapped, knew Sid was a secret agent, knew that she was supposed to possess information about that mythical marvel . . . There had been an assumption, even, that Bella had become interested in the fate of the device on her own account. Sid saw, something he hadn't known for sure until this moment, that the messages had all been read. They were like colleagues, exchanging notes about the game in which they were rival players. It was a version of reality that felt strangely comfortable and good.

⟨I don't suppose you'd consider telling me Aditya's travel plans? My boss thinks we ought to know—⟩

His illusion was shattered by the sudden hurt in her eyes.

⟨Ask him yourself,⟩ she snapped. ⟨Ask 'Kershaw'.⟩

Briefly, her whole body drew itself together, twisting into the animal configuration. He saw the effort it took her to relax that betraying pose, the tensed limbs of a small beast poised to flee. She managed it, but she looked so unhappy, so *cornered*, it was all Sid could do not to burst into tears.

Formally erect, she accused him. ⟨*I need you desperately*,⟩ she quoted, with bitter irony. ⟨I didn't think that was very funny, Sid. What is it you *really* need, you and your boss? Don't tell me you still believe I can lead you to the treasure, because I know that's not true. *I don't understand*. Why won't you leave me alone?⟩

And he couldn't answer. He hung his head like a bad child.

⟨I can't explain.⟩

Dry curls of quarantine floated to the floor, twisting like dead leaves in the faint warmth from her bedside lamp.

⟨You'd better go,⟩ she said.

⟨All right, I'm going.⟩

He didn't move. It was so strange to be *talking to her*, in the intimacy of silence. The only time they'd done this before was in the travellers' camp.

⟨The bombs were part of a plan I don't understand myself. *But it's true that I need you.*⟩ He made this confession staring at her bedspread. It was pink and blue, it had a vaguely nasty pattern. He looked up, not sure how far he could bear to abandon his pride. But in the Common Tongue you can say anything.

⟨Possibly even desperately. But it's just too bad, isn't it?⟩

She sighed. She nodded. ⟨Yes. It's just too bad.⟩

They glanced at each other, sidelong.

Kershaw had agreed that this interview would be private. Sid assumed that the machines were watching, anyway. They'd learn nothing. Even the nuances of body language by which Sid 'called Bella she' – exasperating to the librarian – would be invisible to an old earth monitoring system.

The cameras, if they were running, recorded that the alien and Sidney Carton sat silent and almost unmoving for several minutes. Finally they turned to each other and embraced: at first sadly, like parting lovers – and then, as the universal balm wiped away all complications, all reserves, with perfect confidence.

The Castlefield site was domed to keep out air-raids. This was an area of the city notorious for terrorist action. There were several clubs under the dome: gaming hells, history worlds, adventure playgrounds of all kinds. The Aleutians arrived at dusk, in quarantine film and shrouded in chadors. It was a small party. To Kershaw's evident relief the Silent had elected to stay behind.

Aditya was in a bad temper. Last night he'd commissioned the Kershaw women to buy nightclub masks for the little clan. Today specious apologies had been delivered. The beauty knew that Kershaw had interfered, afraid of the scandal of an alien tourist openly dabbling in the deadworld. Kershaw was always a narrow fool. But he should know by now that Aditya the beauty never cared for scandal, and was accustomed to do exactly as he pleased . . .

At the gates they met a male group of African, Russian and Chinese journalists who were in Europe covering the war. They were in on the secret. Thereupon a party of foreign visitors and their veiled wives entered the dome. The disguise should be adequate for most circumstances. Kris Kershaw led them into a darkness shot with sound and light (it reminded Bella of the spectators' gallery at the mall in Trivandrum). They passed through a transparent marquee of scintillating purple stars. Inside it there was music, a dancefloor and leggy groups of tables and chairs. The floor was empty. They settled around a table. One of the Africans, Roy Ifekaozor, rounded up extra chairs.

'What is a sensei club?' asked Bella. 'I thought a sensei was a deadworld entity running a game?'

Roy started. 'You're a talker? A signifier, excuse me.'

Mr Kershaw leaned across the table. 'Bella speaks excellent English. Be careful of your "formal statements"!'

The cleric smiled. 'A sensei is a "deadworld entity". But the nightclub ones are no more than smart sound-and-light systems. There's no need to be afraid.'

To the Aleutians the journalists were priests, who recorded aspects of WorldSelf's myriad variety for religious purposes: this made them daunting company. The journalists, meanwhile, were not sure what they could properly say aloud, in 'formal speech', and were afraid of giving away secrets in the Common Tongue. And Aditya was sulking. Conversation was strained at first. But these clerics, off-duty, proved to be far from solemn. The Russians and the Chinese ordered beer, the Africans ordered vodka. Mr Kershaw ordered Mekong, Thai whisky, in honour of the Aleutians' Thailand connection. It came with a colourless fizzing liquid called 'mineral water' that Roy pronounced to be laced with the house hallucinogen. It was routine, he said. The drug was cheap, and covered the deficiences of the sensei. Their dumb waiter refused to incriminate itself. Roy's pocket analyser confirmed his guess.

'Knock it back! We're here to have fun!'

They had the marquee to themselves. Bella suspected that Kershaw had picked an unpopular spot, to cut down on Aditya's opportunities for mayhem. The void-force entity sensed that there were paying customers looking at an empty floor. It began to fill the space with fx: giant insects, fantastic beasts and birds, the famous dead.

Jungtao the Chinese explained to Albertine that modern telecoms were nothing like as efficient as the aliens supposed.

'Global satellite communication has become a magical operation! The armies shoot ephemerals into orbit with their railguns: where they live briefly and then decay. The USSA does the same, biodegradable satellites is all we have. As an outsider, all you can do is fire up and hope. If you're in the right place, right time, right incantations something happens. It's barely different from *chance*, it's like filing stories by parapsychology. Cable's the thing in civilised countries, has been for a hundred years. But in the battlefield situation either you're out of the net, or those devils have cut the cable, the *bastards*, *destroyers of worlds*. You have to use a receiverless global or nothing.' His vivid face grew bleak. 'Or you can work for the war governments, and then you have no problem. There are journos who do that. But we don't call their kind of reportage the news.'

Andre Chidi Amuta, a Russian of African descent, was explaining to Viloma: 'You'll have noticed that we were frisked. Useless! *Oxfame*, *Shelter*, *Espèces Endangerées*, *Cancercare*: all the splinter groups active in England get their tech from Ochiba. And Ochiba, because of the ex-Japanese background, is *the* high-tech Reformers' orgo. They can get anywhere. Last month there was a massacre in a sex-shop hell right here – er, a game about lying down, you'd say. The machines cleared up. No one knew what had happened until days later when a soft-rubbish cycler threw out a truckload of skulls.'

Bella listened, wondering if in other parts of the giant planet European journalists gathered to talk about *the war* as if it was something that happened to other people. He supposed so. It was inevitable; it would have been the same at home. He had managed to slip out of the conversational matrix as social relations eased. He sipped a glass of mineral water, and watched the company. Viloma had no talent for foreign languages. He sat stonily erect, saying 'How interesting' at random intervals. Bella felt sorry for the medium. He didn't seem to be enjoying the grand tour . . . Aditya laughed and chattered expansively. Kris Kershaw was pretending to be at ease: and inwardly desperately wary. It made Bella feel a little odd to think that, if Sid had been telling the truth, Kershaw now believed that Bella was a double agent: plotting with anti-Aleutians against the Expedition.

Just like Aditya.

He suppressed that thought; the beauty was too close for comfort: and turned to the dancefloor. There were real people among the fx now. He could see them through the rich complexity of their masks: masculine and feminine, male and female, traditionalist and reformers, dancing together in patterns like the patterns of home.

The discs didn't matter. Secret trade with more-or-less hostile locals was part of the life of Aleutia on earth. It was mischief that didn't shock anyone. The humans had a phrase for it, *the grey economy*. But the treasure hunt, though Bella still could hardly believe that device existed, was something else again. *What is it you want from me?* Sid would not, could not tell. But it was as if he wanted Bella to *guess* the answer . . . maybe against his boss's wishes. Sid was not pleading for a superbeing's love, the way the letterbombs pretended. Bella felt, strangely, that they were equals on *that* particular score: both of them with hopeless unspoken reservations. No, there was something else: something more important. *Don't abandon us, be on our side, be one of us . . .* Bella thought he had found the answer, at last. Through Sid's defensive pride, through bluff and double-bluff, he discerned an appeal to the conscience of Aleutia.

What would Clavel, who was the conscience of Aleutia on earth, want to do about the instantaneous travel device? Could Bella, the humble isolate, answer for the Pure One?

The masks intertwined and melded into a single moving field. In this pleasure garden of the void forces, deadworld devices made a truce between the gender warriors, closed the empty spaces between human bodies, brought their flesh to life. The humans had become Aleutians, no different mind. Bella was filled with an immensely clear euphoria. *It belongs to them*, he told Aleutia-of-his-mind. Peenemunde's discovery belongs to the people of earth!

He seemed to hear Seeker-after-truth telling him sadly that this could not be so. Buonarotti herself had decreed that the treasure was not for his own kind. That couldn't be right. Hadn't the saboteurs been the first to use it?

Among the masked dancers, he glimpsed a woman's face. It was instantly recognisable, as if conjured by his thoughts. Surely that was the long-dead saboteuse, Braemar Wilson! Aditya had seen it too. ⟨Hey! I saw a 'Braemar'!⟩ The beauty sprang up, outraged. ⟨Those lying clawfaces! 'Kershaw'! Your women told me a 'Braemar' mask couldn't be had! They said there was 'no demand'! I want an explanation! I want that mask!⟩

He threw off the chador. There were people at other tables by this time. They pointed at the tall figure in film-covered dun overalls, there was a scatter of ironic cheering. Mr Kershaw whispered to Bella, 'They think it's a mask. But we'd better leave. The Protest's over, but aliens in here—!'

Braemar Wilson had emerged again: a pale-skinned woman with a crown of dark red hair, in a dress of grey frost-fern lace over silver taffeta. Frost-fern detached sleeves rose almost to her shoulders, leaving them naked. Silver-grey tendrils cupped her breasts, barely veiling the dark nipples, and clung to her small waist. 'Oh, I *want* that!' shouted Aditya, in English. 'Albertine! Gilberte! Morel! Charlus! After her! Follow that frock!'

Mr Kershaw moaned. 'Stop them . . . !'

The aliens had shed their cloaks, even the sullen materialist obedient to his patron. While the journalists hesitated, not keen to grapple with the superbeings, Aditya was gone: leaping over tables, dropping to four feet; Gilberte and Albertine close behind. Something, a projectile of light, zipped through the marquee. It passed overhead: a nothing in this sea of illusions. But next moment sirens began to wail. 'Air-raid,' yelled Roy Ifekaozor, in relief. This he could deal with. He grabbed Bella, the only Aleutian still in reach. 'Quickly, er, sir, this way—'

Bodies milled wildly under the purple stars. Bella slipped free from his cloak and left Roy holding it. He stepped on to the dancefloor, into a mêlée of panic and a stink of cooked flesh. Braemar was there, waiting to take his hand.

Green emergency tracks sprang into being. Clubbers ran jostling for the exits down the bands of light. A Godlike voice boomed *PLEASE KILL YOUR FX. PLEASE KILL YOUR FX.* The hand that gripped Bella's, hard and damp and infinitely characteristic, tugged sideways into the dark. He sensed a cumbered, patched and makeshift nakedness of mechanical things, the reality behind the blossoming void. They came to a wall, found a heavy mechanical door that stood ajar, and squeezed inside.

Sid hauled it shut. They were in a large, gloomy shed. Strange creatures loomed, their pens outlined in thin red strips of light. Bella went up to one of them. He thrilled to its antiquity – the quality unknown in Aleutia. The monster's flank was cold to the touch, under a pelt of sticky dust. But it was imbued with the life of the people who brought it into existence.

Sid killed his Braemar mask. He sat on the edge of the display floor, dressed in a shabby singlet, cutoff leggings and plastic slippers. It was cool in here. He rubbed gooseflesh on his arms, which were grubbily pale beyond the rust-red tidelines of throat and wrists.

'That's *Stephenson's Rocket* you're petting. Now all our pomp of yesteryear is one with Nineveh and Tyre. I love the old engines. This is my town, you know. I'd've liked to bring you here one day, if things had been different.'

⟨Are we watched?⟩

'You aliens are so paranoid. No, we're not. This hall belongs to the Office of Museums and Libraries. They haven't any money for livespace. It doesn't matter anyway. Nobody *watches* that stuff. Except Cactus. He monitors the malls for us: a little late, but he's thorough.'

Bella leaned against the engine's flank.

⟨But things aren't different. Sid, you shouldn't be here.⟩

'I was taking your advice. I still need to know Aditya's travel plans. The Braemar mask was my lure. I thought we could meet on the dancefloor, we'd get talking: a random social encounter, he'd tell me about his trip . . .'

She looked at him with an expression of serious disbelief, which confirmed everything Sid had been told about the notorious Aditya the beauty: and touched a fading scorch mark on the slick film that covered her sleeve. ⟨What were the burning things? Was that your anti-Aleutians?⟩

'The fireworms? It was an air-raid, nothing to do with you people. It was the Reformers. I'm not strictly an anti-Aleutian, not like Kris. I belong to a splinter group.' He flicked his pillbox so the beautiful woman's aura rose like a flame. 'I don't try to kill aliens,' he quavered, falsetto. 'Except by the millions . . . What d'you think? D'you like me in a frock?'

She gave him that smile: Sid is being unreasonable.

⟨I have something of yours, anyway. I forgot about it last night.⟩ She came over, leaving the engine as if she was sorry to give up its support, and held out in her filmed hand a sheet of crumpled purplish tissue. ⟨It's your reward for rescuing me. It's ten heads. That's a lot of money . . . What's wrong?⟩

Sid could only shake his head. ⟨I don't want it.⟩

⟨I'll keep it for you,⟩ said Bella, looking mystified. She sat down: folding suddenly, as if her legs had given way, into the aliens' informal crouch. She propped her head on her hands.

⟨Out there, a moment ago, everything was so clear.⟩

Sid grinned. 'Crystal clear, eh? Someone should have warned you not to drink the well water.'

⟨Oh yes, someone did. But your drugs don't work on us.⟩

'Is that so?' She didn't notice the irony. The clubs were such cheapskates: she'd be down again in no time. The Bella who had taken his hand so sweetly, who had run with him into the dark as if they could run away from the world, was already fading.

She lifted her face, frowning at him very soberly.

⟨I tried to tell you last night, maybe you didn't get it. I used to be afraid of you and your boss. But now you're involved in something that's between Aleutians and Aleutians. You have to leave Aditya alone. He's dangerous.⟩

Sid twisted the pillbox on his wrist moodily.

'That's what we think. Dangerous and crazy. So why are *you* travelling in his company, dear mild-mannered librarian?'

⟨It's different for me.⟩ The nostril slits in her starved-child face were drawn together in concentration. ⟨I have to do what I can, you see. In the wrong hands, your treasure could destroy the Expedition. I can't let that happen.⟩ She gave a rueful shrug that acknowledged her meagre resources. ⟨I have to do what I can, however silly that sounds, and however much I sympathise with local interests. Maybe, later, I don't know, I might be able to help you people. Meanwhile I'm a member of the Expedition: and Maitri loves this planet. I owe it to him.⟩

Sid glanced at her sharply: quickly dropped his eyes.

'You don't owe Maitri anything,' he muttered.

She blinked. ⟨What?⟩

'No free man shall be taken,' declared Sid. 'Arrested or imprisoned or disseised – whatever that means – or outlawed or exiled or otherwise destroyed, except by the lawful judgement of his peers and the law of the land . . . It's called the Magna Carta, a bit of it, near enough. It's kind of a code of conduct. We've had it in the architecture for thirteen hundred years or so, a fleabite, I know, by your reckoning. I'm not saying it works but *at least it's there*. Are you a free man, Bella? Or a free woman, if you'll pardon the expression?'

She frowned, her nasal pinched: giving the impression that she was earnestly considering her answer. ⟨I'm sorry,⟩ she said. ⟨I didn't understand a word of that.⟩

Sid laughed. 'Oh, forget it. Sorry I spoke.'

Bella had relapsed into inner space, lost in Aleutia as he thought of it. She was so preoccupied tonight, she hadn't even noticed he was committing the crime of 'calling her she'. He saw the stolen girl he had glimpsed in the shadows of the cistern cave at Mykini. She'd been taking that medicine. She had the wilting-flowerstem look again, which it hurt him to see. But he knew how deceptive her fragility was. He had thought her meek. She was far from meek. He felt the core of obdurate self-respect beside him, hard and fine-cut as a jewel, a diamond in lamb's clothing: and despaired of protecting her.

⟨We're following the 'Braemar Wilson' trail,⟩ she said suddenly. ⟨Tomorrow we're going to the 'Arndale Centre', to see ourselves walking on our heads. Then we're heading for 'East Germany', for a sarcophagus. That's all I know. And, Sid, nobody's going to cancel the 'Himalaya Project'.⟩

The door of the museum hall screeched open. One of the site's lovable old Robbie-the-robots peered in. 'Whoever's in here,' it croaked, 'the all-clear's sounded.'

Bella started, and stared in disgust. ⟨Can it see us?⟩

'Not really.' The robot ambled off like a stringless puppet.

She got to her feet, the origami folds of hips and knees returning to a more human geometry. ⟨I'm glad about last night,⟩ she said. ⟨I don't suppose we'll ever do that again.⟩

He stood. His throat was tight. 'I suppose not.'

⟨Sid, please take care. You only have one life.⟩

'You too. Take care.' He pulled a lumpy paper bag from the daypack on his shoulder. 'Look, here's more of my Aditya bait. You can have them. This is Avalon. You ought to have apples, if you come to the island of apples. They're called Discovery Beauties, by Discovery out of Beauty of Bath.' She took the bag. They faced each other across the unbridgeable gulf.

⟨They'll be looking for me. I'd better go.⟩

The air-raid must have done something to Castlefield's climate control. It was freezing in the engine hall. Sid huddled his arms around himself and hopped from foot to foot, trying to review what she had told him. When she was *there* in front of him, the Common Tongue was transparent. As soon as she was gone it melted in his memory into an intolerable blur.

What can you do with someone who spends a year in fairyland, which to her is but a day, and then takes you in her arms so casually: *not* as if the time between didn't exist – because she knows that you lied to her, kidnapped her, sold her for rent money: she believes you are the enemy . . . Not as if none of that happened, but as if *it doesn't matter*: Never mind, Sid. It was your obligation. He was insulted!

'You're not even my type,' he shouted aloud to the empty hall. 'I wanted a *real girl*. Not a cat-faced shoulder-high marsupial alien, who thinks human gender is just a question of who is bigger and can hit harder. And who WON'T EVEN TALK TO ME!'

The engines stared ahead of them, massively unperturbed.

Suddenly from his fury he plunged into a memory of her body, like fluid in his arms. Her claw shuddering in his gripping hand, the choked wild sounds in her throat. Indignation deserted him. He sat down on the dirty concrete, head in his hands. Shared pleasure had forged the friendship between Sid and the alien into a bond that could only hurt them both. He was enraged that she dismissed the whole human movie plot of secrets and betrayals: *car chases, showdowns, meetings with Mister Big.* She was right. There was nothing to discuss, nothing to be done. She was caught in a trap she couldn't see: and he couldn't save her. He was as helpless as she was herself.

*

Viloma found a body in the car park. The Aleutians turned it over and discovered a swollen, agonised mask, flopping limbs, belly and thighs masked in blood. ⟨It's a 'Man'⟩ explained Albertine, newly knowledgeable. ⟨When the 'Woman' terrorists kill them, they always take the – er – the lying down parts.⟩

⟨They don't like you to use those words like that,⟩ said Bella. ⟨You can be a man or a woman, without being a gender warrior.⟩

Aditya was more interested in Bella's paper bag.

⟨What's that?⟩

⟨It's 'apples'. I found them. Someone must have dropped them. They're something to eat.⟩

In the icy light of the parking hangar the gold and red globes were robbed of colour, but they fitted nicely in one's palm. Aditya enjoyed a moment of triumph. ⟨Don't be silly, librarian. You're meant to smell these, not eat them.⟩

Mr Kershaw spared the corpse barely a glance. 'Get in the car,' he said. 'Please. Into the car.' The soldiers shut them in, and got up in their gun-turret caboose behind.

The cablenet conference facility on Piccadilly Gardens was a large shabby building. The skeletons of some ancient trees decorated the foyer. Sid had thought they were *the last trees on earth* when he was a kid: a romantic notion he'd been quite sorry to lose. The big hall was full of wartime bustle. He finally managed to get one of the 'personal communications experts' to make his connection, using the Fat Man's credit. He had to wait an hour. The 'personal expert', an fxsimile young lady from another age, sat and smiled and occasionally asked fatuous questions. Sid answered with docility. He had tried cheeking the aged data-handlers that lurked behind these images. It wasn't worth it.

At last he was called to a booth. Wherever the Fat Man was (Sid didn't know), he'd decided to answer the cable very straight. He sat at a desk with a red antique telephone on it and nothing else: a bland bulk in a white suit.

'Ah, Sid. How are things in the St Petersburg of the west?'

Sid reported on the substance of the two interviews.

'I don't understand why she won't talk. She must want to know what's going on: I mean *know*, not haze it, for God's sake.'

His boss leaned back, gazing up at an antique virtual fan that hung, ticking gently around, from his virtual ceiling.

'Aleutians have a high tolerance of naked uncertainty.' He spread his Mickey Mouse palms. 'Truth is hard to pin down, not least in interpersonal relations. Humans know this, Aleutians live it. Our librarian prefers to keep the lie direct to a minimum, that's all . . . Hmm. Eastern Europe, a sarcophagus. He told you nothing that you could not easily have found out by other means. But it's a good sign, he's beginning to confide in you.'

Sid tried not to wince. 'The sarcophagus on the Braemar trail could be Peenemunde's place. It would be a plausible cover. I think they have a rendezvous with a spaceplane. They could get away with a secret launch, out there in the battlezone.' He affected a professional tone; his spine prickled with dread. They would take her out to orbit, he would never see Bella again.

The Fat Man pondered. 'It's possible. But remember, Sid. Serial immortality is not the stuff of human fairytales. The phenomenon we have experienced on earth – a group of intimates, centred on the three captains, born in approximate synchrony in consecutive generations – is known to the aliens. These clusters arise spontaneously and break up in the same way. I believe the three captains are all on earth now. Each of them is aware that he may next "wake" many, many generations away: "lost in space" with Dark Ocean triumphant and earth and its secret treasure out of reach in the random void. I suspect that time does not seem cheap to them, at present. None of the three, nor their intimates, will want to leave the giant planet at this juncture.'

He frowned. 'Further than that, I have no idea what Aditya is up to. Consciousness is *work*, Sid. Every kind of mind keeps it to an economic minimum. Aleutians are highly advanced in this respect. In some cases, one might say conscious reasoning is practically dispensed with: which makes reasoned prediction—'

He sat up sharply. 'A sarcophagus on the Braemar Wilson trail! And Aditya has that damned medium with him!' He reached for the red phone. 'Sid, I think we're in trouble.'

8: TERRIBLE AS AN ARMY

A car that 'knew the way to go' had proved elusive. Nightclub masks run by stunning amounts of processing power were available on a wrist-strap. But many kinds of 'machine intelligence' that had been commonplace on Aditya's previous trip had vanished from the market. When they left their private cruiser at the last airport they were forced to fall back on a series of local drivers, who came in pairs and handed the Aleutians on to others of their kind at intervals, in a dour absence of human-alien interaction.

Aditya retreated behind an eye-wrap, and spent hours curled up watching Graham Greene records (Luxembourg M&S had had a glut of them), occasionally emerging to protest that he wished he had an immortal soul, so he could fear damnation.

Following the advice of Mr Kershaw, they lived in the massive cars, driving into open country before they halted for the night. Once they stopped in a deserted town and investigated a large building that turned out to be a hospital. There was a floor devoted to newborn babies. The rooms marked blue for boys were empty. The rooms marked pink for girls were full, but the babies were dead. The other wards were entirely stripped and burned.

Kershaw had offered them an escort. Aditya had declined, but accepted a store of dead weaponry. He drilled the signifiers in firing technique, and posted guards. It was a great game. He stalked away from the cars at dusk and stood, arms stretched across the immemorial battlefield, declaiming:

> *Ah, love, let us be true*
> *To one another! for the world, which seems*

To lie before us like a land of dreams,
So various, so beautiful, so new,
Hath really neither joy, nor love, nor light,
Nor certitude, nor peace, nor help for pain;
And we are here as on a darkling plain
Swept with confused alarms of struggle and flight
Where ignorant armies clash by night

They met neither of the ignorant armies, nor any further random traces of their passage. They forged on, eastward.

The *sarcophagi* were the tombs of giant power generators. Some of them had suffered industrial accidents, some had been bombed or blown up. Many had simply been abandoned as the war made their upkeep impossible: the finicky mechanical suns needed constant attention. In decay they were considered hideously dangerous. The locals would bury the whole thing in instant stone, which they might sculpt into grotesque shapes as a warning to the unwary. Before the war the Expedition had done good business in 'decontamination': and tourists had become fascinated by the tombs themselves. But the spectacular ones were further south. Here, shapeless lumps loomed occasionally on the horizon. Aditya ignored them: only one sarcophagus would do.

After several days of driving they reached the town near their destination. The usual ritual was performed. Pairs of drivers got down, pairs of drivers replaced them. Aditya made his wishes clear, and the cavalcade of three long cars set off. Then disaster struck. The local drivers stopped the three cars by the side of the road, climbed out, went into a huddle: and announced they wouldn't go any further. Aditya argued to no avail. He came scowling to join Bella and the little clan.

⟨Damned fools. What are they afraid of?⟩

⟨Your sarcophagus,⟩ said Bella. He had spent the whole trip diplomatically concealing that he seemed to know more about earth than the beauty. When he was tired, things slipped out. He was weary of the journey, and the idea of staring at a sarcophagus, even one admired by Braemar Wilson, left him cold.

⟨They believe that if you go near the tombs, you'll die young and painfully, and your children will too.⟩

Aditya was too much annoyed to resent the information. ⟨Huh. Cowards. Everybody's got to go some time. Shall I tell them we're decommissioners?⟩

The Aleutians grinned at each other.

The joke was that Aleutian 'decontamination' had consisted of making a big fuss and doing little. There were mechanical sun generators lying about *everywhere*: at the bottom of the oceans, all over. Expedition artisans had established that the things were doing no harm beyond causing a minor rise in the death rate. This didn't make much sense as a cause of concern, when there was a major war going on anyway. The Aleutians did almost nothing to the ones they 'treated', and *nobody noticed*. As Rajath the trickster put it: ⟨They pretend to have a problem, we pretend to fix it!⟩

The local drivers stared at the giggling aliens. They turned and began to walk towards town. ⟨Let them go,⟩ said Aditya. He kicked the front car in its crawltrack, to show who was boss. ⟨Driving these things can't be hard.⟩

Aditya's cook tasted the liquid fuel, and assured everybody that people could eat that too. So they took the fuel cans, as the most economical use of space, and left two cars and the rest of the provisions behind. Nobody stayed on guard. Bella thought this was unwise, but he didn't comment. They went on, squeezed into a single car. It was a rocky and alarming ride with Aditya at the controls. It ended abruptly when the car shied at a boulder and smashed itself into a tree. They climbed out into a little wood where the midsummer leaves, that should be green, hung yellowing and grey. They had reached the exclusion zone. The dead-metal fence that traditionally surrounded a sarcophagus was ahead.

The sarcophagus entry was in an appendix of the *Braemar and Johnny Guidebook*: an obscure item that the book's human designers hadn't troubled to translate into moving image. Aditya could read, but not fluently. Albertine read out the passage of English text for the benefit of the signifiers.

'*The campus of* – ⟨A thing no one could possibly pronounce⟩ – '*University, a greenfields site outside the town of M—* ⟨another⟩,

*Neubrandenburg is believed to be the last location Johnny and
Braemar visited before their departure for the as yet unidentified
secret launch area. A nuclear accident in the Du Pont/Farben
experimental reactor unfortunately contaminated—'*

‹Oh!› exclaimed Bella. ‹This must be 'Peenemunde Buonarotti's'
workplace!›

‹Who's 'Peenemunde Buonarotti'?› asked Albertine.

‹The local engineer 'Johnny and Braemar' came here to visit.
They were trying to recruit 'her' to be an anti-Aleutian fanatic.›

None of the little clan had heard of Peenemunde Buonarotti,
and less did they care. ‹You know too much, librarian,› complained Gilberte slyly. It was a mean accusation. No one can
help their obligation.

The beauty was getting organised. ‹We're in the middle of a
battlefield,› he reminded them. ‹Everybody take a weapon.› Bella
obediently picked up a rifle. ‹Not you, invalid! Don't be silly.
You wouldn't be much use in a 'firefight'!›

They found a broken place in the fence and stepped through.
In the distance Bella saw some massive and beautiful old-earth
science equipment. It was summer, which was supposed to be
the warmer time in the north. But the day was cold.

Bella had been an invalid again at Uji. The bracing empty air
of old earth had restored some of the health he'd found on his
adventure. He tackled the walk to the sarcophagus with a
confidence that would have been impossible at home. But he
was feeling very uncomfortable. Aditya had been becoming more
and more irritable with him since they had left England. The
beauty clearly knew that he was under suspicion. But Bella
didn't know anything more than when they had left Uji. He
wished he had not mentioned Peenemunde Buonarotti . . . A trip
to see a sarcophagus had meant nothing to him. Now it had
turned out to be Peenemunde's workplace, and that must mean
something. What was Aditya doing here, in this place where the
Seeker-after-truth believed *instantaneous travel* had been
invented? What did he know?

Quarantine isolates everyone, but Bella was doubly alone.
None of this company, except Aditya barely, had been part of
his recorded lives. They were blanks with borrowed names to the
isolate: and they served Aditya. They had let him feel, in many

tiny ways, that they were aware of the slackening of their
patron's favour. When at last he stumbled, Celeste picked him
up without a smile and carried him as if he was a bundle of
empty clothes. His joints crept. He felt that some crisis was
imminent, and whatever it was it frightened him.

The sarcophagus loomed in the centre of a waste of ripped
earth. Everything seemed to have been left as it had been the
day they finished building the tomb. It was undecorated: a
chalky brown mound rising at either end into stiff, unequal
towers. It looked like a huge, half-collapsed pudding. As they
got close, the homogenous effect vanished. The froth was folded
into globs and slabs. Shards of it were coming away from the
structures underneath. The entrance port of the smaller building
had been deliberately opened a long time ago, and the material
had not regenerated.

⟨Tourists,⟩ said Viloma intently, touching the stone foam. ⟨I
feel them, faded by the years. This is the right place.⟩

⟨Bella must be worn out,⟩ announced Aditya.

⟨I'm not!⟩

⟨You're exhausted, poor thing. We'll rest and have a picnic
before we go in.⟩

The cook set up the stove. There was plenty of convertible
rubbish about, so he saved his can of car-feed. The signifiers ate
with their rifles slung romantically on their backs. They made a
joke of the inconvenience of the film, through which they sucked
their food. When they were finished the camping stove resorbed
everything. The cook folded it away. And now no quarantine
could contain the atmosphere of intense excitement.

⟨Shall we tell him?⟩ Albertine's round eyes were bright, the
lips of his plump nasal wide. He slipped an arm around Bella's
shoulders. Gilberte, on the other side, pressed against his flank.
Aditya had settled informally opposite. Viloma was kneeling
upright beside him. Around the signifiers, Aditya's Silent were
ranked attentively.

⟨We're going to hold a seance in there!⟩ announced Gilberte.

Bella felt the circle that had closed around him holding him in
place. ⟨What, to raise the saboteurs?⟩ he said slowly. ⟨You know
what I think of that kind of thing. I'll wait out here.⟩

⟨No. You have to come.⟩

⟨I'm really very tired after all.⟩

⟨You can't miss this,⟩ said Aditya. ⟨This is special. I have a genuine relic of 'Johnny Guglioli'. We're going to find out things that nobody has ever known.⟩

Viloma was carefully stripping the quarantine from his hands, his eyes fixed on the isolate.

⟨You are necessary. Everyone must take part.⟩

Bella seemed to have no choice.

An Aleutian medium was supposed to be able to grow a live culture from some decaying trace of the deceased. The thing could be fed, ideally with the blood of the necromancer and others, persuaded to take the shape of some kind of homunculus, and then questioned. Believers claimed that if this was achieved, the creature would tell secrets that the dead person had never confessed: repeat signals that had never entered the living traffic of wanderers. But it was terribly dangerous, and rarely attempted. Things could go horribly wrong.

Bella remembered the seances at Uji, which he had successfully avoided. He was sure nothing much had happened at those. Materialism was a silly and rather nasty parlour game, the rest was baseless fantasy. He would have to take part, he couldn't escape, but there was no reason to be afraid.

They entered the building. It was gloomy inside. Albertine put the guidebook away, and they took out handlamps. Viloma led them now. The medium seemed to grow physically as he followed a faint trail of long-past Aleutian presence through the drab and dead corridors, up narrow, angular stairs.

⟨It is here.⟩

The room was not large. It held a few pieces of furniture. There was a window. The dusty glass, unharmed, was blocked by the mass of the sarcophagus.

⟨This is the place,⟩ announced Viloma. ⟨This site has been passed over and regarded as of no interest. It should be considered the most important location of all. We are standing, buried in a closed tomb, in the space where the saboteurs spent some of their last hours on earth. If any air holds traces of their life, it is here.⟩

Aditya's people prepared themselves. They stripped off their quarantine, their clothes and underwear. From pockets and pouches they produced their occult equipment: phials, mirrors, bowls; a thin knife with a dead metal blade, like an execution-er's. Bella stood uneasily watching. The neat heap of clothing somehow especially turned his stomach.

⟨Um. You know I'm not a believer. Do I have to undress?⟩

Viloma was kneeling in the centre of the room with a bowl at his lips. He glanced up briefly. ⟨Strip off the quarantine.⟩

Two of Aditya's domestics came and helped him.

They had suckered their handlamps to the walls, tuned to a red light and angled so it fell in a ruby ellipse on the dust. Bella remembered the mandorla of dim gold at the head of the cistern stair: the shape like two folded hands that Sid had said was a symbol of birth.

⟨Where's the relic?⟩ he asked.

Aditya's people, signifiers and Silent, were kneeling around the ruby ellipse: except for Gilberte and Albertine, who were standing in front of the door. Everybody looked at Bella.

⟨Is this a joke . . . ? You're crazy!⟩ He felt crazy himself for what he was imagining he saw in their faces. He took a step backwards. Aditya came and stood in front of him, grinning widely: his eyes alight and nasal flaring. ⟨Maitri's librarian,⟩ he crooned. ⟨Maitri's librarian, who was born this time with a rumour attached. Maitri's crippled librarian, the isolate, who is someone important in disguise.⟩

Bella tried to laugh. ⟨I know about that! It was nonsense, it is nonsense. Anyone who told you anything different was lying! Or gone mad, or mistaken, sir.⟩

⟨Who did you think you were, Bella? Which important, vir-tuous person do I see before me? Or would you prefer not to say?⟩

⟨I'm Maitri's librarian!⟩

⟨You know that isn't true. I've seen the knowledge growing in your lonely little mind. You know you're suddenly important, suddenly not the person you were. You've been mistaken about the *kind* of importance.⟩ The beauty grinned. ⟨Poor Bella. You've been so brave, trying to get to the bottom of the plot. You simply couldn't grasp, not even when it was staring in your face, that *you* were the object of it all.⟩

⟨You're crazy,⟩ he repeated.

⟨Rajath wanted me to seduce you,⟩ said the beauty pensively.

⟨*Rajath?*⟩ Bella looked wildly around, as if the trickster might suddenly step out of a corner of the room. ⟨Is he here?⟩

⟨I told him not to be so stupid. But I want you to know, librarian, I would have been glad to lie with you. Good health isn't everything. I like your mind. I'm sorry about this.⟩

Bella understood that every slight he had suffered, on the way to this seance, had been without malice. It had been Aditya's insensate, necessary preparation of himself and his household for this moment. He gave up hope.

⟨*I don't understand!*⟩ he pleaded.

⟨I think you do. You are 'Johnny Guglioli'.⟩

⟨That's ridiculous! I'm Maitri's librarian!⟩

⟨Think about it. 'Johnny' was executed for sabotage, in the shipworld. His body, of course, we returned intact. Have you never wondered? Don't lie to yourself. You know we sneaked an inert tissue sample. Not for use, absolutely not. But *just in case*. It's one of those things everyone denies but everybody knows. That's the way it was: a scrap of tissue kept in secret. Then somebody, we won't say who, had the sentimental idea of bringing 'Johnny' back.⟩

He watched Bella's face. ⟨You don't remember. There's no recognition. You're still sleeping like a baby, and no one knows how to wake you. But you were there when the saboteurs reached our shipworld, using the instantaneous travel device. If anyone alive knows anything about the secret, you're the one. You used it. *You know* what happened. You will tell.⟩

⟨I don't know! I don't know!⟩

⟨We're not sentimental,⟩ said Aditya. ⟨We don't need your mind. For this questioning, your body will do.⟩

Bella dropped to his four feet: flight was irresistible. It was useless. Albertine and Gilberte caught him and pulled him upright. Celeste the Silent peeled back his sleeve. Viloma used his thin knife to remove a piece of flesh from Bella's arm, sealed the wound carefully with a secretion from his mouth and divided the flesh among the bowls.

⟨You're crazy!⟩ wailed Bella.

Albertine was getting squeamish. ⟨Can't we just kill him?⟩

⟨No.⟩ The medium licked blood from his fingers. ⟨We kill him when we have a successful culture. His death is an important

trigger, but that's been my mistake before: to kill prematurely.
The last culture is as likely to succeed as the first. It must be
equally fresh.⟩

⟨You know what that means?⟩ cried Bella. ⟨It means he's never
known this awful trick to work. He means you can chop me to
bloody slivers, and *never* get a 'successful culture' – ⟩

Aditya had taken his place, kneeling in the ellipse. He stared
up at his victim: wide-eyed and exhilarated.

⟨Loyalty is important,⟩ he breathed.

Viloma made a gurgling in his throat, and spat a stream of his
own blood into the first bowl. Everybody took a mouthful, mixed
it with saliva and spat it on to the little pieces of Bella's arm. The
signifiers began to invoke the last formal name of the deceased.
'JohnnyJohnnyJohnnyJohnnyJohnnyJohnnyJohnnyJohnny.'

The participants stared into their bowls. Albertine and Gilberte's grip on Bella didn't slacken.

⟨It doesn't make *sense*,⟩ protested Bella. He was too frightened
to feel any pain from the wound in his arm, or maybe Viloma
had numbed it. He could not believe that they would go on
cutting him into bits until he died. But Aditya's mad exaltation
terrified him.

⟨If I was really made from 'Johnny Guglioli's' tissue: *this
doesn't make sense. You mustn't do it! Don't you see*—?⟩

The cultures began to stir.

⟨Keep quiet!⟩ warned Viloma, electrified. ⟨Let them grow!⟩

They grew fast. There was a brittle explosion of sound. The
first bowl had shattered. Something stood out of it, the colour of
raw flesh, limbless: a small tube of muscle lined with a mass of
teeth. It did not wait to be questioned. It coiled itself and shot
across the room. Whether by accident or by volition, it wrapped
itself round Gilberte's naked throat. It set to work. It ate. With
astonishing speed, it grew. It split into two: they ate, they
burgeoned and divided. Another bowl shattered, and another.
The room was full of flailing limbs, screams and blood.

Bella woke out of blind flight and found himself running in a
greyed darkness, blood-spattered hands and arms stretched out
ahead of him. He didn't know where the blood had come from;
it was not his own. He fell against a door and bounced back. The

door was barred and plastered over with danger signs: ⟨*die young and painfully*⟩. There were letters incised over the lintel, not printed or grown there but cut in an amateurish way and filled with black pigment. He stared at them, agonisingly concentrated. *Get out of here . . . OUT*. To get out he had to go down. He spun around and ran. Wherever he found stairs going down he went down: and finally came to a strange kind of engineer's den. Big place, shining under dust, curved giant pipes. No way out. He'd come too far, have to go up. But he saw light coming in at a window. He broke it and scrabbled through, and out from a crumbled rent in the base of the tomb.

He stumbled back to the front of the smaller building. The can of car-food was there. He felt the way he'd felt when he was on the run with Sid: so exhausted he could hardly breathe. Eat something. He couldn't lift the container. He managed with difficulty to squeeze some liquid into his palm. He tried to drink: and spat, gagging and coughing.

He remembered what car-food could do. There was more in the car at the fence. With luck, he'd find a way of striking a spark.

Sid and the Campfire Girls arrived at the site in a personnel truck that had been deposited at a cautious distance by air-frame. It rumbled through the abandoned campus and pulled up outside the tomb. Sid got down with the rest of them, thirty suits. The shells were tattoo-skin camouflaged with Allied insignia and colours: a disguise that could be rapidly switched. The Campfire officer, Colonel Janet Ezra, came up to Sid. She'd told him to call her Colonel Jez.

'What d'we do now?'

He found it hard to cope with the suit's helmet controls, or the voice that seemed inside his head. He was too frightened. He counted the suits and was awed at the Fat Man's bargaining power. The boss had said: *you were right and I was wrong. We should take Bella away from those people. By force if necessary, but a show of force should be sufficient*. He had called in favours with the USSA Special Exterior Force, and sent Sid to Germany with a miniature secret army.

He had explained what he thought Aditya meant to do. As Sid

understood it, the alien necromancers would kill Bella slowly, once they got themselves set up at this significant location. The aim had been for the secret army to reach the sarcophagus first, and prevent entry. The Fat Man had believed that Bella would be handed over without a fuss. Aditya might be prepared for a pitched battle with rival treasure hunters in the middle of the Gender War. Luckily, the Fat Man said, Aditya would not be making the decisions. But they'd found the car at the fence, and the Fat Man's mysterious deductions had become irrelevant. It was too late. The Aleutians were here before them.

A colonel of the USSA Special Exterior Force was taking orders from Sidney Carton in a very limited sense. She just wanted to hear his opinion.

'We go inside,' he said, 'ma'am.'

The colonel thought so too. They had found only one breach in the tomb. The suits went inside, armoured. They left the breach guarded. They were experts. They moved through the smaller building like a phalanx of ghosts. They quickly found the place where the seance had been held. It was three floors up: a room spread with a welter of blood and other tissue, the rags and tatters of flesh completely unrecognisable.

The two suits who found it had called Sid and the colonel.

'*What happened, Sid*?' demanded Colonel Jez, inhumanly calm. 'We came here to defuse a dangerous stand-off and secure the release of an innocent hostage, hopefully without violence. This doesn't look like the same situation that was described.'

Sid couldn't speak. The bloody stillness overwhelmed everything. He and the Fat Man hadn't told the SEF about the alien necromancy. But nothing the Fat Man had said explained this. The Campfire Girls moved around, examining the spattered walls and stooping to the floor. Sid's helmet was slaved to the colonel's, he had the Radio Suit band and not much else. He didn't know what they were doing. How could they be so calm! Ezra's suit moved its head from side to side.

'They say these nuclear-accident places are haunted.' The helmet turned, as if Sid had made some comment. 'I don't rule out the possibility. The aliens didn't come to an evil place like this for any good reason. Maybe they woke something.'

Then someone shouted in his head. The voice was human, but

Sid couldn't understand the words. Something like: *it's still going on, it's still happening!* For a moment the helmet printed across his eyes a burst of full SEF head-display. He glimpsed dark scenes rimmed by flickering callibration that he couldn't read: a corridor full of flames: naked, bestial running things. The same voice yelled, '*We've found the nest!*' The colonel and the two suits rushed out of the room towards the action. Sid blundered after.

The Aleutians had left their lamps behind in the seance room, and the local lighting commensals that clung to the ceilings were still either dead or sleeping. Everything happened in a gloom in which the sharp edges of local walls and doors connected painfully, cruelly, with people's elbows, knees, flanks, *places* (that made them giggle). At last a lamplighter managed to coax a glow in some material he found lying about. They laughed at each other's nakedness, and laughed even more at the absurdly provident who'd snatched up clothes when the magic went so awfully wrong.

Some people grumbled against the person – whose identity had better remain veiled – who'd led their lord astray. But without rancour. People cannot help behaving like themselves. There were no thoughts of appealing to the local police, who had arrived on some kind of tip-off. They assumed the police would be as hostile as they'd be at home in the circumstances. Necromancy, especially when practised on a subject who is still alive at the start, isn't a respectable pursuit. It would be better if everybody died. That way, there'd be less scandal. There were no regrets. One paid for the glamour of life with Aditya in episodes like this. They reminded each other of pleasant times, and looked forward to pleasant times to come. They embraced, groomed, shared wanderers; composed themselves.

Aditya and his housekeeper were the two signifiers left alive. They had thrown together a barricade on a landing in front of the room to which the remaining Silent had fled. Viloma's corpse was being devoured on the stairwell above them. They'd failed to drag it away from the creatures.

⟨What are those police *doing?*⟩ howled Morel.

Part of the barricade was a filing cabinet. They tossed withered papers and heaps of chargeplastic over it. The creatures of the seance pounced on anything that moved. They devoured and grew and divided and devoured. The weapons Kershaw had provided were useless. The situation needed fire, gouts of flash heat; nothing else would stop these things.

⟨I assume they came for Bella,⟩ answered Aditya coolly. ⟨To rescue her from us. If I was the police, I'd be here.⟩

⟨That's not what I meant! I meant why don't they *do something*?⟩ The space between the barricade and the doors was filled with the sound of their own breath. Snaking, toothed arms of raw flesh were seeping through every crack.

⟨They're like weapons,⟩ Aditya murmured, fascinated. ⟨If they were real weapons, this could be the end of the world!⟩

Morel glanced at him, and shuddered. ⟨But when the police get things under control,⟩ he realised, ⟨I mustn't be here! I mean, somebody has to get away, warn the people round about, report to our employers, tell Yudi . . .⟩

An endless tongue, thin as a whip and razor-edged, lashed at Aditya's cheek, laying it open to the bone. He laughed. ⟨My dear coward, stop babbling. So it's goodbye again. As the locals say: 'I'll see you on the other side.'⟩

Morel vaulted for the top of the cabinet, jumped from there on to the stairs. The monsters, intent on the numerous warm bodies they sensed beyond the barricade, let him go.

Aditya thought of Clavel, who had started this affair for his own benefit and then given up halfway. Always the same Clavel: always having regrets and pulling back from his own desire. *Sorry it's come to a bad end . . .* he told the poet, in the Aleutia of his mind. *But I believe you'll understand my part.* The Pure One should. What could be more pure than loyalty that was totally undeserved?

One of Bella's terrifying offspring reared over the cabinet: my, they were getting big.

Who would have thought the librarian had so much savagery in him? All those mimsy lives of holding it down: *yes sir, no sir, please protect me, sir.* Then *whoosh*, what a reversal! He thought of those idiotic walking hatstands at Uji and laughed again. The traders had despised Bella, because he had no commensals! *More than ever, I'm sorry we didn't lie together.* He had forgotten or he didn't care that the librarian was not the librarian. His wanderers spoke, he spoke to Bella in the Aleutia of his mind. *Another time – ?* He had no last thoughts for the third captain, the engineer. Aditya knew when he was not appreciated.

He had taken poison, which he habitually carried. To enjoy life to the full – as the beauty did – it was necessary to have a little door inside, a secretion that could be triggered to provide a swift exit. The toxin in his body should slow the quasi-weapons.

He made a speech.

> *I know that I shall meet my fate*
> *Somewhere among the clouds above;*
> *Those that I fight I do not hate,*
> *Those that I guard I do not love . . .*

Aditya had never hated anyone. He loved those he guarded, the ones still alive behind this barricade, though he'd led them (not for the first time!) to a premature and unpleasant death. Yet the flavour was right: a fine carelessness. That was the way with these locals. There was something about them as familiar as a remembered dream. But like a dream, it vanished.

He covered his face. The creatures swarmed through.

Bella had collapsed on the stairs, a makeshift torch in either hand, the fuel can from the car on his back. A figure leapt into his smoky view. 'Morel!' he gasped. ⟨Is anyone alive up there?⟩

It was not Morel. But it was an Aleutian face that Bella recognised almost instantly. With one wild glance the figure flew past him and disappeared downwards. Bella struggled to his feet. He had to get on. The creatures were slow to attack him, he'd discovered that. If he was alone in a room with them he guessed he wouldn't last long, but in the open they hesitated and he had a chance.

The suits had a floorplan of the campus, which they'd hooked out of Youro library sources. It turned out to be seriously inaccurate for the building they were in. Their ionising radiation count was alarming; it had gone off the scale of the suits' dosimetry: it was *hotter than hell* in here, must be the most contaminated spot in Prussia. They couldn't work out where the ordinary fires had come from, either . . .

Sid crouched in a doorway, listening to the Campfire Girls on Radio Suit. He had seen Bella. She was alive. He had known she was still alive, somehow, when he was standing in that bloody chamber. He had to get away from the suits and find her.

The Campfire Girls had undertaken to help the Fat Man, to defuse a touchy situation involving rivalry between aliens. They'd agreed to hand Bella over to the Fat Man's agent, and modestly retire. But the SEF knew about the treasure hunt, and they knew Bella was important though they didn't know why. Sid didn't trust them. He tongued Radio Suit to a murmur, to cut the distraction. He'd still hear, if anyone started wondering where Sid was. They could soon find him. But he should have a few minutes before they came looking.

He followed the figure he'd seen, down the stairs. He was near the front entrance of the smaller building. He'd have to brazen it somehow to get past the guards. But once he had Bella everything would be easy. The light from his helmet showed a counter and pigeonholes. An ancient monitor on a keyboard stand gazed at him. The floor was scattered with scraps of litter: how long had it been lying there?

'*Bella?*'

She was in a corner behind the counter in an animal crouch, her overalls smeared, blackened and torn. He could see a red gash on the chicken-skin flesh of one forearm. She had never looked less human. He was consumed by pity and fury.

'What did they do to you?' he whispered, his voice shaking, sweat breaking out inside the cool, safe shell. 'What happened, Bel? It doesn't matter. Come with me, quickly. I'm kidnapping you again. I'll get us out of this. Trust Sid.'

⟨I told you to keep away from me. Get away! *Go!*⟩

He realised how terrifying the suit must look. He wrestled, pulled off a gauntlet and held out his bare hand.

(felt the thunderous fall of invisible death on his skin)

⟨Bel, sweetheart: it's me . . .⟩

The half-human thing erupted from its crouch. It bowled him over. Sid yelled. Something lithe, terrible, wild fell on him, teeth trying to meet in his protected throat. He rolled on the floor, scrabbling for his gauntlet. *How did she suddenly come to be naked?* What he'd thought was Bella wasn't even wolf below the waist. It was a red serpent, a python as big as a man's thigh, made of raw flesh. It had wrapped itself round him. Something was trying to pull him free, but the monster wouldn't let go.

The sound of his own screaming –

He woke surrounded by suits, feeling blissfully dizzy. His right hand throbbed slightly. He rolled his helmet and saw a slick of burned *stuff* that looked like melted plastic smeared thickly across the floor beside him.

⟨WE GOT IT, SID. WE THINK WE GOT THEM ALL. HOW D'YOU FEEL?⟩

⟨Good, I suppose. My hand throbs a bit.⟩

He realised they were talking radio, not Aleutian, and said that again aloud.

'YEAH. IT WOULD. WHAT DID YOU TAKE YOUR GAUNT-LET OFF FOR, YOU STUPID DICK?'

'I can't remember.'

They carried him to the truck. Sid missed some time. When he became conscious again he told them he felt well. They took him to the colonel's office. She sat at her broad desk, below the obligatory portrait of Carlotta de Leyva: the one where she had the parrot on her wrist and heaps of gold braid on her shoulders.

The first President of the United Socialist States of America, a small-boned little woman, putting on flesh in middle age, looked down at him with bold and friendly eyes. She was no more really here than most of what he could see inside this segment of a personnel carrier pod. The impressive acreage of unreality was a sign of rank, like a key to the executive toilet. His sense of the cabin's cramped physical dimensions crept through the matte and the dope, making him feel slightly sick.

'That was not funny, Sid,' said the colonel, in that calm, mysteriously lilting, forgotten accent. '*What happened in there?*'

'I don't know. Ask the Fat Man.'

She heaved a sigh. 'Well, as far as we can tell there's nothing left alive and we've sealed the tomb. We came here to secure the release of a hostage. I think we can safely say that that situation is over. Shit. I hope and pray the gender-warriors never find out about this affair. They'd love some alien biological weapons. Thank God for hard radiation. But why do I get this vile idea that what they were doing was for *fun*, some kind of gross, ugly, alien sex-ritual game that went wrong?'

⟨It's your dirty mind.⟩

She pointed a square-tipped brown finger at him. 'I caught that. Don't bother to translate.' She stared ahead of her. 'I suppose this is the end of the treasure trail. No one's going to be getting any information out of the young alien woman whose career we've all been following with such interest. You, me, the Fat Man, those other aliens. I'm glad. Nothing good ever comes out of old earth, and the aliens are best left strictly alone. In my opinion, *God says no*. The space race is over. We have to learn to make things work right here.'

She attended to a voice he couldn't hear, and then stood up from the desk. They got out of the truck. It was parked in a wood outside the fence. A suit was walking away from a beacon planted in the open space (contaminated farmland) beyond the trees. There was a bullet-shaped German car parked on the road. A local, a Prussian male, was waiting beside it, smoking a tobacco cigarette.

'I sent for the taxi. Excuse me if we don't offer you a lift. We're going straight back to Tracy Island.' Jez grinned. She leaned on the roof of the Prussian car and pushed up her sleeve: studied a silver bracelet that she wore. 'In the middle of the Protest,' she mused, 'one of my guys was in Macedonia, or one of those places, on this very same trail. The last records we have, she was in the alien trading post. She'd found something that looked like crushed beetle wings in one of the trashed rooms. She thought it was the remains of a receiverless global: a suggestive discovery, she felt, in a nest of telecoms-allergic telepaths. She never came back. You wouldn't know anything about that, would you, Sid?'

He shrugged. His expression moved, minutely, through a subtle shift of ignorance and reproachful puzzlement.

'In English, Sid. I'm not a funxing alien.'

'Maybe they *were* beetle wings.'

'All that for, "*maybe they were beetle wings*"? What a ridiculous language.' She let him off the hook. 'Okay. But you tell the

Fat Man the SEF currently owes his private anti-Aleutian alien-watcher splinter group nothing. In fact you are in debt, but don't worry about paying us. We'll call you, got it?'

'Absolutely, ma'am.'

Sid had just discovered that the right sleeve of his borrowed pullover suit ended in a white stub much smaller than a human hand. He was staring, trying to assimilate this knowledge. The colonel turned the bracelet on her wrist so that tiny jewels caught the light, and looked at him without perceptible sympathy. She tucked something into his breast pocket.

'Cash it in where you can and don't forget to take your rad tabs. G'bye, Sid.'

The big silver bird came and picked the personnel carrier up, bearing the Campfire Girls off to their secret base. Sid made the Prussian drive around the exclusion zone. There was nothing moving. He had promised never to leave Bella alone, but he did not dare to go back inside. He sat in the car, clutching a chit for a new hand, and cried and cried.

9: THE DECAY OF THE ANGEL

When everyone had gone, Bella crept slowly from her hiding place in the blighted wood. She didn't go near the crashed car that lay where Aditya and the others had left it. She had seen the suits crawling all over it, and she was afraid. She sat with her back against a tree bole, shivering in the June morning in her singed and blackened clothes.

She was Bella, Johnny Guglioli's daughter.

She grasped at this construction of events, not sure where it had come from. She had been kidnapped as a human female child, disguised by gene therapy and brought up in Aleutia. Kidnapped? *Rescued* from this awful place: from the war, from human misery. But she had been stolen from her guardian by the anti-Aleutians, and pursued by Aleutian traitors and others for the sake of her father's memories. It was a misunderstanding. She remembered nothing. Everybody knew that now.

There would be no more silver suits coming halfway round the world to track her down, no more letterbombs from the anti-Aleutian fanatics, no more showers of mysterious favour from reckless society beauties. She was safe. She realised she was kneeling, covering her face. She dropped her hands, mugging self-consciously. Silly me, praying in the middle of a field.

Stop laughing, everyone!

Aleutia-in-her-mind was laughing at her. She'd been such a fool about the 'disguised prince' rumour. She was Johnny Guglioli's offspring: prey, treasure, a negotiable object. She wasn't important *as a person*, not to anyone. That was proved. Silly librarian, who had walked into the jaws of death, to a fate worse than death, as the locals said, certain that that her secret lover, watching from afar, would rescue her in the nick of time if things went wrong. Convinced, just as she had been in Athens.

She looked at her hands. The pallid skin, where you could see it through blood and smuts, was puckered and visibly pored. I'm a human disguised as an Aleutian, she thought. We – the executive 'we' of Aleutia still came to her naturally – made me into a halfcaste. I am the first true halfcaste. If I had tape of Johnny Guglioli here I ought to watch it and watch it. He is the nearest thing I have to a past self.

What had been done to her was cruel. If you don't know who you are, you are cut off from the WorldSelf. You can't know God if you don't know what aspect of God, the WorldSelf, is you. If you don't know who you are, you are mad. It isn't romantic. You have to be kept in hospital, because you can't look after yourself. She began to tremble, remembering the bridge over the Uji river . . . Maitri's librarian standing there with Aditya, frightened by the beauty's sudden attention, had protested silently, to everyone: *please stop telling me I'm not who I think I am. Don't you know you could drive a person crazy?*

But was that me on the bridge? Where did I, this I, begin? Her identity lay in fragments, shards of used quarantine film. She couldn't get back inside.

the librarian!

She clutched the sides of her head, as if like the locals she believed her self, her identity, was held in there. The memories! So many memories! So many lives! The years going down one from the other, deeper and deeper into invisibility, and all that was still this *Self*, tied to this *person*, the continuity into this immense depth, a lived and living thing going down into the impossibly faraway dark . . .

The borrowed memories fell away. The presence of Aleutia fell away. She was left alone.

A different kind of memory struck her.

Inside the sarcophagus, she had seen Rajath the trickster. Morel had been Rajath in disguise! She didn't know when the substitution had happened. She was isolate, and she'd never known Aditya's housekeeper well. She had told Aditya, that day in Karen city, 'I've heard you're fairly harmless if Rajath's not around.' She'd said it to make Aditya feel unsuspected: she'd

known that if Aditya was a traitor to the Expedition, Rajath the
trickster must be somewhere near. She hadn't known how close.
Seeker-after-truth had told her there were 'traitors with Sanskrit
names' who meant to sell the secret of instantaneous travel to
the Expedition's enemies. She had been looking for the traitors,
and the traitors had found her . . .

She thought Rajath had escaped alive. He must be somewhere
near, right now. She was not afraid, she was in no state for such
a rational emotion, but she felt it would be *horrible* to meet
him. She got up and began to walk towards town. She was
hardly aware of what she was doing. Something came rumbling
behind her out of the empty plain. An Allied jeep pulled up.
There were two men in it. The door of the cab opened.

'*Quelle est votre nomme?*' He shrugged, jerked a thumb.
'*Montes.*' She climbed in. '*Tu t'as trouve dans un peu de* firefight?
*Mais comment? On ne s'battre pas autour d'ici, depuis bien des
jours –*'

Bella said nothing. *Let them make up their own story.* The
jeep thundered on. Soon they reached the spot where the tourists
had abandoned two hired cars. One of them was still there. Its
half-dismantled body was hardly visible under a mass of human
scavengers. The other had gone. She realised as they passed this
spot and the vastness of the plains opened, that she could have
died of exhaustion before she reached town on foot. The dizzying
scale of the giant planet, invisible to a pampered tourist,
returned to her. That was good. Room enough to get lost and
stay lost.

On the outskirts of town the men stopped and sat for a short
while, discussing in their broken dialect whether to force Bella
to lie with them. Boy or girl, they were not fussy. They discounted the risk of disease: they had remedies. But with a face
like that, who could tell what went on under the clothes? They
decided against it. They drove into the centre and gently pushed
her out into the street.

Buildings closed around her like tall broken teeth. She learned
that food was being dispensed and followed this rumour, aware
of someone insisting that she needed to eat. Before she reached
the canteen, she came upon the entrance to a gaming mall. It
was basically similar to the one in Trivandrum. She went inside,

for no other reason than that it was something she had done before. She stood with a group of thrill-hungry children by the pay gate. Someone came in, slotted a cashcard and beckoned. He spoke in a dialect she didn't know, but it was easy to understand.

'You, the little halfcaste – '

In the blue darkness of the spectators' gallery there was a whispering like an overheard dream. She lost her first patron, maybe she missed his signals. She found an exit from the arena and waited. A player came out of the game, pulling off his visor and breathing hard. 'I shouldn't do this. You don't want to get addicted, kid. It'll ruin your life.' He tossed his half-charged kit to her and walked away quickly.

It was like Trivandrum, but better. There was much more of everything, and everything had the richness of detail of the masks in the Castlefield club. The game did Bella good. It was better than food. She came out of it when the kit went dead, feeling alive and focused. She went to the entrance and flopped against the wall, thinking of nothing. Her vision had gone grey, with black at the edges. She had no idea what she'd been playing, no memory of the book at all. She didn't care. Someone came and sat next to her.

'Hey.' It was a girl, a kind of a girl. She was dressed like one of the sextoys on Regent Street Market. Bella was afraid her own bloody and filthy clothes had been recognised as alien. Apparently not. Maybe in this town smoke-stained bloody rags were unremarkable.

'You're good.' Tiny bead-like things moved over the pale skin of her face. They glittered and fell into the air continually.

Bella was surprised to see a halfcaste so far from the enclaves, and wearing imitation Aleutian cosmetics. She said so. The girl made no coherent response. She had the physical appearance of a halfcaste, but she did not 'speak Aleutian'.

'I'm Lotte. You're new here. What's your name?'

'Bella.'

'I'm a spider. Are you? You play like one. What were you doing in there? You're wasted on that stuff. Sword and Sorcery is for the clawfaces: dickheads and kids. If we had money we could play the money games. I could get you in. Have you?'

She searched her pockets. Bella had travelled with Aditya as helplessly as an infant. Of course she had no money: she had nothing. But Lotte's predatory stare demanded to be placated. She found a creased wad of thin tissue and, unthinking, handed it over. The halfcaste girl spread it carefully. It was Sid's tenhead note.

'Aaah!'

The note vanished in a tightly knotted fist. The girl's sigh of delight didn't reach her nasal. Its constructed lips did not plump or quiver, but her cheeks glowed red under the patina of synthetic wanderers. She declared, rapidly, that she did not steal, she was not a thief, she did not know what Bella's resources were and didn't dare steal outright from a stranger of her own kind who might have some spider-means of revenge.

'You need a friend, don't you?' she said aloud. 'I'll be your friend. Let's go. I know where we can change this.'

Bella tried to get up. Her legs would not obey her. Lotte laughed, and grubbed around in the pouch that she wore on the front of her tiny skirt. She took hold of Bella's slack jaw and thrust something into her mouth: something crumbly and hard that softened and burst when it met saliva, with electrifying effect.

'Don't be scared, it's only sugar.'

They left the mall, Lotte with her arm around Bella: laughing and holding her up. Bella could not walk straight, but she was awake enough to register that a halfcaste gamer, living deep in old earth, had instantly recognised an Aleutian banknote. She put this fact away, to think about it later.

Lotte took Bella home with her, fed her, cleaned her up and gave her some clothes. She taught Bella how to play the money games and introduced her as a friend to the tiny halfcaste community. This last was exceptionally generous, because before Bella had arrived Lotte had been the best, most authentic halfcaste in town. It seemed there was not much change after these services from the Aleutian note. Bella never saw a scrap of the money. She didn't complain. She considered the exchange fair, even after she understood what a stack of local credit or cash – at the worst rate imaginable – Lotte should have got for the tenhead.

Eventually Lotte decided to move out east, towards Russia. There were bigger and smarter malls in the resort towns along the fashionable Baltic shore. She bequeathed to Bella – informally; she didn't make any goodbye speeches before leaving – her room, her '*petit trou*' as she called it, in a big derelict block near the halfcastes' favourite mall. The cabal of scavengers who ran the block then discovered substantial arrears of 'rent' and descended on Bella. She didn't mind. She was on a winning streak. She paid Lotte's debts and accepted it as a fair trade for the halfcaste girl's last gift of information: one can move on.

She moved to a big city. She dug herself into her own *petit trou* near the mall the halfcastes favoured, which was inevitably the best – if not the smartest or the most salubrious – gaming venue in town. She was imitative, she was methodical, she did exactly what Lotte had done and everything fell into place. The pattern of her life was set. She had found a way to disappear.

She learned that in every city of the war there was a community of these strange creatures, Aleutian groupies surviving without any Aleutians. They lived around the virtuality 'hells', grifting a marginal living out of the games: some of them resorting to prostitution, or preying on each other. They were a different breed from the *neti-neti* of the south. They did not 'speak Aleutian', they did not study character records. Their clumsy transformations were usually enhanced with makeup. Yet their devotion was real. And sometimes (they insisted) it was satisfied – mysteriously, secretly. But beyond Lotte's acceptance of the tenhead note, Bella saw no evidence of actual contact with any Aleutians.

She lived on sugar and naturlait, and diet-supplement patches handed out at the free canteens. One day she bought bread and a pack of vegetable stock cubes. She broke the bread and the cubes into a naturlait carton and ate the slops. She ate the whole loaf. Her gut struggled painfully and messily, but survived that first assault. The old-earth halfcastes had the same dietary ideal as the *neti-neti* of Trivandrum. They dosed and starved themselves in a regime that produced no more than a liquid drizzle of excrement. They used 'Aleutian' toilet pads as religiously as they used cosmetics to flatten their hair and pucker their skin. Bella, travelling in the other direction, bought shampoo to make her leathery hair curl (it didn't) and trained her gut to make turds.

She became obsessed with hard food. She took it home and gorged on the hardest she could find: raw vegetables, nuts, corn, crackers, cocoa beans. It was an ugly process but she persisted doggedly. She was frightened of this unhuman body. She wanted to kill it if it refused to change. She wanted to be *normal*, ordinary, acceptable. Nothing more, was that too much? She forced herself to eat until she vomited; and then eat again.

Her flesh filled out, her arms and legs were swollen and heavy. But her skin did not become smooth, her hair didn't become fine. Her claw did not wither away. The moist cleft in her belly did not shift towards the cloaca. The scale around it didn't turn to hair. Her torso, with its two small marks like the ghosts of human nipples, remained hard and flat. The grooves that slanted along the muscle from her collarbones to her *place*, and down either side of her spine, did not close. They longed as much as ever for the touch of a lover's mouth and hands.

She made herself ill, and couldn't do anything but lie in her pallet bed: running her hands over her body, hunting for changes and finding none. Her *petit trou* was a bare slip of space. Its furniture was the food she bought (she never thought of cooking) and the meagre grey envelope of un-living pallet rolled out on the floor. She never thought of buying a mirror.

Being ill was good for her. It was a pattern, like walking into the gaming mall but far more potently familiar. She rediscovered the librarian, the invalid: and the ghostly paths of common experience knitted together, making a bridge between the present and the past. She had been the librarian, she could not go home any more, she was Bella now. She remembered Sid: the feel of his body in her arms, the awkward shape, the warm, damp weight. She remembered him in the 'beautiful woman' mask, and the way the mask had failed utterly to hide the person: the irremediably contrary *not this-not that, I won't-ness* which was Sidney Carton. She would never see him again. In this world, her loss was too ordinary to be tragic.

When illness had made this bridge, she was able to think about Aleutia again. She dreamed of a library. In the dream it had become a human library of long ago, made of images gleaned from her beloved 'local records'. She saw shelves of printed books, some of them shabby, old, handwritten jotters. It was someone's personal collection, personal history. Outside there was an empty land of baked, cracked clay going on and on. She was thrown out of the library. The people who threw her out were sorry, but their first loyalty was elsewhere. She pleaded with them, but she did not feel they were wrong. Her time in the library had been borrowed time. She was not the person who belonged there, that was someone else.

No longer pleading, because there was no point, she woke up crying. *Ochiba*, the discounted, the rejected wife. She had been naming herself a woman, Johnny's daughter, since the morning when she had crawled out from under the sarcophagus, her place in the world lost for ever. Now at last she understood the word, and it was true. She was a woman. In gestalt, she always had been.

In the gaming hells of the war years, play was an ingenious compromise between the physical and the virtual. You wore a visor, an eye-wrap, that delivered the environment of the game to your visual cortex. But you remained normally conscious, and moved about in an arena: which you perceived as the whole length and breadth of fairyland. The software entity, the sensei that controlled the game, presented your actions and persona in the fantasy as perceptible experience for everyone who shared the *envie*, the visor-mediated environment.

According to legend – halfcaste legend – it was an Aleutian who had discovered that a game visor would accept eccentric direct-cortical commands: that there were trapdoors and loopholes in the processing architecture which could be exploited for fun or profit. This was clearly untrue. Players had started to subvert game software long, long ago. What the 'trapdoor spiders' did was the continuance of an ancient human tradition – of truly obsessed players finding tricks and random short cuts unplanned by the manufacturers, and spreading the word.

In effect, two virtual worlds occupied the game *envie*. In one, the punters played for the experience alone and behaved as if the laws of the game were immutable as those of reality. In the other the lucid dreamers, the spiders, knew that fairyland is a place where magic works.

Bella picked up something of this history, of the gamer contro-
versies; and a little about game technology as she settled into
her new life. There were spiders who loved to talk. But mostly
she learned by imitation and then gradually discovered why she
did what she did. She learned how to handle the complex and
sophisticated old-earth sensei: how to choose a role from the
book when she first put the eye-wrap on, and avoid the *charac-
terisation* that was strictly, like game drugs, for fools and
punters. She learned how to make money in the money games,
and in side bets on the fantasy battles. But she had been a player
before she knew anything, in that crude and basic gaming mall
in Trivandrum: when she had found something she could do and
insensately started *doing it*. She remained, like an Aleutian,
incurious about theory. Maybe that was why she was so good,
arousing other spiders' envy.

*The Vanaras had surrounded Lanka like a tumultuous sea.
Shouting, 'Victory to the Vanara king! Victory to Rama and
Lakshmana! Perish Raakshasas!', the Vanara army rushed on the
doomed city. Some hurled big boulders against the fortress wall
and on the city gates. Others armed with huge trees torn up by
the roots rushed on the Raakshasas. Ravana sent forth a big
army of demons. They beat their drums and blew their trumpets
until the sky resounded. They fell upon the Vanaras. The valiant
monkey people used boulders and trees and their own nails and
fists to oppose the Raakshasas. Thousands fell dead on either
side. The field before Lanka's gate was covered with blood and
mangled bodies.*

*In the midst of this gruesome engagement there were many
duels between individual warriors, and many momentary quiet
corners where one or two combatants briefly dropped their
weapons and flung themselves on the ground to rest. If the
warriors were the kind called spiders, they did not converse in
character.*

*'D'you know something?' said Angada, tossing aside a severed
demon limb. 'I've played this book in virtuality malls all over,
the worst to the best. And it is always the monkey battle at the
demons' palace. I've never found out how the story begins or
whether they rescue wossername, or what happens at the end.'*

He'd lost an arm. The dripping stump seemed to bother him. He kept feeling it tenderly.

'Give the people what they want.' Indrajiit picked monkey flesh from between his fangs.

'In my first game,' said Sugreeva, 'I thought the trapdoors were it. I thought you were supposed to find every one of them, or you hadn't got it right.'

'Like bunkers on a golf course,' murmured Indrajiit. 'I thought that about bunkers.'

The two monkeys scratched their heads. 'What's a golf course?'

Indrajiit was a demon: a splendid creature. His face was like a great fanged flower, his ornaments blazed with magic jewels. He was a demon, and yet there was something godlike about him: a great nobility. When he fell in battle angels would weep. This was true to the book, reflecting the fine even-handedness of Hindu mythology. However, it gave an edge to the friendly chat. You got more legitimate powers as a demon: but to a pure spider, that was a reason to be a monkey. Legitimate power was not spiderlike.

He didn't answer the monkeys' question. Instead, laughing hugely, he said, 'Sugreeva, how about a duel?'

A fist burst from the ground beside them and proffered a velvet-lined casket in which lay two pearl-inlaid eighteenth-century pistols. Demons can do that sort of thing. It's in the rules.

'Accepted,' laughed Sugreeva. He took a pistol. It turned into a banana, which he stripped and ate.

Monkeys can't do that.

A huge severed head flew across the air above them. Blood rained from the sky, deluging the remains of the coconut grove in which they were sheltering. Sugreeva, who knew a spell against flaming blood, shook the drops harmlessly from his fur. 'That was Kumbhakarna! Damn! I wanted that kill. You distracted me, Indrajiit. This means war!'

Towards midnight, the monkeys entered the city with torches. The battle had been long and varied. Sugreeva was surprised that Angada was still beside him. His arm had regrown, but now he'd lost a leg and it appeared not to be regenerating. He *also had a grisly head wound. He hopped gamely on a whole-tree crutch. This monkey was a spider of sorts. But he wasn't very good. The clumsier rule-benders usually avoided the experts. Angada wasn't going to make any extra kills around Sugreeva. Sugreeva's count in this tranche was respectable. Angada was barely scoring.*

Indrajiit still lived. He and Sugreeva seemed well matched.

The city, oh the terrible sights of that city! Monkeys and demons stumbled through its fire and blood-dabbled streets: limbs shattered, eyes blinded, choking in poison fumes. A huge building suddenly melted into a sheet of liquid stone and poured down upon the combatants. A demon crouched over a fallen monkey, drinking blood: a monkey held a demon child by its two heels and impaled it screaming on another's spiked iron mace.

'Whatever turns you on,' muttered Angada. 'I suppose it's therapy. Maybe they've got a right; it's not as if real life out in the war was much different. But you notice in these battles it's animals dressed up, monsters or something classical. Anything to sidestep the issue. D'you think they enjoy—?'

'I don't care.' *True spiders had absolute-zero interest in what the punters did, or why.*

'That Indrajiit fancies himself, doesn't he? Do you think he's someone rich and famous in the real?'

'I'm not interested.'

'I just noticed! You lost your tail. How d'you do that?'

It was not an injury. The tails were a fearful liability.

Sugreeva shrugged his massive furry shoulders.

'Sorry. If you have to ask—'

Indrajiit, dreadfully wounded, saw them coming and shot serpent darts from his chariot. Arrows in the form of poisonous snakes whipped around the monkeys' bodies, pinning their arms to their sides and searing flesh to the bone. Sugreeva knew a spell against serpent darts. He grew to cosmic size. The fiery snakes burst from his sky-filling limbs, he reached a great clawed hand and dragged Indrajiit's magic chariot from the clouds.

Indrajiit immediately became invisible and threw himself on his enemy. Cosmic size doesn't last. Sugreeva, back to his usual dimensions, struggled with the unseen foe. Angada, who was

*still trying to remember the spell against serpent darts, rolled
over in his bonds to the spot and attempted to set his teeth in a
demon ankle. A demon or a monkey heel spurned him. Sugreeva
drew back his mace for a mighty blow: and the demon
reappeared in death, shattered, his head almost split in two.*

*It was a game kill. In the book Indrajiit was killed by Rama
with a sacred arrow, which would still happen when that
tranche came round. But book kills were in the decor. They
required no skill and had no negotiable value.*

*Sugreeva finished the work and stepped back from his foe,
grimly satisfied. Down and out! Then Indrajiit's cloven head
reformed, his limbs gathered. He rose fluidly to his feet. It's hard
to tell with demons, but he could have been grinning. He
vanished. Angada looked up from the puddle of blood in which
he was lying, trussed in snakes.*

'Hey, Sugreeva. I hate to say it, but you've got a tail.'

Bella went home to her *petit trou* and counted bruises. A virtual
clinch was a stage fight, bodies did not connect. The mall games
were psychically very dangerous, but physically – aside from
terrorist subversion – hardly at all. However, because of the
demon's insolent behaviour, Bella had a lower score and had lost
some of the side bet she had made on that game. That wasn't
important. What *was* important was that Bella had never met a
spider better than herself before. She hadn't given much thought
to this. Now she wondered about Indrajiit.

She could not resist returning to the Lanka game to seek out
one special opponent; and returning again. She did not win. She
thought about this situation, and decided it was time to move
on. Another city, another mall, another *petit trou*. She could
travel around the war like this for the rest of her life, buried
deep.

It was a bad thing, a stupid thing, to get into a duel. It was all
right once in a way, but for a spider to duel with a spider
consistently just made you both poor. She had heard of it
happening to people. You started playing to beat another gamer
instead of playing to win. You fell into a fatal spiral. *Start
taking risks, start losing. Start losing, never stop.*

That was Lotte's wisdom. Lotte, however, had lost heavily

sometimes. She had been destitute, despite her sideline in prostitution, the day that she met Bella. Bella felt she had a long way
to go before she need worry about a 'fatal spiral'. When she
realised that she was sliding into a duel again, she did not try to
fight it. She made no attempt to discover if it was really the
same person following her around. If it was some rich human,
they might be wearing the visor in a private arena on the other
side of the world.

She moved on.

It was four a.m. in Akashi, wherever Akashi might be. Philip
Rao, of the Office of Aleutian Affairs, could read the hour on a
small digital clock, a black lozenge with minimal red numerals.
It stood on the floor beside the Aleutian's couch in the room
from which the alien was speaking to him. He believed the room
was somewhere in old earth, but nobody had tracked down the
location. Or if they had, then no one had told Philip. He was a
contact worker. There was a great deal he didn't know and
therefore couldn't reveal. The aliens weren't true telepaths, but
it was safer to behave as if they were.

'This was months ago,' the alien pointed out reasonably. 'Why
didn't you come to us at the time?'

Philip was wearing his uniform, a dun tabard with a codpiece
bulge in the groin. A woman's tabard had a breast bulge in the
front and a buttocks bulge in the back. It sounded ludicrous and
humiliating, but Philip genuinely felt neither ridiculous nor
shamed. He knew that to the person who was looking at him
physical lumps and bumps had absolutely no *mana*. They simply
wanted to know which brood they were talking to. It would
have been different, perhaps, if he'd been another Aleutian with
a poor supply of wanderers.

The convention, which had been adopted since the First
Gender War, was that you wore a Woman tabard if you knew
you were what the Aleutians regarded as feminine; a Man if you
felt you were masculine. There would have been problems if the
aliens had to cope with the idea of talking to 'brood traitors'
during a war. There would have been problems, too, if a human
was liable to appear, in Aleutian eyes, *in the wrong suit*. It
didn't happen. Anyone in Aleutian contact work had to be clear

about that aspect of their identity: and ready to be open about it.

In these conversations there must be no covert fear, and no lying. (Not because the Aleutians were so terrifying, but because if you gave them crossed signals in the two modes of words and Common Tongue it *snarled things up impossibly*.) But he was alarmed by the audience he'd been granted, and frankly expressed it. Since the Protest, there'd been no communication except recorded messages flown down by freight from Uji. Suddenly he had an interactive screen interview with one of the three captains. In the circumstances, this was not reassuring.

'We didn't think much about it at the time. But gradually we started to worry.'

'Trespass in a battlefield area,' pondered the alien, reclining on his couch in a dark robe: a lazy, graceful baboon in imperial purple. 'That sounds more dangerous to the trespassers than anyone else, as long as they weren't carrying weapons . . . no weapons to speak of, anyhow.'

A story had reached the Government of the World, concerning an incident *involving Aleutian weaponry*, in Prussia many months ago. It was known that the Aleutians had a science, which they themselves regarded with dread, of breeding weapons of mass destruction; a process that somehow involved the 'inert tissue' of the enemy. The Aleutians on the shipworld were a single brood. If they were building weapons, it could only be against humanity.

The Aleutian Affairs Office was reasonably sure that the aliens were *not* building weapons. But though details were meagre and investigation on the spot impractical, it seemed that *something* had happened in Prussia, and they could not let it go by. Aleutians do not respect people who don't seem to know what's going on around them.

The question, *Are you preparing to destroy us*? hung in the air: unspoken, and dismissed . . . *Not this time*.

'No one's concerned about local weapons carried for reasonable self-defence,' Philip said. Since the Protest, that had had to be agreed. 'But we have to remind you, we can't ensure your safety out there.'

'We appreciate the reminder.' The alien swung himself upright into a very human pose, leaning forward from the couch. 'And now I think we should forget the whole thing. Least said, soonest mended, as you people say.'

'Agreed,' said Philip Rao. 'Thank you for seeing me, sir.'

The old man in his tabard dissolved; the virtual screen out of which he'd been peering vanished into thin air. Clavel sat gazing at the place where it had been. Was it bright day in Krung Thep? Did the hot, wet air smell of jasmine and exhaust fumes and rot? Did the river pulse, glaucous and flotsam-strewn, under the strange spire of the Temple of the Dawn? But the Thais had moved their capital to the north, away from the drowned and befouled Gulf of Siam. There was nothing left of the past.

Yudisthara had begged him to handle the interview with the Office of Aleutian Affairs. Poor Yudi was so abjectly dumb about the locals he didn't know he had terrified them by treating this 'incident' so seriously as to involve the great Clavel. But Clavel thought he'd convinced the old alien-watcher that there was nothing to worry about. And the Aleutian Affairs Office could be trusted to do everything possible to keep it out of the records.

He spoke to Yudisthara, in the Aleutia-of-the-mind. ⟨Be calm, merchant. The horrid humans won't bother you again.⟩

He leaned back on the couch. The robe, that was deep indigo blue with purple shadows, fell away from his throat and arms. He lifted his hands in front of his face. They were well-kept, middle-aged hands, the claws trimmed, pads heavy and grainy. A second life here, he thought. And decades more of it. Will there be another, or is this the end? Bhairava, his master at arms, the security officer who had been Maitri's mate in his previous life, came into the room.

⟨Sir?⟩

⟨Just to say I know about the intruder. I'll bring him in myself.⟩

He stepped through long glass doors on to a stone terrace and into his garden, the midnight robe floating behind him over the damp caress of the grass. It was September, more than a year on earth since the seance. The night was cool and heavy with thunder. He let his fingers run through dark spires of flowering plants that surrounded the sloping lawn. Momentarily, they turned blue and turquoise. The glow of the opaque sky became visible. Was that glittering shower a spray of meteors? It could be tracer fire. Reformer 'terrorism' in the Thames Valley had reached guerrilla warfare levels. There were rumours of an imminent Ochiba invasion.

He had called his house Akashi, because it was a name like *Uji*: with connotations of sadness in the Japanese culture of his old friend Kaoru. The old Japanese had called that riverside manor far from his home Uji, after a place that was gone for ever beneath the sea. Akashi was the retreat where Clavel mourned a loss equally irretrievable. He went to his sea-shore – a part of the garden which had been laid with sand and shingle, and planted with marram grass and stunted pines. The scent and sound of the waves came to meet him. In daylight the ocean would stretch to a false horizon all around, and lap the sand.

Clavel's security, like the insect flier he used, was a hybrid system, shamelessly taking the best from living and from 'dead' technology. It was both his quarantine and his defence. It rarely had to deal with intruders. Something had come up against it tonight. The barrier had been adjusted to let the flier through, but to give him a bumpy ride. He sat and listened to someone blundering about among the breakers. He'd brought a handful of gravel from the garden path. He shied pebbles into the dark, where the waves sounded from. In reality it was a part of the garden that he had not reclaimed: a rank patch of stinging weeds and rubble. A yelp rewarded him. A muddy and bedraggled figure came loping up the beach.

⟨Is he here?⟩ demanded young Rajath excitedly.

⟨Who?⟩

The trickster collapsed beside him. ⟨Who! The librarian, of course! You knew I was coming, why didn't you let me in? I think my flier is ruined.⟩

⟨This is a war zone. We need security. Why didn't you announce yourself more clearly? The librarian? He's dead, isn't he?⟩

Rajath had been so terrified by what had happened in Prussia that he had abandoned disguise and fled to Uji. He'd been having an uncomfortable time there. The trickster's attempted treachery remained a decently veiled rumour. But Yudisthara was prostrate with grief. He had lost Aditya: and when they next met the beauty surely wouldn't even look at him. Everybody blamed Rajath, so that his life was a soup of reproaches. Plus he was threatened with a passage home, which would be highly inconvenient.

⟨You said he'd turned up. I came at once!⟩

⟨Did I say that? You must be mistaken. The librarian, as far as anyone knows, is a smear of carbon and burnt grease, rotting in the tomb of a defective mechanical sun. What I said was come, if you're tired of Uji, and I'll put up with you here for a while.⟩

Rajath and Clavel had not met since that midsummer night in a wood near Athens. Nor had they been in communication by local means. The conversation they spoke of had taken place in the Aleutia-of-the-mind. Rajath picked at his muddy sleeves, scowling. It had been very clear to him, in his inner model of the situation, that Clavel wanted him at Akashi, and that this was because the librarian had survived.

⟨Oh, well. I thought it was too good to be true.⟩

Clavel patted his arm. ⟨Let's go inside. I've sent people to look after your 'bird'.⟩

As they reached the terrace the rain began, streaming through the selective deflector dome, a resilient barrier against larger collisions or unfriendly chemical attack. Rajath followed the poet to a small room that was furnished as something between a study and a chapel. A character record of old earth was playing. Bhairava rose as they entered.

⟨Oh, hello,⟩ said Rajath. ⟨Er, I'm sorry about Maitri.⟩

The master at arms responded conventionally: ⟨It was in another lifetime.⟩ He didn't mention Rajath's own bereavement. It would have been tactless. ⟨You'll want fresh clothes, sir.⟩

Rajath brightened. ⟨Yes, please. And something to eat—⟩

Clavel forestalled him. ⟨Make sure everything's ready in our visitor's room. But first, trickster, you and I need to talk.⟩

The screen hovered in the air above a local-make low table with no visible support. The moving images were in shades of grey. Rajath peered at the picture. ⟨Who is that?⟩

⟨It's a famous local cleric by the name of 'Goebbels'.⟩

Rajath's nasal pouted uncertainly. ⟨I don't know the name.

But I'm sure I've met him, or someone very like him, in
'Moskva'.⟩

⟨It's possible,⟩ said Clavel dryly. ⟨If I were him, I'd have
changed my name this time.⟩

For a short while they watched the story of this thin, bright-
eyed, elegant person, and his distorted processing of human
confessions. His congregations foamed in battered-looking local
streets, swarming in and out of big grim character shrines. It was
very familiar to aficionados of old earth – except that nowadays
there'd be no character shrines like that, only gaming hells.

Rajath murmured softly in horrified admiration.

⟨You know, with priests like that it's not surprising they've
turned against religion. Genocide! Brrr.⟩ He glanced at Clavel
uncomfortably. ⟨Are these 'Jews' still around? Or did he finish
them off? People like that tend to repeat themselves. I wonder, if
he is the chap I saw in 'Moskva', who's he after now.⟩

Clavel laughed softly. ⟨Don't panic, trickster. The Protest was
a pitifully innocent affair. If 'Josef Goebbels' is back again, in a
sense, it isn't Aleutians who should be worried.⟩

Rajath visibly relaxed. ⟨Of course: the war. But *genocide*! It's
incredible how little the idea upsets them.⟩

⟨To them, killing one person is genocide of a kind. It is
permanent death, the kind of death we only know in the
destruction of a whole brood. Heaps of murders piled together
have no more bite than the first, I suppose.⟩

The record ended. The virtual screen vanished with a tiny,
decorative sparkle, making Rajath start. Clavel was silent.

Rajath contemplated the ruins of a dream.

⟨I never did believe in instantaneous travel. I don't know if
the Dark Ocean people even believed in it. You know what I
think? I think they wanted the librarian so that they could
pretend the device *might* exist. They thought that would be
enough to get people to agree to leave earth. They're supposed to
be the party that wants us to dedicate our lives to getting home,
but it's not true. All they care about is *doing down the
Expedition*. I suppose they'll want their advance back,⟩ he added
gloomily. ⟨No librarian, no deal.⟩

Clavel watched the trickster, with a bleak and lazy enjoyment
of his sufferings. ⟨Myself, I never meddle in politics. But there's

a pleasing symmetry to it, don't you think? We played a cruel trick on them. We pretended to be superbeings, come to rescue them from their troubles. They have managed without knowing it to play a trick on us: and the gates of heaven have slammed shut in our faces. It was nonsense. One sees that now. This 'device' never existed.⟩

He smiled, with a glint of tooth. ⟨Please tell me: had Viloma the medium tried that curious kind of 'materialism' before?⟩

Rajath drew his shoulders together. ⟨Not exactly. I think he'd used, er, fairly fresh corpses.⟩

⟨Wonderful!⟩ remarked the poet sardonically. ⟨He's such a nice person, our Viloma.⟩

⟨It wasn't *my* idea,⟩ protested Rajath. ⟨It was Aditya who took up with that loopy medium!⟩

Clavel laughed. ⟨That's not what I heard. But didn't anyone – Viloma's mad, but the rest of you – consider the risk? Even if there'd been nothing unusual in the librarian's makeup, you were growing commensals from someone close to mental collapse *having driven him into a state of terror* . . . Do you know how near necromancy is to weapon-building?⟩

⟨They weren't real weapons,⟩ muttered Rajath sulkily.

Clavel snorted. He stared into space.

⟨I do not take Dark Ocean's pay. But I knew we should leave after the sabotage crisis. I was helpless. I could not force myself to fight all the rest of you, to make us leave Johnny's world. It was too much to ask. So I tried to do good. I tried to teach the locals how to defend themselves: to become a heterarchy, to disperse their power and diversify against us.⟩

⟨Whereupon a grateful fanatic shot you and Bhairava in the head.⟩ Rajath injected a note of realism.

⟨Yes,⟩ agreed the poet absently. ⟨I thought it meant they were learning. But I came back and found every change I'd tried to nurture had prospered and had ruined them. There are no monster corporations, no giant states with starry banners, no Big Machines. There's only the war, and us.⟩

⟨I think you make too much of your part, and ours. We didn't do anything, except take advantage in a normal market-place way. Anyone would've done the same. And, you know, these phases do happen. They'll have better times.⟩

'Broken when we found it, officer,' murmured Clavel, in English. 'Never laid a finger, honest . . . *Oh*.' He moved restlessly. Rajath felt him tense as if for flight. ⟨You are wrong. We are to blame: and *it doesn't matter*. Everything must happen. In a way I'm comfortable here with my curios, dreaming of Johnny. But something inside grows lean and hollow-eyed. Something that this planet emptied from me has never been replenished. I'm famished in my soul. I don't know how I can ever be young again.⟩

Rajath felt boredom creep over him, the boredom that (in Rajath's model) was the whole Expedition's chief response when *The Grief of Clavel* came up. In Rajath's view the true reason that Clavel hid himself away at Akashi was because he couldn't stand to face that boredom: *Oh, no, here comes Clavel the Miserable* . . . He kept the idea to himself. He was a little afraid of the poet, and at this age not good at concealing his fear from himself. However much they irritate you, it is daunting to know that someone you honestly admire (though you think he's a kind of holy fool) *seriously wishes you did not exist*.

⟨Why don't you get out more?⟩ he offered at last. ⟨Old earth would solve your problem. Someone would put another bullet in your head.⟩ He warmed to his theme. ⟨You could work with refugees, you'd like that. Just don't make it obviously suicide. You know how people talk. It brands you, suicide. You never live it down.⟩

Clavel suddenly smiled. It was like the old beautiful smile of the one they used to call *forever young*. But in his eyes a chill weariness lingered.

⟨I don't think you quite understand, my friend—⟩

Somewhere else in the house there was noise: doors opening, voices. No known new *person* entered the air. Rajath started nervously. Clavel wasn't alarmed.

⟨They won't bite you.⟩

Two faces peeped around the study door. ⟨In a moment,⟩ called Clavel to the hovering domestics behind. He turned to his guest. ⟨The charming detritus of the days of alien fever. They are not so intellectual about it as those in the enclaves, but I prefer them.⟩ Two concave profiles, two pairs of dark-on-dark eyes. Small clawed hands with horny knuckles but smooth skin. Two

lightly made bodies with sloping shoulders and angular hip-
bones. They were barely more than infants. They were barely
dressed.

Clavel stood, sweeping the midnight robe behind him. ⟨I'll
wish you good night. I've promised Yudi I'll keep you here until
your passage home. Don't try to leave. *His* folk would be too
embarrassed to wrestle you to the floor and frogmarch you to
your room. My people and I feel differently. Don't make us prove
it.⟩

Rajath, after standing for a moment with his jaw dropping,
followed Clavel into a cavernous hall. A stairway swept
upwards. The little halfcastes were up there with the
Expedition's Pure One! The thin, dead effluvia of their skin
tainted the air.

⟨*Well!*⟩ exclaimed the trickster, scandalised. ⟨One had heard
rumours, but—!⟩

Bhairava was at the foot of the stair, holding a lamp. He
turned to Rajath with an eloquent lift of his shoulders.

⟨May I show you to your room, sir?⟩

Rajath shrugged in equal forbearance. Maybe it was a good
sign, a kind of recovery. He ordered food, comfort and company.
Don't try to leave . . . Cheek! He had no intention of leaving.
He'd accepted an offer of hospitality, and he planned to enjoy
it.

In the virtual casino the punters lost money (real money) in
imaginary luxury, and for some mysterious reason found this
delightful fun. The spiders practised direct-cortical telekinesis
on the software of a virtual roulette wheel, a virtual baccarat
pack. The house tolerated their depredations, within reason. The
spiders were part of the decor. Some punters came for them, not
for the games.

Bella went straight to the roulette wheel when she came in. It
was her preferred game, though it was the most difficult to fix.
Later she would move to baccarat. The liveried attendants knew
her. They rushed to push in her chair, to take her coat, to bring
her coffee and petit fours. The hour was late (in the virtual
casino it was always late). The room was full. Jewels sparkled
in the yellow light of many electric lamps. Footfalls and voices

were muted by the acres of thick red carpet, the gold and crimson
hangings that swathed the walls. Croupiers murmured their
time-honoured lines, players chattered between the tables,
glasses clinked. Music played softly. There was no jarring note.
A man-high bipedal reptile moved through the crowd, grinning
affably as the punters gave way. Covertly, Bella watched its
progress.

This slight young person, with glossy cropped hair that lay as
close as scale or feathers, with her 'concave' face and 'oriental'
eyes – so dark there was no visible distinction between iris and
pupil – was not as bizarre in appearance as some players at the
table. Among the merely perfect humans in their archaic evening dress there was a woman's naked body with the head of an
owl, a tabby cat in white tie and tails; a Black Dog in a skirt of
pleated linen with the torso of a man and the Key of Life lying
on his muscular breast. One of the perfect humans wore (rising
from the shoulders of his classic black dj) a pair of rainbow-
burnished wings that soared halfway to the ceiling.

The house provided a choice of masks, or it would accept most
standard formats if you brought your own. If you preferred, it
would scan your appearance and present you in your own image
in the game. Halfcastes traditionally chose this option. Masks
meant nothing to them. Status among halfcastes was tightly
bound up in the reality of your transformation. But the punters
who were queer for imitation aliens didn't trust the convention.
They prowled, flitting from spider to spider: unable to make up
their minds which would remain most truly weird outside the
envie. Bella ignored them. She'd never had to stoop that
far.

She won some small bets. The attendants were attentive
because the house knew what Bella was. She wasn't making sly
random gestures – playing imaginary piano under the table,
pulling her earlobe, shuffling her feet: however, the house knew
she must be doing *something*. But the attendants were decor.
Bella kept half an eye out for the deinonychi. The deinonychus
dinosaurs with the teeth and raking claws were big solid humans
in the real. If they threw you out it would not be a virtual
experience. It would hurt.

She began to lose. The heap of plaques and jetons at her elbow melted. The dowager on her left commented sympathetically: and stopped following Bella's 'system'. The tabby cat on her right gallantly continued to lay the same bets as the little halfcaste, saying that luck is not everything, he preferred to throw in his lot with youth and beauty. They were all of them, in a sense, striving to control the spinning wheel and the tumbling ball. Most of them were submitting to the fantasie, in which the wheel was a real object *out there*. But someone else besides Bella was nudging the virtuality software. The person was not necessarily at this table. They could be anywhere in the environment. She fought back. She won, and lost again. She saw that she'd lost forty thousand ecu, which was her limit for a night's play. She tussled briefly with her addiction, and left the table.

On her way past the baccarat she dropped a couple of green plaques over the shoulder of the player known as the tinman. It was a habit some people had in this *envie*. It was supposed to bring you luck. The tinman was not a beggar. He had to be rich to afford to play so badly. Bella had no idea what the player in the clunky robot mask thought of these whimsical handouts. She had never spoken to him. She tipped him because he appealed to her: with his spirited determination to lose. He jerked around his cylindrical head and cranked out a shy, jagged gash of a grin.

The balcony overlooked feathery tamarisk trees and a shore of yellow sand. Masses of magenta-flowered bougainvillea tumbled over the white-painted stone balustrade. Sparkling waves swept across the beach. Further out great walls of colour broke over a spit of rocks: cobalt, emerald, turquoise.

Bella stared through the illusion. She was tired. In the virtual casino the hours you spent at play were real hours of the world outside. The punters preferred it that way, but it could be exhausting. This was getting strange. She had moved into the casinos, out of battle games, to escape from her adversary, and chose the purest game of chance to discourage his attentions. But if someone wants to duel, they'll find a way. She had no idea who the duellist was. It could be the tabby cat, the owl woman, or someone she'd never had any overt interaction with at all. She didn't know if she wanted to find out.

'Have you ever seen the sea?' The Angel had come out to join her. He still wore the mask of a man in evening dress, in a cut that matched the casino's mid-twentieth decor. The wings had vanished. 'Around here,' he added, with a faint smile.

'I had a chance once. But I missed it.'

The black 'higene tomboy' Bella wore left her limbs and shoulders bare, and closely outlined her breastless torso. The Angel studied her frankly, in character; and in character his eyes awarded her the approval of a connoisseur of womankind. Some players clung to their mask-persona in a kind of desperation. Some of them were having fun. Bella wasn't sure about the Angel. The smile in the mask's eyes deepened. He took out an untipped cigarette, tapped it on his cigarette case.

'What's your name, child?'

'Bella.'

'I'm surprised that you play the tables. The virtual casino is for middle-aged punters on a nostalgia binge for a world they never knew. You're young, and so fast: I'm impressed. I should have thought Death Lizards of Venus would be more your style.'

So the Angel had decided to tell her he was another spider.

'I play for a living. There's money here.'

'I see.' He smiled again, the smile that might be desperate or assured, or both. He drew on the cigarette, which had become lit but was shrinking without dropping ash. 'A rational explanation. Too rational. How much more sensible to be a punter, and enjoy the delights of fairyland. For you and I, I would guess, there's as much pleasure for the senses here as in a game of virtual noughts and crosses. Yet such absorbingly complicated noughts and crosses!'

'But what's in it for them?' asked Bella, feeling both wary and oddly relaxed. 'I can't make it out. Why not a *real* casino? If they like throwing money away.'

'With old earth in the state it is in? How can you ask? Make-believe is cheap. How many nights in hell d'you think you could trade for one real five-carat diamond earring?' He considered the glowing tip of the cigarette. 'If you are trying to be like an Aleutian, Bella, you should hate the games. Or so convention would say. But are these really *deadworld* devices, in the alien sense? It's a debatable point. Maybe you've thought about it. On the scale at which direct-cortical impulse technology operates, where lies the threshold between "death" and "life": or between the material world and the void? It's a puzzle for alien philosophy.'

Bella laughed. 'Someone once told me something like that. I'd like to have tried one of the old games,' she added shyly. 'To be able to fly. I've been able to fly in dreams.'

'Ah, that takes coralin. The indefinite potential of the dreaming state is not an easy thing to model or sustain. There are no wings in the waking brain, not so much as an abandoned stump that can be made to twitch. We are not dreaming, Bella. This is only a game.' The mask grinned wryly. 'There are practical considerations. A flying tank is not a place one can easily evacuate. A body pod is not a nice place to wake up in a powercut. Or an air-raid! We're safer in the hells, these days.'

He tossed the end of his cigarette over the balcony. 'You and I should be friends, Bella. We seem to know each other, don't you feel that? It's almost as if we had met before somewhere.'

With a nod of farewell, he returned to the brilliant room.

Bella stood looking at the sea, listening to the waves. The illusion had the same effect on her as printed words did. It was there, but it felt like nothing. *So*, she thought mechanically. *I've found him. So that's him.*

Bella kept irregular hours. When she came out of the hell she was never sure whether she would find daylight or darkness outside. Sometimes there was a plane raid, and she would run and fling herself into a shelter along with everybody else. Sometimes the shattering percussion of a ground-level explosion would throw her flat. Once she was shopping in the covered market when there was an outbreak of fireworms: singed flesh, crackling threads of light, bodies milling and trampling. The halfcaste store in this city ran short of everything. The other spiders in her block were washing out toilet pads in cold water. Bella was very glad she'd house-trained herself.

But in the virtual casino, the electric lights were blazing. Supplies of caviar and champagne were unlimited. Bella imagined more and more hells springing up, and the locals crowding

into their shelter: rich and poor, halfcastes and purebreds, men
and women together.

She didn't move on. The secret duel continued.

A session came when things were bad before she arrived, play
began badly; and continued worse. Bella had spent an hour at
the roulette table. The heap of coloured counters at her elbow
shrank to nothing. She left the table smiling, and went to a cash
desk. The hells, no matter how opulent their decor, were
accustomed to cater for clients who didn't have a credit line.
Inside the cubicle she pushed up her visor and fumbled for paper
money in her waistbag. The pouch was empty. She searched it,
turned it inside out. She ran her hands over her Tomboy. She
must have more paper somewhere. Must have left the last of
her wad in the *petit trou*. But she never left money in her
room.

The cash desk was a hollow, opaque cylinder with an automat
in one curved side for receiving cash and recharging your house
account. Bella slid into a crouch, in a state of shock. I have lost
everything, she thought. She could not believe she had let this
happen. It was the duel; it had become an obsession. She did not
take game drugs and avoided the company of the hopelessly
characterised. But spiders didn't spurn game drugs for the sake of
mental hygiene. It was because they wanted nothing to pollute
the purity of the fix. They were as much at risk as anyone. *It
will become real*, people warned you. *One of them will become
real, and suck you in . . . and you'll be gone.*

Through the wall of the cylinder, she could dimly see the
casino hall. It looked strange and bare. The masked gamblers
were still masked but they stood and sat around on battered
plain furniture in a big, poorly lit room. Their hands and eyes
moved intently over empty space. If she stayed in here any
longer, the cylinder would retract and the deinonychi would
come and take her away. She left the desk, and went looking for
the Angel. He was with the owl-headed woman, playing cards.

'Excuse me—' She didn't know what to call him.

The owl woman started. ⟨Nasty little pervert! Taking honest
women's work!⟩ Tonight she was dressed in a wide hooped skirt
and bodice that left her breasts and furred lower belly bare. The

Angel was in his basic black. Bella steeled herself. The Angel and she were friends. It was a reasonable request.

'Excuse me, sir. I've come out without my purse. Could you lend me twenty thousand?' The owl woman laughed unkindly.

He shrugged. 'Of course.'

She returned to her place before she consulted the pillbox on her wrist. Forty thousand ecu. That was nice of him. She rejoined the play. She would win. She played on *noir*. The jetons were swept up by the croupier, Bella's winnings were pushed towards her. The kind tabby cat patted her hand with his soft furry paw.

The punters placed their bets, and won and lost, in a vanished world where everyone was rich – or at least the poor were far away. Where the war had been over for millennia, where women accepted their defeat and used it wisely; and men were secure enough to be magnanimous in victory.

'*Rien ne va plus!*'

Bella sat, elbows on the green baize, intent on the illusory wheel. The Angel had asked her, in one of their little chats, what it was she *did* to control the fall. Truly, she didn't know. The roulette wheel was made, essentially, of pure images: ordered and indexed. When some task is part of your obligation, you don't *word* it, you do it. 'I used to be a librarian,' she had told him. 'Checking through packets of information is my métier, I suppose. It isn't hard. There are many things you can't do. If there's one you can, I get there.' But tonight she kept thinking of the mall in Trivandrum, that primitive scrabble between the monkeys and the demons. She was back there and this time the demon warriors were too much for her. As fast as she re-ordered the library stacks, the demons slyly jumbled them. If her adversary had needed to win, as she did, she would not have been in trouble. But he only needed to make Bella lose. The wheel slowed, the ball rattled into rest.

'*C'est fini.*' '*Rien ne va plus . . .*' '*Faites vos jeux.*'

She was concentrating fiercely and intently. She pushed a stake on to the *rouge*. The ball rattled and fell. Lost. Well, it wouldn't happen again. She was in control. She woke, with a start, to find the masked faces turned towards her. A voice murmured in her ear, 'Mademoiselle's stake is not covered. How will you settle?' She was grateful to find that she could.

She walked out on to the balcony to say goodbye to the view. It was misty dawn. The ocean was viscous pink and grey, moving sluggishly in the brimming bowl of beach and rockspit and horizon. She realised that she would miss the illusions very much. She had come to depend on them, the way the punters depended on them. Reality is such a drab and cruel place.

In the dingy foyer, players leaving and arriving brushed past her. The Angel, still masked – it was just a mask now, not part of the *envie* – was leaning against the wall by the checkout gate, one ankle tucked over the other. She owed him forty thousand ecu, and she didn't have a sou in the world. His great wings curved high over his head. They had an air of offering luxurious shelter. He was smoking a cigarette.

'You look worried, Bella. What is it?'

'Money.'

'I was afraid it might be.'

'I can't repay you.'

He studied the tip of his cigarette: and threw it suddenly aside. It vanished in midair. 'I have a home nearby. If you wish, you might make it yours for a while?'

So it was her turn to fall. She had lost everything. The game had become real. She wondered where Lotte was now. And others, friends she'd made in the *petits troux*, friends who'd dropped out of sight. Halfcaste whores in the war cities didn't last long.

'You will come home with me? Come, and repay all debts.' The Angel reached out to her, desperate and assured: '*Compagnero.*'

Bella put her hand in his, and felt the warm and living grip.

'It's agreed?'

Bella said nothing. She stood, trembling.

'Do you want to pick up any luggage?'

'No.'

They went out into the street. 'I don't run a car,' he said easily. 'It's no distance.'

He stepped into a dark doorway. Bella glimpsed touches of colour on walls and floor where the daylight found traces of decoration in the grime of years. The Angel's wings shone, white and rainbow-burnished, as he descended into the black pit of a stairwell. Bella followed.

10: Victimam Sacrifici

The Angel had said his home was nearby, but by the end of the journey through the tunnels he was carrying Bella in his arms. She was set gently on her feet in a darkened hall. Daylight entered from behind her, stained by the coloured glass that it passed through. There were signs of decay. Paint and plaster had fallen in chunks from the walls. Yet she knew that the hall was alive, as infested with Aleutian commensals as the fabric of Uji manor. The Angel still wore his mask, the wings sweeping into shadow, above the evening dress that glowed in black and white.

He watched her, deeply expectant. ⟨Who are you?⟩ he asked.

'I am Bella Guglioli.'

'No,' said the other, aloud. 'You're not Bella. She died not long after Johnny, while she was still a child. I would have done a great deal for her. But I didn't understand quite who she was, until too late.'

'Clavel?' The Angel, named, shattered into a thousand liquid fragments. Bella collapsed on to the floor.

She woke in Aleutia, in a clean, comfortable Aleutian bed. The virtuality casino no longer held her in its grip. She was out of the game. She remembered how Clavel's domestics had gathered her up and carried her off, exclaiming at her pitiful weariness and scolding their lord. She had sipped a bowl of gruel, while they hovered: and tried to climb into this pallet as if it was a local bedroll. It had resisted with the dumb indignation of a mistreated commensal until she gave in and let it enfold her.

They had said she was ill: poor thing, poor cripple; the usual things. She was not ill. She hadn't been eating well, or sleeping much. That was all. She lay cuddled in the living warmth and

looked around. It was a pleasant room, crowded and cosy and
softly lit. Images from Aleutian and local records played, in the
exquisite clarity of local-made screens. The furniture was
adapted for an isolate, not 'half-killed' sterile like products for
the local market, but only mildly alive. On a pretty couch
someone had laid out fresh clothes, including a light blue robe.
She realised that the room seemed familiar because it *was*
familiar. Someone had reproduced her study-bedroom, down to
the last robe Maitri had given to her, which had been destroyed
at Mykini.

Maitri! How glad he will be, she thought, when he comes back
and finds out how the story ended. He'd told his invalid child so
often, silently, *everything's going to be all right*: without ever
explaining what was wrong. She understood that he'd been
forbidden to tell his ward the truth. Clavel had decreed that
nobody must know, not even the librarian with the secret
destiny, until the day when everything was revealed.

Beside the couch where the blue robe lay, a closet stood open.
There were other clothes inside, folded and hanging. They were
human clothes. The folds had an air of permanence, as if this
stranger's wardrobe had been waiting there for a long time.
Bella, half dreaming still, wondered if those things were meant
for her too. If not, then for whom? A door opened. The owners of
some of the air's life came crowding in and clustered round her
bed.

⟨Hello, dear child. Are you feeling better?⟩

⟨Would you like something to eat?⟩

⟨You've had such an awful time, poor thing. You must rest.⟩

She struggled to sit up. ⟨I'm isolate,⟩ she reminded them.
⟨You'll have to excuse me. Should I know you?⟩

One of the Silent took her hand. ⟨You don't know us,⟩ he said
sweetly. ⟨But we know you. And we love you dearly. We're so
glad you are here at last.⟩ His eyes were brimming.

At dawn, Bella had truly felt that she was destitute and forced
to submit to shameful employment or else starve. But that had
been the game's version of events, and it no longer existed. But
somewhere in her, Maitri's librarian recoiled from this welcome.
It was all very well for Aditya, whose self-respect was impervious
to slights. Maitri's librarian couldn't stand to be seen as a *bride*:

someone contacted to be the bed-partner of a more powerful character. But there wasn't a shadow of contempt in the domestics' attention. There was nothing but the usual possessive kindness of their obligation: and a trouble that they were eager to share. She managed to contain her involuntary reaction. Of course she was not a bride! She was the great Clavel's other self: such a momentous promotion, it was hard to take it in.

⟨You must make our Pure One happy again,⟩ pleaded someone.

⟨If you can break him of his sad habits – if only you can!⟩

⟨You could lie a little,⟩ offered another, ingenuously. ⟨It wouldn't hurt to lie a little. You mustn't tell him I said so, but I can assure you he wouldn't mind.⟩

⟨After all, he is everything to you.⟩

⟨You must love him so!⟩

They fussed over her, grooming and petting. Some teased the bed into softer warmth, while others helped her to change her underwear. She asked for her medication. This request produced nervous giggles. They were uncomfortable at having to refuse her anything, but: ⟨Not at first,⟩ explained one of them. ⟨After so long, it might upset your insides. Maybe later.⟩ They left Bella alone with another bowl of pleasant gruel. The Pure One had ordered them not to stay, in case they tired her.

She ate the food, set the bowl aside and stretched herself out: purely luxuriating in cleanliness, in the feel of having proper underwear. It had been so long! If her neighbours in the *petits troux* could see her now . . . !

To ask for the medication had been a reflex. She didn't want it. She knew that the isolate's drugs had been making her ill all her life. She tasted the information-laden air. Soon, she thought, her 'reverse-therapy' would begin, the opposite to the kind she'd risked in Trivandrum. She would be an Aleutian, but not an isolate. She thought of Sid. He had known who Bella was all the time. She saw that now, and accepted fate. Some beautiful things are wasted: it's just life. There was no question of where her duty lay. And when the moment of recognition came, it would be 'duty' no longer. It would be the end of a long and vivid dream and the beginning of real life: no regrets, all debts paid.

She dressed, noting sadly that the modest light blue of Maitri's present was no longer at all to her taste. Nobody came, so she ventured out into the house. Poetry in still and moving images hung on the walls. Bella moved from one to another slowly: thinking of Clavel's own poems about first contact and the giant planet. Maitri's librarian had passionately admired those melancholy strains of colour and form. There was nothing by Clavel himself on these walls, but everything was sad.

She saw how the work of the commensals was controlled. They had been trained to hold the damage done by time, warfare and neglect in a poignant stasis. It was a lovely effect, and inexpressibly mournful. Might such unrelieved grief become a little tedious? The thought felt heretical. She reminded herself that she was here to bring the grief of Clavel to an end.

She found her way downstairs to the wide hall that she had seen when they arrived. Several rooms opened from it. The first she went into was large, and furnished with a collection of local antiques. It felt like a museum. A young local, a man, in old-fashioned clothes, was sitting on a bow-shaped couch in earnest communion with a screen that was showing war news. He glanced up. Bella saw a childlike, open face: a pair of alert black eyes. The person was familiar, but for a moment unplaceable.

'Oh, Excuse me.'

She backed out, unwilling to interrupt the young man's prayers, suddenly conscious that she wasn't in quarantine—

Bella shook herself. *Quarantine?* That was a thought from the past. She had passed through so many worlds since 'Goodlooking' the innocent tourist had arrived on earth.

One of the Silent had appeared in the hall. He acknowledged Bella's presence with a friendly smile, and walked into the room she'd vacated, carrying a large vase of dead flowers. Bella saw him place the flowers, taking a path directly between the young man and the screen. He opened tall glassed doors at the far end of the room, returned, briskly closed the news and moved the local screen (with the practised distaste of the Silent who have to handle deadworld ware) into a closet. The young man with black eyes did not protest. The domestic offered to Bella a room that was, to him, clearly empty.

⟨Please, make yourself at home. Clavel won't be long.⟩

As soon as Bella was alone with him the young man stood up.

He was unmistakable now but subtly *wrong*: too old? Too muscular, too tall, too serious? He crossed the room and vanished, around the moment when he would have reached the glass doors.

'I hope you are rested.'

The Angel had become a tall, loose-limbed Aleutian, no longer young. His modest air reminded her of Maitri. But Maitri was truly unassuming, by obligation. Clavel was awkward like a perpetual adolescent, hopelessly unable to wear his power with grace. It was a discomfort that people loved in him. He folded himself on the bow-shaped couch: watching and waiting, as the Angel had watched and waited. 'Did you know it was me when you met Indrajiit outside the walls of Lanka?'

She was glad of the cloak of formal conversation. 'It seems to me now that I knew at once who you were. But I couldn't be sure, because you didn't say, and we only met inside the games.'

She could not take her eyes from the spot where the figure of Johnny Guglioli had disappeared. Clavel's smile acknowledged her curiosity. He lifted his wrist, to show the pillbox he wore.

'Among some of the locals,' he said, in his perfect 'Japanese' English, 'there's rumoured to be a rule that if you save someone's life, you are responsible for that person for ever, as far as their "for evers" go. I have learned that there is the same bond if you have caused someone's permanent death. It was because of what I did to Johnny that he became a saboteur and was executed. When I raped him I murdered him. Long ago, I realised that I would always be haunted. That for all the lives to come his figure, profoundly unreal, would come and sit by my side. He would be with me, quiet as an old friend, every time I raised my eyes. The deadware ghost I can invoke and banish at a touch makes it easier to endure the other's company.'

Bella felt how incongruous it was that she should be uneasy in this person's company. But she was still like Maitri's librarian: thrust into intimate conversation with his idol; longing to escape and get back to his nest of records, actually much happier with Clavel on a screen.

⟨I'm truly sorry.⟩

Clavel laughed, aloud like a human. It sounded strange.

It was a relief to have something practical that must be said, that was unaffected by this strange and delicate situation. But it was oddly difficult to speak. She felt as if the crowded air was trying to close her throat.

'I couldn't take the risk that it wasn't you. After the seance, I had to hide. I was confused, I admit: and then the games sucked me in. But I never forgot that I was hiding. You see, I know something. Not what people think—' She stumbled on the words. 'Thought that I should know. But something that might be vital.'

Clavel was not responding. He was staring at the silk rug that covered the floor by his couch. It seemed in the lamplight to be woven out of topaz and rubies. He looked up.

⟨No. Don't tell me. I don't want you to tell me anything.⟩ His tone was gentle, encompassing and absolute. ⟨You are safe. We'll be happy. I never want you to think of that time again.⟩

It was dusk outside the glass doors. Domestics came in: one to rouse and arrange the lamps, others to lay a polished deadwood table for a local-style meal. Clavel stood. 'Shall we eat? I hope you like hard food.' He gave her a crooked smile. 'You're using the "she" expression for yourself, I notice. Is this permanent?'

'I . . . it's a habit I got into. I suppose it will wear off.'

It was a very Aleutian approximation of human cuisine. The main course was a stew of vegetables. Rigid chunks of cabbage, carrots and garlic floated in a tepid watery stock. Bella ate with polite enthusiasm while the domestics watched, proud of their achievement and of Clavel's sophisticated taste.

Clavel poured wine for her. 'I'm afraid you're missing your nightly fix. I know what gaming fever is. But I shan't deprive you. We can go to the Baltic.' He looked at Bella, quizzical. 'How did you end up a spider, child? Was it pure addiction?'

'There aren't many places where halfcastes gather, in old earth. I, well, you know how people talk. I had the idea that if I stayed with them, you'd find me eventually.'

Clavel stared: and then laughed in genuine amusement.

'I live so much like a human, I forget that Aleutia is watching me. Of course, the poet's antics are still entertaining the masses. I can withdraw myself from the traffic of the air. But I can't escape from the Aleutia-of-the-mind.'

He leaned his elbows on the table, lips drawn back. 'Speed of reaction,' he said. 'That's what we have. You, Bella, you see the smooth curve where the locals see a jerky sequence of snapshots. You are at the source, they are snatching at inferences. It's not what we can do and they can't that does the damage. Trade depends on the uneven distribution of skills. It's what they can do that we can do better. Oh, a little better: an edge. It's enough. Not all the games we can play with their systems are as innocent as virtuality Ramayana. You ask Rajath.'

Bella preferred not to think about the trickster captain.

'It's because they're not used to direct assimilation of symbolic data,' she said. 'Their processing machinery wasn't like ours, until they invented "virtuality". You had to struggle through layers of language, the machines were *built* in formal language. I've met local spiders nearly as good as me. They'll catch up, now they're able to manipulate the sensei interface, the same way their mind/brain processes perception—'

'You mean they're becoming more like us, and you approve. You're one of those who wants humans to be imitation Aleutians?'

'It's not like—' Bella dropped her eyes. 'I'm sorry. I don't want to argue.' There was a slight, awkward pause.

Clavel talked on. He spoke of the sights of earth, the poetry on his walls, the progress of the climate improvement scheme (on which Yudi was more determined than ever). He was interesting, insightful and well-informed. Bella spooned the dire stew, listened and offered anodyne formal comments. It made her feel better to know that Clavel was at least as nervous as she was herself about what should happen when the meal was over.

The tinman had followed the Angel and his prey into the deserted underground station. The default lighting had failed, but he had nightsight lenses. With their help he read the blackboard by the gate. It was covered with white chalked copperplate, the mark of the sole literate community left in the ravaged city. There had been 'an incident' on the line. Services were subject to long delays, or suspended. The date was a year old.

But it was dated! You had to admire that.

After months of neglect, the gate had fallen open. He killed his mask and passed unchallenged. He'd trudged the filthy ballast for what felt like hours when he came across the feather. It lay poised on a rail: a white feather twice the size of a swan's primary with a heavy burnish of gold, violet, green. He assumed it was virtual. But when – stupid, but irresistible – he stooped to pick it up, it turned out to be real.

He sat down, studying the Angel's message by glimmering animal vision. There were no giant swans around here, and swans don't have rainbows in their feathers. This was the Aleutian answer to human magic. *You can make illusions. We can make reality. You can do bodiless conjuring tricks, we can create. We can make your wildest dreams come true: easily, easily.*

The feather had been dropped deliberately. Clavel must have spotted the tinman at the casino, and knew he'd been followed when he finally took Bella away. He didn't care. He knew he had nothing to fear. Bella couldn't be *rescued* from Clavel. She wasn't a captive. Her fated lover had taken her home at last.

When Sid was a kid, all the halfcastes knew about the great Clavel and his vow of perpetual mourning. Nearly every half-caste child went through a period of being secretly convinced they were Johnny Guglioli reborn: destined to end Clavel's grief, forgive him for the rape, bring Clavel's benign influence back to the Expedition and heal everything that had gone wrong between earth and Aleutia. Spiritually, it was a noble destiny. On a practical level you could dream of the day the poet-captain would come and sweep you off to a life of bliss.

Sidney had never been through this phase. He was the one who used to point out to the other kids that if you forgot the legend and remembered the records, you could see that the rape was irrelevant. The love story had never existed except in the alien's mind. *Johnny Guglioli barely liked Clavel.* Why should a reincarnated Johnny feel any different?

But then, that was the real person who was dead for ever. With a 'Johnny' who had been purpose-built, how could Clavel fail?

He tucked the feather in the breast strap of his overalls, and tramped on. The Fat Man had ordered Sid to leave Bella alone, when they found her in the gaming hells. He was to wait until

the other player had made *his* move, and then go after Clavel
and fetch Bella from the poet-captain's lair. The Fat Man's
instructions were never less than whimsical and arbitrary, but
this was surely the most senseless errand yet. *It's over*, he
thought. *There aren't any 'latent memories', the seance sorted
that out. Bella's no longer our concern. She never was. I was
right from the start. I don't know why I'm doing this.*

The other Aleutians were together somewhere in the house:
playing games, making music, chatting; slipping off to lie down
together. They would sleep Aleutian style, napping and waking.
The poet-captain was with them: puzzling and fascinating and
delightful as ever to his followers. Bella the isolate did not share
their company. She was alone (she'd grown used to it) for the
long blank of the locals' night. She slept, and dreamed.

He, Bella, was profoundly isolate. It was no longer a physical
disability. He swallowed the broth of presence, it sank into his
pores. But the messages delivered to him were untrue. They were
artefacts of the nerve fibres, mechanical tricks. Some vital
chemical twist had come unravelled and he had lost his faith in
the commonalty of mind. It was gone like a major perceptual
interface disabled: as if he could touch the world but feel
nothing. He was surrounded by ghosts. The persons of Aleutia:
Maitri, Bokr, Rajath, Yudisthara, Aditya, Bhairava. . . various
and individual as the void and distant stars, were like empty
deadworld masks. He was hopelessly, permanently alone. So
were they all, but he was doomed to know it.

Bella stirred, half rising from unconsciousness. *Am I always
he when I dream?* she wondered. She had not noticed this before.
The formless nightmare, without events or images, seemed to
tell her that she would never be part of Aleutia again. In her
half sleep it had the cold touch of truth. *But Aleutia exists*, she
thought. *The commonalty is real, it won't disappear because I'm
shut out.* Comforted, she sank once more into sleep.

. . . and was *he.* He saw a room, which he knew was a room
in this house. There was a wide bed, local-style solid but without
legs. The coverlet was gold, crushed silk. A young masculine
halfcaste sat on the edge of it, wearing a pair of denim jeans. He
was not therapied, but he'd had his nipples and his nose removed

by surgery. He rubbed his hairless unmarked breast and bare shoulders. He was looking round him with frank admiration and hoping that a small deception would not be detected. He knew that the libertine who had brought him back to this house preferred virgins. A halfcaste who had been whoring for perverse locals was spoiled. The boy knew this, and naively spoke of his deception in the Common Tongue. The person who was Bella, the hunter who prowled the gaming malls, watched and smiled.

They began the little play that the libertine liked to play. They talked, the two of them. The young man relaxed into his role. He was acting himself: innocent, greedy, and certain that the superbeing could grant his every wish. Bella grasped the youth's hand and drew him into an embrace. The local struggled, as he had been tutored: pretending that he suddenly didn't like the idea of sex with an alien. *When it comes to it*, whispered someone in Bella's mind, *they never have to pretend this part . . .*

This voice whispered knowingly, and was the voice of the person who was Bella. But he managed to project himself into a different situation: in which he truly believed he was being invited to make love with a willing partner. When the young man began to struggle, and his disgust was unmistakable, Bella couldn't stop himself. His revulsion at what he was doing was overborne by habit. It was the terrible mistake that you can't stop making, over and over again. He held the protesting body down, his belly open and his claw clutching. The young man's soft penis had become swollen and rigid while he sobbed in shame: betrayed by the logic of the human sexual response, where fear of the enemy is so close to arousal . . .

Bella was feeling what happened to the male human body from within. He was racked by an incredible flux of sensations, playing both parts inextricably: as if he and the human were true lovers, twin selves . . . but the rape went on.

so smooth and lifeless, like no Aleutian flesh. Knowing that I am destroying any possibility of a true meeting, but so aroused by horror I cannot ever escape. No other lying down could be so agonised, so intense . . . I bring them here. I make them act Johnny's part. They comply in greedy fear, hoping I'll pay them in supernatural favours. I cannot stop myself. I re-enact the rape because the rape is what is happening. What I did to Johnny is what we are doing to earth. They say they want us because they're too frightened to say no and it's too easy to say yes. And we know what we are doing, but we won't stop . . .

Bella lay open-eyed: the engrossing, orgiastic nightmare draining out of her. She was in her own room, she was Bella again and Clavel was crouched by her bed. He was not looking at Bella. He seemed much younger than he had been at dinner. She lifted her hands to her temples. The fugitive trace of pressure from a visor was already fading.

She must have made some exclamation. The poet started.

⟨I beg your pardon,⟩ he said. ⟨I didn't mean to wake you.⟩

He left the room.

Bella sat up. She touched her temples again. Clavel! She felt that she was waking for the first time since the Angel had brought her here. She knew there would be no gene therapy to remove this disguise. She had never been Clavel's other self. She got up, stripped off her night clothes, dressed herself deliberately and went to find her host.

Clavel's retreat stood among derelict ruins, bedraggled bombsites and big old houses subdivided into teeming tenements. The streets were littered with midden heaps and chunks of defunct machinery, left to biodegrade slowly in the foul air. People sat about on corners and in doorways, wrapped in the bored languor of malnutrition. Sid wanted to hide behind the tinman mask. But kids here would sell their vital organs for an fx generator – if anyone was buying. He kept the pillbox pushed well up his sleeve.

He found a cafe and ordered tea and a slice of cornbread and scrape. He could remember how it felt to be a halfcaste in a neighbourhood like this. It is not good to have to deal with people who envy you without having any reason to fear you. It's a bad bargaining position: it ruins your nerves. It didn't make any difference that halfcastes had no material advantages. They had their faith. For the victims of the Gender War, that was unforgivable. He sat for hours, intermittently scraping with a pocket-knife nail file at a blemish on the heel of his right hand.

He'd decided not to break in until after dark. It would be

better that way, she'd have settled in. He'd make his speech, she'd say *no thanks, I'm sorted*. He'd congratulate the happy couple and leave.

He moved from the cafe to a pub. About ten in the evening, when the looks he was getting were approaching the verge of random violence, he headed for Clavel's protected grounds. He used the Fat Man's gadgets to get in, and prowled like a trespassing sightseer: throwing stones at the sound of the waves on the sea-shore, listening to hooting monkeys and the rustle of tropical rain in the West African forest. He might as well check it out. He wasn't going to be here again. No alarms went off. No one appeared to give him the *can I help you?*, and escort him to the gates.

It was raining hard when he finally dared the terrace above the English country garden. He picked the dead-and-alive lock with his hybrid skeleton key, and pushed the glass door open. His lenses showed him a big room furnished with a tasty collection of antiques.

I just want to talk to her, please . . .

He stepped inside. The room wasn't, as he'd first thought, empty. For an instant virulent orange swamped his vision. The lenses adjusted. Bella was sitting on a soft couch that was the most Aleutian object in sight, a dim lamp at her elbow, dressed in the same black slip she'd been wearing at the casino. She had a whisky tumbler in one hand.

⟨Shut the door,⟩ she suggested.

He shut the door, and stayed with his back to it. The air made him want to cough. It was a long time since he'd lived with aliens. They'd spawned monsters from her terrified flesh and he'd left her there alone . . . He realised, startled, that she was as consciously feminine as if he was looking at a human woman in full gender warpaint.

⟨Why are you calling yourself 'she'?⟩

If she was surprised to see him it didn't show: of course not. She sipped the whisky, giving him a sombre, level look over the rim of the glass. ⟨Now that I understand the term better, I don't know why you don't use it yourself, Sid. Being 'she' has more to do with hierarchy that anything else, far as I can see.⟩

It was a moment of complicity, the small against the great, so unexpected that he could not respond. He put on the tinman, and clanked silently over to her. He shook a closed metal fist.

'You were very generous to the club mascot. Pity a person can't live on fairy gold.'

He killed the mask and felt naked: cruelly exposed.

'I like the outfit. I often wanted to tell you so. Is that what they call a "Tomboy"? It's very old earth, very natty.'

⟨It's made of a new kind of yarn that eats skin waste and gunk. If you can't get fresh clothes, at least you don't have to keep wearing different things, in that odd human way.⟩

'Yeah, I know. Du Pont higene. If you don't think traditionalism is that weird—'

'I don't care which side a company belongs to. I'm not interested in politics.'

Her stillness had an edge to it that puzzled him. It must be his imagination. He wanted to beg her *please don't leave me*.

'I've been sent here by my boss,' he said. 'You know the whole story now, how you were supposed to be able to "remember" things that happened to Johnny Guglioli. We want you with us, but that's not why. We want you for yourself, the person you really are. Come with me, don't vanish into Aleutia. You could be what Johnny should have been, the bridge between two worlds . . .'

She wasn't even listening.

'What's the use?' He collapsed on to a rosewood dining chair. To his shame and fury, tears were stinging at the backs of his eyes. If he didn't give this up, he'd be sobbing outright. Suddenly he realised that *she wasn't listening* because her taut attention was fixed on something going on elsewhere, something behind him . . . Her eyes snapped like a cat's into full dilation, so that a distinction you didn't know you could see in the black-on-black vanished: leaving nothing but a light-eating hole.

⟨Danger? Bel? Are we in danger?⟩

⟨Of course not!⟩ she said, meaning the opposite. ⟨Be calm, everything's fine. No need to look behind you.⟩

Sid instantly swivelled around on his chair. The Aleutian who had come softly into the room was four-footed, looming larger than any natural animal because of the mad, sentient glitter in its eyes.

Hair rose on the nape of Sid's neck. Clavel stood fluidly: a terrifying transformation, animal to fairytale monster. He moved into the lamplight and eyed the intruder with tolerant amusement.

⟨I won't ask how you got in here, Sid. I have my sources.⟩

Sid scrabbled together his control of the Common Tongue, managing to achieve the rigid stare of a rabbit transfixed in headlights. Clavel strolled to a elegant sideboard. Sid flashed a bemused question at Bella:

⟨What's going on? What's *wrong* with him?⟩

⟨Be very careful,⟩ she told him barely: nothing more.

The poet poured himself a shot of whisky and returned to lean on the back of the couch. 'You're right, Sid. Bella is not Johnny Guglioli.' He spoke very deliberately, like a drunk. But Sid didn't think he was drunk. 'When I came back and found I was as trapped in misery as I had been before, I fought with myself for a while. But the heart has its reasons. I knew the weapons people had taken tissue from Johnny's body. I had my people build me a hybrid embryo, and I had Maitri raise you as his own, Bella. Your unwitting host, if that's what I mean, had to be carefully chosen. Luckily there was someone who fitted the profile in Maitri's own household, which was a stroke of luck.'

⟨Someone who wouldn't be missed by anyone,⟩ agreed the librarian quietly. ⟨Not even by himself.⟩

The poet bowed his head. ⟨Yes.⟩ He continued. 'Maitri's librarian fit our profile, which made it natural for Maitri to keep you close as you grew up. I waited. But the moment never came. I gather Rajath tried to have your base-identity read, here on earth. If he'd succeeded maybe we'd know how much of the human material remained recognisable. It doesn't matter.'

Clavel came to the front of the couch, looking down at Bella. 'You are not Johnny. Maybe the best way to describe you is to say you are Maitri's librarian, wearing a rather strange prosthetic body in which you are no longer disabled. That's who you are, that's what we achieved.' Bella looked up. Sid didn't catch what passed between them: something, perhaps, of how it had felt to be the subject of this benign experiment.

For a moment Sid glimpsed the poet-princess of first contact, ashamed and painfully young. Then the older Clavel smoothly recovered. 'I admit, we didn't know exactly what would happen to "Maitri's librarian". But we also didn't realise that the librarian and I would not get on.' Clavel smiled. 'When you arrived, Sid, Bella was about to tell me that she can't help it and she's sorry she's not what I wanted. She was going to volunteer to stay and do her best to make me happy anyway, for the sake of the Expedition. Isn't that right, librarian?'

⟨About right.⟩ Bella lowered her eyes.

'You never thought you were Johnny.' Clavel frowned over a remaining puzzle. 'That's bothered me. You *never for a moment* thought you were Johnny, though you are such a clear thinker. How did you manage to miss that solution? You had enough clues.'

'I knew that Maitri had been going to tell me I was your truechild. He wouldn't lie to me. And Johnny Guglioli—'

'Was never that.' Clavel stood. 'Maitri didn't lie. He told you what I believed. I'm going to turn down your noble offer. You're a critic, I'm an artist. It wouldn't work.' He went over to an ancient, exquisite writing desk. 'Well, Bella – if you like the name, keep it – I am sorry that my fantasy caused you so much grief. It's over now. The silly rumour of the "instantaneous travel device" will die a natural death. But you two young people will need protection for a while.'

(Bella shrugged faintly. There was a forgivable slur in this. In Aleutia pairing crosses a generation. It was an impropriety for *two young people* to be together.)

He handed Bella a sliver of plastic. 'Later I'll make a more settled arrangement.' He walked to the glass doors. 'This is the deal. Sid, you give up your secret-agenting. Leave here, keep going, don't contact your boss ever again. Bella, do not try to contact Aleutia. Stay away from the aliens, both of you. Lose yourselves, I won't lose you. As long as you keep to my con- ditions, I will look after you.'

Sid was paralysed, hypnotised. Suddenly the Pure One laughed, a choked, human splutter. 'What a fool you are, Sidney Carton. Don't you see? The princess is yours. *Go, can't you?*'

Bella took Sid's hand. He found himself with her in the garden under a sky of deep plum and charcoal in crusted layers of cloud, like Japanese appliqué work. There were trees like looming giants, shrubs like crouching animals. There was the false sigh of the waves. Sid pulled up, too confused to take a step further.

'What happened? Did I ruin things for you? Did I let slip something about us having sex? It can't be serious. He'll forgive you. You go back and tell him—'

Bella hauled on his arm.

'Come on! We have to get away.'

The sound of her voice was like a thunderclap. 'Huh?'

'Before you came in,' she said, 'I had woken from a virtual experience of the rape. The rape that he has repeated here, who knows how many times. I didn't volunteer. He put the wrap on me while I was asleep. He was trying to characterise me, without my consent, to make me into what he needed.'

'*What?* Clavel did that! *Clavel?*'

'Don't put your trust in heroes,' said Bella. 'People do bad things when they're miserable: it all has to be forgiven. But when I went downstairs to find him, he was very strange, very strange. *I think we should get out of this garden,* because Clavel is not at all stable tonight.'

The sound of her voice. Her hands gripping his. Sid could hear his own breathing and the pounding of his heart above the wind and the rain that were pummelling the Thames Valley. A tonne of déjà vu fell on him. He could barely see her face. The wave had collapsed. They had stepped out of the game, and into the real. They ran hand in hand out of the poet's garden and into the streets.

Standing at the glass doors, tumbler in his hand, Clavel watched the two mortals hurry into obscurity. '*Since there's no help,*' he whispered, '*let us kiss and part.*' He waited for the changeling to come running back out of the rain, crying: 'Daddy! It's suddenly come right! I *do* know you!'

But the soul of Johnny Guglioli would never look out of those precisely judging eyes: never know him, never remember.

I have guessed as best I could what you would want, Johnny. I have kept the faith. I have tried to be good. I am trying still.

'Oh, God.'

Suddenly he dropped the glass and covered his face. He prayed, as if he naively believed in WorldSelf as something separate from his own being: a Big Person, out there.

'Oh, God, if you ever loved me – *get me out of this.*'

They had to wait for hours until the automat monorail started up before they could travel back to the city centre. At the last station, Bella fed the gate with Clavel's plastic.

'Fairy gold,' she said, 'is dangerous. It leaves marks.' She dropped Clavel's gift on the barrier. Sid gave a faint cry of protest: but she'd walked on. He left it there. The great city was silent in the dawn. The rain had stopped and the sky was clear. A hawk flew out and plummeted from a tower block, pigeons scattered with a clatter of wings.

⟨Your place or mine?⟩ he asked.

⟨Yours. I don't want to go back to mine.⟩

She walked beside him in absorbed quiet, not seeming to notice the cold on her bare limbs. The leaves were turning in the wilderness that had encroached on central London. In vacant lots goldenrod lay in tarnished sheaves, battered by the rain. Seeding willowherb made a ghostly grey tangle, berries glistened. Small animals rustled unseen. Once she asked, 'Are there elephants?'; and he realised what was happening in her silence.

'Sorry. No elephants. No rhinos, no giraffes, no hippopotami. All gone. We have more and more people instead.' He touched her arm and pointed to where a trotting, tawny shadow was crossing the Strand ahead of them. 'Lioness. We have them. Escapes from the old "safari parks", naturalised. They're like foxes. They eat anything, get everywhere and most people admire them sneakingly: but don't forget they'll happily eat you.'

⟨Aditya,⟩ she murmured.

The city began to wake as they walked. It was strangely peaceful, as the cities of the war could be at this time. They walked through a street projection advertising a game that Bella had once played: where? She had no idea.

'I didn't know I was in London.'

Sid's hotel was not far from where the Aleutian tourists had stayed. But it was a characterless modern establishment that rambled on one floor, the rooms opening off a series of drab courtyards. Bella touched the building material curiously.

'Is this stuff an Aleutian product? It sort of feels alive.'

Sid laughed. 'Funny you should say that. It's recycled waste: to be candid it's mostly human shit. You have to use what you have plenty of, right? It's supposed to be sterilised, but you know what European manufacturing is like.'

He bought a litre of coffee and a bag of sugar fritters in the canteen and led her into the warren. He thumbed the lock (his own) on his flimsy pressed-shit door and went to lift down the anti-airborne shutters from the window. He yelped as a blast of pure sunlight hit his lenses: tipped them out into his palm and dumped them on the window ledge.

The walls of the room had been sprayed in a pattern of blue sky and clouds that vaguely attempted an effect of depth and movement. There were two narrow beds-on-legs: a chemical toilet and a washstand stood behind a screen. There was a piece of green matting between the beds, trying to look like grass. Bella stood by the door.

'How is Lydia? And Roger, and the others?'

'The kids are fine. The others are no worse than usual. I've been back to see them: kind of sick leave, some of the time that you were in the hells. They send me tapes here. There's a screen with a decoder that takes Tourviddy format down in the cantina.'

She came over to the window, and touched his fingers.

'I'm sorry about your hand.'

He'd forgotten, momentarily, how he'd lost the original. 'It's as good as new, except for this.' He showed her the place where the kitemark and the logo of the copyright company had obstinately regenerated. 'Don't you hate that? If they want me to advertise for them, they ought to pay me. I've tried shaving it off. It grows back in hours, and if you dig too deep it *hurts*.'

His chatter foundered. He drew a breath like a sob, and pulled her into his arms.

She returned the embrace. But there was something wrong. He had known it as they were walking here: *something very badly wrong*.

Her silence was unreadable.

⟨What is it?⟩

He drew back, keeping hold of her. 'About being a woman. I'm kind of attached to the equipment, but if it's what you want, I'll do it.'

Bella thought of Aditya: the lovely face alight in death. For Aditya being *she* was a reckless abdication of autonomy, a gloriously dangerous game: more alluring than any risk Aleutia could provide. There were so many different ways of being *she*. None of them was very healthy. It was not a habit you would wish on a friend.

'I like you the way you are.'

'We could go to the USSA: like Clavel said, start a new life. Their immigration's tough, but we could try.' He thought of the forbidden territory that had determined *not to change*, a society maybe stranger than Aleutia by now. 'To tell you the truth, I don't think we'd fit in . . . Bella, *what is it?* I can't give back to you what you've lost, I wish I could.'

She detached herself and went to sit on one of the beds.

'I haven't lost very much. I was always isolate. Now I'll die and I won't come back. I've had time to think about it, and it doesn't seem so bad.'

But for Sid, the air of the room was full of her goodbyes.

'Did you know?' he asked. 'About Clavel—?'

'I knew the same as you. That Clavel, who is our conscience if you like, was distraught with grief and only his trueself could heal him and bring him back to us.'

'I knew that I was done for once he'd got you. I knew you didn't love him. You love *me*. But you would never give up your duty. But you can't help him, Bel.'

'Clavel's wrong,' she said. She didn't appear to be speaking to Sid. She was looking away, preoccupied. She lifted her hands and let them fall, with sad finality.

Sid was terrified. 'So it's all over,' he said cheerily, to hide his panic. 'The mystery of how Johnny and Braemar reached the shipworld will return to its rightful place in the scheme of things, along with the *Marie Celeste*, the origin of QV petrovirus and whether you can sharpen razor blades by putting them under cardboard models of the pyramid of Cheops.'

What's wrong? He didn't dare ask again.

'I'm still an Aleutian, you see. I owe you so much. You saved my life when I didn't know it needed to be saved. You knew I was supposed to be Johnny Guglioli and you never told me, but I have no quarrel with that. I was, I am, extremely grateful to you. But you serve your cause, and I have to serve mine.'

'Extremely grateful? That sounds nasty.'

'You've told me yourself, often and often. Race is bullshit, culture is everything. No matter how I was built, I'm an Aleutian. I have to go and look for someone who, I think, will be looking for me, so it shouldn't be hard to find him. And you can't help. I'd never ask you to change sides. Neither can I.'

Sid stared. To Bella's bewilderment he grew mysteriously less alarmed as this speech progressed.

'So this is goodbye,' he broke in solemnly. 'You're off to find your lawful master, wherever in the wide world he may be.' He frowned. 'But didn't we just promise the great Clavel we'd stay away from aliens?'

⟨I didn't promise anything. And I threw the money away.⟩

Sid looked grave, but his eyes glinted blue.

'I think it's time I took you to meet my boss.'

Outside the lodging house Sid hailed a leclec, the three-wheeled London self-service teksi. They shot away in jaunty style, through Westminster and the Monuments, towards the Royal Parks. Bella had a strange feeling that everything was as before. He was Maitri's librarian on the holiday of a lifetime, riding with the halfcaste Sidney Carton through an ancient city: storing up memories for the long, eventless lives to come. He didn't ask where they were going, and Sid was giving nothing away.

In Hyde Park, under the tarnished foliage of the remaining trees, the squatters' camps stirred with morning life. Beside a mobile army barracks Allied soldiers were cleaning a herd of big brick-and-grey coloured vehicles. The leclec bumped over pathways that had been old when the Aleutians came to earth, and stopped outside a curious, angular building that stood alone not far from the dry basin called the Serpentine.

The room inside was large and bare. The air was full of dust. It smelled of the past, of forgotten things. The Fat Man was lying on his bed in the middle of a clutter of baggage: one leg crossed over the other, white gloved hands folded behind his massive head. He sat up as they entered, with the unflappable dignity of an enormous child. Bella didn't wait to be introduced.

'Seeker-after-truth!' she cried. 'Seeker-after-truth!' She ran and buried her face in the engineer-scholar's ample lap.

11: The Light of Other Days

Sid hung back, grinning oafishly. Bella and the Fat Man were all over each other, hugging, stroking, nuzzling, as unselfconsciously physical in their greeting as two animals – one much larger than the other. Bella was babbling: ⟨What a beautiful place, such a lovely atmosphere, so much nicer than the government hotel . . .⟩

Sid looked up into the spidery roof tree, around into the corners piled with ancient rubbish and desiccated human turds, swallowing hard. He'd brought her home. She wasn't talking about the derelict Serpentine Gallery. Aleutia was the lovely place. Their *place*, their main hall: the teeming hollow, you could say if you wanted to get metaphorical, where they all lived, inside each Aleutian body. He saw the physical grappling (always disturbingly animal-like to human eyes). But he felt the force-field, mind-field of the Aleutian commonalty.

He knew that Bella had recognised the third captain, Kumbva the engineer, the moment she met the Fat Man disguised as a Hindu widow in Trivandrum – and had kept quiet about it in her inimitable way (the things she could keep quiet about: it was awesome). He also realised that on some level Bella was not surprised to find that the third captain was Sid's boss. And that from this moment what had been done to her, to Maitri's librarian, had been done with her consent, and the consent of her peers. They had strange ideas about time and consequence. It's no use quoting Magna Carta to an Aleutian, he thought ruefully. They don't understand a charter of liberties. Their society genuinely *does not work that way*.

At last the two Aleutians left off hugging and turned, arm in arm: little cat-faced Bella in her black tomboy, and the big fat bear of an engineer in white linen. What a ridiculous pair! Bella's eyes were brimming.

Kumbva laughed. 'Well, Sid, you rogue, you bold deceiver. What have you to say for yourself?'

He was appalled at the Fat Man's perfidy. 'I couldn't tell you!' he protested to Bel. 'I wanted to! But what could I do? What do I know about Aleutian psychology? I had to trust him.'

Kumbva smiled modestly. Sid thought of everything that they'd done since Maitri's librarian came to earth. Sid had been sure that Bella could not inherit *latent memories* of instantaneous travel from her human 'parent'. He had found Kumbva's pursuit of the librarian callous and incomprehensible. But Aleutians see things differently. Sid had gradually realised that to Kumbva the thriller plot of capture and escape, the pawn exchanged and recovered, was an old, told tale. Kumbva, in his curious way, was intent on looking after Bella.

Sidney felt humbled: a sensation he detested. 'And I did trust him,' he admitted. 'I sometimes hated him. But I kept on trusting him, just hoping I was right.'

Bella pulled Sid down beside her, so that she was flanked by him and Kumbva. ⟨You are very wise,⟩ she told the engineer. ⟨You didn't let Sid tell. They say Aleutians cannot learn, but you made me learn, until the truth was a part of me. And all the while there was Sid, never letting go: never leaving me alone, telling me I belonged to earth, not Aleutia. You were forging a bond between us, a tried and tempered bond, a commonalty of two. You were right to trust him, Sid. The plan worked. I am Bella, I'm whole. I don't want to be anyone else, or anywhere else but here with you.⟩

Kumbva beamed at the lovers, shoulders tucked to his ears.

'But the seance—' Bella shuddered, looking at the engineer. 'How did you know? How did you know anyone could *do* that?'

Kumbva's face fell. 'I didn't. That ceremony was *not* a part of my rough midwifery. But when I finally realised what Aditya was babbling about: I was afraid. You realised, librarian, that the way you were made had to be close to weapons-building?'

She remembered her terror when Aditya had told her *what she was*: and started trying to bring severed fragments of that flesh to life. 'Yes, I did.'

'And then . . . Viloma. I do not believe in magic. But there are strange stories about that person. Whatever it is he does, he is not entirely a charlatan.' Kumbva shook his head, and slapped his knees (he was sitting cross-legged, human style, a trick he'd worked hard to perfect). 'No more of that! It was in another lifetime. To business. I can take it, Bella, that you have accepted the job I offered to you a while ago?'

'Well, yes, but.'

His large nasal crinkled in amusement. 'You want to discuss pay, conditions of service, out-of-pocket expenses?'

⟨No. I have to ask Sid something.⟩ She turned to him.

'I was sure you were an anti-Aleutian fanatic. That's why I was so miserable this morning. I'm *still* sure. I don't see how I could be making such a mistake, because *I know you*. So why are you working for us? Maybe I understand,' she added. 'But tell me.'

⟨Librarian,⟩ murmured Kumbva. ⟨Can't bear to be wrong.⟩

'Why am I—?' Sid was taken aback. 'But I'm not. I'm not working for you people. I know it may look that way—'

They burst out laughing. Always the same Sidney Carton!

He scowled. 'All right, laugh. It's the truth. I am not in this for your benefit. Present company excepted, I want the aliens off my planet. But I'm realistic about the options.' Deeper colour tinged his ruddy cheekbones. He wrapped his arms around his knees and stared at the dirty floor. 'When I was a kid, I lived on the myth of starflight. Then I met the Fat Man, and he had his Aleutian version of the mythology. The longer we work together, the less we find. But I consider it proved beyond doubt that the great scientist Peenemunde Buonarotti had a secret that died with her. I want to know what that secret was. If there is ever an end to this treasure hunt I want to be there for the human race, as a witness. If Peenemunde's secret *is* the secret of efficient interstellar travel, which I find less and less credible, then *nothing would please me more* than for the aliens to use it and leave. Does that answer you?'

She nodded, meeting his eyes: an encompassing ⟨I see⟩ that took in the dogged hope that pride denied, and his secret knowledge that the search had become necessary in itself. If you have a quest – however crazy – you have a reason for living.

⟨One more thing,⟩ Bella ventured. ⟨There's Clavel.⟩

Kumbva stirred. ⟨You're worrying about your dereliction of duty? Don't. Clavel is beyond our help, I think, for this life.⟩

'Will someone explain?' demanded Sid. 'You people overestimate my powers. I managed to stumble on to what Kumbva was doing, in the end. But I can't follow Clavel's line in this.'

The Aleutians glanced at each other.

⟨He could have killed you, you know,⟩ said Kumbva.

⟨He didn't,⟩ returned Bella quickly. ⟨He let us go.⟩

'But why?' protested Sid. 'Why would he kill you? Because you're not Johnny?'

'To protect the secret,' she explained. 'I had to wake as Johnny, and recognise him. Nothing else was good enough; it had to come from me. That's why he delayed our meeting, when I came to earth. I was too old, it was too late, but he was still hoping. Meanwhile Dark Ocean, the people in orbit who want us to leave earth and go off again in search of home, had hired Rajath to get hold of me for the sake of Johnny's memories. Then Clavel was horribly torn. That's why he did nothing for so long. He was waiting for me to come to him, to know him again. Yet he was afraid that if I *was* Johnny he'd have to kill me, to protect the secret of instantaneous travel. He's not always so crazy, but he does believe the device, if it exists, belongs to the people of earth, and we shouldn't have it. That's why he made us promise, Sid: *tried* to make us promise,' she corrected herself, 'to stay off the treasure trail.'

'Hmph,' snorted Kumbva. 'We're flattered by the poet's confidence, I'm sure! I fear the secret is safe for a while longer. However. Sid's honour is cleared, and Clavel we will leave to his grief. You children forgot to eat breakfast. Let's picnic.'

He delved into the baggage that surrounded his pallet and produced a local camping stove, a folding kettle, a carton of naturlait and several paper parcels. Sid made the tea. One parcel contained currant buns. Another, when opened, released a powerful hideous stink.

'Lock Fyne kippers. I get them from Fortnum's. Won't you try some?' Sid and Bella retired to the far end of the bed and breakfasted on buns and tea, while Kumbva devoured his awful

delicacy. Finally he folded up his kipper wrapping. ⟨Yum! Someone told me you should 'cook' them, but I don't see it . . .⟩

'The sad thing is,' he remarked, 'if the poet really wants to
save earth for the earthlings, he ought to be helping us.'

Sid looked from one Aleutian to the other.

'If we can't go home by some positive means,' agreed Bella,
'we'll stay. I have seen that. Dark Ocean's lost the battle: why
else would they be ready to employ Rajath? They were clutching
at stars, as you people say. Aleutia won't go back to wandering
in the dark, when there's a landfall here. Eventually, no matter
what people say now, we will start settling on earth.'

Eventually, all of earth will be like the Uji valley.

There was a grim silence: grim on Sid's part anyway. It was
one of those moments when he lost his *unspoken dialogue* trace
on the Common Tongue. He knew from the way they looked
everywhere but at him that he wasn't keeping his feelings to
himself.

Kumbva slapped his knees again. 'No moping! One trail ends,
another begins, and now we are three!'

'But I don't know that this trail has ended,' said Bella.

Suddenly, the bare room became preternaturally quiet.

On that night in Mykini, Sid had cried *I am going to destroy
you.* Bella remembered that now. No one else, not even Kumbva,
had seen the affair of Johnny Guglioli's 'latent memories' in
quite that light. Maitri's librarian had been destroyed indeed . . .
And for nothing? For a stupid mistake? She remembered how
Clavel had paced, in the dark house full of sad beautiful things.
Clavel had been prepared to kill Bella, because he divined a
secret that owed nothing to the failed experiment.

She heard idle shouts from the soldiers in the barracks; traffic
muttering faintly further off. Sid and Kumbva were waiting.

'I saw something, under the sarcophagus.'

⟨You saw something?⟩ repeated the engineer intently.

⟨I don't know. It was probably nothing . . .⟩

'*What did you see?*'

Bella's nasal compressed. Her limbs drew together, trying to
twist around for flight. She was so afraid to be wrong.

'Lettering: words. I think I could draw it.'

Sid and the Fat Man looked at each other in wild surmise.

⟨She can't read,⟩ protested Sid.

⟨She can remember.⟩ The Fat Man reached over and took a battered flat notebook from by his pillow, opened a blank page. 'Use the stylus. Take your time.'

She formed the letters awkwardly, barely managing to fit them on the page: *DEUS PROVIDEBIT.* ⟨And the rest of it. The password you showed me.⟩

'*Where?*'

Bella quailed: ⟨I told you.⟩ 'Inside the sarcophagus.'

Sid laughed at the anticlimax. 'Well, obviously. It's Buonarotti's secret password, you were in the place where she used to work. It's not surprising you saw her mark. But it's no use. There's nothing left at the university. Any data stored there was *certainly* destroyed, rendered useless by the accident.'

Kubmva was bending hungrily over the scrawled letters.

'Sid, remind me. What do we know about the accident?'

'Not much. Du Pont/Farben were running a mini-reactor. One fine day it went down with a touch of non-linear positive feedback. Boom. Everybody relocates off campus for five thousand years. It wasn't a famous disaster. These things happen – happened – in the mid-twenty-first: maintenance running down, no money, civil disruption, communal violence. Things was coming apart.'

'And Buonarotti?'

'Was working on her quantum simulation – officially, that is – for her corporate sponsors. You know. You get some fantastic number of Craysworth of computing power, and calculate every bloody quantum mechanical feature of a bunch of nonexistent atoms, real bottom-up, absolute "virtuality". Same work that got her the second Nobel: organo-metals. She was modelling the behaviour of hybrid materials that didn't exist but might be useful if they did. In her spare time, according to some, she was going for jaunts around the galaxy in her prototype starship, which has never been found.'

'Thank you, Sid.' Kumbva was gazing into the distance. 'A mini-reactor. What needed so much power?'

'A carbon-based plasma atom-smasher. Dinky little thing, lab-sized. We don't know what it was for. Du Pont were developing a new brand of support hose: who knows?'

'Mmm.'

Sid looked at Bella. She was ignoring the strange terms. She was attending vividly to the wordless communication that was flying: to the meaning, not the words. What he saw in her face alarmed and thrilled him.

'Oh, now,' he protested. 'Fat Man, let's not get excited.'

'I think we need to know more,' said Kumbva mildly, 'about this *accident*, which we have previously found uninteresting . . .'

The treasure hunters stared at each other. The password! It had acquired such a numinous glow. Sid grinned, wide and nervous.

'She's a librarian. Let's take her to the library.'

There was a spurt of ominous firecracker noises in the distance as they came out, but the incident was too far off to worry about. Someone had taken Sid's leclec. They hurried on foot along Rotten Row, where a party of veiled women were riding on showy thoroughbreds flanked by armed grooms. At Hyde Park Corner a traffic jam had formed around a van hawking green fodder for drom-drawn carts. Here they picked up a group of little boys who, thanks to the Fat Man's skill, did not see a noseless alien, but who grasped the entertainment value of a fat foreigner in a white suit. ⟨Enjoy,⟩ murmured the Fat Man. He broke into a run down Piccadilly, and lost the jeering children by diving into the second-hand clothes mart opposite the Ritz hotel.

It took Sid and Bella some time to track him down and prise him away from the stalls. It must have been nearly noon before they reached the library. It was in a short, quiet street near Whitehall. There was a breadqueue opposite. Bella called them all *breadqueues*, though it could be anything desirable and rare. The entrance to the library was chained and barred.

⟨Good heavens,⟩ she exclaimed. ⟨That's a 'Henty Moore'!⟩

Kumbva tapped his lips. ⟨Ssh! No need to tell everyone.⟩

'Closed for major refurbishment,' Sid read from a crumbling lettered sign. Kumbva moved in. It became clear that the barrier was not functional. The queue watched incuriously as three scavengers: a halfcaste dressed for clubbing, a ruddy-skinned blond in 'alien' overalls, and a big fat man wearing animator's gloves and a white suit, dismantled it and vanished inside.

The 'new' library was in the basement. Sid, who had a bag of Fat Man tricks slung over his shoulder, shone a torch around. 'We found this place years ago. Everyone has forgotten it exists, we reckon: that's how it survives. But it's cabled-up, still functional and powered, but it's better to bring your own.' He went to the central island, and removed a panel with an accustomed air. He tugged out a meltoptic cable, broke it, spliced in a plump brown disc.

'Just in case some Allied monitoring spots a little user-surge where none should be: it could happen. Besides, this part of London, the Monuments, greys out every five minutes or so. It shouldn't matter to a system like this, but it does: and *I'm* not the one to try and funx-out what's wrong. Lights. Service.'

The room woke. Bella saw ordered booths and dusty display cases that had beem emptied of their mementoes long ago. This was not a library in the sense she understood: not a private collection.

⟨Cover one's face?⟩ she suggested uncertainly.

⟨Are we in church? I don't know. The Self is everywhere.⟩ Kumbva followed suit cheerfully, briefly. He cocked his massive head. ⟨What are you waiting for, librarian?⟩

⟨What is it I can do that you two haven't done?⟩

'Ah.' The secret agent and his master looked at each other.

'We don't know how to use the databases,' confessed Sid. 'We didn't have public libraries around where I was dragged up. What d'you think this is, the twentieth century?'

⟨At home,⟩ put in the engineer humbly, ⟨I have people to look things up for me.⟩

'We ask them stupid questions,' explained Sid. 'It's like one of those random counselling generators. Sometimes we get a blizzard of stuff, and we don't know how to persuade them to sort it. Sometimes they say "Yes", or "No": and we get no further.'

Bella still looked doubtful. ⟨But this isn't a virtuality game. How can I *do what I do* with an antique data-processing system designed by humans?⟩

The Fat Man chuckled. ⟨This isn't an antique! Try it.⟩

Bella sat down. Kumbva and Sid took booths on either side of her. She picked up the dusty visor – thinking, as she clasped it around her eyes, what a life-changing, fearful gesture it had been the first time she had put on a humans' contact wrap. Her field of vision became a coruscating mass of blue on blue on blue.

'Hello, friend. There are no human librarians on duty at the moment. Can we help? Or would you prefer to leave a message?'

'Coralin!' breathed Bella, putting her hands up to the human wrap that held *life*, in astonishment. 'Is this coralin?'

'Yes, we are,' answered the sweet, multitudinous voice.

'Coralin,' agreed Kumbva placidly. 'Living on here, undisturbed, unsuspected. Coralin, whose trademark is to be *compatible with anything*. The polymorphously perverse blue-clay, the processing medium that the human race abandoned in horror when the aliens arrived and they were faced with the reality of *compatibility* sans frontiers. Goodness knows what they get up to in here when nobody's asking them stupid questions.'

'We catalogue,' they answered. 'We cross-reference. There is always more to be done in a library.'

Coralin, thought Sid. *Performing animals, I hate 'em*. It was a horrible idea, really. The entity (our name is legion) that lived inside this casing: sucking up the news, the shows, the music, sucking up hordes of new books from the publishers before they even hit the hells. Sucking in *everything*. Changing, in another space and time, becoming what? Never knowing that they/it had been abandoned, that in this world humanity had taken another turning: their swift ages passing uncounted. How did coralin perceive time?

'What do we want to know?' asked Bella.

'I can't tell you,' confessed the engineer. 'We had no hope of finding anything at that site, because of the effect of accidents of the kind on stored data. I hardly know what I'm hoping, in fact I'd rather not say. Suppose we survey anything on record about the accident in Neubrandenburg and see where that leads. Don't be afraid of going over old ground.' The Fat Man's tone took on a touch of hauteur. 'Sid and I may have overlooked a few details.'

There was a silence. The blue screen in front of Sid's eyes shifted with enormous rapidity through an algebra of data-

netting tools that meant nothing to him. It slowed to Bella's eye-
blink. He glimpsed a map of Europe dotted with tiny pyramids.
It settled on a monochrome video sequence which he'd seen
before.

'That's it!'

'This is the accident,' said Bella's voice. 'From the campus
monitoring.' A mushroom cloud billowed silently, small figures
scattered. Sound had been lost somewhere along the years.
'There's a little more of the entombment: and some text and
figures from various sources. I'll run through it. Stop me whenever you like.'

'Thank you,' murmured Kumbva.

The accident had happened in an off-shift, when there were
few people in the building. There were two presumed fatalities,
technicians whose remains (at this point in the reportage) had
not been recovered from the reactor chamber. With such a pitiful
body count, coverage outside the immediate locality concentrated on Buonarotti and her departure for New Delhi, where
she would pass into retirement and be forgotten.

'Can you raise anything anomalous?'

'These are figures for similar accidents.'

Aleutian 'figures' were false-coloured spirals, fans and mushrooms: intensity of colour translated into closeness in time, in
geographical area, in the type of reactor, in the pathology of the
accident, in the behaviour of the plume, in the data on short
and long-term contamination . . . It was all too direct for Sid's
intuition. He could not sense these gradations as measurement;
he wanted numbers and graphs and printed words. But Bella, the
librarian who couldn't read, flipped over them at dismissive
speed. 'Entombment looks interesting . . .' she remarked,
absorbed.

'Mmm,' agreed Kumbva.

Back to ancient and very basic video, as translated and
preserved by the coralin entity. Now they were scanning several
emergency clean-up operations, one of which was the crucial
accident, frame by frame. The team that poured the tomb for Du
Pont/Farben was a Russian outfit. The greyed-out images still
held the raffish swagger of those legendary tough guys of the

Devolution. 'Differently marked vehicles,' noted Bella. 'But some faces are the same.'

When Aleutians say 'face' they don't mean eyes-nose-mouth. They mean the whole presence. Sid peered intently. She could be right.

'Clean-up teams were usually Russian,' he told the aliens. 'Rasputin types: breakfast on strychnine sandwiches, smoke a pack of fifty heavy tars, pick up a few hours of cell-destroying radiation, break for lunch on scrapie sausage. They thrived on it. Environmental disaster was good business for them.'

'Too good, maybe. Look.' .

The screen flipped rapidly and settled on a courtroom: a prosecution for fraud. There was clear dialogue, for a change. The coralin helpfully lipsynced the speech into English. There had been an expensive industrial accident. It was suggested that no accident had in fact occurred: that in collusion with the hiring company the clean-up team had faked evidence, doped emissions and tampered dosimetry.

'There's more of the same.'

It transpired that under different company names and personal aliases, several members of the team who handled the accident at Buonarotti's university had had brushes with the law. They found only one, minor, successful prosecution. The informal exchanges in livespace court records left little room for doubt about other cases, for two Aleutians and a halfcaste. In one incident, it seemed clear that the 'clean-up' team had arranged, with inside help, a substantial conventional explosion in a chemical plant. .

'The contamination?' asked Kumbva sharply.

'That's difficult,' admitted the librarian, after studying more 'figures'. 'The clean-up team had a contract to monitor soil and site: but they seem to have gone out of business after the first year. Then in the second year there was a similar accident nearby, and the campus and surrounding area were affected by that plume, confusing the traces.'

'Let me study some of the raw stuff.'

'Buonarotti spent wads of money that year,' murmured Sid. 'D'you remember, Fat Man? She emptied her account; and no

trace of where it went. We thought she was financing anti-
Aleutians.'

'Ssh . . . But so cumbersome!' The engineer's lips drew back
from formidable teeth. 'So dangerous and elaborate! Such a risk!
I have been searching for *information*. Everything I knew of her
culture, your culture, pointed to that. Why do it this way?'

'If you mean what I think you mean,' answered Sid, 'I can tell
you. Why would she hide a secret under a blanket of nonexistent
hard radiation? Because she knew what was coming. She could
see a future where no one would notice a faked nuclear accident
among so many real ones. She could see coralin tape knitted into
blankets, discs cut up and used to stop teeth. She was smart,
remember. You people couldn't fool her, when they fooled
practically all the world.'

At last the Fat Man sat back. He pulled off the wrap. Sid
glimpsed the dimpled sea of blue as Bella signed off before he did
the same.

'She faked it!' exclaimed Kumbva. 'Peenemunde Buonarotti
faked an environmental disaster!' He twisted the wrap over and
over in his hands. 'I don't know,' he corrected himself. 'Nothing
here amounts to proof. All we can say with certainty is that we
are no longer sure we can dismiss Peenemunde's workplace . . .
Whereas, as Bella once wisely pointed out to me, if it *wasn't* for
the nuclear accident there, the campus would have been the
obvious place to look for our hidden treasure.'

There was silence in the forgotten room.

'The Campfire Girls,' Sid remembered suddenly. 'In the sarcophagus. They were having trouble with their rad counters – !'

He stared ahead of him, his heart thumping. He was thinking
of the last great scientist of the global civilisation: getting old
and tired, frightened and reckless as her world collapsed around
her. It was strange to think that *this* world, the day-to-day mess
that Sid took for granted, was to Buonarotti a dreadful,
unplumbed abyss.

Kumbva moved suddenly, the bear-body full of urgent energy.

'We'd better be on our way. No time to lose.'

They travelled to Hamburg by air-cruiser and checked into one
of the runway hotels. Their room was a drive-in lockup with

space to spread their bedding beside the vehicle slot, a compacting toilet-cum-wastebin, a cablepoint; nothing else. Kumbva at once plunged into a tussle with the cable service to secure transport and provisions for the trip east.

Sid walked out into the cold, dusty afternoon. The vast expanse of the old airfield was dotted with caravanserai like their own. There were people wandering about. Bella was looking through the perimeter fence. He stood beside her. In the distance a cruiser grew by tiny degrees, a silvery blob grazing the rim of forest that blurred the horizon.

The engineer was travelling in his preferred old earth disguise: as the mysterious but respected alien-watcher known as the Fat Man. Sid wondered what the alien-watching circuit was making of Bella, if it had picked up on her.

She'd swapped the higene for Aleutian-style clothes. Over her dun suit she wore an open-sleeved robe in fine black and white wool, a local version of the alien style. The patterns on it were too sharp-edged to be Aleutian. Sid called them *geometric*. Bella and the Fat Man called them *scientific-looking*: meaning an effect of the wildest imagination.

They had not been alone together in the day and night it had taken to set up this journey. Somehow the gulf had opened between them again: *something wrong*. He wanted to touch her but he couldn't. The tug of physical attraction, which had become so necessary to him, had been shut off at the source.

⟨I wish I knew what was wrong. Can't you explain?⟩

Bella turned, arms folded over her breastless torso. From the starved, dead-child face alien eyes surveyed him.

⟨I feel exactly the same.⟩

She walked off, back to their room.

Right, fine. That put Sid in his place.

No one would rent them a car so the Fat Man bought one, a lumbering armoured camper-van convertible. Sid did the driving. The Aleutians stayed in the back. He sat and held the juddering bar through long, hypnotic hours, thinking about the sarcophagus and what they were likely to find there. He was appalled at the thought of going inside that place again. He had bought himself an army surplus suit on the Fat Man's credit. Kumbva and Bella

planned to walk in without any protection, whether the accident was fake or not. The Fat Man had brought surprisingly little
in the way of equipment. Sid assumed this meant that there
would be reinforcements and supplies joining them at the tomb:
but he'd been told nothing directly. He felt left out and bitter.

They avoided towns and cities as much as possible as they
passed through the fragments of what had once been Germany.
The satellite receiver in the van picked up snowflake trans-
mission swathe by swathe, most of it heavily coded and unintel-
ligible. When they found a cablepoint they stopped and filled up
with local news and public information. It was hard to get a
coherent picture, but it looked as if their route might lead them
into an active battlefield. But they were well defended.

Sid dreamed, in his top bunk in the back of the camper, that
he was still driving along the juddering roads. He was leading
hordes of noseless humanoid monsters to a sacred place. He was
taking them to the treasure, and selling humanity into oblivion.
He woke up sweating with horror, and the nightmare was true.

One night they stopped by the side of the road near an old
intersection, a nest of enormous concrete vipers. Sid went to
sleep and didn't dream; and woke to find himself alone.

The Fat Man was totally distracted by now. He barely spoke,
formally or informally. He looked through you and his glance
was like a blank veil over writhing, churning pools of industrial
processing. Sid presumed he was performing superbeing mental
experiments on whatever he expected to find in the tomb. The
effect was like travelling in the company of a large, dumb
animal. He often got out and wandered around in the dark. It
was foolhardy, but Sid couldn't stop him.

But where was Bella?

Sid climbed down from the back of the van. The night was
warm and clear and moonless. He saw her at once. She was
sitting with her back to him on one of the outer lanes of the
autobahn, in the meadow grass that had grown on either side.
Beyond her a fence of forest trees stood black. He was going to
join her, hoping that the invisible barrier might have vanished.
But she was looking up, so he looked up. He saw the stars: the
brilliant embroidery, the blue-black void veined with skeins and

needlepoints of light. Overhead spurted the frothy, divided arc of the Milky Way.

Did the night have skies like this on their home planet? They lived 'indoors', but some of them ventured into the wilderness. Were there names, in the unknown Aleutian language, for their share of the galaxy's enfolding arms – as homely and immediate and evocative? He didn't know. He thought what a crass fool he was to blame her for seeming *distant* on this trip. He stood, an enormous bubble of clear sadness swelling inside his ribcage. Someone began to sing. He thought it was in his head, and that he was remembering the nights when he used to lie hearing the voices of the Silent mimicking English: lost and sweet and strange. Then he realised that the voice was Bella's.

> *Oft, in the stilly night,*
> *E'er slumber's chain has bound me,*
> *Fond memory brings the light*
> *Of other days around me . . .*

The light of other days blazed down. She looked so pitiful under that immensity. He moved abruptly, meaning to run to her, to comfort her somehow.

A voice behind him said, 'Let her be.'

Kumbva was sitting on his haunches against the housing of the van's retracted treads, his bulk softened and blurred in dim starlight. 'She'll need you,' he said. 'Don't doubt it. You'll need each other. But not tonight. Go back to sleep.'

He lay awake for a long time. He thought the camper and the whole night air was filling up with years upon years: of smiles and faces, fragments of music, expressions, colours; the view from a window, the sound of a beloved voice. Outside in the dark Bella was alone, guarded but alone: mourning her dead.

In Neubrandenburg, halfway between the town and the abandoned campus, they ran into a firefight. Armour snapped over the windows. Sid's field of view became a false-coloured moving picture. The lights came up, the air inside the van was rent by faint squeals and zips and rumbling thunder. Sid panicked and yelled: 'We're ambushed!'

'Keep driving, it's nothing to do with us.'

The Fat Man was right. The soldiers treated the camper as if it didn't exist. A troop in unmarked dark armour charged across the roadway. A personnel carrier heaved over a clay embankment and thundered after them. The forward turret was a fused mass of hybrid metal. It was equally anonymous, wounded and on the rampage. Something thumped them. The images on the inside of the van's armoured eyelids shook and lost depth.

'We've lost a cam!' shouted Sid. 'Who *are* they?'

'I've no idea.' Kumbva was not curious.

Then they were on the other side. The armour retracted from their windows, and the naked plain stretched out before them. The sounds of the skirmish pursued them, but nothing else. When they came to the wood where the Campfire Girls had landed, Sid slowed. There was another aircraft there now, darkly camouflaged and hidden close under the trees. Three Aleutians came to meet them from the insectoid flyer. They weren't in quarantine.

'Sid,' said Kumbva, laying a hand on his arm. 'You have met Clavel. This is Rajath, the trickster, of whom you've heard so much; and Bhairava, Clavel's master at arms.'

'Pleased to meet you,' said Bhairava gravely.

The trickster grinned, like the bad boy he was.

'Hallo, Sid.'

Sid saw that Bella was not surprised. He knew he shouldn't be surprised himself. No doubt the Fat Man had told him, or thought he had. They took so much for granted. They never understood that you didn't understand . . . Clavel had changed. He seemed calm and sane. 'Rajath has something to say,' he prompted.

⟨Do I? Oh, yes – ⟩ The trickster spread his palms low and open against his sides: ⟨Peace?⟩ He made a speech, in English.

'I am sorry about the seance, librarian.'

Sid, coping with his own feelings, felt Bella steel herself.

'Don't mention it,' she said. 'We've all done stupid things.'

⟨But it was Aditya's idea—⟩

⟨Trickster, be quiet,⟩ said the poet. He looked at Bella, with a glance that Sid could not read. Bella put up her arms like a child for his embrace.

*

The Aleutians went to fetch things from Clavel's aircraft. Sid retired to the van. He suited up and sat on Bella's bunk in the back. He hoped Bella was going to be safe in there. He'd seen how quickly she healed; that should mean something.

He shouldn't be shocked that the other two captains were here, but he was hurt. It wasn't *fair*. This was the end of the treasure trail. It belonged to Sid and the Fat Man and Bella, no one else. His belly felt at once hollow and disgustingly active.

Bella appeared at the open tailgate, climbed in.

⟨What does your suit say?⟩ she asked cautiously, as if unsure of his temper. ⟨About the 'radiation'?⟩

He shrugged. 'You can't trust anything that's made in Europe. It says there's no heat. The background rads are not *good*. Not what you'd call ideal for bringing up your family. But not too bad for an old-earth battlefield. Wait till we get inside.'

⟨If the 'radiation' isn't there, the 'Campfire Girls' must know there's something strange about this tomb.⟩

Colonel Janet Ezra probably thought the evil demons spawned by hard radiation had found a way to escape detection in order to tempt humans to their destruction. Sid thought he could believe something like that himself.

Bella looked at him with sympathy for his superstition. ⟨Do you want to wait for us out here?⟩

'Oh, no. I'm coming in.' He donned the helmet and jumped into a crouch, arms akimbo, leapt down the steps of the van kicking out his heels: a pillow-limbed Cossack in faded urban-camo of rust and grey. *'Ra Ra Rasputin! Pass the strychnine sandwiches!'*

⟨'Sid's' right,⟩ whimpered Rajath, on the ground beside the insect flyer. ⟨We should all be in armour. I want one of those suits.⟩ He eyed Bhairava's approach unhappily. ⟨Why couldn't we bring a few more people? A few hundred, maybe?⟩

Clavel sighed impatiently. 'We're alone, trickster, because we are *trying* to be discreet. We won't be far ahead of the pack. Remember the saboteurs? The locals will be on to this soon, the same way as they found the shipworld.'

⟨Sir,⟩ said Bhairava, coming near. ⟨Weapons cannot be built outside a laboratory. It's a complex process. There is no danger.

Please try to be calm in front of 'Sidney Carton'. It's a question of prestige. Never forget that we are few and they are very many.⟩

Rajath noted bitterly that Bhairava, while saying there was 'no danger', was arming everyone to the teeth with superheat.

He accepted his own firearm with disgust. ⟨I *hate* these!⟩

The breach at the entrance to Buonarotti's building was still massively sealed. The signs were that no one had been near it since the Campfire Girls left. The party made their own entry through Bella's exit and the broken window in Du Pont/Farben's basement. They had to melt the rest of the glass before they could squeeze in the bulkiest item that Clavel had brought with him.

It settled on the dust-layered floor: a mass of brownish pulp. A monstrous sea anemone, a giant ox heart? The pulp looked as if it would have the texture of raw flesh. But it was warm and hard to the touch, like baked earth.

'That's a *big* disc,' remarked Sid.

He heard his own voice emerging from the helmet speaker as a high-pitched squawl.

'I hope we find a use for it,' said the Fat Man.

They stood in the dusty dark. The Aleutians were in their dun overalls. Sid felt like the native guide in full witch-doctor kit. The Fat Man carried a bag of tricks that Clavel had brought. He took out a pointed bar of what seemed to be dark metal. The surface moved sluggishly: the whole substance was heavily alive.

'What's that?'

'It's a cattle prod. Or an *ankus*, maybe.' He poked the pointed end at Sid. 'It's a thing for herding bluesuns. It can smell those things you call hard rads.'

They prowled, shining handlamps on the vacuum pipe, yoked and coiled, that snaked around the hall. Its metal still gleamed through the dust. The whole array seemed intact as if it had been in operation yesterday. They went exploring. They found the reactor chamber and looked in through panels of heavy glass. The reactor had been shut down. Sid's suit hummed a mild warning, the *ankus* stirred. The chamber was orderly, undisturbed. A couple of fuel rods lay on the floor.

'Adding a touch of verisimilitude,' murmured the Fat Man, 'to an otherwise drab and ill-seeming narrative. I wonder what happened to the technicians who were supposed to have been killed here. They disappeared from the later reports, didn't they? I'd be glad to think there were no real casualties. I don't like to think of Peenemunde causing permanent death.'

They reached a place where the passage floor in front of them was sheared away, and shone their lamps into a chaos of shattered walls and ceilings that had been pumped full of glassite stone. It was obvious that the centre of the explosion, the one recorded on that ancient videotape, had been here: not in the reactor chamber. Kumbva's *ankus*, held casually in his large bare hand, agreed with the tally Sid was getting from his suit. Radiation levels were not significantly above the Prussian background.

⟨We've seen enough,⟩ said Kumbva.

Bella led them through the basements until they hit the Campfire Girls' barrier material. Kumbva smeared it with stone-devouring commensals. They passed through.

⟨Shall I leave this open, Bhairava?⟩ asked the engineer.

⟨Close it,⟩ said the master at arms, after brief thought.

They passed walls scarred black from the fire of Bella's torches; found the stairwell above the lobby and began to climb. Now it was the Aleutians' turn to feel the dread. Sid caught the trickster's eyes, glittering wide and dark in the beam of his lamp. They had sealed the way out behind them. They would rather die in here than have one of things they called *weapons* escape. The empty tomb was haunted, for Aleutians and humanity alike, by the ghost of the king of horrors: Death the invincible in His most terrible form; the invited guest.

At the third turning of the stair they heard the sound of footsteps, light and human. Something appeared in the corridor. Before Sid could make out more than a vague bipedal shape it was rocketing towards them, a projectile of blood and bone. Bhairava was ready. It dropped in a whoosh of superheated flame.

The master at arms knelt and touched a patch of unburned skin, put his fingers to his mouth. ⟨It's dead.⟩

There was stir of relief among the Aleutians.

Bhairava addressed Sid. He did not speak formally, for none of this was to be evidence, but he expressed himself slowly and clearly. ⟨When I say 'it is dead' I mean that the products of the seance were not weapons. They have not proliferated. The air is empty of them, this was a lone survivor. There is no danger.⟩

⟨Good,⟩ mugged Sid clumsily, since a response seemed correct. ⟨I'm glad to hear it.⟩

Bhairava slipped a hand inside the neck of his clothes. It came out weeping blood-red wanderers. He shook his fingers over the burned flesh. ⟨Go, *little selves, take this commensal back into the Self* . . .⟩ The Aleutians covered their faces. Sid, after a moment's awkwardness, did likewise.

⟨It wore my face,⟩ whispered Bella.

Bhairava stood and put his arms around her. ⟨Don't cry, isolate. Your fierce offspring are all safe home.⟩

With a casual gesture, contrasting strangely with his ritual reverence of a moment before, he raked the charred body again. They left the streak of black, dry ash behind them.

They reached the room where Viloma had held his seance. The door was rent and shattered and burned. There were thick black stains on the walls and door jambs.

⟨Don't go in there!⟩ Bella led them on, shuddering.

They reached the other door. They saw the letters, incised clumsily and filled with black pigment.

DEUS PROVIDEBIT SIBI VICTIMAM SACRIFICI

On the other side of the door there was a narrow metal stair leading up. Sid finally took off his helmet and gauntlets and they climbed: the Fat Man, Sid, Bella and the two captains, Bhairava last. The door at the top was sealed. When Kumbva opened it they looked into a cave. They were outside the building, on the flat roof of the residential block, but still inside the glassite shell. Beside them, within the canopy of the lava-like instant stone, rose a wall of dark metal, with ladder rungs set into it. Kumbva applied more of his stone-eating commensals to clear the way upwards. They climbed again. The thin sheet of glassite that wrapped them was in places as translucent as coffee-coloured alabaster. The light of their dimmed lamps filled it with a red, moving glow. Sid thought of Buonarotti, the massively built Aryan goddess. He saw the Fat Man climbing through walls of flame to Brunnhilde's high couch.

The head of the ladder was guarded by a metal cage, which

had kept most of the stone foam at bay. Kumbva squeezed into it. They seemed to have reached the top of a metal tower on the roof. A broad metal plate lay at Kumbva's feet, sealed by extrusions of glassite. A slotted ring was set into it. The Fat Man was actually *shaking*. Sid could feel the shudders in his own arms as he clung to the top rung of the ladder. ⟨Go on! Go on,⟩ he begged. Disdaining commensals now, Kumbva heaved on the ring and shifted the hatch by brute strength. He dropped it at once. He covered his face. ⟨Oh, my God!⟩

⟨What did you see!!⟩

'I don't know,' whispered the Fat Man, his eyes dazzled, his voice trembling. 'I don't know!'

When the whole party had climbed down into the secret room, Kumbva stripped off the heavy plastic shrouds. They looked at a chunky workstation of unfamiliar design, the casing humbly worn and scratched, the symbols on the alphanumeric keypad faded with use. Beside it stood a foam couch, a kind used in early whole-body virtuality. There was a narrow cot, a bed-on-legs with a deadstuff blanket folded on it. On the wall above hung a gallery of sepia-framed blurs. The still images were faded beyond recall.

⟨Is this it?⟩ asked Rajath at last.

⟨I don't know,⟩ repeated Kumbva distractedly.

⟨But where's the ship? The device, whatever?⟩

The engineer drew a deep breath. He settled himself in the moulded seat of Peenemunde Buonarotti's desk. 'In London, at the headquarters of the Royal Society, there is a doorbell powered by a battery that was built by Michael Faraday. I have rung it. I ran away: what else are doorbells for? But it works. A machine like this had what they called an integral recycling powerpack, and its memory is not volatile. I don't see why it shouldn't be functional.'

He laid his hands on the keys reverently. Nothing happened.

⟨Tsk,⟩ remarked Sid: came up, leaned over the Fat Man's shoulder and poked the 'on' switch. ⟨Sometimes helps.⟩

'My friend, my dear lord,' said Kumbva. 'I'm here.'

The upright monitor screen fizzed and cleared. Dust showered from it. An image of the room itself appeared. A large woman with a mass of greying yellow hair was sitting on the edge of the cot. She wore an ugly blue suit. Her hands were knotted in her lap in an agony of livespace shyness.

'Hallo,' she said in an accented English. She smiled, a petrified grimace. 'Who are you, I wonder? And how many years have passed? I am almost sure that you are an Aleutian, and I do not know if I am glad or sorry that you have found me. The lord himself will provide a victim for the sacrifice.'

An editing shift: Peenemunde Buonarotti leaned forward. 'Now, listen. I am going to tell you a little about my discovery. You *must listen* because I will not repeat myself. You can stop this record and start it but you cannot replay it, and it will play once only. Are you listening? In the basement of the Du Pont/Farben building there is an accelerator. Beside this desk is a Kirlian couch, which maps the quantum properties of a human physical entity – particle by particle. I will leave you to consider the mathematics of the compression. The couch is connected to the accelerator. The entity modelled by the Kirlian couch becomes a particle source. A stream of energy packets is accelerated to the threshold of the speed of light, divided and set on a collision course with itself. At the collision something happens, uniquely because of the way each energy packet in this stream "remembers" the complex perceptual state of the entity of which it is a part, because, it seems to me, it is what we call *conscious*. Lightspeed, the state of having no location, is achieved. The person who lies down on the couch almost reaches this state: and borrows energy from beyond the threshold to make the leap possible. From the state of having no location, one can step out on to the surface of a distant planet. *I have done so.* All that's necessary is a clear knowledge of where you want to go. The informational entity takes material form from the surrounding environment. You are flesh, you can bleed and can even die. Yet to return to the couch (as far as my experiments have shown so far) requires only an effort like the effort of recognising that you are dreaming and deciding to wake.'

An editing shift. 'Are you ready? First, you must find a powersource. In your time, that may be the most difficult part. In the case that you have a reliable power supply, go down to

the accelerator chamber and I will lead you through the set up:
if this is still possible. But *only once.*'

'Oh, my God,' breathed Sidney Carton. 'Is that what they did?
Is that what Johnny and Braemar did?' To be torn apart, particle
by particle, literally ripped to shreds, sent hurtling to shatter
against your self . . . 'It gives a whole new meaning to the term
"smashed".' He giggled.

'They didn't know,' murmured Kumbva. 'She didn't tell them.
She said: "Lie down on my magic bed, and you can be wherever
you desire to be – "'

Sid and the Fat Man looked at each other.

'*What are we waiting for?*'

They ran part of the way. In the Du Pont/Farben basement,
Buonarotti was looking from a monitor screen, the paused video
frame making it seem she was nodding shakily in approval. They
patched the giant disc into twenty-first-century power cable,
and set to work, under Peenemunde Buonarotti's orders.

The two captains, Bella and the master at arms kept well out
of the way, and Sid, at least, was barely conscious of their
presence.

As they followed Peenemunde's instructions – which were not
particularly clear – they kept catching each other's eye and
mugging ecstatic disbelief. They laughed wildly (it was all right,
she couldn't hear them) when the professor lost her thread,
degenerated into mumbling apologies, made them undo a
sequence and start again. *Unbelievable*, Sid kept muttering,
unbelievable. Sidney Carton! You have won our star prize.

She told them to go back upstairs.

They returned to the secret room. This time they met no
monsters. Buonarotti was on the screen, sitting on her cot. Her
notes (she'd been projecting scribbled equations for them) had
disappeared.

She said: 'Now you are ready. Now I will tell you the problem.
If you are human, beware. For human beings, the experience is
too much like a dream. Your mind/brain will enact meaning on
what happens, as it does on the images that pass through your
consciousness in sleep. *It is impossible for a human being to take
action in the visited world without falling into a psychotic
episode.* The dream becomes a nightmare, in which the traveller

is trapped. I have found no way out of this impasse, and because
of the way we construe our consciousness – the mind in the
machine – I am not hopeful that a way can be found. We
humans may travel only as ghosts, shadows, spectators.'

She paused, and went on calmly, 'If you are an Aleutian, as I
believe you are, the case is different. It is the pattern of
consciousness that "travels". For you, the pattern of consciousness is diffused through your air, your tools, your whole world.
You, I believe, may find a way.' She looked out, eyes brimming.
'Not on this mountain,' she said. 'Nor in Jerusalem. But in spirit
and in truth, we shall worship together. Well, my unknown
friend. "Good Luck", as the English say. Until we meet.'

The screen went blank.

Kumbva gave a smothered cry, reaching out. He seemed to try
to haul Peenemunde physically from that dead space. But she
was gone.

Sid stood staring dumbly at the empty screen.

'Oh, no,' he said. 'No. You hear me? You can't have it! It's
ours!' His head was spinning. There were hordes of noseless
monsters round him, and the human race was fading, like
Peenemunde fading, under her strange skies: becoming meaningless. Meaningless!

'I am sorry,' said Clavel, coming forward. 'Kumbva told me
that you understood: I was afraid he was wrong. Now you've
heard it from Buonarotti herself. Why else do you think she hid
the device away? The instantaneous travel device is not for
humans. If you didn't want it to be ours, you should have taken
my offer and walked away from the treasure hunt.'

Sid felt Bella and the Fat Man looking at him unhappily. He
thought of Peenemunde's trail of dreams. Peenemunde had told
him plainly enough that that was all she had . . . unless some
alien stranger came along to make the dreams come true.

He rubbed his hands over his face, which was glistening with
the sweat of joy and labour. He wished he'd kept his helmet on;
it was good camouflage. He struck as careless an attitude as one
can strike in an ill-fitting army surplus noddy suit.

'Sorry, folks. I don't know what came over me. You can keep
your sympathy, poet. The Fat Man and I understand each other,
we always did.' He grinned at Kumbva. 'It's yours. We knew

that. Peenemunde left the trail for you. If my compatriot, *the greatest mind in the known universe*, wanted you shipwrecked refugees to have the secret, who am I to argue?'

Kumbva wrapped his large arms round the suit. ⟨My true friend! We will build you your starships: and we'll ride in them together!⟩

By common consent, then, the three captains drew together and the others moved aside. It was as it had been at the beginning: Rajath the trickster, who had the idea of making landfall and a quick profit; Clavel the Pure One, drawn into the plan because Clavel was never content, never satisfied anywhere; Kumbva the engineer, whose curiosity was boundless: whose motto was *enjoy*.

Rajath peered at the couch, nasal puckering. ⟨This needs research. Several lifetimes of research and generations of unlucky complex-commensals need to try that ride before I do!⟩

⟨Study, yes,⟩ agreed Kumbva. ⟨I have very little idea how this works. Or how we can 'make it real' as Peenemunde says . . .⟩

⟨No one knows what it does to an Aleutian,⟩ said the poet. ⟨I want to go.⟩

Kumbva looked at him, smiling. ⟨I think it may kill you.⟩

⟨I think that too.⟩

There was no discussion of the destination.

Kumbva made a speech.

'The lord himself will provide a victim for the sacrifice. That was the message Peenemunde left for us. I have tried to understand the story in your Bible, from which she took her password. It isn't easy, but I have a glimmering. Abraham was ready to sacrifice his child, his futurity, to secure his continued existence in the goodwill of the WorldSelf. To sacrifice your future for your future is curiously like a description of what must happen when the traveller leaps the threshold, and thereby finds the power to make that leap. But perhaps, as in the story, there has to be an actual sacrifice too. Someone has to pay the price, without stealing it back again. Abraham did not sacrifice his child. There was an animal there, a ram caught in the thicket, and he offered up the animal instead.'

Clavel, transfigured by profound emotion, came and took Bella's hands. 'I never loved Johnny,' he said. 'I wanted him, and could not accept that he would not play my game. I have been so stupid, but finally – with your help, librarian – I understand. Since it wasn't love I felt, it wasn't love that fell into corruption in my soul. I am very glad to know that.'

Turning to someone unseen, he said: 'Have I paid?'

He went to the couch and lay down. The foam closed around him. The power surged. In an instant, in less than no time, the body on the couch had vanished.

It returned to a room silent and dusty, lit by dim shoulder lamps, a room in which alignments had shifted, though Sid was unaware that any time had passed. Kumbva and Rajath stood on either side of the head of the couch, Bella and Bhairava beside them: Sid was a few steps away. Clavel's eyes opened.

'Well, poet? Where have you been?'

There was no answer. The eyes closed again. Sid thought the air smelled different. He thought of light: a clear, icy sunlight and a branch of new leaves opening their palms to a sky of shining indigo. He felt the shock that went through the aliens.

Kumbva smoothed away the foam, and folded Clavel's arms crosswise over his belly: the well of life.

And the dove came back to him in the evening, and lo, in her mouth a freshly plucked olive leaf.

Time Regained

Bella and the halfcaste had left. In the secret room, the two living captains moved away from the couch, leaving Bhairava to make his farewells in private.

⟨I don't know what you see in him,⟩ Rajath grumbled. ⟨Someone had to look out for Maitri's librarian, and we're very glad you took that on board—⟩

⟨Indeed?⟩ murmured Kumbva. ⟨All of us?⟩

⟨Of course,⟩ said the trickster huffily. ⟨You made things harder for me, but I can be grown up about it . . . But you should get rid of the other one. I think he's insolent. And crafty.⟩

The engineer chucked. ⟨You would know best.⟩ He looked at Rajath speculatively. ⟨Years ago, I found 'Sidney Carton' in the enclaves. I recruited him for the qualities you don't appreciate, and for the sake of a familiarity that I couldn't quite place. Maybe his 'insolence' reminded me of the old days. One day, to be polite, I watched his favourite piece of character record with him. It's the story of a young man in some kind of clerical orders. A not entirely admirable person, embittered by circumstance, who becomes embroiled in politics in a time of unrest. Finally he goes to the scaffold in an act of self-sacrifice that redeems his whole life. Listen: *It is a far, far better thing that I do, than I have ever done; it is a far, far better rest, that I go to, than I have ever known* . . . Well?⟩

Rajath was stunned. ⟨Good heavens! That sounds like—!⟩

⟨Exactly. The very voice of 'Johnny Guglioli' facing an unjust execution, noble at the last, giving his life so that his lover could escape. An absolutely typical Johnny exit!⟩

⟨You think your 'Sid' is the real 'Johnny Guglioli'?⟩

Kumbva shrugged. ⟨No. I do not. I believe they die, and they do not come back. I was struck by the coincidence, nothing more. But what are the selves that you and I wear, trickster, if not constructs that we choose to perform? If 'Sid' is not 'Johnny' he is no less 'Johnny's' self, the Self in its human aspect. I like to think in some sense a debt was paid when he and I stood here and saw our quest achieved.⟩

Sid had taken a pack of stone-eaters and let himself out, while the Aleutians were occupied with their dead poet and the chemical messages that he'd brought back. Outside the tomb he extricated himself from his suit. He went to the front of Buonarotti's building, sat on the steps and took an Aleutian ration pack from a sleeve pocket of his overalls. It tasted like oatmeal gruel mixed with liquid soap: not too bad, really. He squinted up at the grey sky, stared around at the scattered debris, untouched since the crooked Russians drove away a hundred odd years ago.

In another pocket he found a scrap of tough plastic tissue: the cover note for the insurance on his new hand. Insurance was an item that turned up on bills for fancy products, one of those commercial words that nobody used in real life any more. He wondered what it was supposed to mean.

THIS SCHEME DOES NOT COVER

a) loss or damage directly or indirectly caused by, or arising from, ionising radiations or nuclear waste from combustion of nuclear fuel.

b) loss or damage directly or indirectly occasioned by, happening through or in consequence of war, invasion, acts of foreign enemies, hostilities (whether war be declared or not), civil war, revolution, military or usurped power or confiscation or nationalisation, or requisition or destruction of or damage to property by or under the order of any government or public or local authority.

c) change in clinical prescription.

He laughed, and held it up for the wind to carry away.

Bella came out of the hole he'd made. She was carrying two incongruous-looking packages. She came over to him doubtfully.

'Hallo,' he said. He sniffed, and wiped his knuckles across his stubby lashes. 'I suspect I've been difficult to live with these last days. I'm sorry for anything offensive I did or said . . . I knew the score. But it was hard.'

In bringing back chemical messages Clavel, dying, had achieved more than Peenemunde Buonarotti ever managed.

'It's all right. I knew how you were feeling. If it helps, I didn't enjoy accepting Rajath's apology much.'

She sat beside him, close enough to touch but not touching. 'In a way, you have the best result possible,' she offered. 'One of your clerics says: *call no man happy, until he carries his happiness with him down into the grave.* That's you, Sid. It will take years, lives, before interstellar travel is a going concern. You've achieved your quest, and you don't have to be here when it all goes horribly wrong.'

⟨Thanks, Bel.⟩ It was an odd comfort, but you couldn't fault the logic. ⟨I love the way you think.⟩

She remembered the packages. ⟨Look: presents from Kumbva.⟩

They were gift-wrapped, in dark green foil with Christmas bells. Sid had a receiverless phone. Bella's present was a pouch of white and puckered skin. It opened at her touch, revealing a row of small containers of the same material.

⟨It's my medicine. I can be an Aleutian again. Sometime – if I need to be.⟩ She held a vial on her palm, studying it intently. ⟨What is it about power?⟩ she wondered. ⟨Am I what people call 'good', because I am a cripple, and have fewer chances to be wicked and make it stick? Or is it because I am naturally 'good' that I'm Maitri's librarian, and will never be powerful?⟩

⟨You're not a cripple any more.⟩

⟨I'm not Maitri's librarian any more.⟩

He saw how the pouch grown to match her own skin would become a treasure kept with heartache: and one day thrown away with heartache because the meaning had leached away into alien years. *Deus providebit sibi victimam sacrifici.* To the three captains, it was Clavel who had become the victim. But what had the poet lost? He'd be back. To Sid it seemed that it was Bella who had been sacrificed on Buonarotti's altar. Aleutia would know about her part. but mental-model telepathy is no more reliable than any other form of historical record. Kumbva had taught him that. This would be the three captains' story.

Aleutia would know the truth: but they'd prefer the version with the big stars in it.

'Bel?'

She blinked, coming out of sad reverie.

'I'm not your other self. I'm nothing like you. I frequently don't know what is going on in your head, even when you tell me.'

Bella's shoulders lifted. 'I'm not your other half. I'm not female and I'm not feminine, not seriously. I don't want to upset you, but at home people thought Maitri's librarian was *masculine*, if anything: because I hate getting emotional, and so on. And I don't care which you are. You're just . . . Sid.'

'Oh well,' he sighed. 'So much for the movies.'

They turned towards each other: face to face. Stubby lashes flickered apart, unveiling the blue windows of Sidney Carton's stubborn, gentle and contrary soul. Bella put her arms around him and kissed him the way Aleutians kiss, her mouth and nasal nuzzling his throat and the angles of his jaw.

The cold breeze was stirring the litter and rustling the yellow fallen leaves. Over Bella's shoulder he watched a sheet of giftwrap fly into the chill air.

'And the north wind will blow.'

The aliens weren't going to leave tomorrow, because Clavel had tried a local magician's trick and it had seemed to work. From this hollow place on the other side of his heart's desire, Sid could see how much would be unchanged. He saw that the Himalaya Project would go on: and since he knew that it must happen, he stopped fearing it so much.

'Maybe it won't be so bad. Natural disasters never do what they're supposed to do. Maybe levelling the Himalayas actually will turn earth into a tropical paradise.'

Bella said, 'I think the north wind is blowing now.'

Cold wind of misfortune, blowing away a civilisation. Blowing away the principalities and the powers, the unkept promises, blowing away the riches and the lies. In times like these you do what you can: save what you can, make what new beginnings you can, for a recovery you'll never see.

'I've felt the north wind before. It blows in Aleutia. But it's better to be out in the storm instead of indoors and helpless. So long as you have someone to keep you company.'

'Ahem!'

Sid and Bella sprang apart. Rajath had come out of the tomb. He was followed by Clavel's master at arms, and they were carrying the superheat weapons. Bhairava's eyes were still brimming and shining with tears. Rajath's mourning seemed to be over. He acknowledged Bella, but looked at Sid with far more interest than he'd shown before: enough interest to make Sid uneasy.

⟨We're on our way,⟩ he said. ⟨The Government of the World and the padres and who knows who else will be turning up here soon and getting sniffy about quarantine.⟩ He waved vaguely at the sky. ⟨They have their methods of keeping track. I'll take those commensals.⟩ He took the pack of stone-eaters. ⟨Well! We owe you a debt of gratitude, 'Sidney'. The other thing will be the boffins' business now. It looks to me as though nothing profitable's going to come of it for lives . . . But it'll be good to have the poet on form again. Which it seems likely he will be when he comes back. You know, we can't do without our Clavel.⟩

He glanced at the tomb. There was no sign of Kumbva yet.

⟨The engineer's staying for a while. Could I offer you two a lift? It'd probably be healthier for you to be with me rather than on your own when the authorities turn up.⟩

⟨No, thank you, Rajath,⟩ said the librarian politely. ⟨We wouldn't want to trouble you.⟩

Transparently, he considered making the invitation more pressing, glanced at Bhairava as a possible ally in a kidnap: and decided against it. He stared hard at Sid.

⟨Kumbva's been telling me about you, you sly person. Are you *really* 'Johnny Guglioli'?⟩

Sid barely hesitated. 'Nah. I'm Braemar Wilson. Everyone knows that!'

Rajath's stare became comically blank.

⟨Thanks again, librarian,⟩ added Bhairava, ⟨for all you did for him. There's a bond between us for ever. See you later.⟩

The Aleutians loped off to Clavel's flier. By the time it dawned on Rajath that *Braemar Wilson* might satisfy his backers just as well – if he could get the reincarnate out to orbit before they

realised the significance of the events here today – he was
strapped in a comfortable net of take-off webbing and Bhairava
had lifted the insectoid above the trees. He resolved not to worry
about it. ⟨*Nice idea*,⟩ he told Kumbva in his mind's model of
things: glad to score over the engineer. ⟨*But you're completely
wrong. He's not Johnny! He told me so himself. Take my advice,
stop trying to understand 'em. You never will.*⟩

When they'd stopped laughing at the look on Rajath's face, they
decided that the Fat Man didn't expect them to wait. The road
stretched grey across the empty plain. Bella and Sid began to
walk, in the opposite direction from the firefight and the place
where Bella, reborn, had played her first old earth game. Sid
thought there was another town further along. A rumbling
started behind them. They stood poised for flight. The vehicle
was a truck: an old, slow, alcohol-fuel truck. It had no military
markings and it wasn't armoured. They stuck out their thumbs.

It stopped. Three fat headscarfed women in a close-packed row
stared down from the cab. One of them gestured. The truck's
tailgate (it was open at the back, piled with some kind of
vegetables) lowered with a painful whine. They climbed in. The
vegetables were apples.

'I'll have my back pay.' Sid counted on his fingers. 'By which I
mean, there'll be some random amount in credit for us from the
Fat Man, when we can find a working automat that recognises
me. He'll have done that. And there's that tenhead note—?'
Bella was not attending. He shook his head resignedly. Never ask
a gamer for money: 'Achcha, forget about the tenhead note.'
The apples were surprisingly comfortable. He lay back and stared
up into the dusky clouds.

'You know what? Peenemunde Buonarotti may have been the
greatest thinker in the cosmos, but she never played the games.
She knows nothing about how I *construe myself*. Or you. Nor
does the Fat Man, bless him. He likes gadgets, but he's not an
aficionado of the hells. You wait and see. Humans can and will
go to the stars! You build them. We'll get in that car and drive.'

Goodbye, thought Bella. *To the library, to Maitri, to
uncounted trivial precious things*. In one of their conversations
in B. K. Pillai's house, Kumbva had told her that the world we

know is perhaps one of indefinitely many. Each time you make a decision, you step into a new universe created out of nothing. It was a good thought. In one of those worlds the librarian would live on, a modest signifier of Aleutia. She wished that person well. In this world, Bella would die.

A rapping noise alerted them to a face at the back window of the cab. One of the Prussian women mimed violently, cramming her hand to her mouth:

‹Eat what you like!›

The north wind cut through her clothes. She would die before instantaneous travel was more than a fragile dream. She would go out of this room and shut the door and never return, having known nothing in this life on earth but war and danger and spreading dissolution. No home, no safety, no permanence. Sid's body warmed her side. The prospect of dying had never worried her before, why start now? Bella who had been 'Goodlooking' took the apple that Sid held out and bit into it. The juice spurted into her mouth.

ACKNOWLEDGEMENTS

A short bibliography:
The Way of an Eagle, Ethel M. Dell, Ernest Benn London Ltd 1912; *On the Face of the Waters*, Flora Annie Steel, Heinemann, London 1896; *Kim*, Rudyard Kipling; *Lost Horizon*, James Hilton, Macmillan, London 1933; *Lonely Hearts of the Cosmos*, Denis Overbye, Macmillan London 1991; *Bright Air, Brilliant Fire*, Gerald Edelman, Penguin 1992; *The Ape That Spoke*, John McCrone, Macmillan London 1990; *The Autobiography of an Unknown Indian*, Nirad C. Chaudhuri, Macmillan London 1951; *Casino Royale*, Ian Fleming, Jonathan Cape London 1953; *Remembrance of Things Past*, Marcel Proust, tr C. K. Scott Moncrieff and Terence Kilmartin, Penguin Books 1983; *Black Dog*, Alison de Vere, Lee Stork, Channel 4, 1987; *Wings Of Desire*, Wim Wenders; *The Marriage Of Figaro*, W. A. Mozart; *A Tale of Two Cities*, Charles Dickens.

Quotations:
Breakfast song at Aditya's cottage: from 'The Ghost', Walter de la Mare, courtesy the Literary Trustees of Walter de la Mare, and the Society of Authors, as their representative; Sid's quote from Magna Carta trs Harry Rothwell, MA, Ph.D.; Aditya on the battlefield: from 'Dover Beach', Matthew Arnold; Aditya's death speech: from 'An Irish Airman Forsees His Death', W. B. Yeats; Intro to the virtuality Ramayana: from *Ramayana*, C. Rajagopalachari, Bharatiya Vidya Bhavan, Bombay 1978; Bella's mourning from 'The Light Of Other Days', Thomas Moore; Sid at the sarcophagus, from *Rasputin*, Boney M.; Bella's consolation to Sid, from *Oedipus at Colonus*, Sophocles.

Also available in Vista paperback

White Queen

GWYNETH JONES

It's 2038. Japan has been destroyed by a geologic catastrophe. The global economy is in chaos. And Johnny Guglioli, a young wirehead cyberjournalist infected with a very deadly computer virus, meets a mysterious young woman who puts him on the trail of a group of extraterrestrials who have landed in West Africa.

But when Johnny finally finds the aliens, they're far different from anything he could have imagined – and driven by a dark imperative that may cost humanity its future.

'Seductively weird . . . populated by characters that live on in the mind long after the book's been put back on the shelf' Iain Banks

'One of those rare books that stretches the intellect while it engages the heart. One of the key sf novels of this decade' *Time Out*

ISBN 0 575 60378 X

VISTA

Phoenix Café

GWYNETH JONES

It is three hundred years since the Aleutians arrived on earth. In a city that was once Paris, Michael Connelly – son of the *quartier*'s game warden, keeper of the virtual wilderness – meets Catherine, human ward of the alien Lord Maitri.

Both damaged by the consequences of the Aleutian Invasion, Misha and Catherine recognize in each other a capacity for suffering and a need for pain that will draw them into a strange and shocking private world.

But there are worlds within worlds, in these last days of the alien empire on earth. The Buonarotti Device, disputed and perilous key to the kingdoms of heaven, has not given up all its secrets.

'Hyper-imagined, strenuously intelligent'

Observer

ISBN 0 575 60075 6

VISTA

Sacrifice of Fools

IAN McDONALD

They're ancient, they're enigmatic, they're alien and they're here. The Shian arrive on Earth, not as conquerors, but as settlers. Outwardly similar but inwardly deeply different, the Shian are a challenge to all mankind's established notions of society, family, gender, sex and law.

When a prominent Shian family is brutally murdered, human and alien cultures find themselves on a collision course, with only Andy Gillespie, ex-con and aspirant to the mysteries of the Shian law, standing between them.

His search for justice takes him through corrupt religious sects and sinister political organizations with the police and paramilitaries hot on his heels – for Shian justice always comes at a price . . .

'One of the finest writers of his generation' *New Statesman*

'Powerfully good storytelling . . . cleverly written, intelligent and unflinchingly truthful' *SFX*

ISBN 0 575 60059 4

VISTA

Fairyland

PAUL J. McAULEY

WINNER OF THE ARTHUR C. CLARKE AWARD

In twenty-first-century Europe, endlessly ravaged by the changes of war and technology, gene hacker and psychoactive virus designer Alex Sharkey is a bare step ahead of the police and the Triads. But when he helps a scarily super-smart little girl called Milena to turn a genetically engineered doll into the first of a new, autonomous species, the Fairies, he doesn't realize he's giving history a dangerous shove.

Milena has her own reasons. Some of the folk, as fey and malign as any in legend, have other ideas about their destiny . . .

A giddying baroque journey through the crumbling counter-cultures, obsolete magic kingdoms and war-torn realities of post-nanotech Europe.

'McAuley is part of a spearhead of writers who for pure imagination, hipness, vision and fun have made Britain the Memphis Sun Records of SF'
Mail on Sunday

ISBN 0 575 60031 4

VISTA

Other Vista Science Fiction titles include

VISTA books are available from all good bookshops or from:
Cassell C.S.
Book Service By Post
PO Box 29, Douglas I-O-M
IM99 1BQ
telephone: 01624 675137, fax: 01624 670923

VISTA